DAWN OF FOREVER

JEWEL E ANN

Copyright © 2016 by Jewel E. Ann

Second Print Edition

ISBN: 978-1-7359982-6-8

Cover Designer: Jenn Beach

For my readers, I "adore" you.

CHAPTER ONE

DAY

*"J*UDE*! S*TOP*!" Sunny Day held up the long skirt of her evening gown as she chased her seventeen-year-old son out the front doors of the de Young Museum.*

Jude couldn't breathe, yet his legs propelled him ... away from the woman impersonating his mom. Away from what he saw. Away from his life falling apart.

"Stop! You don't understand."

She was right. He didn't understand. How could he? No explanation on Earth could justify what she did.

"Please ..." Her plea broke with a heart-wrenching sob.

As if he hit an invisible wall, he stopped—chest heaving, heart hardening into a four-chambered prison of bitterness.

Sunny rested her hand on his shoulder. He jerked it away, keeping his back to her.

"I love him. I've loved him my whole life."

Jude laughed. "Don't sugarcoat it."

"You're old enough to hear the truth. I'm not going to lie to you."

Jude didn't want the truth. He wanted to un-see his mom

kissing a man who wasn't his father. He wanted to un-hear her saying that she "loves him."

"Fuck you."

"Jude!"

He turned. "If I'm old enough to hear the truth, then I'm old enough to tell you what I think of it."

Why was she crying? The tears she wiped from her eyes meant nothing.

"We met when we were five. To say we were inseparable would be an understatement. He was the first boy who held my hand, the first boy I kissed, the boy who took me to all my homecomings and proms. He was my first everything. Then he enlisted in the military and left me. I waited for him for five years, but he kept reenlisting and his career ambitions crowded me out of his life. I wanted a family ... I wanted a life."

"I don't care." He gritted his teeth. Heat flushed through his body as his muscles tensed to the point of quivering.

The stranger before him clutched her body, holding herself together. Her voice thickened with pain. "Someday you'll understand. Someday you'll fall in love and it will brand your heart forever. And if life keeps you apart, you may invite others into your heart, but it will never truly be theirs. One stamp. One person."

Sunny gazed at Jude with vacant eyes. "I hate him for leaving me. I hate him for coming back when it was too late. I hate him for still loving me. But after seventeen years I'm just so tired of all the hate. I was in it for you and Jessica."

"Was?"

She cast her eyes to the ground on a long, slow sigh. "I'm leaving your father after you and Jessica start college next fall. I wanted to wait until next summer to say anything. I know Jessica will take it hard, but she's a strong

2

young woman. I know you two are close and you don't have secrets, but if you love her, then you need to think about what's best for her during her last year of high school."

Jude leaned forward, demanding she look at him. "If I love her? Do you hear yourself? How can you preach to me about love when the only person you love is yourself and that fucker who had his hands all over you!"

A second round of tears filled his mother's eyes. He felt nothing.

"I love you and Jessica—"

"No! You just said one stamp. One person."

"It ... it's not the same." She shook her head, pressing the back of her hand beneath her nose as sobs racked her body. "The love I have for you is a different kind of love. It's unconditional. You and Jessica are not my heart, you're the beat. You're my life, my world. There's nothing I wouldn't do for you, and I've spent the past seventeen years proving it. I'll spend the rest of my life loving you, being here for you, protecting you ..."

Jude narrowed his eyes. "I don't want your protection. I don't need your protection."

"Don't say that."

Love didn't exist, at least not the way he thought it did. Jessica was daddy's girl, but Jude idolized his mom. Sunny was president of the PTO, organizer of fundraisers, keeper of schedules, the bright face in the front row at all their school events, the hug before bed and kiss on the cheek in the morning. She kept a tidy house, baked, cooked, mended clothes, and always ... always made everyone feel loved.

More than that, she was the loving wife. Jude knew it. He saw it in the adoring looks she exchanged with his father, the hand-holding, the playful banter, the patience she showed when his job got stressful. She was the glue that held everyone together.

No longer.

She was a fraud. A liar. An adulterer. She could not be trusted. Women could not be trusted … except Jessica. That night his sister became his everything and all other women became objects to fuck. Period.

CHAPTER TWO

KNIGHT

JACKSON KNIGHT MADE one call to set everything into motion.

"Dodge, it's Jackson Knight. Sorry to disturb you on Thanksgiving, but I have some bad news ..."

AJ's head rested against the PT Cruiser window. It felt as cold as the voice outlining the events of his death ... only he wasn't dead—*yet*.

He died in his sleep. Jillian found him. The body was taken from his house to prepare for transport back to Portland.

The car slowed as the hum of pavement turned to crunching gravel beneath the tires. Jackson cut the engine.

Silence.

AJ blinked open his eyes.

Nothing.

"W-w-where a-are we?" The option of dying with dignity no longer existed.

"The end of the road."

AJ nodded.

"S-she'll h-a-a-te you."

The lack of Jackson's response confirmed it. Jillian would hate them both.

"You can't keep anything down, so I can't really offer you a last meal. Do you have any other last requests?"

When Cage flew to Portland for the weekend, AJ said his final goodbye. Neither of them acknowledged it was the last goodbye, but when his college quarterback son clung to him with the desperation of a five-year-old boy, the tears said all that needed to be said.

Life is not fair.

I'm sorry.

I forgive you.

I love you.

His father would understand. His mother would not, and neither would Brooke. Women were built to nurture and carry hope beyond all reason. Even Jillian, with her ironclad heart, succumbed to her own vulnerability when she begged him to go back to Portland with her. In that moment she was no longer his *real*. If he were honest with himself, he lost that Jillian on a private jet from Houston to Omaha. She died in his arms that day, but he didn't know why.

"Ji-Jillian. I w-want ... to k-know."

"Know what?"

"Ever-ev-er-ything."

"Everything?" Jackson grunted a laugh. "If I tell you *everything*, there's no going back. Right now, you could ask me to take you back to her and I would. Once I start this story, the only way it will end is with you dying. Understood?"

AJ married the first woman he truly loved. Minutes after Brooke gave birth to their son, he watched Cage's tiny fingers wrap around his pinky finger, claiming his heart. He took a bullet for a comrade on the battlefield, serving his country with pride. Fuck the PTSD. AJ lived a good life. A life that ended with the love of a woman who took him in a show-me-your-worst-and-I'll-love-you-even-more way.

"Un-der-stood." He closed his eyes and never opened them again.

"Her name was Jessica Mauve Day, born and raised in San Francisco—daughter to Grant and Sunny, sister to Jude. She has elite tactical and self-defense skills. At seventeen, she and her best friend were kidnapped by a serial killer. Her friend died from forty-four slashes to her flesh, the final one to her femoral artery. Jessica survived because that's what she is ... the ultimate survivor. One of the kidnappers died from forty-four slashes to his flesh, the final one to his femoral artery. The other kidnapper died at a rest stop in Wyoming several months ago from a broken neck, but the official report called it heart failure. Can you guess who killed them?"

AJ had no more to say.

"She fell in love with her psychiatrist and they lived together with their dog until our parents were killed last year. Our father was an undercover DEA agent until someone blew his cover. As a result, Jessica and Jude had to die too, so that Jillian and Jackson could live. She's fucked-up in ways I don't think anyone will completely understand. But if I'm honest, all she's ever really wanted is a sense of normalcy and someone to love."

Silence.

Pain.

Regret.

Then ... nothing.

One.

Jude Day took the lives of twenty-three people. Jackson Knight killed one man—a mercy killing. After Jillian killed Trigger, Jackson swore he'd never let his sister take another life. AJ would have asked her to take his. Pain makes a person desperate, and Jackson had never seen so much pain bleed from one man.

She would hate him. He would accept it. They would survive. It's who they were.

A single candle flickered on AJ's dining room table. Jackson stepped over the shards of glass and scattered roses in a pool of water on the floor, the wall still wet from impact.

"If you touch me ... I. Will. Kill. You." Jillian's hoarse voice ripped through the silence.

He stood over her. She hugged *the* cloth napkin to her chest, body curled into fetal position on the floor.

"Then you're just going to have to kill me." He bent down to pick her up.

A stabbing pain stopped his motion. Wrath-filled eyes narrowed at him. Jackson grabbed her wrist—her bloodied hand still gripping the long dagger of glass lodged into his shoulder.

"When did cutting become your thing again?" Jackson seethed, squeezing her arm until she winced, releasing the glass. He wadded the front of his shirt to grab it, then pulled it from his shoulder with a grunt.

"Did you kill him?"

He was wrong. The pain that bled from her eyes held as much desperation as AJ's had possessed. The blood oozing from her hand that stabbed the glass into his shoulder signified her lack of readiness to hear the truth.

"I took away the pain."

"You murdered him. You're a fucking murderer!" The napkin from her non-bloodied hand fell on the floor, absorbing the water from the vase. The black words disappeared into blotchy stains. "No! No! No!" Jillian snatched it up, holding her breath as the ink-stained water dripped from the edge.

Jackson watched her fade ... watched her die right along with AJ's last words to her. She'd risen from the grave so many times, but even she had her limits. Would she ever come back from this?

"I hate who I've become." Jackson applied more pressure to his stab wound.

Jillian hugged the napkin to her chest. Silent sobs racked her body.

"I hate our past. I hate not feeling human. And the list of regrets in my life grows more every day. But I will *never* regret taking AJ's life."

"Oh God ..." Jillian cried.

He picked her up, wincing as more blood seeped from his shoulder.

"You killed him ... why ... why ... why?"

"To save you," he whispered in her ear, carrying her to the door. There was nothing he wouldn't do for his sister. If it meant taking all her anger, all her tears, and all her pain, that's what he would do. Death was AJ's fate—a painful, undignified, miserable death. His sister couldn't see past her blinding love. Jackson couldn't save AJ, no one could, but he could save his sister.

"I hate this world. I *hate* it so fucking much." Her voice broke, shattering with each word.

"I know, Jess."

Jillian looked up at him through puffy eyes. He kissed

her forehead. "Don't look at me like that. You'll always be Jessica to me."

"Fin de journée," she whispered.

End of Day.

He didn't respond. Day—maybe it wasn't the end.

LOVE AND LOSS became the unbreakable pattern of Jessica and Jillian's life. She hated her brother for taking something that wasn't his to take. Maybe she hated herself too. Did her pain overshadow AJ's? If he would have asked her to take his life, would she have been able to do it? The questions haunted her, but so did the answers.

"Eventually you're going to have to talk to me again."

Jillian shoved clothes into a bag.

Jackson sighed, plopping down on her bed. "I should be going with you."

She stopped, leveling him a death glare for a few seconds before resuming her packing.

"How's your hand?" His hand pressed to his own shoulder still bandaged from the stitches.

Jillian received fifteen stitches of her own from grasping the glass dagger to stab Jackson two nights earlier.

"Mrs. Baker left me a message that she no longer will be taking lessons from me. Maybe I did overreact."

Jillian paused again to give him the *ya-think?* look. Hating Jackson wasn't easy, but it's all she had. The anger served as motivation to keep moving, and she needed every ounce of life-propelling effort she could muster to make it to Portland for AJ's funeral.

What would she tell his family? They believed she'd been with him when he died. The self-imposed silent treatment prevented her from asking Jackson about AJ's last words. The last words AJ gave her were nothing more than blotchy ink on a blood-stained napkin. How fitting that her entire past be tainted with blood.

She just wanted one decision to be her own. When G.A.I.L. chose to have their fake deaths be suicides, she didn't have any say in the matter. Leaving Luke behind meant leaving him with the belief that she didn't love him enough to live for *him*. He spent almost a year believing she gave up on herself ... gave up on them. If only he could have known that he was *everything*.

Jillian zipped her suitcase and hauled it toward the front door. Feeling a rush of anger, she turned.

"I'm not coming back after the funeral. I need some time alone to figure out if I can forgive you, because right now what you did feels unforgivable. Don't call me because I won't answer." She tossed her phone on the table.

Jackson stared at it, overwhelmed with defeat. They'd been through the unimaginable and survived the un-survivable, but what he did broke a bond that should have been unbreakable.

"The texts?"

She shook her head. "They can come for me and we'll see who meets their maker first."

THE PLANE HEADED TO PORTLAND, but Africa was her first choice—Africa, the middle of China, Antarctica, or anywhere that qualified as the farthest possible distance from AJ's dead body, Jackson's messed-up intentions, and the painful memories of Luke.

Exiting the secured area of the airport, she homed in on

a large sign with her name on it held by a middle-aged woman wearing a black pantsuit and dark red hair pulled tightly into a bun. Jillian paused a few seconds as the anxious people behind her brushed past with a few shoulder bumps and bags jolting the one slung over her shoulder. The woman's eyes surveyed the oncoming storm of people, not stopping on Jillian with any sort of recognition.

The uncertainty of how AJ's family would welcome the woman who stole their son's last days felt like a brick resting on her heart until that point. One of them had arranged to have her picked up at the airport and just like that ... her heavy heart lightened a bit.

"I'm Jillian Knight." She forced a small smile for the lady. The smile felt foreign to her lips. She couldn't remember the last time she'd truly smiled.

"A pleasure, Miss Knight. Do you have any checked bags?"

Jillian shook her head.

"Very well. If you'd like to follow me, I have a car waiting for us."

Jillian followed her to the exit like a zombie, having not slept more than a few hours each night since she and AJ arrived back in Omaha. It had begun to take its toll on her body and mind.

"I'll put your bag in the back."

Jillian forced another smile as the woman held open the door to a white SUV with tinted windows. After relinquishing the bag, she climbed into the back seat and sighed, feeling her whole body deflate. In twenty-four hours she would be on a plane to someplace far away from the men who all claimed a piece of her heart, a shred of her humanity, and had a hand in her feeling of utter ruin.

The driver opened the back hatch. Jillian's bag landed with a *thunk*. "Traffic is not too bad today. We should be at our destination before too long, Miss Knight."

Jillian barely registered the voice behind her until it was an icy whisper in her ear. "Or do you prefer Miss *Day*?"

A needle plunged into Jillian's neck two seconds before everything went black.

CHAPTER THREE

Frigid shock sent Jillian's body into jerking convulsions. Her eyes flew open. Sharp pain cut through the skin along her wrists and ankles bound with rope and zip ties. She winced from the pain and piercing light, the kind that felt like staring into the sun until everything burned white and then faded to black again. Every inch of her body shivered with pin-pricking goose bumps because every inch of her skin was exposed.

"Funny how you're the crazy one, yet I got sent to the psych ward for five. Long. Years."

Jillian squinted one eye open, twisting her head side to side, searching for the slightest reprieve from the light and a glimpse of her abductor. No such luck.

"But you know what happened in those five years?"

"You lost every one of your fucking marbles?"

Another wave of icy water crashed into Jillian's face, wedging her restraints deeper into her skin as she jumped in response. The stitches in her hand ripped away from her wound each time she tugged against the zip ties.

"Try again, whore. I'll help you out a little. I've been

texting you hints for months now."

The infamous biblical texts.

"You memorized verses in the Bible for five years?"

"I found God."

Jillian chuckled. Giving up on trying to see anything, she closed her eyes, dropping her chin to her chest. "God was in the psych ward?"

"I met a man in there who was a preacher. His wife committed suicide then something inside of him snapped. Love can do that to you. He read the Bible to me every day. It was so cathartic to purge my sins. God has forgiven me."

"Forgiven you for what?"

"We'll get to that."

Jillian gasped as cold water doused her naked body again. "Dammit!"

"Consider this a sort of baptism—a washing away of your sins."

"W-what sins?" she shivered, teeth chattering.

"Sex with a married man."

"N-no ..."

"Yes! You fucked my husband and so did your mother."

Her captor's insanity knew no boundaries. Jillian squeezed her eyes tight, continuing to shake her head.

"What are you ... talking about?"

"I-I apologize," the woman said, in a tight, labored voice. The hollow breath of an exhale followed a long puffing. "I won't lose my temper again. I need you to trust me so you will repent and I can absolve you of your sins before I put an end to your life."

Jillian had no qualms with death, but repenting and *trusting* the baptizing psycho for some twisted sort of absolution of her sins wasn't ever going to happen. She grew up going to church, and in spite of the times in her life that felt like the opposite of a blessing, she believed there had to be something—*someone*—greater than the whole of humanity. The voice before her did not represent anything greater than the grimy floor beneath Jillian's bare ass.

"I have a funeral to get to. Sorry my mother and I had an imaginary threesome with your husband. Sorry I cheated on a history test in the seventh grade. Sorry I dodged a speeding ticket when I was sixteen by claiming to have just started my period. Does that do it for you?"

"Yeah, about that ... Sergeant Monaghan's funeral was yesterday. You've been out of it for a little while. I may have overdone it a bit on the tranquilizer, but with your history I couldn't take any chances."

Aric James ...

Jillian clenched her teeth like an animal ready to tear apart its prey. Cage, AJ's parents, Dodge and Lilith, they paid their final respects to him without her. Some things could never be undone. AJ—she'd never see him again. The coward hiding behind the glare of lights would die. Two men were ripped from her life. Her actions no longer mattered. Jessica and Jude—Jillian and Jackson—would always be killers. New identities in a city surrounded by miles of manure changed nothing.

"I'm going to kill you."

The woman returned a cynical laugh. "That's quite the declaration coming from someone naked and hog-tied."

"Fuck!" Jillian seethed. Pain radiated down her arm from the razor-tipped arrow that had just sunk into her shoulder.

"I can't break your neck. Hell, it took me thirty minutes to get your body dragged down here. But I can land these in any part of your body with laser precision. So keep that in mind as you plan my death."

"What do you want?" Jillian grunted, holding still to prevent the arrow tip from moving.

"I want to prove that I'm not a fool. All of you will see that I'm smarter than the rest of you combined."

"All? Who's all of you?"

"G.A.I.L."

Releasing a slow breath, Jillian let the pain in her shoulder go and concentrated on the reality of her situation. The woman knew G.A.I.L., therefore she knew everything.

"Good girl. You were trained to not say anything. That's fine. I'll do the talking. Guardian Angels for Innocent Lives. It's quite poetic and beautiful. Wouldn't you agree? Named after Gail Brighton, wife to founder, Edgar Brighton, mother to Peter Brighton and *me*."

"They only had one child."

"Speaking already, are you? Not as good at following the rules as I thought. You are correct. *They* had one child together, although we both know Peter was never actually born. He died in the womb the day she was murdered. Gail had two children. I was her first. My father left when I was seven. My mother married Edgar five years later because she was pregnant with his child, Peter. Edgar never liked me. He thought of me as the poster child for childhood obesity, and I looked nothing like my mom so all he saw in me was my father. He shipped me off to boarding school. I returned home three weeks shy of winter break to attend the funeral of my mother and brother—half-brother."

Jillian did the math. Her captor had to be about forty-two.

"I didn't know your mother. I've seen Edgar maybe a handful of times, but I've only talked to him once, when my father first introduced us."

"I concur. You see, I know more about you and your

family than you do. No worries. Before you die—because you and everyone else will have to die of course—I will enlighten you. The look on your face will be priceless. It always is when someone has their dreams shattered."

Jillian didn't have dreams or anything left to shatter. The mentally-unstable woman would be sorely disappointed.

"Who's your accomplice?"

"What makes you think I have an accomplice?"

"Your intention to make *everyone* pay. Surely you have help."

"Once again, there's a ridiculous amount of irony in your words. I have the great Jessica Day at my mercy, and I did it all by myself. I know how you've been trained. But let me tell you a little secret: the most dangerous weapon is revenge with the brains to execute it."

"I don't even know you. Never knew you existed."

"Would you have let my husband fuck you if you would have known about me?"

The impossible comprehension sent pain sledgehammering through Jillian's head, obliterating all coherent thoughts. Aching muscles screamed for a reprieve from the restraints. A cold tingling sensation settling in her fingers as blood oozed from her shoulder.

"Who's your husband?"

"Does it matter? The correct answer is 'No. I would never commit adultery.'"

"I'm not a home-wrecker."

"Bullshit! Both you and your mother lusted after my husband."

Again, the hollow breath of an exhale followed a long puffing noise. It sounded familiar, but Jillian couldn't place it. Her mother was not a home-wrecker either. Sunny Day loved her husband and her children. She lived a good life. Jessica would have known if her mother cheated on her father. Furthermore, the idea of Jessica and her mother sharing a lover was beyond preposterous.

Jessica and Jude both had many lovers—one-night stands—over the years. The difference was Jessica wanted a relationship. Jude did not. The women Jude fucked threw their phone numbers at him. The men Jessica fucked threw her out the door with a string of expletives that included "psycho" and "sick bitch."

Not Luke. He loved her. Completely. Unconditionally. Eternally.

Jones

JESSICA WAS ALIVE.

Time didn't exist for Luke, neither did his job. After waking in his bed with a slight concussion and Jessica's forlorn expression branded into his memory, he drank six Heineken and passed out again. He woke eight hours later scrambling to the bathroom. Heineken wasn't his friend that day.

Reality ripped his world apart, holding him hostage in his home. Those people watched him, followed him, and knew his every move. Luke shot out texts to his family, Charlie, close friends, and his secretary, informing them of his bout with the flu and requesting they stay away for a few days. Then he polluted his body with an insane amount of alcohol over the next several days.

Jessica was alive.

He needed to save her. He needed to tell someone. He

needed to know why she would leave him if no one was holding her against her will.

If he went to the cops, his family would be in danger. The only person who could help him was Jessica. Luke believed with every cell in his heart that she did not commit suicide. That's how he knew she'd been murdered and the suicide was just a cover-up. But in the past year ... not once did he imagine she was still alive. That realization knocked him on his ass. She might as well have committed suicide. Either way, she made the conscious choice to leave him forever.

Teetering on the edge of dehydration and death, he crawled into the hot shower, followed by a tall glass of water and two Advil. Then he tore into his closet. Luke ignored his own insanity that had led to all of Jessica's belongings remaining untouched nearly a year later. Coat pockets, purses, shoes, boxes marked "childhood," he plowed through it all over the following four hours.

Nothing.

"Fuck!" he roared, fisting his hair and falling to his knees in the middle of the ransacked closet.

There wasn't a single clue, not one dear-Luke-if-I-fake-my-death-come-find-me-here note. He knew her better than she knew herself, and yet ... in that moment, he didn't know her at all.

"Luke?"

He jerked his head up.

"Luke?"

In one swift move he jumped to his feet and combed his fingers through his hair.

"Coming," he called, emerging from the closet.

"What the hell is going on with you? My God, you've lost weight."

Luke drew in a breath of courage to explain—lie—about his whereabouts and his condition. His sister, Lake, stood inside the door with her hands fisted on her hips. She'd mastered the tough role, even with her prosthetic leg that still tripped her up a bit.

Hell seemed to be the only fitting word to describe the previous year. Lake survived a car accident then flirted with death, locked in a coma for three months before waking to find her leg amputated below the knee. As if that wasn't enough to take in, they had to share the news of her boyfriend not surviving the crash and Jessica's death three weeks after the car accident.

Luke held it together for his family. The only time someone wasn't by Lake's side during those three months was the day of Jessica's and her family's funeral. How could Jessica do that to him? How could she leave him when he needed her the most?

Luke hugged his sister. She didn't return his affection.

"I've been under the weather."

"I see that. You look like shit. But that doesn't explain why you stood Charlie up in Houston. She flew out there just to be with you. She rescheduled patients and a speaking engagement because you led her to believe that you were ready to commit."

"Tea? Coffee?" Luke walked toward the kitchen.

"Neither. Don't blow me off, too." Lake followed him like a nagging dog.

An empty refrigerator stared back at him. No Heineken. He'd finished it all off. Fetching the wine opener from the drawer, he grabbed a bottle of Pinot Noir from the rack.

"You're drinking *wine*?"

"Yep."

"It's not even noon, and you stopped drinking wine after ..."

With his back to her, he paused, closing his eyes for a brief moment. "I know. After Jessica died."

Lake sighed. "Please tell me this is progress and not some sort of backslide."

He chuckled, uncorking the bottle. It was progress for sure. He'd gone from shock to devastation, finally settling into a sinking hole of anger and denial. At one point he told his best friend, Gabe, that he'd rather slit his wrists than ever taste wine again—ever taste Jessica again. Then he met Charlie, Lake's physical therapist.

The accident happened in San Francisco. Lake wanted to stay after she awoke from her coma instead of going back home to recover. She claimed it made her feel closer to her boyfriend. Luke knew it was because she wanted to be closer to her grieving brother.

Their parents rented a place near the hospital that was handicapped accessible. Tom and Felicity took turns staying with her while the others kept their bed and breakfast going in Tahoe. Once Lake received her prosthetic leg, Luke watched after her, taking her to her physical therapy appointments so their parents could have a break and much needed time together.

"I'll talk with Charlie. It really is disturbing that you're closer to her than I am. That's a big part of my 'commitment' issues. If it doesn't work out, I'll be letting you down too."

"That's it?"

Luke winced at the incredulity in her voice. He couldn't bring himself to look at her. If he did, she would see it. She'd see the lies, the pain, the truth that could put her life in danger.

Stopping an inch short of taking a long pull straight from the bottle, he grabbed a glass and filled it to the rim.

"That's it." He took several numbing gulps.

"She *flew* to Houston. You weren't there. You didn't call. You didn't answer your phone. Jesus, Luke! She was worried about you. Have you even looked at your phone? We've all been worried about you since you stood Charlie up and then sent out the I'm-sick-stay-away texts."

He turned. "*We?*"

"Yes. Mom and Dad—"

"Wait. Mom and Dad know about the Charlie incident?"

Lake rolled her eyes. "Yes. I called them after Charlie called me about the 'incident.'"

He swirled the wine in his glass, giving it his full attention as if the answer would appear on the surface. "I would have called Charlie but my phone died."

"And you didn't have a charger?"

"I lost it."

"You could have replaced it."

"I told you I wasn't feeling well. I just wanted to get home to hug my own toilet. I'm fine. Charlie's fine. You're fine. Just ... I'm sorry." He looked up again. That much was true. "I really am sorry, and I'll call Mom and Dad then I promise I'll call Charlie."

"Flowers, buddy." Lake pointed her finger at him as she narrowed her eyes. "Lots of flowers. Chocolate too. She loves chocolate and sex."

"Lake!"

"I'm serious. I'm not a kid anymore. Girls talk about this stuff. She told me you two haven't had sex yet. Okay ... I asked, but whatever. She thinks it has something to do with

23

Jessica. I told her that's not it. You're a psychiatrist for God's sake, you've worked that out."

Luke denied her eye contact again.

"You *have* worked that out. Right?"

He *had*. After keeping Charlie at a safe distance for months, he decided it was time to move on. She wasn't Jessica, and it didn't take a doctorate degree to figure that out, but he couldn't stop his heart from missing its sole purpose. Luke thought if he let his mind and body move on, eventually his heart would catch up. Houston presented the perfect opportunity, someplace that felt detached from Jessica, their bed, their life. What were the chances of finding her in the very place he went to escape her?

"Jones!" Lake greeted the small horse as he plodded into the kitchen, carrying his usual security blanket. "You and that crazy sweatshirt. Why are you always carrying that thing around?"

Jones dropped the red sweatshirt at Luke's feet.

"When I came over to let him out and feed him, he nearly bit my hand off when I tried to take it from him."

"It was Jessica's. Well, it was mine, but she laid claim to it." She'd slipped it on every morning over her naked body. Luke could still see her sitting at the table with her knees tucked up in it, using the extra six inches of sleeves as hot pads to hold her mug of coffee. There were never enough stars in the sky to count how many times a day he fell in love with her.

"Aw, Jones, poor baby." Lake stuck out her bottom lip. "Mommy's not coming home."

Reality gashed Luke's heart. He wanted to bleed out right there on the floor. Anything to take away the pain of knowing the truth.

CHAPTER FOUR

KNIGHT

THE DAY after Thanksgiving Ryn received a call from Jackson stating that AJ had died. His voice held no emotion. It felt like a service announcement from a stranger. She cried silent tears, barely able to say goodbye before he ended the call.

Flying to Portland for the funeral would have been financially straining, and Ryn wasn't ready to see Jackson, even if she did want to be there for Jillian. Something unexplainable steered her car to AJ's house on Tuesday morning. She wanted to clean his place one last time. She needed to say goodbye and that was her way.

The shambled dining room took her by surprise. Wilted flowers and shards of glass lay scattered on the floor, amidst smudges of what looked like dried blood. Two place settings remained on the table, but not a crumb of food. Depositing the glass, one piece at a time into a trash bag, Ryn tried to imagine what events led to the scene before her. They weren't going to have Thanksgiving dinner. AJ couldn't keep food down. So why the formal setting?

"What are you doing?"

"Shit!" She jumped, sending a sliver of glass into her finger. "Dammit," she seethed while holding her finger.

Jackson hunched down beside her. "Let me see."

She shook him off as she stood and headed to the bathroom. "You scared me. What are you doing here?"

He followed her. "I saw your car parked in the driveway."

Opening several drawers, she found a Band-Aid. "No. What are you doing in Omaha? Why didn't you go to the funeral?"

Jackson grabbed the Band-Aid from her. She narrowed her eyes.

"Sit."

"I don't want—"

He lifted her onto the counter. His touch still heated her skin. For some reason her body didn't get the memo that it was no longer supposed to be attracted to Jackson Knight.

"You have a piece of glass stuck in your finger." He held her finger.

She held her breath.

Retrieving tweezers from the same drawer as the Band-Aids, he washed them under hot water. Ryn couldn't stop staring at him.

"Here." He held her finger between his index finger and thumb. "Jillian didn't want me at the funeral," he said, keeping his eyes focused on her finger as he eased the sliver of glass from the cut.

"Why?"

With a shrug, he rinsed off the tweezers again then bandaged her finger. "She blames me for AJ's death."

"Why would she do that?"

He rubbed his thumb over the Band-Aid. What she wouldn't have given to read his mind at that moment. The intensity in his expression held the possibilities of a Trojan horse. One crack and his whole world could escape. What then? Would it crush her more than he already had?

"Because nobody wants to believe bad things can happen for no reason. She needs someone to blame." He brought her finger to his lips.

Ryn sucked in another breath and held it.

"So I'll take the blame. I'll let her hate me if it makes it easier for her."

Ryn eased her finger from his grasp. "That doesn't make any sense. How could she possibly blame you?"

Jackson's gaze lifted to meet hers. "Because I was with him when he died."

"Where was Jillian?"

"Waiting in his dining room."

Ryn's brow tensed. "Oh. He must have went quickly."

He nodded. "Like flipping a switch."

It wasn't until Jackson brushed his thumb along her cheek that she noticed her own tears.

"I miss you," he whispered. The pad of his thumb brushing along her lower lip evoked both desire and anger.

"Don't." Ryn pushed him away. Her feet reached for the ground as her heart reached for the door. It needed to escape before her brain served it up on a platter for Jackson to break again.

"I can't do this."

"Ryn, I'm sorry." He touched her hand.

She pulled away. "I forgive you." Her words were honest. She grabbed a broom to sweep up the glass, not risking another cut.

"But?" Jackson shadowed her every move.

"But nothing. I forgive you. Period." She moved around the dining room keeping her back to him.

"You forgive me but you 'can't do this?'"

"Correct."

"Why?"

A palpable pain in his voice tugged at her heart. She inhaled a deep breath to break the hold he tried to get on it.

"I did the dysfunctional relationship thing. It nearly killed me. The next relationship I have will be with someone who adores me and wouldn't hurt a fly. I need someone who will sit on my porch swing, rub my feet, and discuss what color of paint I should use when I get the money to repaint my house. I need a guy who wants to be with me forever *every day*, not just some days. And I think I'm worth a proper proposal. My guy will drop to a knee and look up at me like I'm his whole world. He will promise to spend the rest of his life making me forget that any man touched me before him."

A shiver paralyzed her movement as the heat of his breath washed over the back of her neck.

"No man will ever erase my touch."

Truth. And Ryn knew it.

"Which touch? The one that made me love you or the one that made you leave me?"

Jackson stepped back with a sharp breath. Ryn waited for the release, the string of reasons why she was wrong, the promise that it would never happen again. Instead, he blew out her candle of hope with a long breath of defeat.

"I asked you to give me two weeks."

"No. You asked me to give you everything, and when I did you threw it back in my face. *You* told me what *you* did was unacceptable. And you know what? You were right. I don't know you and I can't be with someone I don't know." She pressed her lips together, closing her eyes for a brief moment to regain some control. "I'm sorry. You didn't mean to hurt me—physically or emotionally. I know that. I really do. I ... I just want something easy for once in my life."

"Ryn—"

"No. Please don't say anything. You know who I want? I want the guy that kissed his sister on the head and whispered, 'You've got this.'" A laugh of incredulity bubbled up her chest. She shook her head with a painful grin. "That sounds so ridiculous, doesn't it? That touch ... the one that made me love you? It wasn't even *me* you touched. I fell in love with you because of how you love your sister. Betcha never heard that one before."

"My sister hates me."

Ryn shrugged, bending down to sweep the pile of glass into the dustpan. "She'll forgive you. That love you have for her? It runs deeper than any hate, and it takes so much more to hate someone than to love them. Hate is so exhausting. Trust me, I know."

"You don't hate me?" He held open the trash bag for her.

She dumped the glass into it. "No. I love you. But for the first time in over twenty years I love myself more. For the first time in over twenty years I feel worthy."

Pushing up on her toes, she kissed him on the cheek. He didn't move.

"Thank you, Jackson Knight. You gave me that."

"You don't have to watch me clean. Your place is next."

Jackson couldn't drag his eyes away from Ryn. Her words stunned him into total disbelief. He didn't give her up. He didn't let her go. And he certainly didn't want her to walk away and *thank* him.

Another guy? Ryn had things all wrong. Her guy, her *forever* stood in the same room. Jude Day wanted a lifetime of women for one night. Jackson Knight wanted one woman for a lifetime. But not just any woman. Ryn Middleton—he wanted her and only her.

"I know you're composing some epic speech. But I'm working and you're done swimming in my pond."

"Low blow." He narrowed his eyes, but she kept working as if she didn't just sucker punch him in the junk.

"Go." She chuckled. "I'm working."

"And why is that? I don't think you'll be getting paid to clean here anymore."

She drew in a shaky breath then glanced over her shoulder at him. "I just ... I just *need* to. For me."

Jackson nodded before leaving her to clean AJ's place for some sort of closure. He moved with the focus of a zombie through two piano lessons, giving undeserving praise to women who had no desire to do more than shamelessly flirt with him. They weren't ugly. Jude would have classified them as doable. Maybe if Jackson would have bent them over Black Beauty and fucked them like their eyes begged him to do, he'd forget about his sister leaving and Ryn rejecting him.

He'd lost himself in so many women over the years. Meaningless sex became a cleansing of sorts. That release that lasted mere seconds gave him a sense of relinquishing control. Ryn thought hating someone was exhausting—so was needing control. Sex should have meant more. Life should have meant more. But they didn't.

Jude Day killed people, more people than his sister could ever have imagined. Jude Day fucked women, but not for the reasons anyone would have imagined. His parents gave him the fairytale and then they ripped it away. Love, the kind that's not bound by blood, it didn't exist. He hated Jessica for pretending that it did. She would break Luke or Luke would break her. The inevitability happened the day Luke sobbed over her empty casket.

Jessica let Luke go because she thought it was the right thing to do. Jackson knew Luke would *never* see it that way. Jude Day never gave women the chance to break him. He could never be his father.

Jessica never knew her dreams of normalcy and love were built on illusions. She idolized their parents' marriage. Sunny Day's blood ran through her daughter's veins. Their mother loved another, then she built a family on pillars of altruism and loyalty.

Had Jessica and Claire not been kidnapped, Jude would have told her the truth. Before Claire died, they had no secrets. After she died, Jude's life revolved around protecting Jessica from herself, her past, and anyone who might shatter her dreams.

"Jackson?"

He lifted his head from his arms crossed on the ledge of the piano. It wasn't like him to not hear things, but Ryn stood before him.

"Hey."

"Were you sleeping?"

Relinquishing a sad smile, he shook his head. "Just ... deep in thought."

"Oh. Well, do you want me to come back?"

"Nope." He stood. "I'm gonna take off. Go for a ride on Jillian's bike. Supposedly it's good for clearing the mind."

"It's like ... thirty degrees outside."

He shrugged then giving her an easy nod, walked past her toward the back door.

"Jackson?"

"Yes?" He turned.

"Are you upset with me?"

"Why do you ask?"

"Because of the cold shoulder and curt nod."

Tipping his chin down, he chuckled and shook his head. He would never understand women.

"My body temperature runs pretty warm, so it's unlikely I gave you the 'cold' shoulder. And it was just a nod, not a 'curt' nod."

"So ... we're good?"

He sighed. "Are you good, Ryn?"

"So you are upset with me."

"Oh for the love of—" His frustration released as a growl. "Cheese cubes on a blanket, stable boy my ass," he grumbled. "I don't speak 'woman'. Never have. Never will. When it comes to relationships I have a master's degree in fucking. You were the exception, but clearly I should go back to what I'm best at. So you go enjoy your porch swing masseur with an eye for the perfect paint color, and I'll do what I do best. For a brief moment in time I believed monogamy was possible for me. So thank you for reminding me why that's not possible. It seems as if we've both helped each other realize our self-worth."

The tears in her eyes would not break him. No woman would break him.

Ryn blinked them away. "I ... I deserved that."

Jackson forced a breath out his nose—a half-suppressed, cynical laugh. "No. You didn't. But until you realize that, you'll always be the victim."

CHAPTER FIVE

DARKNESS.

Finally. The lights were off or Jillian had died. The latter being her preference. The desert heat pulling every ounce of moisture from her body intensified as she came to. The question of Heaven or Hell for the duality of Jessica and Jillian seemed to be answered.

"Welcome back. Hungry?"

Of course, the psycho daughter of Edgar Brighton would be in Hell too. Or maybe she was the Devil. It all began to make sense until the wretched smell of animal carcass infiltrated Jillian's nose.

"Sorry. The chef doesn't accommodate vegetarians."

Jillian opened her eyes, taking a slow survey of the room. "Oh my God," she whispered.

"So you remember this place? I thought you might. I had two places in mind when I planned this *years* ago, but this one felt like the best fit to give you closure. The other place would have given me closure, but I'll make this work for both of us."

The odds of leaving that room alive for a second time felt stacked against her. Jillian's captor was one sick bitch.

"I can't tell you how disappointed I was that they painted the floor. The thirteen-year-old blood stains would have added to the effect I'm going for, but I bought it anyway."

They were in San Diego, in the same basement where Claire died. The red glow of heating elements from at least a dozen space heaters gave the dungeon a dim light like a piece of meat under the broiler. Jillian preferred the bright lights and icy water that left her blind to her surroundings and the memories they evoked.

Psycho Bitch perched on a stool in the corner, holding a personal fan up to her face.

"You knew Four."

"Four." She laughed. "I heard that's what you called him. Monsters don't deserve human names and all that crap, right?"

Correct assumption by *Psycho Bitch*. The bow and arrow on the floor next to the stool caught Jillian's eye. She tipped her chin to see the wound on her shoulder minus the arrow.

"No. I didn't know Edwin Harvey until he cut your BFF forty-four times."

Jillian bared her clenched teeth like a rabid animal.

Psycho Bitch shrugged. "What? Is that not how it happened?" She rolled her eyes. "I'm kidding. As I told you earlier, I know more about you than you do. Now, Matthew Green? I did get the chance to make his acquaintance, but just via phone conversations. It took me a little while to track down that slimy little worm, but when I found him he couldn't resist a hundred grand to kill you."

"I killed him."

Psycho Bitch shrugged. "I thought you might. It was a win-win for me either way. If he killed you, I wouldn't have had all the fun I'm having now, but the end result would have been the same. And if you killed him, which you did, then I didn't have to dish out a hundred grand *and* you—Jillian Knight—officially had blood on your hands, and it opened the door to fuck with your brain when I decided to send you all those messages."

"It's all about the mind-fuck."

"I spent five long years in a mental institution so yes ... I get a high from manipulating everyone else's brains."

She sighed. "Anyway ... as I was saying, Edgar took pity on me after I graduated college. My exemplary grades in school earned me a job with G.A.I.L., working in intelligence and logistics. A behind-the-scenes position. Before Jude Day was allowed to snap anyone's neck, I made sure the intelligence we had was accurate. Very few people saw or knew me. I had a small cubicle and a computer with security access that rivaled the Pentagon. Edgar gave me a code name, and that's all anyone knew."

The heat. Jillian's brain lagged several steps behind the long explanation. Hunger and dehydration vied for her attention more than the story behind Edgars's stepdaughter and her road to insanity. The bowl of brown sludge on the floor brought bile inching up her throat.

Dog food. Psycho Bitch didn't miss a thing, including Four feeding Claire dog food.

"G.A.I.L. did a psychological evaluation on you afterward. The report said you refused to eat. Are you still a vegetarian? I bet I'll break you of that. I bet you'll be licking the contents of that bowl before you die."

Jillian had a lot of bets going on too. She bet Four's murder would look like child's play compared to what she had planned for Psycho Bitch. Jessica Day had been young, still valued her life and possessed a few give-a-fucks in her conscience. Not Jillian Knight. She would blow up the whole city of San Diego to seek revenge on one person.

Jessica had two parents, Luke, and a brother that loved her. Jillian had the memories of a dead lover, a brother that had lost the last breath of his humanity, and a feeling of certainty that Luke hated her. How could he possibly not?

Day

A SMALL HORSE disguised as a black and white Great Dane sat next to the bed like a statue—a drooling statue. Jessica peeked open one eye, puckering her lips to blow Jones a kiss as she reached for the birthday boy.

Naughty intentions curled the corners of her lips—lips that she wanted to wrap around the world's most beautiful cock. She never imagined thinking of a penis as beautiful, until Luke. Everything about him screamed beautiful, perfect, and slightly anal-retentive ... in a sexy way. She loved early-morning-mussed-hair Luke, but during their nearly two years together, she'd also come to crave the stunning, polished man in a suit. He bled authority, control, and an overall fuck-me vibe.

Her hand found smooth, folded sheets and a fluffed pillow. Jackknifing to sitting, she frowned at his side of the bed with its military-style order: sheets pulled tight and tucked under his side, the top folded down a perfect six inches with no sign of wrinkles.

"Luke?"

Swinging her feet to the side, she landed nose to nose

with Jones. She loved the beast of a dog, but he had a knack for always being in the way.

"You have *got* to control that drooling problem of yours." Her face wrinkled as her foot landed in a pool of drool on the wood floor.

No Luke in the bathroom. Her beastly shadow followed her to the kitchen. No Luke in the kitchen.

"Luke." A soft sigh floated past her lips, being pushed out by the swelling of her heart.

She grabbed the card on the counter next to a gardenia bonsai with three perfect white blooms.

Did you know I wake up early just to watch you sleep? It's how I start each day with purpose. You remind my eyes to see, my lungs to breathe, my heart to beat. Then again ... sometimes I feel blinded by your beauty, breathless to your touch, paralyzed by your love.

I know what I want for my birthday, but I had to go into the office to deal with a sticky situation. Meet me for lunch at my office at one. (Yes, I'm lifting the office ban for one day.) ~Luke

"Lunch at Daddy's office. What do you think of that, Jonesy?"

Jones tilted his head.

Jessica bent down and kissed him. "Don't worry. You're invited too."

After a shower and breakfast with Jones, Jessica sent off a text to Luke.

Jessica: On R way. We're walking. Gardenia bonsai *sigh* UR my whole <3

Jones: *C U soon. Just finishing a few notes.*

Grinning like a fool in love, Jessica made the six-block journey through the hills to Luke's office with her gallant K9 steed by her side. On the elevator ride to the twenty-seventh floor, she realized her heart could no longer remember what it felt like to not love Luke. What if her heart loved him with its very first beat? Her heart bore the scars of war and near death ... all to find its way home. Home to Luke.

Since they ended their professional relationship two years earlier, Jessica made a grand total of three trips to his office. Once to surprise him with lunch, which earned both of them a raised brow from his secretary, Eve. It also earned Jessica a long lecture about *never* coming to his office. The whole us-being-together-is-extremely-unethical thing really made him paranoid.

The second visit was a year earlier on his birthday. The argyle thigh-high socks and stilettos earned her a double brow raise from Eve, who insisted on taking Jessica's trench coat from her. Not really believing Eve could be so naive and trusting her to not end Luke's career, Jessica relinquished her coat, revealing a pleated miniskirt and white button-down blouse exposing ample cleavage. Eve showed no reaction, probably because the pigtails left little to the imagination of what was under the coat.

Jones plopped down in the lobby. He had been there more than Jessica, but Luke had a strict no-dog-in-his-office rule that Jones seemed content with obeying. Eve wasn't at her desk since Luke was supposed to have the day off.

The door handle resisted Jessica's effort to turn it. "It's rude to invite me to lunch then lock me out, even if it is *your* day."

"Just making one last note, babe."

"If you're screwing some bimbo on your desk, I'm going to take a sledge hammer to your car."

Jessica grinned at the sound of Luke chuckling on the other side of the door.

"No, you won't. I think you love that car more than I do. You might even love it more than you love me."

"I do love your GTO, baby. But I *adore* you."

Luke's voice grew nearer. "You adore me?"

"Yes. This guy I once knew, told me adoration is better. It means to love and admire." She tried to turn the handle again, knowing he was right on the other side of the door. "Let me in." She laughed.

"How long?"

"How long what?"

Luke waited a few long seconds to answer. The lock clicked.

"How long will you adore me?"

The birthday boy had some crazy questions. How could he not know that answer?

"Forever, you know tha—" She opened the door. Shock paralyzed her entire body.

A glorious technicolor of sticky notes covered every surface of his office, floor to ceiling. Her favorite Staples aisle exploded in Luke's office. There must have been thousands of sticky notes. In the middle of the paper sea: Luke on *two* knees. He held a small box with a neon pink sticky note on it that read *"Marry me?"*

"This is where it all began. This is where you ruined me for every other woman. I think I loved you before I ever knew you because it's never felt like a choice for me. It's just something as certain as the change of the seasons, the tilt of the earth, the dawn welcoming a new day."

He looked around the room. "I know flower petals would have been the normal thing to do, but my girl has a Staples obsession—"

"It's not an obsess—"

"It is." He grinned.

She did too.

"Jessica Mauve Day, I want you to marry me more than I want my heart to beat. This love I have for you is beyond any kind of insanity I've ever encountered. Every second we're apart it feels like I'm holding my breath, and the moment you walk through the door I gasp for air. You fill my lungs and flow through my veins, giving me life. I know all you see is your past, but all I see is our future. I don't want a wall of pillows between us. I don't want to talk about your past anymore. I want you to let go. I want you to free fall into my arms and know I've got you. I'll always have you."

Loving Luke became the most beautiful redemption for a life filled with stolen innocence. Giving herself to him in body, mind, soul, and name would close the door to her past and open the door to *life*. A real life.

"I'm messy." She bit back her grin.

"You're the worst." Luke refused to hide his smile. It looked truly stunning on his handsome face.

"I'm stubborn."

"Contumacious."

She giggled. "I can't cook."

"I'd rather starve than eat what you make."

She pinched her lips together and nodded. "I think this could work."

He flipped open the box. Her brow furrowed at its contents.

"I thought the future Mrs. Luke Jones needed her own key to my GTO."

"Oh ... well this is ..." she grimaced.

Luke rolled his eyes to the ceiling with a sigh and head shake. "You made your own key already, didn't you?"

Jessica nodded slowly. Luke chucked the box over his shoulder.

"Luke Thomas Jones?" Dropping her purse, she inched closer.

He rested his hands on her hips while she pressed her palms to his cheeks, relishing the feel of his soft stubble, the blue depths of his eyes gazing at her with pure, unequivocal love.

"Hmm?"

Tears pooled in her eyes. "If there were only one path to you, I'd take the heartache, the deaths, the loss, the pain ... the insanity. I'd spend an eternity in Hell for one single breath with you." Taking his hand, she pressed it against her chest. "Do you feel that? That's you, Luke. You're my heart."

He turned his face to kiss her palm. "Please tell me that's a yes."

She blinked, releasing a laugh and fat tears filled with a lifetime of relief. "Yes!"

He reached into his pocket and retrieved a brilliant solitaire diamond set atop a platinum band. Then he slipped it onto her finger.

"Best. Birthday. Ever." He looked up at her with complete nothing-could-ever-compare *adoration*.

CHAPTER SIX

KNIGHT

Hating Jackson came easy to Ryn after he rode off on Jillian's Harley. His words tore through her heart with the brutality of a serrated knife.

Rip. Rip. Rip.

She didn't want to think about him *fucking* other women. She didn't want to be the victim anymore. And she definitely didn't want to clean his house. Just the opposite. Starting in his bathroom, she squeezed all the shampoo and shower gel onto the floor and TP'd the rest of it. Then she proceeded to his bedroom, stripping the bed and dumping all the contents of his dresser drawers onto the floor. Saving the kitchen for last.

Eggs.

Chocolate syrup.

Beer.

Red Bull.

Ketchup and mustard.

It all painted the floor. She prayed Jillian didn't return until Jackson had a chance to clean up everything, but something told her—woman to woman—Jillian would understand.

No man had brought out the crazy side of her. She despised Preston, never wanting to draw his attention to her because it always came in the form of a fist to her face or foot to her ribs.

Jackson's attention? She wanted it. All of it. And that's exactly what she would get.

Before she managed to make her escape, Greta hollered to her. "Wait up!"

Ryn swallowed back the nervous lump in her throat. Greta had no idea Ryn just left the Knight's house looking like ground zero.

"Hi, Greta." She lifted her shoulders and flipped up the collar to her red wool coat, protecting her ears from the biting wind.

"Just checking to see if you received your uh … *toys* from my party." Greta's black, full-length down coat with a faux-fur trimmed hood covered nearly every inch of exposed skin. Ryn dressed for the low forties, Greta dressed for the arctic.

Ryn smiled. "I did. UPS delivered it last week."

"Swell, just swell." Greta looked around before meeting Ryn's eyes again. "Have you tried any of them out?"

The lump inched back up her throat as the rumble of a motorcycle drew near. "Uh, not yet."

Greta winked. "Clearly you don't need them when you have him."

They watched Jackson speed into the garage. He climbed off the Harley and shut the garage door without a single glance back, leaving a dust cloud of anger suffocating Ryn.

"I'd better go." Ryn squeezed her car key to steady her

shaking hands. She needed out of there before Jackson's anger blew the roof off the joint.

"Do you want to come over and warm up with a cup of coffee or—"

"No. Sorry, I don't have time." She slipped into the driver's seat, just as Jackson stormed back outside.

"There's my handsome neighbor," Greta said. "How's Jillian? We sure have been thinking of her."

Ryn cowered under his narrow-eyed glare fixed solely on her.

"She's fine. Taking some time for herself," Jackson answered calmly, never shifting his eyes from Ryn's.

"That's good. She needs it. Well, nice to see you again, sweetie. I've got to get my caboose inside before it freezes right off."

Ryn shot Greta a pleading look. Silently begging her not to leave. She needed a distraction to get away. No such luck.

"Okay ... bye." Ryn's voice wavered.

"Too-da-loo," Greta sang crossing the street.

"Get out," Jackson growled. The chilly afternoon felt like a tropical island compared to the icy intonation of his voice.

Ryn's heart stopped in self-preservation like an animal waiting for its predator to pass by. The impulsiveness of her destructive behavior began to lose its justification the longer Jackson towered over her, his anger multiplying with each passing second.

"If you touch me, I'll scream."

Jackson recoiled. His anger replaced with a look of shock, maybe even pain. The resentment hung between them as thick as the cloud of condensation from their breaths.

Ryn would always be the skittish dog, no matter how

hard she tried to put on a brave front. At some point, Preston's physical abuse ingrained that reaction into her.

"I'm sorry—"

He shook his head as he turned, retreating back toward the house. "Go home, Ryn."

A mishmash of emotions warred in her mind and her heart. Sliding out of her car, she slammed the door and pounded ten steps on the driveway toward Jackson's front door. Then she spun around and retraced those same steps back down to her car, repeating it two more times until her nerves gained enough momentum to make it all the way to his door.

In the middle of her incessant knocks, Jackson opened the door, holding an amber bottle of beer. He said nothing and neither did his expression.

"I trashed your place." She hugged herself. The heat of her anger enveloped the onset of shivering nerves.

He took a long pull, unaffected by the cold and appearing bored with her stating the obvious.

"You trashed my heart. You and your relentless pursuit of me have completely wrecked this life I've fought so hard to get back. I didn't want to love you, but I did. I didn't want you to promise me forever, but you did, and then you took it back. Now I'm left with what? What's left when someone takes back forever?"

"Don't cry." His brow furrowed.

"I'm not crying!" She wiped her cheek. "Dammit," she whispered to herself, making haste to dissolve the rest of the evidence. Her frayed nerves and uncooperative hormones deserved reprimanding with a full bottle of wine as soon as she got home.

The lines on his forehead deepened with her outburst.

"For God's sake." She fisted her hands at her side, her

voice escalating despite her effort to stay calm. "You asked me to marry you. I said yes. I. Said. Yes!"

He took another pull of his beer, leaning his back against the door to keep it open.

"You're supposed to fight for me. You're supposed to get down on your knees and beg for my forgiveness because you were a complete jerk. Instead, you seem hell-bent on teaching me some lesson about not letting men step all over me, as if having the shit beat out of me for years wasn't enough of a lesson. And that crap about you acting like the only thing you're good at is fucking random women ... that hurt! What is wrong with you? Why ..."

Fuck the tears. It no longer mattered.

"Why can't you just love me?"

IT HAPPENED. She broke him.

He always imagined it would be his sister. Both Jessica and Jillian had tried over the years. Somehow he knew his sister's strength would allow her to persevere.

Not Ryn. She wore a brave face over the hollow shell of a woman she used to be. Jackson never knew that woman, but he saw glimpses of her. It made him want to end Preston Iverson's life for beating it out of her. It made him want to shake some sense into Maddie for not seeing the amazing woman before her.

"So that's it? You don't have anything to say?" She sucked in her quivering lips, tipping her chin to her chest. "It would hurt less if you hit me." Her words were nothing more than a soft murmur to herself, but Jackson heard every single one.

He turned, letting the storm door close between them as

he set his beer on the table. When he walked back toward the door, the woman who owned him had made it halfway to her car, head down, sobs racking her body.

He was a jerk. He didn't deserve her. And if he could live without her, he'd let her get in her car and hate him forever. *If* he could live without her. But he couldn't.

"You're going to regret loving me."

She jumped, gasping for a breath, as he scooped her up in his arms and hauled her inside the house.

"But that's just too fucking bad." He deposited her on Jillian's bed, smashing his mouth to hers before she could protest or speak any words for that matter.

There were so many things left to say, but he needed her physically before he could even think of articulating the vulnerable, emasculating emotions in his mind. Her fingers curled into his arms and he felt them gripping his soul. When she wrapped her legs around his waist, he moaned like a wounded animal.

They became a tangle of limbs, ripping off clothes. He peeled away from her body. Standing to remove his jeans, he left her breathless on the bed. Her tongue eased out to wet her lips while her fingers traced the C-section scar before resting a hand over it. He'd seen it many times before. Her insecurities saddened him.

"Don't," he whispered, kneeling between her legs.

Keeping his eyes fixed on hers, he pushed her hand away from the scar. She swallowed hard. It broke him a little more.

"I love you."

Ryn closed her eyes. A lone tear trailed down to her ear.

"I love your imperfections. I *need* them. They give me hope that you will love mine too."

47

Could she love him if she really knew him? He prayed to God she could.

Ryn opened her eyes. Sitting up, she shifted to her knees, facing him. He clenched his teeth, afraid to breathe, as she pressed her palms to his face. Her gentle touch dominated his strength. Ryn's ineffable beauty stripped him raw, leaving him a slave to her mercy. In that moment only one truth existed: he would protect her with his life, and she would make him human again.

"There's nothing about you I couldn't love ... if you'd just let me," she whispered.

He kissed her, palming her breasts until she moaned, opening her mouth wider to him. The slide of her hand from his face to his chest ended wrapped around his cock, annihilating his last bit of control.

"God, Ryn ..." He thrust into her touch, biting and sucking at her lips. "I'm so fucking sorry ... this isn't going to be gentle."

She answered by curling her fingers into his hair, yanking hard while plunging her tongue into his mouth. Jackson slipped his hands behind her legs and lifted her up. When she wrapped her legs around him, he pushed inside her, swallowing each other's groans.

He fucked her. He loved her. He drowned in the sensation of being lost inside her. And when Jackson Knight emerged ... he was one. His duality vanished under her touch. Jackson loved Ryn to the depths of eternity, and so did Jude Day.

CHAPTER SEVEN

"**W**HY ARE we in Jillian's room?" Ryn lifted the sheet, peeking down at Jackson, who seemed content sprawled out on his stomach between her legs, head resting on her stomach. She combed her fingers through his hair in a lazy rhythm. The look on his face led her to believe he could start purring.

"My ex-cleaning lady went berserk."

She stopped her hands, fisting his hair. "*Ex?*"

He chuckled. "Yes. I feel her attention to detail isn't what it used to be."

Her smile faded, washed away by the memory of his parting words. "Can you be honest with me?"

His answer took its time. It bothered her that he needed to consider his ability to be honest with her.

"Yes," he said, turning his head until his lips pressed to her C-section scar.

"Were you just angry or were you serious when you implied that all you're good at is … 'fucking.'"

A slow breath escaped his lips, warming her skin. "Both. I wanted you to show me I'm more than that guy. He's all

I've ever known. But then you went off about foot rubs, porch swings, and paint swatches. I knew I would never be *that* guy. I felt like the guy who helped you see what you want, but it wasn't me."

"Jackson ..." Ryn's chest ached beneath the weight of his words. "I fear you more than I've ever feared any man."

He turned, resting his chin on her stomach. Confusion lined his brow.

"Preston hurt me. He broke my skin and even a few bones, and I survived. But you ... you could do something Preston could never do. You could break my heart, and I don't know if I would survive that."

"I'm going to hurt you," he murmured over her skin, inching up her body. "I'm going to do everything wrong nine times out of ten." He rested his lips between her breasts for a long second then looked up at her. "But I will never cross that line. I'll never break your heart."

Ryn nodded once. Her dreams clung to his words ... to his promise.

"What happened?" She traced the outline of the large adhesive patch on his shoulder.

"Jillian."

"Sibling feud gone wrong?" She smiled. He did not.

"Were you serious?" he asked.

Ryn continued tracing the patch on his shoulder. "About?"

"About there being nothing about me that you can't love?"

Her heart raced just from the tone of his voice, as if she somehow knew what he was about to say would forever change her life. But if given a thousand lifetimes to contemplate the possibilities, she never would have imagined his next confession.

"Yes," she whispered past the asphyxiating fear in her throat.

"The glass on the floor at AJ's?"

Ryn nodded slowly.

"She stabbed me with a long shard of it."

"What?" She shook her head. "Why?"

"I took AJ's ..." Jackson laced his fingers with hers, holding them next to her shoulders as if his words required her to be restrained.

Her body tensed beneath his, preparing for impact. Of what? She didn't know. "You took AJ's ... what?"

"Life."

He didn't say that. She knew that's not what he said, and if he did there was no way it's what he meant. It had to be metaphorical.

"W-what do you mean?"

"He was in a lot of pain. Jillian was in denial."

Ryn shook her head, trying to wriggle from his grasp, but the more she tried, the harder he held her down.

"What are you saying? You ... you killed him?"

"Yes." The firm resolution in his answer held no regret.

Jackson killed AJ. Jackson. Killed. AJ.

"It was his decision, not mine."

"What?" She tugged against his grip. "Let me go!"

He released her. She flailed to sitting then scrambled to collect her clothes, tripping on to her face.

"Are you okay—"

"I'm fine." She yanked away from his hold, skidding back onto her butt with her clothes hugged to her chest.

"Whoa ... what the hell?"

"You killed AJ! You took someone's life. How can you stand there like it was nothing? That's ... that's ... *something.* Like illegal and immoral and ... and wrong on so many levels. It doesn't matter that he asked you to do it. He wasn't in his right mind. I mean ... for God's sake, if I get embarrassed and mumble the words 'kill me now' are you going to put a gun to my head and pull the trigger?"

"What?" He jerked his head back.

She wasn't crazy. Okay, she had a little crazy going on, but nothing to warrant the shocked look on his face.

"Ryn, stop. Just stop. I didn't put a gun to his head. He. Was. Dying." Jackson moved toward her.

She retreated until her back pressed against Jillian's armoire. "What if his family finds out? You could be charged with murder."

"They won't find out. I know what I'm doing."

"You know what you're doing? H-how? Did you Google euthanasia?"

He chuckled. That fueled her fire.

"Oh my God. You're laughing about this?"

Jackson shook his head, lips twitching as he tried and failed to hide his smirk. "No. I just didn't expect this reaction from you."

"Oh ..." She shoved him out of her way, dropping the wad of clothes onto the bed. She sorted through them to find her bra and panties. "Do share. What reaction did you expect from me?"

"Stop!" He grabbed her arms and forced her to sit on the edge of the bed as he knelt on the floor in front of her. "I know you don't know what to do with this information right now. You're in shock. I get it. AJ had terminal cancer. He couldn't control his personality and he began to get violent with Jillian. He was going blind and losing his ability to even form words. He couldn't eat. He was having seizures. He was suffering, Ryn. Can't you see that?"

She couldn't see anything. There was a reason behind the term *blindsided*.

Blink. Blink. Blink. She stared, searching for reason.

"How?" she whispered.

He sighed. "How what?"

"How did you kill him?'

Jackson flinched. A barely noticeable flinch, but she saw it.

"Does it matter?"

"Yes."

"Why?"

"It just does."

His hands slid from her arms to her legs as he sat back on his heels and stared at the floor. "I did what I did to Preston in the restaurant. After AJ passed out, I broke his neck."

Who was this man?

"How did it make you feel?"

"Confused."

"Why?"

Jackson's response came without hesitation. "Because he didn't deserve to die."

Jackson was right. Ryn didn't know what to do with his confession. She stared at his hands and tried to imagine him using them to kill another human being. Her hands rested on his, squeezing them. He looked up and she gave him a sad smile.

"I still love you ... all of you."

His whole body deflated with relief.

"Ryn?"

"Hmm?" She rested her hands on the back of his neck and leaned forward, kissing his forehead.

"It's ... nothing"

JACKSON PLOTTED A FOUR-STEP, fool-proof process.

Step One: Confess the mercy killing first.

Step Two: Wait for Ryn to acclimate to Jackson's ability to take another's life.

Step Three: Make her fall so deep in love with him that not even the assassin confession could drive her away.

Step Four: Be prepared to gently hold her in captivity until she snaps out of her inevitable conniption fit because realistically there is no way Step Three would ever fly.

"Done." Ryn sighed, tying the last trash bag.

Jackson nodded from the seat of Black Beauty, where she put him in timeout when he tried to help her clean up the disaster she made hours earlier.

"You can come out of timeout now." She smiled, tilting her head to the side, much like Gunner.

Jackson continued to play a Bach piece, looking only at her. "I'm good. I rather like watching you work, especially when you're on your hands and knees, scrubbing my kitchen floor." He twisted his lips to the side, making a quick downward glance as his hands made a transition. "Does that make me a pervert or an attentive boss?"

Ryn narrowed her eyes. "A pervert since you fired me, therefore you're no longer my boss." She picked up both bags, lugging them toward the back door. "Nice knowing ya, Mr. Knight. Thanks for the opportunity. Sorry it didn't work out."

Jackson grinned. "I'd like to rehire you, but just to dust the pedals of my piano, in a low-cut shirt—sans bra. And maybe to do a little spit shining of something else while you're under there."

The door slammed shut. He chuckled to himself. A few

moments later she returned, hands on her hips that swayed gently as she walked toward him with a newfound confidence. Or maybe she'd always had it, he just brought it out of her again.

"I need to go take Gunner for a walk before it gets too late."

Jackson nodded as he kept playing. "Show me your tits one more time before you go."

She walked behind him, draping her arms over his shoulders. Her teeth tugged at his earlobe. "I'm going to pretend you didn't just say that because I'm forty, you're thirty, and we need to meet at a thirty-five age level of maturity if this is going to work. I don't know too many thirty-five-year-old men that say 'show me your tits.'"

"Clearly you don't know too many thirty-five-year-old men. Or really any men for that matter. We come out of the womb in search of a woman's tits. That desire never goes away. Our use for them simply changes as we age. I guarantee you every man that you encounter thinks, at least subconsciously, 'show me your tits, Ryn.'"

"So every woman you encounter, you want to see her breasts."

"Tits. And yes. It's genetic, sweetheart. So you can't be pissed. Well ... I stand corrected. There are a few women in this particular development whose 'breasts' best stay hidden."

"I bet Greta would go all Mardi Gras on you in a heartbeat."

"No! No. No. No. That's what I'm talking about. Don't say that."

Ryn laughed. "Goodnight, Jackson," she whispered in his ear.

He stopped playing and flipped his legs over the bench

to face her. "Goodnight? You're not coming back?" Hooking an arm around her waist, he yanked her onto his lap.

"I don't live here. Besides, I'm exhausted. Physically and emotionally it's been the most draining day ever. Anyway, I need a shower."

"I like showers." He bit back his grin, wondering if she would remember the last time he said that.

Her eye roll and soft laugh confirmed her memory was still intact. "When is Jillian coming home? I heard you tell Greta she's taking some time for herself. Did she stay in Portland with AJ's family?"

Good question.

"I don't know."

"Well, have you talked to her since the funeral?"

"No. She left her phone here. Symbolically, it's the biggest fuck off she's ever given me."

Ryn brushed her lips against his a few times before kissing the corner of his mouth. "I didn't love AJ and I flipped out. You're going to have to give her time and space to grieve, not only AJ's death but also the trust she had in you."

Jackson wasn't sure if Jillian would ever forgive him. She left having hit a new level of rock-bottom in her life. He had to believe a spark of life would eventually resurrect her. He used to be that spark, but he was no longer.

His hands slid up the back of her shirt. "Don't go."

"I have to."

He let her wriggle out of his hold, righting her shirt when she stood. It was for the best. He needed an outlet and if she stayed, her body would've been that outlet. It took considerable strength to not bend her over Black Beauty and fuck her into another dimension. But he knew that would not sate him. He would physically break her before his own body reached the exhaustion it needed to calm his nerves and numb his worries.

"Drive safely."

"You okay?" She cupped the side of his neck. Her fingers played with the hair at his nape. "Your pulse is racing?"

Jackson swallowed then cleared his throat. "You're touching me. My dick is hard with a racing pulse as well. You've got ten seconds to get your sexy ass out of here before I have you face-down ass-up on my piano." He gave her a cocky grin to hide the dim reality of his true intentions.

Ryn's eyes widened a fraction before settling into their own smile that matched lips he imagined wrapped around the aforementioned pulsing erection. She needed to leave. Stat.

"We'll do face-down ass-up another day." She winked, blowing him a kiss as she headed toward the door.

Jackson forced out a hard breath after the door clicked shut. He needed to run ten miles, burn out every muscle group, and figure out a way to tell Ryn *everything*.

CHAPTER EIGHT

JONES

ONLY ONE THING remained for Luke to do in his lifetime: find Jessica. Even if it took a hundred lifetimes, he would never stop looking for her.

On his way to meet Gabe for a jog, he ran into Charlie in the lobby of his building. The timing could not have been worse. His list of fires to extinguish included a sincere apology to her, just not at that exact moment.

"Luke, hi." The forgiveness in Charlie's smile twisted the growing knot of guilt in his stomach.

Charlie was kind and genuine, a real catch for any man. Luke wasn't any man. He belonged to Jessica and she belonged to him. Not even death could change something as certain as that.

"Charlie, this ... God, this is the worst time for me, but—"

"Are you okay?" The touch of her hand on his arm continued to feed the guilt monster. "My God, I was so worried about you."

There was no easy way to tell her he didn't have time for more than a five-second explanation of his behavior that seemed to be carefully monitored by people willing to kill to keep their identities protected. The I-was-abducted-by-aliens explanation seemed like a bad choice, but it really was as close to the truth as he could get.

"I owe you an apology the size of the state in which I abandoned you, but I'm meeting someone in a few minutes."

Her shoulders turned inward as she looked at her feet.

"There's nothing I can say to make what happened okay. I can't even explain it myself. I just ..."

"You got cold feet." She looked up at him with blue eyes and long dark lashes that matched the color of her chin-length hair.

He had to be an asshole, but not by choice. Honesty put too many lives at risk. Had he not seen Jessica, Luke would have taken the next step with Charlie, an enormous step away from his past and the woman who should have been his wife.

"Yes. I got cold feet. My past won't let me go. I'm so sorry. If you hate me, I wouldn't blame you."

Charlie blinked away her tears. "If she was as wonderful as you remember, she'd want you to move on."

Luke returned a slow nod as Charlie leaned up and kissed him on the corner of his mouth. Every instinct told him to pull back, but it was a goodbye and she deserved that.

"I hope she lets you live your life someday." Charlie walked out of his building and his life.

Taking time to sort out his feelings about her and what he could have said differently was not a luxury he had with Gabe waiting. He jogged to Pier Three where Gabe stood with a what-took-you-so-long look distorting his face.

"Heard you went MIA." Gabe met Luke's pace.

"I need a favor."

"What kind of favor?"

Luke picked up the speed, making sure they weren't being followed. "The kind that could get me killed if anyone finds out."

Gabe laughed. Luke did not.

"Shit. You're serious?"

"I need you to go to Texas for me."

"Luke, you're not making any sense—" Gabe rested a hand on Luke's shoulder.

"Keep jogging. If we stop, someone could hear us."

"What are you talking about?"

He sounded crazy. That couldn't be helped. Gabe was his only choice. The only person he could trust.

"Jess is alive."

"Luke, buddy ... what's going on with you? She died. We were all at the funeral."

"I saw her in Houston."

"Sometimes we see people or things we want to see. You, better than anyone, know how the mind works."

"It was her. Blond hair. Too thin. But it was her. She saw me too, for all of ten seconds before I was hauled off, injected with a sedative, and interrogated by some psycho."

"What the fuck?"

"It's a long story, and I don't know half of it, but she's alive, Gabe. These people, they're watching me and they've threatened to kill me and my family if I try to find her or tell anyone. But for Christ's sake ... I saw her. I can't pretend she's dead."

"So you want me to go to Texas to find her?"

"I need you to get a flight to someplace within driving distance. I don't want you to fly directly to Houston. It would be a red flag. The hotel I stayed at in Houston ... you need to do whatever it takes to see security footage of when I saw Jessica. You'll see me in a line at the concierge's desk around seven-thirty in the morning. Jessica was the second person in front of me. Blond hair in a bun. Make them retrace the footage to see what room she was in. Find out what name was on the room and any other contact information."

"What if they won't show me?"

"They will. Everyone has a price. Figure out what it is and I'll pay it." Luke stopped, his breath too labored to say much more. Hunched over, he rested his hands on his knees. "You can't say a word to anyone, not even Kelly. Just make up some business trip excuse."

"What if they don't have footage of her coming out of her room?"

Luke shook his head, not wanting to think about that real possibility. "I don't know, but it's all I have right now."

Two DAYS and two burner phones later, Luke went back to work while Gabe flew to Dallas then made the two-and-a-half hour drive to Houston. Dr. Jones had a full schedule and not a brain cell left to devote to his patients. Only Jessica.

Finding her without anyone dying in the process required Dr. Jones to get back to work, giving the appearance of resuming his normal life. Jones got his usual walk with Luke around Fort Funston, and Lake came over for dinner.

"I talked to Charlie today. She said you ended it. What the hell, Luke?"

He set two bowls of lobster bisque on the table and sat

down across from her, draping his napkin over his right leg. "I shouldn't have stood her up in Houston."

"No, you shouldn't have dumped her in the lobby. Please tell me this isn't about Jessica."

"It's complicated."

"Complicated? How can it be complicated? I get it. Jessica was the love of your life and what happened was tragic, but it's time to let go."

"How's your love life?"

With an eye roll, Lake smirked. "Nice diversion. It's not the same thing. You lost your fiancée, I lost my boyfriend and my leg. I have yet to find a guy that thinks my bionic leg is sexy. I'll probably die a virgin."

Luke narrowed his eyes. "Mom caught you having sex in one of the guest rooms."

"You know what I mean. It's just an expression."

"It's really not." He sipped a spoonful of soup.

"Why can't you let her go yet?" Lake tapped her spoon on the edge of her bowl. *Tap. Tap. Tap.* Waiting for Luke's answer.

"I guess I still can't believe she's gone. There's a certain amount of closure that comes from seeing the body. We never got to see her body."

"I know what you mean. When I came out of my coma to the news of both Ben and Jessica's deaths, I couldn't wrap my head around it. It's like you spend the rest of your life waiting for that last goodbye."

Luke never said goodbye. He didn't want to say goodbye, and he didn't care that God gave him 86,400 seconds in a day—he didn't want to say thank you for taking her away.

Jessica. Period.

Luke wanted his life back.

"What happened with Charlie in Houston was terrible on my part. I like her ... a lot."

"But she's not Jessica."

Luke nodded.

"So you're just going to spend the rest of your life pining after someone you can never be with?"

He shrugged. "For now. I didn't get to marry her, but my heart is still married to the memories I have of her."

"Luke I'm—"

"Don't. It's not your fault."

"My accident was on the morning of your wedding day."

Luke reached across the table, squeezing her hand. "And when Jessica found out, she ran to find me, ripped off her veil, and drove me to the hospital."

Lake blinked back her tears. "I miss her too, ya know? But I also miss my brother. I miss the man you were with her. She made you normal." Lake smiled.

Luke chuckled. No one in his family ever knew Jessica's whole story. Despite the irony in his sister's statement, she was right. He found the best possible version of himself with Jessica. She gave him a life.

A life he wanted back.

———

THE VIBRATING buzz of Luke's burner phone brought him out of a light sleep a few minutes shy of midnight.

"What did you find?"

Gabe chuckled. "Not how much of your money did I have to spend?"

"Fuck the money. Tell me."

"I saw the tapes, man. You were right. My God ... it was her."

"No shit. The room, Gabe. Whose name was on the room?"

"An Aric J. Monaghan. Omaha, Nebraska address."

"Message it to me."

"You can't go. You said it yourself. It's not safe."

"Well I can't not go. She's there. I have to—"

"I'll go. You stay put. I'll get a flight out in the morning. Kelly thinks I'm going to be gone for another couple days anyway. Don't be stupid and risk yourself or your family. Nobody will be looking for me. Besides, if she's with some other guy, I'm not sure you showing up unannounced is the best idea. In fact, if she's with some other guy, I'm not sure why you're even pursuing this."

The muscles in his jaw twitched as he clenched his teeth. "Just send me the address."

"I just told you—"

"I'm not going anywhere, but if your wife doesn't know where you are going, I think I should."

"Good point. I'll send it and call you when I know more."

"Gabe?"

"Yeah?"

"Thanks."

CHAPTER NINE

KNIGHT

Held hostage in a constant groggy state, the lines between Jillian's dreams and reality blurred. Time became indistinguishable. Had she been there days or weeks?

"Good morning, sunshine. I'm done running my errands, so I eased up on your sedative. Your food is attracting maggots. That's not going to taste good when you eat it. And believe me ... you *will* eat it."

"Go to hell." The words scraped across Jillian's throat like sandpaper.

"You first." Psycho bitch cackled.

She peeled her eyes open. A shiver erupted in bumps along her skin, a welcome contrast to the oven.

"What the fuck?"

"I thought the zip ties were poetic given our location, but I had a devil of a time trying to get the IV in with your hands tied behind your back. Or are you questioning what's beneath your bare ass? That would be your own piss. Now *that* I'm sure brings back memories, huh? Freaky, isn't it? C.A.I.L. insisted on knowing everything about your kidnapping. They needed every little detail to assess your mental state. It didn't take long for them to conclude your psyche was irreversibly damaged."

The duct tape securing her arms to her body didn't allow an inch of movement. A mottling of bruises covered her forearm from her elbow to her wrist. In the middle, an impaled IV needle was taped in place.

"Your whole I-don't-care-if-I-die attitude is not acceptable. You don't have to eat *yet*, but I can't have you dying of dehydration before the fun even begins. Getting the IV and saline was the easy part. Following the YouTube instructions for inserting it ... not as easy. No worries. I swabbed your skin good with alcohol. Or did I? Hmm ... I just can't remember. But let's face it. The puncture wound on your shoulder and the nasty cut on your hand aren't looking too good right now, so I highly doubt my little IV experiment will make much of a difference at this point."

Psycho bitch maintained her usual spot in her chair under a lone hanging light bulb, wearing a wicked grin matched only by Satan himself. The gleam in her eyes expressed her pleasure as Jillian glanced up to take notice of her—specifically what she wore.

"You like?" Her smile grew, exposing her crooked teeth.

Jillian focused on that instead of her military fatigues and boots—big, repeated-blows-to-the-ribs boots.

"It's funny how you fooled everyone into thinking you were cured—normal. Your near-wedding nuptials had everyone fooled. Jessica Day found love and was going to live happily ever after with her Prince Charming. But the second you became Jillian Knight, your true personality came out again. How do you explain your fascination with fucking your neighbor? And not just any neighbor. Sergeant

Monaghan. Was it the camouflage? The boots? Or just your need to be a total whore again? Because that's what you are. Like mother like daughter."

It didn't take long to figure out her game. Psycho Bitch had no intention of physically torturing Jillian. It was all about the mind games. The ache in her heart from the mention of both Luke and AJ had to be ignored. Jillian knew her captor waited for her to break. She would wait a long time. The memories of Luke and AJ only made her stronger.

"Who was your husband?"

She sighed. "We'll get to that before too much longer. He'll be joining us. Then we can really get all the details." Fake-nailed fingers combed through her red, wet hair.

She showered while Jillian slept in her own piss. That alone set her apart from Four. He didn't shower. Drugs. Alcohol. Cutting. That was it.

"I haven't decided on all the party guests quite yet. You, of course, are the guest of honor. Jackson should join us too. Don't you think? Maybe I can have a piano hauled down here and he can play the Doomsday music. After I fuck him, of course. He is unquestionably the best sex I've ever had. Your brother knows what he's doing." Another cackle escaped her lips that were too big for her face. "The crazy part is he didn't even know who I was when he fucked me against the locked bathroom door of the club."

An inward grimace tugged at Jillian's stomach that was already eating itself alive. She hated the reminder of Jude and his past. A past she never fully understood. Jessica had an explanation for her behavior. Jude never did, or so she always assumed.

"This has really turned into a family affair, hasn't it?

You, Sunny, and my husband. Jackson and I. Maybe I should have gone after your father too. He would have been a harder sell because he actually loved your mom. I think. It's hard to say. I mean ... the man married a woman who was in love with another man. He had to know she didn't love him. Then again, she was pregnant with his babies. I guess he thought she'd eventually love him the way he loved her."

The tape cut into Jillian's skin as she tugged against it. Psycho Bitch would die for saying that to her. A lie. It had to be a lie. The foundation for which she had worked so hard to build her sanity, her life with Luke, was the desire to find a love like her parents'. The devil before her kept crashing into that foundation, leaving Jillian on the edge of collapsing.

"I'm getting ahead of myself. We'll finish that later. Now where was I?" She tapped her fake nail on her lip. "Oh, yes, Luke. I think he should definitely join us. I heard he and Agent McGraw had quite the run-in after your brief reunion in Houston."

"You're going to die. I will sacrifice my own life to make it happen. But I swear to God if you lay a finger on Luke, I will kill you so fucking slowly you'll regret the first breath you ever took."

"Ha! That's ... wow. Please don't swear to God. Not until you've repented your sins."

She wasn't without a few cracks of her own. Jillian could almost feel the race of her captor's pulse. As much as she tried to wield her intelligence as the ultimate weapon, Jillian made her nervous. No amount of intelligence could overcome fear.

"I'm going to cut off your lying tongue and make you

swallow it. Then I'm going to carve every Bible quote you sent me into your skin. If *you* repent, I'll show mercy and cut your heart out first. If you don't, I'll dissect your body, leaving your heart for last."

Psycho Bitch cleared her throat, breaking eye contact first. "I think I gave you too much sedative. It's messing with your perception of reality. One of us is restrained with duct tape the other is not."

"Then you'd better kill me before I show you my Houdini trick."

"I think we're done talking." Psycho Bitch stood, fists clenched a moment before snatching a syringe off the table and charging towards Jillian. Her hands fumbled the cap, each breath shallow and labored.

"You can't even look me in the eye. I don't think you have what it takes to kill someone."

The jittery, wheezing woman paused. The syringe tip just millimeters away from the IV line.

The mouse inched closer to the trap. "I can and *will* kill —FUCK!" Blood flowed like striking oil as her captor covered her broken nose, tumbling backward on to her butt.

Jillian dismissed the instant headache she gave herself and the blood trickling down to her own nose and into the corner of her eye. The satisfaction of seeing the bitch curled up on her side, moaning like a woman in labor, was worth it.

"I've dealt with broken noses before. Why don't you let me take a look, *sweetie*?"

A growl interrupted the moaning as she glared at Jillian over the hand covering her nose. Staggering to her feet, she stumbled hunch-backed to a table and grabbed something off it before heading toward the stairs.

The familiar puffing sound followed by the slow exhale

was the last thing Jillian heard before the slam of a door. An inhaler. That's what she grabbed from the table. Psycho Bitch had asthma.

Luke was right. Monsters were weak. Survivors were strong. Jillian was a survivor.

CHAPTER TEN

DAY

WE'RE NOT INVITING Cathy to the wedding." Jessica shot her mom a warning glare over the kitchen table as they narrowed down the guest list.

"Jessica Mauve Day, she's my best friend. Of course she's invited."

"Your best friend is a cheater. I can't believe you've sided with her. Daniel is the perfect guy. Who cheats on perfection?"

"I thought I was the perfect guy." Luke surprised her from behind, kissing the top of her head. "Good morning. It's Saturday. Why is my bride-to-be and her lovely mother not at Samovar?" Luke ruffled Jones's ears on his way to the coffee pot.

"You are the perfect guy ... for me. You'd like Daniel, babe. He's a middle-school guidance counselor and track coach. Incredibly nice guy. And Saturday tea has officially been relocated to here until the wedding because we need more space. Your mom and sisters are coming next weekend to get fitted for their dresses. Have you taken Jones to your tailor yet to get fitted for his tux?"

Luke narrowed his eyes over the rim of his coffee cup. Jessica bit her lips together.

"My mom's going to knit him some argyle socks too."

Sunny looked at Luke then rolled her eyes. They never forgot the shitty dog incident at Kelly and Gabe's wedding. Jessica didn't want to deal with Jones on their wedding day any more than Luke did. She just enjoyed his reaction to the possibility.

"Jones is not going to be at your wedding, but Cathy is." Sunny grabbed the list and wrote Cathy's name next to the scribbled area where Jessica had crossed her off the list.

"She's not—"

"What if I had an affair? Would you never forgive me and ban me from your wedding?"

Jessica's head jerked back. "Why would you even say such a thing?"

Luke raised his eyebrows, leaning against the counter in his navy pajama pants, no shirt. He seemed to enjoy the show.

"Because I didn't raise you to be this way. I've never seen you be so unforgiving ... so judgmental. You're getting ready to marry the man of your dreams. You're a few months from happily ever after and you're letting Cathy's affair eat at you. I just don't understand why. She fell in love with another man. She didn't kill—" Sunny slapped a hand over her mouth as her eyes filled with regret. "Oh, God. I'm sorry, sweetie."

Jessica restrained her response behind tight lips and a slow nod. "I think we're done for today."

"Jessica!" The pain in her mom's voice wasn't enough to stop her from retreating to the bedroom and answering with a slam of the door.

Stripping off her clothes, she pulled on a T-shirt and

jogging shorts, yanking at them as if they too had offended her.

"Want to talk about it?"

Her chin dropped to her chest on an exhale as Luke's body pressed to her back. His arms wrapped around her shoulders, protecting her, loving her, reminding her that he was her home.

"I don't need Dr. Jones right now. I need my Luke."

His lips brushed the side of her neck. "And he needs you."

She closed her eyes. "I'm scared."

"Of what?"

"Of having ..." The words caught in her throat.

"Of having what?"

"Everything I've ever wanted."

"Oh, baby ..." Luke turned her in his arms. "I *adore* you. This is happening. You deserve everything you've ever wanted. Instead, you're getting me and Jones." He grinned. "But the three of us are going to make it work anyway. Forever."

The feel of forever beneath her lips as she pressed them to his bare chest, brought happy tears. "Cathy and Daniel were my and Jude's godparents. I idolized their marriage, just like I do my parents'. Through everything, I've held this shred of hope that there is truly someone for everyone ... that happily ever after really does exist. But when Cathy left Daniel, I questioned everything I held on to. Then my mom stood by her side without question, as if she somehow empathized with Cathy, and that's bugged me for years. Why would she do that? I get forgiveness, I really do. But not once has my mom acknowledged that the affair was wrong and then today ... Can you believe she asked me how I would feel if it was her and Dad instead of Cathy and

Daniel? Talk about fucking with my mind and kicking my dreams in the gut."

Their embrace intensified as if he could squeeze every last drop of doubt and insecurity from her.

"It was hypothetical."

"What if it wasn't? Hypothetical questions are often-times reality in disguise. I have this 'friend' who might be pregnant. What do you think 'she' should do?"

Luke pulled back a fraction, brows arched as he peered down at her. "Baby, are you pregnant?"

She pinched his sides until he buckled at the waist, chuckling.

"I'm not pregnant, you dimwit. I'm trying to be serious."

"So Kelly is pregnant?"

"Luke!" Her pinch turned into a gut punch.

He grabbed the back of her neck and kissed her so hard breathing became an afterthought. Walking her back into the wall of his dress shirts that hung from hangers spaced evenly apart, he lifted her up until her back pressed to the wall. A few perfectly-starched shirts surrendered, falling to the floor.

Jessica gasped for air as lips devoured every inch of skin along her neck. "I love the way you love me. It's ... *everything*."

"It's forever," he whispered in her ear, sliding her T-shirt up her body and over her head.

Their bed waited twenty feet away. Luke deemed it too far as he laid her on the floor of the closet, several dress shirts trapped beneath her."

"Your shirts—"

"Fuck the shirts." He smirked, eyes hooded as he removed her shorts and then his pants.

"Dr. Jones is going to be pissed at you."

Luke settled between her legs, rubbing his erection against her clit as she closed her eyes on a soft moan. "Not when he smells sex with Jessica on them."

"Oh ... God ..."

He pushed into her and she let him control her body, dominate her thoughts, and erase all doubt.

"So WHEN DID you make your decision?"

Luke reached for the shared red sweatshirt wadded on the floor a few feet away and draped it over Jessica's back. She seemed content sprawled out on his chest, but he felt goose bumps along her skin.

"What decision?" he asked.

"The one where you had to choose between orderliness and me. Surely you knew you couldn't have both." She teased his nipple between her teeth so he pinched her ass, eliciting a squeal and the release of his hostage nipple.

"The first time we kissed. Orderliness doesn't turn me on like you do."

Jessica giggled. He loved that giggle. Every day she seemed to reclaim a piece of her innocence, and he felt honored beyond words to be the one to help her put those pieces back together.

"I bet you get at least a semi from a spotless mirror and perfectly-folded hand towels."

He shrugged. "It may twitch a bit."

The most beautiful lips ever planted a soft kiss on his shoulder. "I love you and I would never cheat on you. You're it for me. If a runaway cable car flattens your ass tomorrow, I'll never be with another man."

"Don't say that."

"It could happen."

"I'm talking about you not moving on if something— probably *not* cable car related—were to happen to me. You're young and you have so much love to give. It would be a crime for you to not share it with someone."

"Nope."

He scooted out from underneath her until they sat facing each other, holding hands. "I want ... I *need* you to promise me that you'll love again."

She shook her head. "It wouldn't matter. I'd never find someone to accept me the way I am."

"The way you are? You mean strong, resilient, beautiful, smart, funny, sassy, kind, giving, thoughtful ... I could go on all day. But I see what you mean. No man would want that."

"Luke," she whispered, staring at their interlaced fingers holding on for life, just like their two souls.

If he'd had one wish, it would have been for her to see herself through his eyes for just one moment in time.

"I want to be your everything, but only while I'm here. If the day comes that I'm not, then let me go. Let me be your greatest memory."

She looked up at him with the eyes that served as a looking glass into his entire existence. Luke didn't want to think of them looking at another man the way they looked at him, but if it meant someone looking back at her the way he did, then it made the thought bearable ... just barely.

"And you? If I die will you love another?"

No. The world's biggest fucking double standard ever, but he wouldn't. She needed love. He had enough to last his entire life.

"I'd try."

Jessica nodded slowly, but it didn't feel like a nod of

agreement, more of the nod someone gives when they're trying to process something.

"I need to apologize to my mom."

The change in subject was fine by him. "We're not your parents or Cathy and Daniel, we're not even the crazy skinny dipping couple from Tahoe. I know you've used them as a litmus test for your own chance at happiness, but you ... *we* don't need them. I got you. I'll always have you."

He prayed his words held truth.

Wearing her playfully deviant smile, she crawled onto his lap and wrapped her arms and legs around him like a monkey. "What would you have said if I was pregnant?"

"Nothing." He kissed her shoulder then bit it.

"Nothing?"

"Nope."

"Why not?"

"Because the best things in life leave me speechless."

CHAPTER ELEVEN

KNIGHT

JACKSON KILLED AJ. So what?

Ryn captured two hours of sleep after Jackson's confession. Of course they were the two hours before her alarm went off. She downed three cups of coffee then cleaned two houses on autopilot. By the time she carried her supplies to the car, three inches of snow blanketed the ground. A smile grew on her face.

As she slowed to pull into her already-shoveled driveway, Drew waved from his sidewalk. Ice melt crunched beneath her feet as she walked toward her front door. Gunner flew out his dog door, tail wagging.

"Drew, I've told you a million times you don't need to shovel my drive. And holy crap, what's with the ten pounds of ice melt? I can't even see my driveway beneath it. Is this some joke?" She laughed.

Drew stabbed his shovel into a drift of snow and rested his hands on the handle. "Yeah. Don't be surprised if a photo of your driveway shows up in the newspaper tomorrow with the title *Ice Melt Hoarder*. I think your friend bought every bag from the hardware store. Don't even get me started on the fact that he didn't drive here. He had on shorts and a sweatshirt and he made six trips on foot carrying the ice melt and I think a new shovel too."

Ryn laughed, shaking her head as she reached in her pocket for her phone that vibrated. "Speaking of Jackson." She held up her lit screen. "Bye, Drew."

She nearly slipped on the inch of ice melt, navigating the porch steps.

"Hi," she answered.

"Have you left for home yet? It's snowing. I don't think you should be driving."

Ryn laughed, shutting the door and toeing off her shoes. "Ya don't say?"

"I cleared your driveway and sprinkled some ice melt, but it's still snowing so you might need to reapply when you get home. I left a couple bags in your garage."

"How did you get in my garage? The side door was locked."

"Oh, I have ... um ..."

"A universal key? Like your sister?"

Jackson chuckled. "That would be correct."

"Well I'm home already." She plopped down in her favorite chair and threw her feet up on the ottoman. "Did Gunner growl and bark at you the whole time?"

"I brought treats."

"I see. So you thought of everything. My neighbor, Drew, saw you. Did Woody break down? He said you made a few trips on foot with the ice melt."

"Of course. No one should be driving in this weather."

She giggled. "You act like you've never driven in snow. It's the first snow, it's not that cold, and all the main streets have been plowed. Don't try to tell me it didn't snow in New York."

"Well, yeah, of course it snowed in New York. I just ... I ..."

"Let me guess. You lived and worked in the city, therefore you didn't even own a car."

"Bingo."

"Pathetic. Well, I'd invite you over for dinner, but that would require you to drive."

"Or walk. I'll see you in thirty minutes."

Ryn laughed some more. "Don't slip on the side walk."

"I've got that covered. The guy at the hardware store sold me some sort of yak things for my shoes."

"Yaktrax?"

"That's it. See ya soon."

Gunner cocked his head sideways as she tossed her phone on the ottoman. "So all it takes is a few treats to keep you quiet, huh? I fear you're going soft on me."

Gunner jumped to attention from the quick rap on the door.

"There's no way he's here already." Ryn grinned as she made her way to the door.

"Preston." Her smile dissolved as her body stiffened.

Gunner sat idle next to her, a mild growl vibrated in warning.

Preston glanced down. "Easy, mutt."

"What do you want? You can't be—"

"Be where, sweetheart? Here? You dropped the restraining order. Remember?"

Ryn tried to swallow past the familiar fear. "Why are you here?"

"It's snowing. Aren't you going to invite me in?"

"No."

Preston slipped off his black leather driving gloves and

shoved them into the pockets of his long wool overcoat. "I need to talk to you about Maddie."

"Your phone stop working?"

Preston grinned the same grin that got her knocked up twenty-one years earlier. She loved it then, but not anymore. It made her want to knock out every single shiny, white tooth that peeked out from behind his lips.

"Come on. You have your guard dog to protect you. Besides, I come in peace."

She glared at him. Nothing about Preston Iverson was peaceful.

"Five minutes and then you can let him chase me out the door. Deal?"

The asshole ex-husband needed to be gone before Jackson arrived. Preston didn't deserve a blink of her concern, but a tiny part of her feared for his life.

"Five minutes."

Gunner stayed glued to her side, ready to attack on command as she stepped back.

"I see you bought the smallest place on the block." His beady eyes appraised his surroundings. "Does it have indoor plumbing?"

"Four minutes."

He smirked. "You could have bought a place ten times the size of this one."

"I'd live on the street before I'd take a dime from you."

He nodded, still taking in her belongings. When she finally got the nerve to leave him, she did it with only the clothes on her back and even those ended up in the trash.

"Well you're not far off."

"Three minutes."

"I want you back, Ryn."

All she could do was laugh.

"I'm serious." He stepped toward her.

Gunner growled. Preston glared at her dog.

"I want a two-headed horse with magic wings. Maybe when that happens, I'll come back to you."

"We were young. We both made some mistakes—"

"What did you just say? *We?* Are you serious?"

"We both had our whole lives ahead of us, then you went and got pregnant."

"Oh. My. God." She shook her head. "Time's up."

"Think about it ... for Maddie."

"Go to hell. Now ... out."

Preston backed up as Gunner bared his teeth, moving slowly toward him.

"That tattooed asshole is trouble. I don't trust him, and I sure as fuck don't like that he's trying to take something that's mine."

"You beat the living crap out of me because I over-cooked your steak. You threw me down the stairs because I wore a dress you deemed too short to a holiday party and some asshole friend of yours commented on my legs."

"I'm not that guy anymore."

"You're *exactly* that guy. After all these years you still think you own me."

He clenched his teeth. Ryn recognized the muscle twitch in his jaw and the vein on his forehead. Had Gunner not been a foot from castrating him, Ryn had no doubt Preston would have backhanded her for being "disrespect-ful." It was always his signature first strike.

"He's a speeding ticket away from being thrown in jail. Chances are they'd find drugs, illegal weapons, or whatever I'd want them to find in his trunk."

Ryn narrowed her eyes. Why couldn't he just let her go? Why did he have to destroy her entire life?

"Think about it." He opened the door and turned to a large man in a hoodie, jeans, black boots with Yaktrax, and murder on his face.

"Be easy on her. She'll need some recovery time after what I did to her." Preston wore his usual asshole smirk as he rested a hand on Jackson's shoulder, attempting to side step him.

"Fuck!" Preston squeaked out when Jackson grabbed his neck with one hand, shoving him into the siding. Preston's face turned crimson as he clutched at Jackson's iron hold with no success.

"I'm going to end you."

Preston maybe had twenty seconds before passing out, but even then he was too stupid to shut up.

"Is ... t-that a threat?"

Jackson's head turned side to side slowly as he leaned in and whispered in Preston's ear. Ryn heard every chilling word.

"It's a promise." He released him.

Preston fell like dead weight to his hands and knees, gasping and coughing.

Jackson stepped inside and shut the door without a single glance back at Preston.

"You let the man, who put you in the hospital, into your house?"

"It was the only way to get him to leave." She hugged herself to ward off the chill from the door being open so long and the icy wave of anger that radiated off Jackson.

"What the hell do you have that dog for?"

She narrowed her eyes. "*That dog* has a name and you know it."

"That dog should be feasting on the corpse of your ex-husband right now."

"Stop calling him—"

"What?" Jackson shoved her against the wall and covered her mouth with his hand.

Gunner growled.

"That dog is growling at me, Ryn."

Her heart pumped so fast all she could hear was its pounding pulse.

"But he's not attacking me. Why is that?"

She blinked and struggled to get out of his hold.

"Do something, Ryn. Knee me in the groin. Bite my hand and tell *Gunner* to attack me. But stop being the fucking victim. Stop inviting the enemy into your house."

Tears stung her eyes and when she blinked they spilled over.

"DO IT!"

Her body fell limp. Jackson removed his hand and grabbed her as she released her first sob. He just yelled at her. He scared her. He made her cry. Despite all of that ... she clung to him.

"I hate him ... I hate him so much for breaking me."

Jackson leaned against the wall and slid down it with Ryn hugged to his body.

"He ... he took everything."

"I'm going to give it back to you—all of it." He took her face in his hands, forcing her to look at him. "Baby, you have an attack dog that won't attack. What the hell?"

Ryn sniffled. "Gunner doesn't do anything without my command, including that."

"But you didn't say it."

Anger remained in Jackson's voice. Ryn flinched. Old habits.

"I'm afraid."

"Of what?"

She blinked out more tears. "Everything. You don't understand. I lived like a prisoner in my own home for so many years. I couldn't get up from the table without permission. My hair, my weight, my clothes, my exercise routine, my friends ... they were all controlled by Preston. His verbal abuse did so much more damage than the physical abuse. I became anorexic, stopped having my periods, and eventually ended up in the hospital because I kept having fainting spells."

After all those years the pain felt as raw as the day it happened. "Preston had to come home from a business trip to 'deal' with me. They discharged me two days later, and he bashed my head into the dash before we left the parking lot. He said that's what I deserved for ruining his trip." She shook her head. "He bled every ounce of self-esteem from me. I don't want to be this way. I hate that I don't have a shred of confidence. Inside ... I have so much anger, so much hatred, but the fear is so crippling I can't do anything with it, so it just festers and eats me alive."

HOLDING Ryn was like holding an egg with a dozen cracks. Jackson knew he could never completely mend her. He could give her the self-defense skills to fight off a small army, but he couldn't make her use them any more than she could give Gunner the go ahead to attack her enemy.

Brushing his thumbs over her tear-stained cheeks, he smiled. "So Vera Wang and Ed Sheeran?"

Her laugh came out as a half sob. "Don't ... you can't possibly still want—"

"You. I want you, Ryn. I know you've lost so much of

yourself ... maybe so much that you don't know where you belong in this cruel world. But I do. You belong with me."

"My God, that was ..."

"A better line than swimming in your pond?"

Ryn laughed. Jackson smiled back at the forty-year-old with freckles and innocent blue eyes. She was truly beautiful in every way. He knew he would destroy anyone who ever tried to take that smile away again.

"Jackson Knight, I'd marry you in a paper bag, with a boom box playing Boyz II Men."

"What's a boom box and Boyz to who?"

She grabbed his hair, yanking his head an inch away from hers. "Knock that shit off."

Perfect. The woman who feared everything, dominated the heart of a killer. What were the chances?

Jackson surrendered the final inch, resting his forehead against hers. "I'm sorry for what I did to you," he whispered.

Her hands released his hair and slid to his cheeks.

"I didn't understand, but now I do. I'll protect you. I promise."

"What you said to Preston ... you wouldn't really *kill* him, would you?"

They danced around his past, giving him ample opportunities to tell her everything. Telling her would break the rules—G.A.I.L's rules. Members weren't allowed to share that information unless they were married. It was ridiculous. What kind of wedding gift was that? A marriage certificate didn't buy the kind of loyalty and trust required to keep G.A.I.L hidden. Yet, somehow they'd managed to keep everyone silenced for years. Jackson knew their tactics were rarely worthy of "Guardian Angel" status.

"Ryn ..." he whispered.

"Tell me. Would you kill him?"

"Yes."

Jerking back, her gaze bored into his, searching for truth. For the first time in his life, he wanted someone—Ryn —to see that truth.

Yes. The ultimate truth. A drop-all-weapons-hands-up surrender to only the second woman in his life for whom he would lie down and die for.

She swallowed hard, choking on that one little word. Jackson didn't blink. He kept his eyes trained to hers because in spite of the number of lives his hands taken ... he didn't regret one.

He knew her next question before it passed her lips.

"Aside from AJ ... have you ever killed anyone?"

As sure as he knew her question, the intensity in her eyes said she knew his answer.

"Yes."

Did she see him? *Really* see him?

Her eyes closed. Jackson said nothing. All he could do was wait for her to open them again and pray they'd look at him the same. Love him the same. Accept him ... accept Jude.

"I don't want to know." She shook her head. "I-I can't handle it."

"Ryn?"

Fluttering open, her eyes focused on his chin, his chest, his arms ... but she didn't look him in the eye. "The answer is yes. I fear it will always be yes."

What was the question?

When those blue eyes met his again, he couldn't read them. Was the sparkle in them the beginning of unshed tears or the light of life drawing him from the darkness?

"You want to know if I still love you."

More than the secret to life.

"The answer is yes," she whispered.

"But?"

Ryn slid her thumb along his bottom lip before pressing a soft kiss to it. She smiled. It held more pain than pleasure, but nonetheless it was a smile. "No buts."

He should have felt better—relieved—but he didn't. What was that? Unconditional love? Jackson told him to take it and run without ever looking back. Jude? He wanted Ryn to love him too, but he wanted her to know everything first. Jude had always been too biblical for his own good. The need to confess his sins to Ryn and cleanse his conscience would cut Jackson off at the knees, preventing him from ever running from his past again.

CHAPTER TWELVE

JONES

Gabe turned on his burner phone when the plane touched down in Omaha. He left his personal phone with Luke so he could text Kelly at least once a day on his behalf. On his way to the rental car counter he texted Luke's burner phone to remind him to do just that.

He lied to Kelly about his fake meeting. She trusted him and he never gave her any reason not to until that point. Somewhere between Luke's unbelievable story about his abduction, Jessica not dying, and his plan to get her back, he'd convinced himself if ever it was okay to lie to his wife that was the time.

It didn't take him long to get his rental car from the airport and drive to Peaceful Woods. A fresh layer of snow blanketed the ground, but the streets were plowed and dusted with a salt and sand mixture. After parking along the side of the street at the entrance, double and triple checking that he had the correct address, he continued into the development. Not even schools had as many speed bumps as the short private drive that he traveled to get to the home of one Aric James Monaghan.

Gabe spent the entire flight thinking of what he would say if he saw Jessica, but he landed in Omaha without a single word figured out. What if she wasn't there? What if Aric Monaghan answered the door?

The sun signed off for the day on his way there. Most all of the houses had their front lights illuminating their driveways, except Aric's. Gabe squinted to see the house number embedded into the brick front. The black windows indicated the likeliness of anyone being home to be about zero.

He called Luke.

"You found her?"

"Not yet. I'm parked in Aric Monaghan's driveway. It doesn't look like anyone is home."

"Check."

Gabe grinned. "Brilliant idea."

"Well then, why are you calling me if you haven't checked yet?"

"To make sure you texted Kelly. Why are you so on edge?"

"Because I'm fucking anxious. I'm dying here!"

Luke out of control was rarer than a UFO sighting.

"What if you're putting her in danger by tracking her down ... by having me track her down? If she's in some kind of witness protection thing, I'm not sure her past is her friend. You're her past, Luke."

Gabe waited then looked at his screen. "You still there?"

"I'm not going to put her in danger. I just need to know that she's okay."

Even with Luke's attempt to sound resolute and sincere, Gabe knew his friend too well. Luke would never be able to go on with his life if she were alive and not with him.

"I'm worried about you, buddy. She's with another guy. It can't end well."

"The guy who took me said the man Jess was with has cancer. If she ..." Luke's voice cracked.

Gabe flinched.

"If she cares about him and he dies ... I fear she could too. It's too much for her. I know things about her that would make you shudder. Just trust me ... we're saving her."

"What if she runs? If she knows she's been found, she could run."

"Call me ... when you find her .... I want you to call me and hand her the phone. Okay?"

"K. I'm going to the door. Wish me luck."

"Gabe?"

"Yeah?"

"Thank you. You're my best friend and you're getting ready to be a dad. I feel like such a prick for asking you to risk yourself for me. I should tell you to just turn around and get your ass back home to Kelly, but ..."

"But she's your whole damn world. I get it. I get it better than anyone. I've always thought of you as family, Jessica too. Let's get her back."

The line went dead after a few seconds. Gabe frowned at his phone. He thought of Kelly and then he imagined her missing, then he climbed out of the car with steadfast purpose.

After a dozen or so knocks and incessant ringing of the doorbell, he concluded nobody was home, but for good measure he added a few more rings and raps against the cold glass storm door.

"Can I help you?"

Gabe turned to the sound of a woman's voice. An elderly lady stood on her front stoop wrapped in a fluffy robe and boots. Holding up a friendly hand as if to say "I come in peace" he crossed the street.

"I'm looking for Aric Monaghan."

The woman's friendly smile faded. "Young man, can I ask your name?"

"Um ... Andy."

"Are you a friend?"

"Actually, I'm a friend of his ... girlfriend."

Her eyes widened. "Oh, you know Jillian?"

Jillian? "Yes. We go way back. It's been awhile since I've seen her. I wanted to surprise her."

"Well I'd tell you to try her house, but she's out of town. I take it you haven't talked with Jackson."

Gabe shoved his hands into his pockets to ward off the cold breeze. "Jackson?"

"Her brother."

"Oh, yeah ... I wasn't close to him, just Jillian. Sorry I'd forgotten his name." Gabe couldn't help but grin a bit. Jessica and Jude had become Jack and Jill—brilliant.

She nodded behind him. "They live in the unit next to Sarge's. But we saw Jackson leaving earlier to go to his lady friend's house. She recently got her sex toy order from Jillian's party at my house, so I don't expect him back for quite some time if you know what I mean." She winked, an awkward wink, but Gabe was pretty sure it was still a wink. "Any who, he walked over to her house. Said it was too dangerous to drive. Crazy guy. I assume you're from New York too? Surely you all see as much snow as we do."

No. He wasn't from New York and neither were *Jillian* and *Jackson*. They were all from San Francisco. That explained Jackson's apprehension over driving in snow.

"Sex toys?"

"Come on in, honey. It's too cold to have this conversation outside. I'll make you some hot chocolate. Are you a marshmallow guy?"

Gabe smiled. He was a red-eye guy—black coffee with a double shot of expresso. "Sounds perfect, thank you."

WAITING for Gabe to call left Luke on the verge of committing himself. The woman who came to him for reasons of insanity had him flirting with it himself. After three Heineken, he tore his hands from his mussed hair to answer the phone. It had to be her. How could he be so stupid to drown himself in alcohol before giving the speech of his life? It didn't matter. Just the thought of her made the world fall away. The time between hearing of her death and seeing her in Texas was the longest fucking single heartbeat ever.

He was ready to breathe again.

"Jessica?"

"Sorry."

"Gabe." Luke deflated as his hand grabbed for his hair again. Tears stung his eyes.

"She wasn't home and neither was Sarge. However, I talked with her neighbor for over an hour, a Greta Housby. Quite possibly the funniest and most interesting lady I have ever had the pleasure of talking to. But ... she didn't have good news. I'm not sure what you want me to do now."

"Who is Sarge?"

"Sorry. AJ, Aric James Monaghan. They called him Sarge because he was a Senior Master Sergeant, career air force.

"Called? Was?"

Gabe sighed. "He died on Thanksgiving."

"Where is she?"

"They don't know. She flew to Portland for the funeral.

Jackson told them she wasn't coming home right away. Apparently she needed time alone."

"Jackson?"

"Sorry. You're never going to believe this ... Jude is alive too. They live in the townhouse next to AJ's. She's a consultant for Lascivio. Have you heard of that?"

"No."

"Sex toys. She sells sexy toys and he teaches piano lessons." Gabe laughed. "And that's not the best part. Jessica and Jude Day are now Jackson and Jillian Knight. Jack and Jill."

Luke closed his eyes and shook his head.

"Do you want me to stay and talk to Jude ... Jackson?"

"No. I mean ... fuck! I don't know. Who'd you say you were?"

"An old friend of Jessica's or Jillian's."

"I'm sure the neighbor lady will tell Jude someone was asking about them, which could cause them to disappear again. But he's not the most stable guy and he could snap your neck so fast you'd never see it coming."

"He knows me, he's not going to kill me."

"Something tells me he would to keep his sister safe."

Jessica had a conscience. He never got the chance to make a definitive assessment of Jude's stability.

"You're not helping. What am I supposed to do?"

Luke flopped back on the couch and stared at the shadows on the ceiling. "God, I didn't think this through enough and I'm ... I've had too much to drink."

Gabe chuckled. "How about I leave a burner phone with your burner phone number on it by their front door. He probably won't be back until tomorrow anyway. He's at Ryn's."

"And Ryn is?"

"His girlfriend."

"Try again. Jude doesn't do the girlfriend thing."

"Well this Jackson guy apparently does. Greta said she's older by ten years and 'utterly adorable.'"

"Now, do you want to know more about 'Jillian' and AJ or shall I wait until you're completely drunk?"

The chances of Luke ever being drunk enough to handle hearing about Jessica with some other guy? Nil.

"Leave the phone and my number then get your ass home to Kelly before we both get caught."

"I'll get a flight out tomorrow."

"Thanks, Gabe."

"Luke?"

"Yeah?"

"We'll find her."

He nodded to himself then pressed *End*.

CHAPTER THIRTEEN

KNIGHT

HUNGER.

Jillian awoke with her stomach churning. Time vanished, leaving her lost for any sense of how long she'd been in the dungeon—for sure longer than she'd been with Claire. If she made it out alive, the house would be permanently leveled. No one would ever suffer in that basement again.

"I'm going to break your nose with this steel pipe, but not until we have an audience."

Only part of Jillian's body had feeling after sitting in the same spot for ... days? The parts that still registered life, throbbed with a dull ache: shoulder, head, back. Her groggy eyes shifted to her captor in her chair, black and blue face, nose taped, and a three-foot steel pipe resting in her hands. The maggots multiplied in the bowl of dog food. The stench roiled her stomach even more.

"What's your name?"

Psycho bitch laughed. "Does it matter?"

Heavy eyelids blinked with lethargy. "No. It doesn't."

"So you don't care who I am and what I know?"

The ugly bitch wasn't worth the effort for Jillian to open her eyes again, so she rolled her head against the wall from side to side. "You're a psycho bitch and you don't know shit. Fucking hell!"

Ice water drenched her body, sending her heart into her throat and making it impossible to breathe.

"Look at me when I'm talking to you."

She had Jillian's attention—a death glare to both her wretched face and the empty five-gallon bucket in her hands. Pure rage burned off the chilling effects of psycho bitch's favorite form of torture.

"So what's wrong with you? Why can't you keep your husband from fucking other women? You have to take too many breaks during sex to suck on your inhaler? You don't give good head? Or is it just that you're ugly as fuck from the inside out and there's just no cure for that?"

Taking a seat again, she looked over at her inhaler. Jillian grinned. She'd rattled her, but taking a puff of it would make her feel weak. Jillian sensed her conflict. Instead, she twisted the lid off her bottled water and took a long swig, buying time to calm her nerves before sharing what would surely be a revealing comeback.

"When Luke joins us, are you going to give him the play-by-play of how you fucked Sargent Monaghan?" She laughed, delighting in the illusion of the upper hand. "Of course you are ... or I'm going to use him as target practice." She tapped her foot against the bow propped up against the leg of the table.

Luke would always be her Achilles' heel, and her captor knew it. Knox had his usual hissy fit when Jessica insisted Luke be "guarded." They were an hour from being married, an hour from Luke earning the right to know everything about G.A.I.L., everything about Jessica. Like most men,

Knox couldn't keep his dick in his pants and the minute he forced it into the ass of his comrade's daughter, he surrendered to a life of granting Jessica's every wish or dying at the hands of her father or brother. Knox knew he was lucky to still be alive.

"You won't hurt Luke."

She rolled her eyes. "What makes you so sure?"

"Because you shot an arrow in my arm, but you refuse to look at it. I broke your nose and all I get in return is a bucket of cold water. But most disturbing is the claim that I fucked your husband and yet I'm still alive." Jillian grinned. "Tell me ... after I fucked him, what scars did I leave ... because I *always* leave my mark."

She stood so fast the chair flew backward. Jillian waited for the confession of a pierced lip, clawed back, or bite marks on a shoulder. But she never imagined the words that her captor spoke just seconds before grabbing her inhaler and fleeing for the stairs.

"A broken nose, two missing teeth, three fractured ribs, and a punctured lung."

CHAPTER FOURTEEN

RYN SLEPT ON HER STOMACH, sheets kicked off, bare ass beckoning Jackson back to bed. The piano lesson gig got in the way of him following his compass that morning, which coincidently pointed north and had him adjusting himself several times while getting dressed. He made a mental note to remind her that sleeping naked on her stomach was forbidden ... unless she lifted the anal sex ban.

"I have to go," he whispered in her ear then pressed his lips to the back of her neck.

Her shoulders jerked up. "That tickles," she said in a groggy voice.

"If you don't hide this, it will be *mine*." He palmed her ass.

Ryn flipped over, blond waves of hair matted to her face, and grabbed the sheet, pulling it up to her chest. "Hot flashes. I get them occasionally. Doesn't help when I'm in bed with a guy whose body temperature is abnormally high all the time."

Jackson smirked. "You think I'm hot. Nice." He pulled his shirt on slower than necessary. For the first time in his life he wanted a woman to ogle his body. Seemed only fair since he worshiped hers in search of redemption, salvation, and eternity.

"You realize all those tattoos are going to look hideous when you get older and your skin starts to sag from losing its elasticity and muscle atrophy."

Twisting his lips, he tilted his head to the side, hands shoved in his jean's pockets. "Hmm ... but you'll still love me right?"

She shrugged. "Depends. I might have to trade you in for a newer model."

"So basically someone young enough to be your grandchild?"

Her jaw dropped on a quick inhale a split second before she launched a pillow at his head. "I was going to offer to drive you home, but after that comment you can huff it through the snow, buddy."

He tossed the pillow back to her then sat on the edge of the bed to pull on his socks. "You shouldn't be driving in this weather anyway."

She giggled. "*This weather?* What? A couple inches of snow that's been plowed from the streets? Not that I'll need it but my Rav is 4-wheel drive. Well ... I may need it to get out of my driveway through the solid foot of ice melt."

He narrowed his eyes and grabbed her knee, squeezing it until she squealed and begged through a string of mercy apologies.

"Enough!" she squirmed out of his grip, breathless and beaming with a smile bright enough to melt all the snow in Omaha that day.

"Is this how it's going to be? For the rest of our lives are you going to critique my domestic skills? Mocking them?"

Her smile faded a fraction. Then she bit her lips together as if she needed to suppress her response.

"What?"

She shook her head. "Nothing. Well, it's just I like when you say that, and yet is scares me to death at the same time."

He leaned over and buried his face in her neck, tasting the most addictive skin imaginable. She threaded her fingers through his hair. Her body arched into his, calling "come hither."

"It's you and me, babe. Deal with it," he mumbled.

"I'd rather you deal with me." She freed a leg from the confines of the sheets and wrapped it around his waist to pull him closer.

"I have to go." He laughed, grabbing her leg to remove it from his waist.

"Mr. Knight, are you telling me no?" She yanked his hair until he looked at her.

He squinted, looking at her clock, then sucked in a breath through his teeth. "I'm afraid so." After dropping a quick kiss on her lips and then one on the tip of her nose, he pulled away and sighed. "I'm going to quit my job after today. Then you can tie me to your bed for eternity. Deal?"

"It's a mattress on a simple frame. There's nothing to tie you to."

He walked to the door and grabbed the handle. "I'll buy you a new bed."

"How are you going to do that if you quit your job?"

Jackson opened the door, lifting a single shoulder. "I'll dig up a coffee can or something ingenious like that." He winked and shut the door behind him.

"I love you!" Ryn yelled

He paused at the top of the stairs. The distant echo of

her words brought back the flash of a memory from his childhood—his mother yelling downstairs "I love you" to her twins before they left for school. He still hated what she did. He hated his father for living a lie. He hated his sister's circumstances that prevented him from ever telling her.

The entire Day family had to die so the man, who fell for the woman on the other side of the bedroom door, could find the ability to love again. And he did ... Jackson loved Ryn.

"I love you too, hot pants!"

LIGHT FLURRIES SWIRLED in the breeze as Jackson made his way home. He inwardly grimaced at his overreaction to the first snow. He should have ventured out of San Francisco more in the winter months.

Stan waved from Greta's driveway. He wore some sort of coveralls and expertly wielded a snow shovel. The guy was seventy and worked circles around men in their twenties.

"I thought our association dues covered snow removal," Jackson called from his driveway.

"They do, but those idiots don't know what they're doing. If you don't get all this snow cleared better and throw down some ice melt, it's just going to get packed on the driveways slick as snot."

"An ice melt guy." Jackson grinned. "I hear ya. Lots of ice melt."

He grabbed the small snow-covered box by the front door on his way inside then slipped off his boots.

It was a phone with a number on a small note. It had to

be Jillian needing to contact him, but he had a phone, she didn't. Why send him a burner phone?

Without hesitation, he called the number, eager to hear her voice.

"Where is she?"

Jackson closed his eyes with the immediate recognition of the voice on the other end of the line. "Do you really have such little regard for your life? Your family's? Hang up. Destroy your phone. And forget about her."

"Jude," he whispered.

Jackson felt Luke's pain, his desperation. Since meeting Ryn, he felt everything. Feelings had no discrimination. They were all or nothing. Humanity existed in the balance between the polarity of pain and pleasure.

"Where are you?"

"Home," Luke answered.

"How did the phone get here?"

"A friend."

"How did you get the address?"

"The hotel in Houston. Where is she?"

"Luke ... you don't—"

"So help me, if you try to tell me I don't understand I'm going to fucking lose it. I know about Aric, I know he died, I know—"

"What? You know our parents were murdered? You know we faked our deaths? Bet you didn't know she could have brought you too. She chose to leave you behind. It was *her* choice. Jess loved you, but she fell in love with another man and she's mourning his loss. I don't know where she's at and that's the truth. Her phone is sitting here on our table. She's upset with me ... she's upset with life. I can't bring her back until she's ready. I respect you, Luke, I really do, but

Jessica doesn't want to be found. Not by you and not by me. If you love her, you'll let her go."

"I was an hour away from marrying her. I feel like my wife died. I feel like another man took my wife. I feel like my *wife* needs me now more than ever. I can't let her go ... I can't fucking breathe. Let them kill me because I'm already dead."

"I'm sure your parents and siblings would disagree."

"Don't make me feel like some selfish bastard for loving her. Long before the day of our wedding, I chose her—over *everyone* else."

"But she didn't choose you."

Luke chuckled, it had a condescending tone. "You're wrong. She left me because she didn't choose herself. She's never chosen herself because she's never felt worthy of that kind of happiness. That was supposed to be my job. I was supposed to spend the rest of my life proving to my wife that she is worthy of every goddamn thing she could ever want."

Jackson plopped down in the chair. Defeat crept into his conscience, a conscience that had been a sealed vault for over a decade. Ryn cracked that vault, infecting him with unwelcome feelings of empathy. With that empathy came accountability. He didn't want to be accountable for Luke's inability to breathe or his suicide mission to find Jessica.

"I'll let her know you're looking for her if she decides to come home."

"Dammit! How can you be her fucking twin and not see that something's wrong? She's not like you, Jude. Holing up as a recluse has never been her thing. The strength on the outside masks the most fragile soul on the inside. She *needs* people, it's why she clung to Kelly in college and had tea with your mom every weekend. It's why she craved every minute in the garage working on cars with your dad and sparred with you. If she loved this Aric guy, then she has to be in so much pain, and whatever you did to piss her off has driven her away from the only person she has and now she's alone. Jessica doesn't do alone. We have to find her. Something's wrong. I saw her that day in Houston, a hollow shell of the woman I knew. So whatever the hell you did, make it right and help me find her."

Jackson, *Jude*, never saw the desperate, out-of-control side to Luke. The great Dr. Jones carried himself with control and authority. His analytical mind insisted he always think before speaking. Jessica got under his skin. She ran through his veins and infected his mind.

"I can't make it right—*ever*."

"I don't believe that."

"I don't give a fuck what you believe. You weren't here. You didn't see her dying right along with him. I had to put a stop to his pain. I had to save her."

From one highly intelligent man to another, Jackson knew no further explanation would be necessary.

"I'll find her." Luke ended the call.

Jackson sent the phone flying across the room, crashing into the stone around the fireplace. "Goddammit!" Pressing the heels of his hands to his forehead, he gritted his teeth. "Fucking suicidal shrink."

Luke's total disregard for his own life would get him killed. Jillian would never *ever* take another breath if Luke died. Claire, their parents, and AJ seemed impossible to handle, but she did.

Luke? Never.

Jessica had what their parents never did. She had *everything*. If Luke died she would officially have *nothing*.

CHAPTER FIFTEEN

DAY

Eyes of desire and complete *adoration* roved Jessica's body.

"Never stop looking at me like that." She lifted the floor-length skirt to her red strapless evening gown and crossed the bedroom to straighten the matching red tie of her handsome fiancé in his black suit and crisp white shirt.

He grabbed her hand. They both knew it was already straight. Messing with Luke's tie had become the proverbial ruffling of his anal-retentive feathers.

"And how is it that I'm looking at you?"

Her eyes focused on his fingers adjusting her engagement ring. He did that a lot, as if he needed to reassure himself that she was still there—that she really said yes. It always made her smile.

"Like I'm a dream."

"Are you?" His hand moved from her ring to her wrist, feathering up her arm until her skin prickled with goose bumps.

Twisting her red lips, she looked up through painted

black lashes at the world's most gorgeous face. "Hmm ... maybe. But a wet dream? Yes."

Luke smirked. "You strip me of all dignity and self-control with just one look. I'm pretty sure all that's left is a walking erection in a suit."

She laughed. "Let's go. Rumor has it, this holiday party has an open bar. If you're lucky I'll get a little tipsy and you might score later." Turning on silver, open-toed heels, she clacked down the hall to the front door.

"Ten bucks says you'll be riding one of my legs on the 'dance floor' before you've finished your second glass of champagne."

She narrowed her eyes, tossing her lipstick into her clutch purse. "Once. That happened once, and I'd had a lot to drink *and* nobody saw because the dance floor was so crowded."

Luke opened the door as she kissed Jones on the head before sashaying to the elevator.

"It was an award ceremony and I was the guest of honor. There wasn't a dance floor. You basically gave me a lap dance in front of my colleagues to background elevator music after downing an entire bottle of wine during my acceptance speech."

The elevator door opened to the parking garage. Jessica held her head high as she made her way to the car.

"You were giving me bedroom eyes during the whole damn speech. It made me nervous like everyone could see what you were thinking, so I just kept drinking to numb my nerves."

"I wasn't giving you 'bedroom eyes.' I don't love speaking in public and I was using you as a friendly face to calm *my nerves*." He opened the car door for her, then walked to the driver's side.

They drove to the party, exchanging flirty looks the whole way. Jessica loved Luke's playful side. Not too many people got to see it, and that made it even sexier.

"Behave," he whispered in her ear as they stepped into the hotel lobby. His deep voice elicited all kinds of deviant thoughts, not one falling under the heading of "behave."

As they approached the entrance to the Grand Ball Room, Jude stepped around the corner from the women's restroom, straightening his jacket and tie.

"Don't," he warned his sister before she had a chance to say the words that matched her scowl. "Luke." Jude smirked, giving him an easy nod.

"He's not going to give you a high five or fist bump or any other approval of your terribly inappropriate actions, so don't *even* smile at him."

Jude's brows peaked, his attention focused on Luke. "Man, are you really going to let her speak for you? That's kind of emasculating, if you asked me."

Luke's eyes flitted between the Day twins, both daring him to take the other's side. "Was she married?" He gestured toward the restroom.

"No."

"Condom?"

"Yes." Jude smirked.

Luke shrugged. "Well, I believe my job here is done."

"Holy fucking hell! What is that supposed to mean?"

"Well ... well ... well ... I thought I heard my daughter out here." Grant opened the door to the ballroom and stepped aside to let his children and the traitor inside. "I don't know too many women that use 'holy,' 'fucking,' and 'hell' in the same sentence." He kissed Jessica on the cheek then pulled her in for a bear hug, as if to let Luke know she still belonged to him.

"Hi, Dad. Sorry. It was Jude's fault..." she narrowed her eyes at Luke while still in her father's arms "...and Luke's."

"And why are you boys getting my little girl all riled up?"

Jude snagged a glass of champagne from the waiter passing by. "She doesn't approve of my extracurricular activities or Luke's freedom of speech and his right to think for himself."

Jessica wriggled out of her father's arms and lunged for Jude, but not before Luke hooked his arm around her waist to prevent a scene.

"Man whore!" she seethed.

"Jessica!" Grant warned.

Jude emptied his entire glass of champagne down his throat then merged into the throng of people, giving her a sly look over his shoulder, the proverbial sticking his tongue out at her.

"I don't understand how he ended up that way. You and Mom have the perfect marriage. He should be settling down and starting a family, not sticking his dick in every open hole."

The thoughtful look on her father's face gave no reassurance. If anything, his expression held an air of sadness. Then he dismissed her without a single explanation or affirmation that what she said was true.

"You're going to have your hands full, Doctor Jones." Grant turned and walked away without giving Jessica a second look.

Her jaw dropped to the floor.

"Don't." Luke pressed two fingers below her chin to close her mouth.

She batted his hand away. "I'm tired of everyone saying 'don't' before I have a chance to say anything, like I'm so fucking predictable. You don't know what I was going to say."

"True. But I know what you're thinking and your words only have a two-second delay from your thoughts."

Jessica planted her fists on her hips. "Funny, I thought you were a psychiatrist not a psychic. But please, by all means tell me what I was thinking."

Luke waited to speak because *his* words had more than a two-second delay from his thoughts.

"And don't you fucking smirk at me, Jones!"

His lips pulled tight, fighting said smirk. As only total-control Luke could do, he took a deep breath, composed himself, and channeled his inner shrink.

"I was in the middle of composing a speech to yet again reassure you that we are Luke and Jessica, not Grant and Sunny and not Jude and every woman he's used to suppress what's really going on inside him. But you're so mad at me I now think this is not about you doubting our future, I think ..."

She leaned in, dying to hear his brilliant explanation. "You think what?"

Then it appeared. *Fucking smirk.*

"I think you're jealous Jude has it anywhere and anyway he wants. He doesn't abide by any set of rules or moral expectations."

"W-what? You think I'm jealous ... of *him?*"

"Are you not? You've been undressing me with your eyes since I put on this suit and tie. You're rarely censored anyway, but tonight you've been dropping f-bombs like marbles rolling off a table. I know you want to take me in the men's restroom and have your way with me. I bet you'd use this red tie to restrain my hands behind my back before riding me, whip in one hand, a fist full of my hair in the other."

The *only* man who could render her speechless, did it again. He was right. She had an anger inside that festered, but the real reason for it had not seeped into her conscience. It wasn't PMS. It was just a feeling, an undefined feeling. Her emotions were an effect without a cause. Jessica hated that feeling.

However, her inability to define what it was did not hinder her ability to know what it was *not*. And it was not the need to take Luke into the hotel restroom and sexually dominate him. She knew it and so did he. Luke Jones was so much more than a doctor and a man. He was a phenomenon—someone who simply existed in life for Jessica. Destiny was real and it stood before her in a sharp black suit, red tie, and argyle socks.

The anger evaporated, giving way to a smile meant only for the man who saved her from her own insanity by drowning it in his love. "I worship the ground you walk on."

A blinding smile grew along his face as he pulled her into his arms and whispered in her ear, "Impossible. When I'm with you my feet don't touch the ground."

LUKE PLAYED it cool like he wasn't counting down the days —to the exact second—until Jessica would be his wife. Holding her together to get to the altar seemed to be his biggest obstacle. Every day she fought the demons that threatened to steal their happiness, the ones that haunted her with self-doubt that happily ever after existed.

It didn't really take a degree in psychiatry to see that Jude was all kinds of fucked-up. Why? Luke didn't know, and Jessica didn't seem to have any clue either. However, her parents seemed to be hiding something. He'd seen it in Sunny's eyes the day she and Jessica had their infidelity argument. Grant confirmed it by not reassuring Jessica, his precious baby girl, that he and Sunny had the perfect marriage. The coward didn't even look at her. Luke knew she saw it too, but denial buffered reality from her heart.

"Hi, sweetie." Sunny hugged Jessica before everyone took a seat at the large round table adorned with cranberry topiaries alternating with votives and cylinder champagne flutes with a single evergreen sprig.

"Mom, everything looks amazing."

Luke pulled out her chair then leaned down and kissed her exposed neck as he scooted her forward. "That smile looks much better on your lovely face," he whispered.

She raised her arm and ran her fingers through the hair at the nap of his neck, as if to hold him close for an extra few seconds. That same hand took the life of a serial killer. It didn't seem possible. He *adored* her touch. He craved it. He lived for it.

"I can't take credit for any of it. Everything was donated."

"But someone had to get the donations." Luke smiled at Sunny as he unfolded his napkin on his lap.

"I have great friends."

"She has influential friends." Jude took his seat on the other side of Jessica.

Grant seemed to tense as much as Luke did. The chances of a food fight or brawl breaking out between the two siblings was higher than average that night.

"I've met people from all walks of life during my years of volunteering. But yes, the influential ones make thousand-dollar-a-plate holiday charity dinners possible."

"Why don't you just give this food to the homeless instead?" Jude gave his mom a pointed look.

Jessica grabbed her brother's leg, knuckles white, but he didn't flinch.

Luke liked Sunny. She always paused for thought before responding, the only one in the Day clan that wasn't a hair-trigger.

"You've been attending these dinners for the past eight years, my dear son. What part about 'everything is donated' don't you get? The hotel donates the room, three different catering companies donate the food, two local florists donate the decorations, and the band is also here tonight free of charge. Every year we pick two local charities to be the recipients of the money. But the reason this is such a success is because we use the holiday dinner as an opportunity to personally thank each donor and let them know how their contribution changes lives."

"Stop being such an ass," Jessica gritted through her teeth.

Jude shoved his chair backward, making a weak effort to give the guy behind him an apologetic look for ramming into his chair.

"Of course I'm the ass because coddled little Jessica could never be an ass." Jude stood, towering over his sister.

She balled her hands. Luke grabbed her arms, her muscles steel beneath his touch.

"Both of you out." Grant stood with an air of authority, attempting to level his twins with a glare that brought the temperature of the room down below freezing.

Jerking from Luke's grasp, she stood, eyes narrowed at Jude. He turned, shoving his way through the sea of people with Jessica on his heels.

"Let them go."

Luke squinted at Grant. He respected Jessica's parents, to a certain degree, but their lack of doing anything to diffuse the situation between Jessica and Jude left him questioning their morals. Pondering their parenting skills had to wait. Luke barged through the ballroom doors, looking in both directions. They were gone.

"WHAT THE FUCK is going on with you?" Jessica grabbed the sleeve of Jude's suit jacket as he stomped toward his black Jetta parked in the hotel's parking ramp.

He whipped around, jaw clenched, anger simmering in his eyes. She didn't back down. Jessica would never back down from her brother.

"Go back to your mommy and daddy and your Prince Charming. Go live your fucking fairytale."

She shook her head, anger in her belly, tears in her eyes. "Fairytale? Are you serious?" She shoved him.

He growled, fists clenched at his sides.

"I've pulled off the greatest illusion in the history of the world. Luke *loves* me. He thinks I'm redeemable." Her voice cracked on the last word as tears spilled over. She motioned between them with her finger. "We both know I'm not, but *you* are."

Jude widened his eyes. "You've taken one man's life. A fucking serial killer who murdered your best friend. Do you have any idea how many people I've killed? I'm a killer disguised as a computer engineer. I fuck women like most people chew gum because I know things about love that would break you." He leaned down until she could see every speck of pain in his eyes like shards of glass embedded into his soul. "I could obliterate your last shred of sanity."

He stood, his jaw set like chiseled stone. "Now go before I do or say something I'll regret."

"Stop protecting me," Jessica whispered.

Something gutted him and she felt it. That was their bond. It would forever be an inseverable bond. There was nothing worse than feeling his pain but not seeing it.

"Sorry, princess. It's my job to protect you."

"Hit me, asshole. But don't take the coward's way out with all your bullshit name calling." She shoved him again. His degrading comment rekindled her anger. "Do it. DO IT!"

Jude looked over her shoulder. "Not today. Wouldn't look good in your wedding photos."

"Fuck you, coward."

Pressing his lips together, he gave her one last look then turned and walked to his car. "Yeah…" he mumbled in defeat "…fuck me."

Jessica turned, tugging at the hem of her dress stuck to her heel. She looked up and froze, ignoring the black Jetta that sped past her.

"Let him protect you."

"Luke, I—"

"Just …" He walked to her.

Would she ever feel truly worthy of him?

"Just let him." He lowered his beautiful body, kneeling before her on the abrasive concrete in his custom-tailored pants.

With a squeeze of her hands, his desperation broke her heart.

"I'm begging you. Let him protect you. Leave your past. Leave it for me."

Sniffling, she nodded while wiping the tears from her face. "It's just that I feel it … I feel his pain and it's so deep."

"I know." Luke stood and hugged her to him. "After the wedding, I'll talk to him. Okay?"

She nodded, but the comfort of Luke's arms didn't over-power the fear that Jude's words embedded in her mind, a bomb waiting to go off without a breath of warning—destined to shatter her world.

CHAPTER SIXTEEN

KNIGHT

The woman who never ran late found herself running quite late to her first job. Sex with Jackson Knight, self-professed murderer, could do that to a woman. His confession demanded her attention, but she didn't want to acknowledge any of it. The most unexpected feeling of happiness felt within her grasp. Just for once, she wanted to take it. Damn the consequences.

A quick kiss on Gunner's head and she scurried out the door, ice melt crunching beneath her feet as she walked to the garage. As soon as she shut the door, her phone chimed. Plopping sideways into the driver's seat, she banged her boots together as she jabbed her hand into her purse in search of her phone.

"Maddie, hi, sweetie. What's up?"

"Hey, Mom."

Despite running late, Ryn paused mid-motion fastening her seatbelt. First, Maddie called her which was rare. Second, her tone was friendly—too friendly.

"Everything okay?"

"I'm having issues with one of my professors."

"What kind of issues?"

"He's ... interested in me."

Ryn latched her seat belt. "Sounds unethical."

"It's kind of creepy. He's old, like your and Dad's age."

Ryn closed her eyes and shook her head. There was always a verbal slap in the face when it came to her daughter.

"Are you certain he's interested in you?"

"He's my International Law professor. I'm not doing so well in that class. He offered me extra credit."

"I'm not seeing how that's a problem."

"There is no extra credit for the class. He summoned me to his office to offer it to *only* me. When I got there he told me if I was interested to lock his office door behind me."

A nauseous feeling settled in Ryn's stomach. "You need to say something to the Dean of Students."

"Dad is friends with the dean."

Just the mention of Preston made the sick feeling in Ryn's stomach intensify.

"Have you told your dad about this?"

"Yes."

"And?"

"He said I need to pass the class."

"What is that supposed to mean?"

"He thinks I'm too close to being done with school to start making waves."

"Making waves? Reporting sexual harassment is not making waves."

"Dad said my professor will deny it and it will be his word against mine, then he'll flunk me."

Ryn rubbed her temples. "I'm still not following. He

doesn't want you to report your professor, but he doesn't want you to flunk the class either. So—"

Maddie sighed her usual sigh, the one that conveyed her frustration with Ryn. The OMG-Mom-you're-so-dense sigh. "So he said that some of the most successful women in the world had to suck a few dicks to get to where they are."

"He said what?" Ryn saw red—blood red.

"Calm down. I was shocked at first too, but the sad part is he's right."

"Maddison!"

"I'm not going to do it, so don't get mad at dad for telling it like it is."

"He wasn't telling it like it is, Maddie. He was encouraging you to turn a blind eye to sexual harassment, but even worse, he basically told you to say yes to your professor! *That* is not okay and I'm not mad at your dad, I'm fucking furious!"

"Oh my God! Did you just say the F-word?" Maddie laughed. She actually laughed.

The girl had no clue how serious her situation was, thanks to her father downplaying women sucking dicks to get ahead in life.

Still parked in the garage, Ryn rested her head on the steering wheel. Thankfully her first client was out of town and would never know that she was late, but it set the pace for the rest of her day. Late. Late. Late. And *pissed*. Seriously pissed.

"I'll deal with your professor and your father. You just stay away from both of them."

"I have class this afternoon. It's not going to help my grade to skip class."

"Fine. Go to class, but don't put yourself in the position to be alone with him again. Got it?"

"Whatever. But if I flunk this class—"

"If you study harder, you'll have no reason to flunk it. And let's just be clear on one thing, my dear daughter. Some of the most successful women in the world got to where they are in life *not* because they sucked a few dicks, but because they stood up for themselves and refused to take it up the backside."

Ryn ended the call before Maddie could shoot back a snide remark. Maddie always took her father's side, but someday—if she were lucky enough to get married and have children—she would finally understand the love a mother has for a child. Ryn's love knew no boundaries, not even the ugly, unappreciative, and deep-cutting jabs to the heart. Her love for Maddie would always be unconditional.

If it weren't for Maddie, Ryn would not have lived to see forty or Jackson Knight. Preston physically and emotionally beat her to the lowest depths of Hell, but Maddie, her little blonde with pig-tails and bright eyes, kept her breathing—brought her back to life again and again.

"Jackson? Did you hear me? Jackson?"

All eighty-eight keys stood idle. Why weren't they moving? It was a fucking piano lesson, the least she could do was pretend to play, anything to drown out the nagging doubt of Jillian's wellbeing.

"Time's up. I have to pick up my kids from school."

His eyes shifted, following the sound of the voice. The curly-haired brunette wearing a low cut mother-slut-of-three-kids blouse that revealed every detail of her lace bra continued to move her lips. The words began to register like someone turned up the volume to a muted TV.

"Great. Practice it again this week."

"But I played it perfectly." She thrust out her chest as if she'd played the piece with her nipples and they were waiting for a reward.

Jackson grabbed the sheet music and tossed it on the floor. "Then let me hear it again."

Shock grew in her eyes as perfectly-glossed lips parted. "I can't play it by memory."

"Then it would appear you still need to practice it. Wouldn't you agree?"

She deflated. He didn't care, not that day. Luke calling, Jillian's proverbial fuck-off still on the table with a dead battery, and his inability to do anything about any of it, severed his last bit of patience. Jackson needed to rid his body of the pent-up anger and anxiety. The woman raping his piano needed to pick up her music and get the hell out of there before he told her how he really felt about her musical talent or lack thereof.

"Fine. I'll practice it more." She gathered up her music, slipped on her gray wool coat, and snagged her purse from the table before shoving her feet into her black leather boots and letting herself out.

Jackson clenched and released his fists several times, but the tension wouldn't budge. The need for a physical release throbbed in his veins, the ticking of a bomb. He threw on jogging pants, a gray hoodie, and a beanie, then hit the snow-mottled sidewalks to run until his lungs burned equally from exertion and the frigid air. The past kept him warm as his memories ignited an anger like a dormant volcano destined to erupt, destroying everything in a hundred mile radius.

Day

JUDE COULDN'T KEEP his mother's dirty secret. Every day he felt a piece of his humanity being chipped away. Two days after catching her in the arms of another man, he took his sixteen-year-old girlfriend's virginity and then told her they were over. No woman would ever have the chance at his heart. If the woman he had on the highest pedestal couldn't be faithful, then no woman could. Fuck them all. And that's exactly what he did.

Jessica became the exception. He would protect her, even from her own delusions of Grant and Sunny Day being the perfect couple—the shining example of happily ever after. She wanted to marry a man like their father and love him with Sunny's passion. Sunny's fucking passion. She had passion, just not for their father.

Jude planned on telling Jessica, then the both of them would break the news to their father. Grant didn't share or understand Jude's interest in computers and Jude had no desire to work under the hood of a car or mess with greasy motorcycle parts, but he respected the man who worked hard for his family and risked his life to protect the lives of others. Grant Day was his father and he loved him.

"Jujube?"

Jude shook his head, staring at his computer screen. "You know I don't respond to that name."

Jessica plopped on his bed, stretching her gum out then wrapping it around her finger before sucking it back into her mouth. "You just did respond."

"Why do you call me that?"

"Because you're just like Jujubes—tough, yet sweet on the inside."

"I don't think Tessa thinks I'm sweet on the inside."

"Yeah ... I heard about that. You dated her for nine months, took her virginity, then dumped her. Was the sex that bad?"

"It wasn't about the sex."

"Then enlighten me. Because after nine months, I don't think the proper protocol for breaking up with a girl is to pop her cherry before shattering her heart. I think you were supposed to promise to respect her in the morning, then cuddle her afterward ... or something like that."

Jude clicked from one screen to the next, not really wanting to have that conversation. He had more important things to discuss with sister dearest.

"Yeah, well, I don't respect any woman."

"Ouch. Good thing I'm not a woman. Just a weak little daddy's girl, according to cock-face Knox."

"You just piss him off. That's all."

"Clearly. And why is that again? Because I work circles around everyone else, including you some days? Or is it because I've knocked him on his ass more than anyone else during sparring?" She giggled. *"Stupid fucker."*

"It's because you're Grant Day's daughter."

"That makes no sense."

"It does." Jude swiveled in his desk chair. *"Shut my door. I have something to tell you."*

"I have something to tell you first." She shut the door and lowered her voice. *"I'm going to San Diego with Claire. Her cyber boyfriend wants to meet her now that she's eighteen and she wants me to go with her. She's telling her parents we're going to L.A. for a concert and that's what I'm telling Mom and Dad too."*

"You're going to San Diego so Claire can have sex with some stranger?"

"Nobody said anything about having sex, and he's not really a stranger. They've been dating online for over a year."

"He could be a serial killer."

"You think a serial killer is going to date a girl for a year and refuse to see her until she's eighteen, only to kill her? I think out of your two brilliantly paranoid assessments, the sex scenario is more likely."

"Rape."

Jessica rolled her eyes. "She's an adult. If it's consensual, it's not rape. Besides, I'll be there. Do you really think I'm going to let anything happen to her?"

"Then why are you telling me?"

She walked behind him and hugged his neck, giving him a loud, smacking kiss on his cheek. "Because we don't have secrets. Right?"

He nodded slowly.

"Now..." she stood and played with her gum again "... what do you need to tell me?"

Twisting his lips to the side, he shrugged. "We'll talk when you get back."

"You sure? Is it about Tessa?"

Jude shook his head. "Indirectly, but it doesn't matter until you get back."

"OK. Dad expects you to track my phone, so when he asks for an update, don't fuck up and say I'm in San Diego when he's expecting me to be in L.A. Got it?"

Jude brought his middle finger to his forehead and saluted her.

"Nice. Is that what you did to Tessa after deflowering her?"

He spun around in his chair again and focused on his computer screen. Bursting her bubble would have to wait until another day.

CHAPTER SEVENTEEN

KNIGHT

Confronting Maddie's professor didn't go well. In college, parents trying to settle disputes between instructors and young adults was frowned upon. Of course he denied everything, saying Maddie came to him and asked for extra credit and he told her it was not an option for his class. Without proof it really was Maddie's word against his. Ryn made sure to let him know that she was also going to talk to the Dean of Students just so the incident would be on record.

It was a risk, but she made sure the professor knew Maddie's father played golf with the Dean of Students. She failed to mention that her asshole of an ex-husband saw nothing wrong with extra-credit blowjobs. Instead, she hoped he would decide it to be in everyone's best interest to pass Maddie, even if she didn't earn the grade. Ryn wanted her daughter as far away from that predator as possible. Period.

Before leaving campus she tried calling Jackson several times, but it went straight to voicemail. She needed to hear his voice to calm her nerves. Instead, she held her phone up to her ear, waiting for Preston to answer his phone. There was no doubt in her mind that he would.

"Calling to apologize for your meathead boyfriend?"

"I'm calling to ask why the hell you encouraged Maddie to give her sick bastard of a professor what he wanted. For Christ's sake, why are you even in her life? She needs a father, someone to protect her from assholes like him, not a pimp. The thing is ... I was so pissed when she told me what you said, but I wasn't surprised. You're a monster and I should have packed up my daughter and moved halfway across the world to get us both away from you. Instead, I stayed and not only have you tainted her with your bullshit about our failed marriage, but now you're making her think she has to spread her legs to get a college degree!"

"First of all, she's *our* daughter, which you seem to forget—"

"You never wanted her," Ryn said through gritted teeth.

"I never wanted you either, but you got yourself knocked up with my child so I had no choice. But don't sweat it, sweetheart, because you both have grown on me over the years and maybe it's just my age or sentimentality, but I want us to work. I want us to be a family again. Maddie needs a father ... a role model, and you need a man with more to him than just a punch card to the local gym."

"Family? Are you kidding me? We were never a family. You ignored your daughter, beat your wife, and stuck your dick between the legs of anything that walked."

"Now, now ... it takes two to tango."

"Tango! Our marriage wasn't a dance. It was a fucking concentration camp!"

"My, your rogue lover must be influencing you with some vulgar language. I don't believe I've ever heard that word come out of your mouth before."

"Fuck you! Fuck your family reunion. Then fuck off, asshole!" She ended the call then screamed, gripping the steering wheel as if she wanted to rip it right off the dash.

Preston Iverson was the devil. He drew the absolute worst from her. All those years later and he still tortured her with his words. She needed Jackson. After escaping an abusive husband, she'd found comfort in the arms of a murderer. What were the chances?

AFTER RINGING the doorbell several times and knocking on both the storm door and side window, Ryn sulked back to her car. She needed the security of Jackson's arms. Instead, she climbed back in her car and let the tears fall. In between sobs she laughed.

"He's just not home. Why are you crying?" she asked herself, resting her forehead on her hands gripped around the top of the steering wheel. Not once in her adult life had she allowed herself to need a man—until Jackson. After dealing with Preston, she *needed* Jackson so badly her chest felt painfully hollow.

Bang bang bang!

Ryn jerked her head up and there he stood in a gray hoodie and jogging pants, face flushed, rapid puffs of air condensing between his lips and her window. He frowned, brow drawn tight.

She smiled, blinking her teary eyes. He opened her door.

"What's wrong?"

Ryn leaped into his arms.

"Hey now ... what's going on?" He hugged her to him.

"You weren't home." Her words muffled into the neck

of his hoodie. "Oh God. I didn't mean it like that." She pulled back, keeping her hands cupped to the back of his head. "It's been a shit day ... and I ... I just really needed to see you. I know that sounds crazy but—"

He kissed her. Tasted her. Claimed her in the deepest recesses of her heart, places no man had ever been before. Ryn wanted to kiss him for eternity, or at least until he filled every inch of her mind, leaving no room for the pain of her past.

"It's not crazy." The whisper of his words over her lips chased away the events of her day, at least for that moment.

He moved to shut her car door.

"Don't!" She gripped him tighter. "If you move then this moment will end."

Jackson chuckled. "And what is this moment?"

Searching his eyes, she smiled. "It's perfection."

He laughed again. "Aren't you cold?"

"Not in your arms."

"Well, I did run nearly ten miles. I feel like a furnace—a sweaty, smelly furnace. I need a shower."

She pinched her lips together, concealing her grin as she shrugged. "I like showers."

His eyes grew wide. "Do you now?"

"I do." She played with the strings to his hoodie.

"As I recall, you don't take showers with men."

"I've recently made an exception."

"Yeah?"

She nodded, biting her lip. "Younger guy. Tattoos. Geeky glasses. Fairly nice body."

Jackson puckered his lips. A stern look appraised her with an unnerving intensity. "Fairly nice?"

"Yes. He could use some fat on his body. Women like little love handles."

"Well if you need something to hold on to, I can offer you something rather large and quite firm."

"Is that so?"

"It is."

"I suppose I could see whatcha got."

Jackson smirked. "Follow me." He took her hand and led her inside.

She sat on his bed, enthralled with every move he made, from something as mundane as untying his shoes to the more erotic show of him undressing. Every moment with Jackson was a pinch-me moment.

"Tell me about the tears."

She looked at his eyes, having drunk in every other part of his body. "Maddie has a professor offering extra credit in exchange for sexual favors and her father condones that behavior. Apparently the job that successful women have to master before making it to the top is the blowjob."

"Don't let my sister hear that. She'd hunt down that professor and castrate him, then she'd do the same thing to your ex-husband."

"So I should definitely say something to her?"

Jackson chuckled, but his smile faded within seconds. "I've had a shit day as well. We should have stayed in bed."

"Want to talk about it?"

"I want you to take off your clothes."

"I talk better with my clothes on."

"I fuck you better with your clothes off."

Ryn opened her mouth to reply. Nothing.

"It was your idea." He crossed inked arms over his chest, completely comfortable standing naked in front of her.

"Yeah, I was emotional yet oddly more confident in the driveway."

Jackson cocked his head to the side. Every look felt

like an assessment. "We can fuck in the driveway, but it's going to be cold and I have a hunch there might be something in the association's code of conduct that prohibits it."

Ryn laughed. "Ya think?"

"Yes. I think the first law is no speeding and the second is no fucking in the driveway. Now strip."

Using borrowed courage from some unknown place, she stood. It was a start.

"You're mine for eternity, so you might as well get used to these eyes looking at your naked body—*only* these eyes."

Her heart drummed against her chest in a terrifying yet exhilarating rhythm. In an unexplainable way, she both hated and loved how far out of her skin she felt when he looked at her.

"Let's start with this ... What part of your body have I not seen?"

The hint of a smile played with the corners of her mouth.

"Better yet, what part of your body have my lips not touched?"

Tugging off her shirt, she smiled. Gone were the compression bras; she didn't burn them, but they were hauled off with the trash shortly after the infamous refrigerator sex. Lace, satin, and underwire took their place.

"What you're doing right now feels more intimate than anything you've ever done to me with your mouth."

"We'll see about that." He wet his lips, eyeing her white lace bra. Approval glimmered in his eyes.

She removed the rest of her clothes, eager to be in his arms. He took a step back as she moved toward him.

"Stop."

She froze. Her hands searched for a place to be: hanging

idle at her sides, covering her breasts, shielding her neatly-shaven pussy?

"Repeat after me."

"What?" Her voice squeaked with disbelief.

He grinned as his ego gobbled up her confidence. "I'm beautiful."

Ryn squinted.

"Say it."

She sighed. "I'm beautiful."

"I'm taking back every bit of confidence that bastard took from me."

It would never happen like that, but someone who hadn't been in her shoes could never understand. However, she loved the naked man standing before her for saying it.

"I'm taking back every bit of confidence that bastard took from me."

"I'm worthy of happiness."

That one hit harder than it should have. She'd never given happiness much thought.

"Say it."

"I'm ... I'm worthy of happiness."

"I'm going to marry Jackson Knight and love him in spite of his multiple fucked-up personalities."

"Jackson—"

"Say it." His voice carried a rare pain and vulnerability.

"I'm going to marry Jackson Knight..." she stepped closer and rested her hands on his chest "...and I'm going to *love* Every. Single. One. Of his fucked-up personalities."

"I've had a shit day," he whispered, brushing his thumb along her cheek. "Until now."

She nodded slowly, then looked up at him. "I've had a shit life ... until now."

"Touch me," he said.

"Where?"

"Everywhere. Make me feel *human* again."

She could do that. She could make him feel human. After all, he made her feel alive.

Jackson looked at her with complete surrender as they stepped into the steamy abyss. His breath caught when she touched him. He closed his eyes and let her move her soapy hands over the firm planes of his body. The pain in his face crushed her. What had happened to him? Could one human take the life of another and still feel whole? Or did he give away a piece of himself with every life he took?

The water washed over her like guilt. What if he needed to tell her? Ryn didn't want to know everything. She loved Jackson Knight now and just like her past, she didn't want to let yesterday taint today and steal tomorrow.

Water clung to his eyelashes as he blinked them open when she shut off the water. Wrapping his arms around her waist, he lifted her up and carried her to the bed, not stopping for towels.

"We're drenched," she shrieked as he threw back his comforter and tossed her onto the cold sheets.

Before she could protest with another word, he crawled up her body while covering them completely with the comforter. Ryn liked their private cocoon. She also liked how he wasted no time warming up her body with his.

"You're so beautiful," he whispered over her skin.

She closed her eyes as his tongue parted her folds, his lips soft on her sensitive flesh. Ryn grabbed his hair and let her legs fall open for him. Everything he did meant something so much greater than physical desire. The woman who survived years of abuse had learned to trust again, but more than that, he'd taught her to believe. When Jackson touched her she *believed* in herself and she *felt* truly beautiful.

"Jackson ..." she writhed beneath him as he kissed his way back up her body, sinking into her as his lips claimed hers again.

Ryn turned her head to the side, relishing the feel of his teeth teasing along her neck.

"Tell me."

"What?" he murmured over her skin.

"Tell me we're not just fucking."

He stopped. Ryn clenched her muscles around him buried inside of her. The fullness stole her breath as much as the intensity in his eyes.

"We're having intercourse." A smile crept along his face.

Ryn dug her nails into his ass.

He teased his lips over hers. "Our genitals are having a play date."

She bit his lower lip. He chuckled.

"I'm holing up for the winter."

Snaking a hand between them, she squeezed a testicle.

"Okay ... okay." He flinched.

"Tell me what this is."

Jackson planted soft kisses on her entire face then hovered over her lips. "I'm making love to you, Ryn. You're the only woman I've made love to. And this? You? It's my whole fucking world."

CHAPTER EIGHTEEN

Some things in life were too overwhelming—too big—to see from Earth. Jillian opened her eyes, feeling a world away from reality. Maybe it was the view from the other side. Her captor's words broke the unbreakable.

Jessica had a long list of innocent victims, but only one man had she left with *a broken nose, two missing teeth, three fractured ribs, and a punctured lung.* And he wasn't an innocent victim.

"I'm sorry."

She jerked her head up, eyes wide. Across from her, bound and propped up against the opposing wall, was *him.*

"Fuck you." She shook her head. It just couldn't be true. It couldn't be her reality.

"I loved her. I've loved her my whole life."

Jillian coughed past the sandpaper feeling in her throat. "You'd better be referring to that psycho bitch, because if you're talking about—"

"Sunny. I loved your mother."

"Don't you fucking say that!" She fought against her restraints, but they didn't budge. Her heart tried to bust through her chest. Could a heart kill someone? Jillian felt certain hers could.

"I loved her before she met your father."

"Stop! Just ... stop." Tears stung her eyes. They were filled with anger. She couldn't imagine how many times her world could be shattered and pieced back together, just to have it blown up all over again.

"She loved me too."

"She would *never* love you." Her words sliced through the air. She wanted them to slice through his throat, gouge out his eyes, and rip his fucking heart from his soulless body.

"We met in kindergarten." He stared at the floor, a smug smile curling his lips.

Jillian squeezed her eyes shut, silently begging for icy water, sauna heat, or even another arrow, preferably to her heart—anything would have been better than the torture his words put her through.

"We lived a block away from each other and became inseparable. She was the first girl I kissed. She was my best friend ... the best of everything. Soul mates."

"Are you two lovebirds playing catch up?" Psycho Bitch descended the stairs, trying to regain some dignity by throwing her shoulders back, as if it could distract from her fucked-up face.

"Let her go, Vic. This has nothing to do with her."

Her polite smile did nothing to enhance her mangled facial features. "It has plenty to do with her, *Special Agent McGraw*. Isn't that what you liked me to call you when you fucked me like a dog, refusing to actually look at my face when we made love? Oh wait ... except on our wedding night. You surrendered to the missionary position, but kept your eyes shut the whole time."

Knox gave Jillian a fleeting glance. She glared at him. How did she not know he had a wife?

"Vicki?"

"Vic." He looked at his ex-wife while speaking to Jillian. "Virtual Intelligence Command. Edgar gave her that code name. Everyone assumed the eyes and ears of G.A.I.L. was a man named Victor. Instead, it was his orphaned step-daughter who happened to know her way around a computer. He took pity on her and gave her a job to let her be part of G.A.I.L. because her asthma prevented her from being in the field. Then I took pity on her and married her."

"Pity my ass. You married me to get your greedy little hands deeper into the inner workings of G.A.I.L. You married me for money and power. You and all your other unscrupulous comrades took something good, something positive that came from my mother's death, and you turned it into a corrupt business."

"Money equals power, sweetheart. You don't protect innocent lives without a helluva lot of power. An army needs deep pockets. Corruption is a fact of life."

"It was never about protecting innocent lives. For you it was always about revenge."

Jillian watched her two enemies sling their words.

"Jesus, Irene! What the fuck do you think *this* is? Revenge! You're out for revenge and everyone is collateral damage."

"Irene" narrowed her eyes, flitting them between Jillian and Knox. "Don't ever call me that again." She gritted out each word then took a puff from her inhaler.

"It's your name."

"It's not my goddamn name!" Her fist slammed the table, knocking over a can of Mountain Dew and her bow that had been propped up against the leg. "Irene died the day she became Vic. You never knew Irene. She was Gail's daughter—innocent and full of hope. Vic fed G.A.I.L's corruption. She married a cheater—a cheater who drove her to the edge of insanity and then shoved her off it. Five years, asshole. I spent five years in that godforsaken place all because of you and your mistresses."

Irene's eyes bore into Jillian's.

"I wasn't his mistress," Jillian said with absolute resolution. It was the truth.

"You fucked my husband." Irene's rage overshadowed her newfound commitment to God. Underneath that self-righteousness stood a human with an ego and bleeding emotions.

"I fucked up your husband. I *did not* fuck him."

The man her mother supposedly loved since kindergarten, sodomized Jessica—raped her. She lacked all ability to rationalize any of that. Even the words caught in her throat. Her mother would never have loved a rapist. It was easy to stay strong when the events in her life held some sort of meaning, some shred of rationale. Knox McGraw and Sunny Day having been soul mates obliterated all sense of reason.

"Let her go, Irene."

She whipped around, snatching her bow from the floor, loading an arrow, and piercing through Knox's shoulder in a single blink. "If I let her go, she'll kill me."

Psycho Bitch with the bow and arrow skills of Robin Hood could predict the future. Except Jillian wouldn't just kill her ... she'd kill Knox too.

"Besides, the reunion has just begun. We have more guests that will be joining the party."

Knox grimaced at the arrow plunged into his shoulder.

"Are you going to resurrect Sunny from the dead?" he seethed.

He ignored Jillian's scowl. The bastard had no right to mention her mother in that context.

"You never know. I have God on my side." Irene tossed the bow on the table.

"I think you're worshiping a false god." He goaded her.

"I think you're going to die first when my original plan was to save you until last. I wanted you to watch those around you perish from your indiscretions. I fear my need to shut you up will spoil my plans."

"I agree. Kill Knox first."

That got both of their attention.

"Or you could let me kill him."

Irene smirked. "You had your chance."

"I wasn't trying to kill him. Had I been ... he'd be dead."

She picked up the spilled pop can and headed up the stairs. "Behave, kids. I have some things to attend to."

When the door shut, Jillian looked at Knox. "You have more protection and resources than the FBI. How the hell did she get you here?"

"She got you here."

"She snagged me in a grief-stricken state from the airport in Portland. I was on my way to AJ's funeral. What's your excuse?"

"I came willingly."

"Bullshit. Where's your phone?"

"Home."

Jillian shook her head. "No way."

"Irene's smart. Crazy, but smart. Every bit of 'intelligence' that came from G.A.I.L for nearly a decade came from her. She can track a mouse through a back alley in New York City. You were trained to kill with your hands, she was trained to assassinate by typing in a password on a keyboard. Trust me. She has eyes and ears on us as we speak. She's resourceful and manipulative." He smirked. "So believe me when I say she has people working for her that don't even know it. They work for cash. No questions. No names."

"The texts ... did you know she was the one sending them to me? Did you know she found God in the psych ward? Did you keep this from me?"

Knox shook his head, a gruff chuckle vibrated his chest. "No. She was admitted and I let her go. I didn't give her another thought—just happy to be rid of her. No need to keep tabs on someone locked up in a mental institution. And I sure as hell didn't know she found God."

Jillian narrowed her eyes. "You keep tabs on everyone. Don't try to convince me that you didn't know she was out."

He shrugged. "I knew she was out, and I had her followed for a month or so, but nothing she did warranted any more of my time or resources so I pulled my men from her. No flags. No threat."

"You were wrong."

He nodded. "I was wrong."

"What did she say to get you here? Why would you willingly walk into the lion's den without someone having your back?"

"You ... and Sunny."

"Don't. I don't want to talk about that."

Knox chuckled, tipping his head back against the wall and closing his eyes. "Then what do you want to talk about?"

"Luke. I want to know what you did to him, what you said to him."

"We chatted about the words you two exchanged in

Houston. I'd planned on having the same conversation with you, but out of respect, I decided to wait until after the funeral."

"Respect? I'm not sure you know what that is."

"I'm not the bad guy you think I am."

"You're a monster."

Monsters prey on others because they have no self-control ... they're the weak ones.

Knox released a long breath. "I told Dr. Jones to forget about you. I told him to fuck as many women as it took to make that happen."

Once a monster, always a monster. Of course he said that to Luke.

"Don't give me that look."

He didn't have his eyes open. How could he know what look she gave him?

"You found another lover. You gave him your heart and he died, taking a part of you with him. Dr. Jones needs more than a memory to keep him warm at night. You could have chosen him, but you left him behind. I told him as much. He needs to be angry and pissed at you to move on."

"I didn't give AJ my heart. I didn't have a heart left to give him." Her words lacked conviction, in spite of her intent to mean them, in spite of wishing they were true.

"I moved heaven and earth for you in your last-ditch effort to save him. People don't do that for a good fuck. He meant something to you."

"Jude killed him, but you knew that, didn't you? I'm sure you had your hand in covering it up ... making it look like he died from the cancer and making sure his body made it back to Portland without suspicion."

Knox smiled, eyes still shut. "Your brother is an unscrupulous lethal weapon. He takes lives without a blink of hesitation. That's rare. Even your father and I battled with our consciences when aiming our guns at known killers, but not Jude. He was born to kill. *But* ... something tells me he blinked more than once before taking Sergeant Monaghan's life. He knew he was also killing a part of you. He killed AJ to save you."

"Fuck you."

"I know. Fuck me. Fuck Jackson. It doesn't change anything."

Irene brought Knox there to torture Jillian. She knew the emotional pain he could inflict would hurt her more than any kind of physical torture.

"He's with someone. Her name is Charlie. She's Lake's physical therapist. My sources told me she's smart, beautiful, and his family seems to adore her."

Adore.

She didn't begrudge Luke a single thing. Jillian wanted him to find happiness. Luke deserved a happily ever after more than she did. Of course imagining him with someone else filled her with pain, but Knox was right, Jackson was right ... she chose to leave him behind. If she had it all to do over again, she would have made the same decision. Luke's family needed him.

"I'm happy for him ... for them."

"Really?" Knox opened his eyes.

"I loved him enough to let him go."

"How kind of you. I'm sure he doesn't see it that way. I never took you for the if-you-love-something-set-it-free type."

Questions whirled in her head. Had her mother let Knox go? Did he let her go? With her mother dead, would Jillian ever know the whole truth? Did she *want* to know the truth?

CHAPTER NINETEEN

JONES

THE UNANSWERABLE QUESTION. Where does one search for someone who doesn't want to be found? For the safety of his family, Luke had to go through the motions of his life until the universe answered that question for him—until Jessica answered that question. He remained Dr. Jones by day, transforming into the man willing to risk his career and his own life to find her.

"Brother dearest?" Lake called, letting herself into Luke's place.

He needed to confiscate her key.

"In my office." He clicked out of his search screens and shut the top to his computer.

"Watching porn?"

He leaned back in his desk chair, resting his folded hands on his stomach.

"To what do I owe this unannounced visit?"

She eased into the leather chaise lounge in the corner of his office. "Nonsense. I announced myself when I opened the door."

"You need to get enrolled in school again or find a job."

"I have a job."

"I mean a paying job, a forty-hours-a-week job." Luke applauded his sister for volunteering to work with amputee children at the hospital, a position Charlie suggested, but it became her excuse to not reenroll in college after her accident. Their parents weren't going to be able to support her living in San Francisco forever and Luke loved his sister, but he was not an enabler.

"Will you drive me home tomorrow to spend the weekend with Mom and Dad?"

"I can't."

"Why not? Mom and Dad want to see you, but they have guests and can't come visit us."

"I have somewhere I need to be."

"Where?"

He gave her a pointed look. "Since when are you my keeper?"

"Since Jessica died and since you blew off Charlie."

Sometimes he swore the woman before him was Jessica. Lake had a strong personality and spoke with uncensored words. Contumacious.

"I'm leaving town tomorrow."

"For?"

"Research."

"What are you researching?" Her eyes grew wide with expectancy.

Luke chuckled. "Stuff for something I'll be presenting at a conference in the spring."

"What's the topic?" Lake's relentlessness was unmatched.

"Life after death."

"Really? Sounds intriguing."

"Very. So let's plan a trip home in a few weeks."

"Christmas is in a few weeks."

"Well there you go. Perfect timing." Luke grinned.

Lake rolled her eyes. "Take me with you."

"Absolutely not."

"Why?"

"I'm going to be busy. I won't have time to watch after you."

"I don't need you to watch after me."

"No."

"Come on."

"Absolutely not. It's too dangerous."

"Dangerous? Where are you going? Looking for ghosts in the ghetto?"

Luke sighed. "The answer is no. No now. No tomorrow. No if you ask me a million more times."

"You're no fun."

"So I've heard."

"I'm not going to watch Jones for you."

"I'm not asking you to. Eve has agreed to watch him."

"I think you're taking advantage of your secretary."

"Probably, but she loves Jones, maybe more than me, so I don't feel bad about asking her."

"So you're just going to leave me by myself this weekend."

"I'm sure Charlie will indulge you in a movie or some female-bonding thing."

Lake shrugged, a pout stealing her full lips. "I'm trying to give Charlie some space. I think being around me reminds her of you."

Luke's brow furrowed. "I'm sorry. That's one of the main reasons I hesitated getting involved with her. I didn't want anything to happen to your friendship." It was a half-truth. Jessica was the biggest reason for his reservations about a relationship with Charlie or anyone else.

"It's fine. I'm actually comforted by the fact that my brilliant psychiatrist brother is messed-up in the head. It makes the rest of us feel less crazy for having a human side."

"Next weekend. I'll go home with you then. Okay?"

"Deal." Lake stood, taking an extra moment to gain her balance.

He walked around the desk and hugged her. "I am messed-up and yes, the whole 'human side' really sucks."

"I love you, Luke. You're still my idol."

"Thanks. But I think you need to set your role model standards a bit higher than me."

"How long will you be gone?"

"I had Eve reschedule my patients for next week so I don't feel rushed. It depends on what I find and how soon I find it."

Her. It depended on how soon he found *her*.

LUKE BOARDED the plane for Chicago. It was the safest destination to take by plane. He would pay cash for a rental car and drive to Omaha where he would pay cash for a hotel. Jude/Jackson was his ticket to finding Jessica. Luke didn't buy his claim that he couldn't find her.

"Sir, we're experiencing a slight delay. Can I get you something to drink while we wait?" the flight attendant asked.

"I'm fine. Thank you." He tipped his head back and closed his eyes. The 6:00 a.m. flight was always a bitch.

A while later the flight attendants began their pre-flight instructions to the passengers. Luke opened his eyes and stared out the window as they taxied down the runway, waiting in line to be cleared for takeoff.

"So Chicago, huh? I've never been. This should be fun." Lake.

Luke whipped around in his seat to blue eyes that mirrored his. Lake smiled, pink Beats covering her ears.

"What the hell are you doing?"

The older gentleman sitting next to her scowled at Luke.

"I thought I'd surprise you. No one really likes to travel alone."

"You can't be here."

She laughed. "We'll be in the air in less than sixty seconds. I think I'm here to stay."

"The second we land in Chicago we're getting you a ticket right back home."

"Um ... okay, Dad." She rolled her eyes.

"Sir, I need you to face forward. We're getting ready to take off."

Luke turned back around. Rage filled his mind. Lake would get a proper ass-chewing as soon as they landed in Chicago. Then he'd put her back on a plane.

He slipped on his own headphones to block out the sound of her gabbing with the passenger next to her. The girl could chat it up with anyone. It would be a long flight.

As soon as they exited the plane, he grabbed her arm.

"Ticket counter. Now."

She tugged out of his grasp. "I'm an adult, Luke. You can't tell me what to do."

"Have it your way." He marched past her. If she wanted to see Chicago, she could see Chicago. He had a rental car to get, and then he would head back west to Omaha.

"Luke! Stop!"

He stopped, closing his eyes and gritting his teeth.

"What the hell? I get it. You didn't want me to come. But I'm here. You can't just leave me."

"I told you it's not safe for you to be here."

"What does that mean? You think I'm going to get mugged or raped? I'm not going to wander the streets alone at night. You can do your thing during the day and I'll do mine. We can meet up for dinner. I promise I won't be a burden."

"I love you and *that's* why you can't stay. You have to trust me on this. I'm begging you, please just go back home."

She crossed her arms over her chest. "No."

"Enjoy Michigan Avenue. I'll see you back in San Francisco." He continued on, setting a pace he knew she couldn't keep.

Thirty seconds later he turned to the sound of commotion behind him.

"Dammit!" he jogged back to Lake.

A crowd of people surrounded her.

"I'm fine. Really, I'm fine."

Two men helped her to her feet while a lady shoved the spilled contents of Lake's purse back inside it. Blood oozed from a gash above Lake's eye.

"Jesus, what happened?"

"I was trying to catch up with my brother." She scowled at him, garnering similar looks and sympathy from the small crowd of people.

"I'm a doctor. Thanks. I'll take it from here." He smiled at the people around them as he took her bags and slung them over his shoulder. "Let's go. We'll stop by Urgent Care on our way out of town."

"We're not staying in Chicago?" She held a wad of tissue to her forehead as he led her through the crowd.

"No. We're not."

———

WITH A RENTAL CAR and a stitched up forehead, Luke and Lake headed west, Omaha bound. Self-preservation didn't matter when it was a solo trip. Lake's stubbornness put her in danger and compromised Luke's ability to find Jessica.

"You can't be mad at me forever."

He could.

"The silent treatment is getting old. We've been on the road for three hours. Tell me where we're going."

"Omaha." Keeping it a secret wasn't an option. Lake could read.

"You know, I haven't been to Omaha either, but I'm one hundred percent sure they have an airport. Did you over-shoot your destination by a couple states on purpose?"

"Yes."

"One word explanations. I can work with that. I like twenty questions. Let's see ... are you really going to Omaha for business?"

"No."

"Hmm ... did you purchase a cattle farm?"

"No." He gave her a quick sideways glance with a single squinted eye.

Lake laughed. "Is Warren Buffett your financial advisor?"

"No."

"Does this trip have anything to do with a woman?"

Luke contemplated his answer, not sure if telling Lake the truth was a good idea. "Yes."

"OMG! Are you serious?"

OMG confirmed she was not ready to handle the truth, but his options were limited.

"Serious."

"How did you meet her? Does Charlie know? God, you're such a pig. Do Mom and Dad know? Is it serious?"

Lake received the hairy eyeball again.

"Sorry. Um ... how did you meet her?"

"She was my patient."

"Shit. Are you serious? That's so unethical ... and completely romantic. Oh man ... you're going to visit her for a lust-filled week and your little sister is tagging along. That's not cool. Sorry, Bro. My bad. Now I feel regretful."

"*Now* you feel regretful? When I told you it wasn't safe and you were putting yourself in danger, that didn't faze you. But now that you think you're putting a kink in my sex plans you feel regretful."

"A bit. Yes. When did she move to Omaha?"

Luke bit his lips together, squinting a bit. "I'm not sure. Less than a year ago."

"Did you meet her before or after Jessica died?"

"Before."

"Oh ... Luke." Disappointment laced her words. "Please tell me you weren't cheating on Jessica."

"It's complicated."

"Asshole," she mumbled under her breath, turning her back to him to stare out her window.

Twenty Questions ended before she got to twenty. Just as well, he wanted Lake to think about Jessica. He wanted her to miss Jessica. He wanted to prime her brain for what he would tell her when they arrived in Omaha. Even then, it would be too much for her to comprehend.

A cold silence settled between them for the rest of the drive to Omaha. They stopped in Des Moines for dinner.

Lake didn't say a word, didn't even look at him. He wanted to tell her, but not yet. The truth was irrational and Lake would need to be in that frame of mind before he could make her see it—make her accept it.

They pulled into the parking garage of the Element hotel, and Lake jumped out before he put the car in park. In an angry march she headed straight to the lobby. He took his time getting their bags and checking them into their room.

"Coming?" he asked, breezing past her to the elevator.

Her flushed face confirmed she was seconds from exploding. He slid the key card in the door and held it open for her. As soon as it closed behind them, she turned, hands fisted, eyes squinted.

"I hate you. You cheated on Jessica. Jessica! What the hell is wrong with you? We loved her. The whole family. I think we preferred her to you. You were going to marry her. How could you? I'm going to hate this woman we're here to see. I don't care what you think of her. I already hate her for trying to steal you from Jessica. The only reason I'm not taking a cab to the airport right this second is because I want to see her. I want to claw her goddamn eyes out."

Tears streamed down her face.

"I idolized you. Jessica was a sister to me. I miss her so damn much. The only thing I have left is the memories of her—of you two together and now you've ruined that! You can't be with this girl, Luke. You just can't. She's not Jessica."

"She is."

Lake shook her head. "Don't you dare say that. Don't you dare disrespect her memory like that. You're such a bastard."

"I'm here for Jessica."

"Stop!" She covered her ears. "Just stop. Jessica wouldn't want you here doing what you're doing."

Luke couldn't deny the probable truth in that statement.

"Lake?" He grabbed her hands.

She fought him, squeezing her eyes shut.

"Lake, look at me."

She opened her red eyes, the ugly-cry grimace still stuck to her face.

"Jessica didn't die."

"Oh my God ... you're seeing ghosts. This won't end well."

He grabbed her face. "If you never listen to anything I say again, *please* hear this."

She blinked, holding her breath.

"Her parents were murdered and her death was faked to protect her from being murdered too."

Lake blinked some more. Anger and fear converged into complete shock.

"I saw her at the hotel in Houston. I was taken by the people who are supposedly protecting her. That's why I stood Charlie up."

"Im-impossible," Lake whispered.

"I'm here to find her. She and Jude moved to Omaha, but some things have happened in her life and she's gone again. I need to find her and this is the only place I know where to start."

"They took you. What does that mean? Took you where? Who took you?"

Her words indicated enough acceptance that he let her go and took a step back. His chin tipped to his chest as he rubbed the tension in the back of his neck.

"That's a little more complicated. Let's just say they

don't have much regard for my life or my family's. Being here puts my life in danger." He looked up at her.

Realization robbed her face of all color. "And mine is too," she whispered.

Luke nodded. "I think you should forget everything we've just discussed and get on the first flight out tomorrow."

"Is that what those people said to you?"

"More or less, just with a little more force and a lot more threat."

"But you're here anyway."

"I love her. I was miserable when I thought she died, but knowing she's alive is a different kind of pain—the kind that will kill me if I can't be with her."

"You're not cheating on her?"

Only Lake could bring a smile to his face in the midst of so much pain. "That depends on how you look at it. I'm searching for a woman with Jessica's build, but blond hair, and she goes by the name Jillian Knight."

"Jillian Knight?"

Luke nodded.

"I can't imagine her as a blonde. How does it look on her?"

"Hideous. Stunning. Disturbing. Mesmerizing."

Lake laughed. "Well, let's get some sleep. We have a blonde bombshell named Jillian Knight to track down tomorrow."

"I want you to go home."

"I know and I love you too, but by all rights I'm living on borrowed time, with a fake leg and a job that doesn't pay. I think doing anything *but* living on the edge would be a crime at this point."

"I'm serious. If anything happens to you—"

She pressed her finger to his mouth. "Shh ... I love her too."

He grabbed her hand and pulled her into him for a big hug. "Some guy, with my scrutinizing approval of course, is going to snatch you up one day and he's going to be the luckiest guy alive."

CHAPTER TWENTY

KNIGHT

WITH MINIMAL CONVINCING, Jackson talked Ryn into staying the weekend at his place. He hesitated for a fraction of a second when she reminded him Gunner would have to come over too. The that-dog-wants-to-rip-my-balls-off look ended with a smile and silent acquiescence.

Jackson loved to eat. Ryn loved to cook. They were a perfect match by any standard. The pang of guilt she felt when he woke up early to go for a run while she nestled back under the covers disappeared the second she realized the kitchen was all hers. A Friday night trip to the store before coming to his place ensured she had everything she needed to make muffins, bacon, seasoned hash, and fresh-squeezed orange juice. It did seem a bit excessive for two people, but Ryn couldn't resist.

Gunner gave a warning growl when the doorbell rang.

"The dope must have locked himself out." She wiped her hands and traipsed to the front door wearing nothing but Jackson's large T-shirt.

Ryn opened the door with a big grin that morphed into a grimace at the two strangers that stood on the opposite side of the storm door that thankfully fogged over within seconds.

"Shoot!" She held up a finger. "Just a minute." Closing the door, she ran into the bedroom and stripped the T-shirt from her embarrassingly-flushed body then slid into her jeans, a bra, and sweater. There was no time to deal with her hair, so she ran her fingers through it on the way back to the front door.

"Sorry about that. I was expecting someone else."

The man smiled. "That's fine. Sorry to disturb you so early in the morning. We're looking for Jackson Knight."

"He went for a jog."

The dark-haired man looked around at the snow covered ground and shook his head with a slight grin. "Of course he did," he mumbled to himself. "We're old friends. Would you mind if we waited for him?"

Ryn assessed them both. The girl looked young, maybe Maddie's age. Harmless.

With Gunner as her backup, she stepped back, welcoming them inside the house.

"I'm Ryn Middleton." She smiled and offered to take their coats.

"Luke, and this is my sister, Lake." They both slipped off their shoes then shook her hand.

Lake had a prosthetic leg. Ryn tried not to stare.

"Nasty car accident."

Her staring didn't go unnoticed. Ryn gave her a polite smile.

"Looks like you're lucky to be alive."

"Most days." Lake ginned at her brother before returning her attention to Ryn.

"So ... Luke and Lake. Your mother must have been a glutton for punishment."

Lake giggled. "You have no idea. We have three other siblings: Lane, Lara, and Liam."

"Wow." Ryn pulled the cranberry-orange muffins from the oven. "So how do you know Jackson?"

"I was closer friends to his sister, *Jillian*," Luke said.

Ryn poured two glasses of orange juice and offered them to her guests.

"Oh no. We didn't mean to intrude on your breakfast." Luke had an earnest smile, mature but boyish at the same time.

"You're not intruding. I never get to cook for many besides myself, and I was just thinking how overboard I went for just two people. Here ... I insist."

Luke and Lake took the juice and thanked her.

"Have a seat." Ryn nodded to the table. "I have muffins, bacon, and hash too. Unless you're vegetarians like Jillian."

"No, we're not," Luke grinned at his sister as if there was some sort of inside joke.

"So you're from New York too?"

Lake squinted her eyes a bit.

"Yes. Yes we are." Luke took a sip of his juice. "So are you and Jackson ... *together*?"

"I know what you're thinking. I'm older and he's ... *younger* and—"

"No." Luke saved her from her impending rant of insecurity. "I was just thinking the guy I used to know never had women making breakfast in his kitchen."

Ryn nodded. "He told me he wasn't much of the relationship type before ..."

"Before you?"

She shrugged. "Yeah. Boy, that sounds conceited, doesn't it? I don't mean it like I think I'm something special or anything."

"You're beautiful. Age doesn't matter. It would seem he's lucky to have found you. I'm sure you make him a better man."

Both Ryn and Luke stared at Lake. Those were mature words coming from a young woman. Ryn couldn't imagine Maddie saying something like that.

"Thank you." Ryn smiled, the kind she could feel across her whole body. "It would seem you showed up this morning just to make my day."

Lake laughed, nudging her brother's leg under the table. "Hear that? I've made *someone's* day."

"So what brings you two to Omaha? I hope not to see Jillian. She's out of town and we're not sure when she'll return."

"Do you know where she is?" Luke asked.

Ryn set two plates filled with food in front of Luke and Lake. "I don't. Did you know she lost someone close to her recently?"

They both nodded.

Ryn frowned. She didn't like the truth behind AJ's death, but with each passing day she understood it—understood Jackson—a little more.

"I think she needed some space, some time to grieve and try to make sense of everything."

"Have either you or Jackson heard from her?"

"I haven't and I don't think he has either. She left her phone behind so there's no way to contact her until she decides to call home."

They all turned as the front door opened.

NOTHING RUINED a long night of sex with Ryn like an unfamiliar car in the driveway that said he would not be having his way with her in the shower. The Martha-Stewart-moved-in-here smell that greeted him when he opened the front door almost made up for the lack of shower sex he would've had. *Almost.*

"Hey, I see you didn't slip on the ice and break your neck." Ryn kissed him on the cheek as he toed off his running shoes.

"Whose car is in the driveway?" Jackson followed Ryn around the corner.

"Ours. It's a rental." The damn thorn in his side smiled.

He and Ryn were good. Jackson embraced his new identity, his new life. Why did the past insist on resurfacing? Only on the rarest of occasions was Jackson at a loss for words, but at that moment he had nothing. He felt stranded in the middle of a mine field, not daring to move a single step. What had they told Ryn?

"So you've met my *friends*." He forced a smile at Ryn. "And you're feeding them my breakfast."

"Yes." She set a plate of food down on the table and motioned for him to take a seat. "And there's plenty of food."

"We thought we'd make the trip from *New York* to check on Jillian. She can't be doing well." Luke held his gaze to Jackson's, probably trying to read his mind.

"What a wasted trip. I'm sure Ryn told you she's not here and we don't know when she'll return." Jackson eyed Lake. He'd only met her a handful of times. Each one of those times he deemed her to be doable. Jessica threatened both testicles if he so much as looked at Lake for more than two seconds at a time. He didn't look at her that way anymore. She reminded him of Maddie—too damn young and immature.

"You brought your sister along. Interesting choice."

"How so?" Luke asked.

Jackson shrugged. "Safety reasons. Plane hijackings. Slamming into a semi on the icy roads. Any number of things could happen. I would have left her at home. That's all."

"Well my dear sister is stubborn."

"I know the feeling." Jackson dove into his breakfast. Reason nine hundred and ninety-nine why he would never let Ryn go: the woman had mad skills in the kitchen. Too bad the Jones siblings had to distract him from fully enjoying it.

"I had hoped since we talked on the phone that you would have reconsidered looking for your sister."

Jackson shook his head, mouth full, taste buds in heaven. "She'll come home when she's ready. Sorry you wasted your time coming here just to hear me say the same thing I told you on the phone."

Luke stared at his food. The guy's brain never shut down.

"Where is your restroom?"

"Down the hall on the left." Ryn smiled at Jackson, eyes big as if she worried answering that simple question somehow crossed a nonexistent line between her house and his.

Jackson grinned at her. He liked how she'd made herself at home. If his plans for the future worked out, they wouldn't need two homes.

"Thank you. Excuse me." Luke walked past Jackson, his expression filled with words he held back from Ryn's ears. For that Jackson was thankful.

"Are you in college, Lake?" Ryn asked.

"No. I was before the accident, but I haven't gotten back on that horse or any other for that matter. I volunteer at the hospital, working with young amputees."

"I heard about your accident. Sorry to hear about your leg." Jackson felt the need to say something, but he wasn't good with emotions and the words that went with them.

"Thanks." Lake stared at her plate. "It's never a good time to lose someone you love." Lake looked at Ryn. "My boyfriend died."

Ryn reached her hand over and rested it on Lake's. "That's terrible."

Lake nodded. "But if it had to happen I wish it could have been on a different day. Any other day."

"Oh?" Ryn's brow furrowed.

"We were on our way to a wedding." She looked at Jackson.

He tried not to react, but his jaw muscle twitched anyway.

"Luke's wedding."

"Oh no. Your poor family."

"Yeah, he didn't get married that day."

"But he did eventually, right?"

Lake shook her head. "I was in a coma so the wedding was postponed."

Jackson looked away the minute he saw tears pooling in her eyes.

"His fiancée died in her own tragic accident before I came out of my coma. I woke up to no leg, no boyfriend, and no Jessica."

Jackson flinched at the mention of her name.

"Life isn't anything if not heartbreaking and unpredictable." Ryn wiped away a tear of her own.

"I'd better make sure Luke didn't flush himself down the toilet." Jackson stood, eager to leave the hot mess of emotions at the table.

The bathroom door was open with the lights off, but the door to Jillian's room was shut. He cracked it open. Luke sat on the bed, holding Jillian's sweatshirt to his face. He didn't startle or show a shed of guilt for being in her room, smelling her clothes.

"You love Ryn?"

Jackson shut the door behind him and leaned against it. "I do."

Luke laughed. "Never thought I'd see the day. I honestly questioned if you were capable of it."

"Jude wasn't. But I'm not him."

"You have to do that don't you?"

"Do what?"

"Separate yourself from the man you were and the life you left behind. It's the only way to keep your sanity, isn't it? She did it too. Jessica couldn't love AJ, but Jillian did."

"I never claimed to have my sanity, even now. This life is easier. Everything that plagued Jude is dead."

"The anger plagued you. You were always angry. Jessica knew it, but she didn't know why. Are you saying your parents made you angry?"

"Listen, Doc, I don't need you to psychoanalyze me. I'm not the one sniffing my ex's clothes."

"If someone took Ryn from you today and you were without her for almost a year, you'd be sniffing her clothes."

Jackson wanted to deny it, but he couldn't. He was a little pissed at her for washing his sheets after they got wet from sex after their shower. He wasted no time getting her naked and rolling around in his bed again. "I don't know where she is. I'm not lying."

"But someone does. Knox knows, doesn't he?"

The brilliant doctor didn't have a clue. Some things in life had no explanation. Some people lived without accountability. Knox was one of them.

"He tracks her phone. She doesn't have a chip inserted into her neck or anything like that. If he were concerned about her whereabouts, then he would have had her followed. She took a plane to Portland for a funeral. He called me after she left, wondering why she was still in Omaha. I told him she forgot her phone."

"You lied?"

"Yes."

"Why?"

"She needed time alone without anyone following her, and I didn't want Knox thinking she went AWOL."

"I have to find her."

"You won't."

"Then you find her."

Jackson shrugged. "I wouldn't even know where to start."

Luke glanced around the room. "Look through her stuff. Find a clue to where she might be. Maybe she went somewhere with him before he died and she's gone back there to feel close to him. Maybe she said something to his family at the funeral. Maybe—"

"Stop with the fucking maybes. I spent years anticipating the behaviors of other people, guessing their next move, where they would be, where they might go. But she's not predictable like that. She could be in Maine or Florida, Indiana, Alaska ... hell she could be staying at your fucking hotel for all we know. She's carrying cash, nothing to track."

"Call Knox. Tell him she's gone AWOL. Make him find her."

Luke had lost it. He wasn't hearing anything Jackson said. "Sure. And if by some miracle he finds her reading a book on the beach in the Keys, he's going to be fucking pissed for the wasted man hours and so is she."

"She's not on a goddamn beach in the Keys. Something's wrong!"

"How do you know? Huh? How the hell can you possibly know something is wrong?"

Luke dropped his head, clenching his hair. "I just ... *know*."

CHAPTER TWENTY-ONE

DAY

THE BELOW AVERAGE January temperature greeted Jessica with a maddening gust to her hair as she emerged from the building. The number of women in her self-defense class nearly doubled from the previous weeks. The holidays sucked the life out of attendance.

"Mrs. Jones?"

She turned around, wrestling with her ponytail whipping her face like a fly on a horse. Luke stood leaning against the passenger's door to the GTO with Jones shoved into the backseat. Her fiancé looked GQ handsome in his black wool coat with the collar up protecting his neck from the frigid wind.

"Mrs. Jones? Really? Not until next weekend." She walked into his waiting arms and just like that she was home.

"I'm just trying it out in public. Seeing how it sounds when I holler it in the middle of the busy sidewalk."

She clenched his lapels, looking up with complete adoration. "And how does it sound?"

"Incredible. Didn't you see those people looking around like a celebrity had been spotted or the queen was in town?"

"I must have missed that." Suspicion pulled at her eyebrows.

"Are you getting cold feet?"

She slid into the car as he held open the door. "No, my socks are a wool/cotton blend."

He looked at her with his typical I-don't-want-to-grin-but-I-am smile as he fastened his seat belt. "The wedding. Are you getting cold feet about the wedding?"

"Nope." She twisted her body, petting Jones on his chest.

"Are you sure?"

"I swear."

Luke laughed as he started the car. "You swear, huh?"

"Yep. I swear on my uncle's grave I'm not getting cold feet over marrying you."

He pulled away from the curb. "That's not very comforting."

"Why do you say that?"

"You don't have an uncle. Your dad's an only child and your mom has a younger sister who lives in Canada."

"Exactly, I've only seen my aunt once in my life. She basically divorced the family when she moved to Vancouver with her rich lover. My mom didn't even send her an invitation to the wedding. Fucking Cathy got an invite, but not my aunt, which is fine. I don't really want either one of them there. But in my dreams I had this amazing uncle who was a NASCAR driver and he let me drive his car around the track as fast as I wanted and whenever I wanted. When I was younger he took me for ice cream—twist cones dipped in chocolate. He tragically died after winning Daytona. An

RV in the parking lot backed over him. So when I say I swear on my uncle's grave, it means a lot."

Luke stared at the road ahead, taking a right into the parking garage. As soon as the car was nestled into its parking spot, he unlatched his seat belt and readjusted his body to face her. She'd seen that look on his face a million times. It was the one that said I love you, but you need help. You need an emergency session with Dr. Jones.

"I'm a little concerned that you've constructed this imaginary world with an uncle that never existed. I've always assumed you and your father had a good relationship, but this makes me question that. Is there something about your father that you've never told me?"

She frowned, looking down at her gloved-hands resting in her lap. "Well ... there was this one incident. The door was cracked to my parents' bathroom. I thought it was my mom, but upon closer inspection I noticed my father standing in front of the mirror in a pink lace bra and matching panties. Beneath the tough guy uniformed exterior, he liked wearing lingerie. I think that day a little piece of me died. The man I looked up to was no longer truly a man."

"Jess ..." Luke whispered, touching his hand to her cheek.

She looked up and grinned. "Just fucking with you. God ... you're so gullible." She hopped out, letting Jones out as well.

"What the hell?" Luke chased after them as they made their way to the elevator. "You were joking? About your father?"

The disbelief in his voice cracked her up. Ruffling Luke's feathers was her favorite past-time.

"Yes, joking about my dad and my imaginary uncle. Joking about all of it."

The second the doors opened, he shoved her to the back of the elevator, pinning her against it with his body. Her heart pounded, certain he would give her a pounding of her favorite kind very soon as well.

"You made the whole story up?" He pinched her sides.

It tickled and hurt at the same time.

Jessica giggled. "The look ... oh my gosh, the look on your face was ..."

He clenched her ass with an iron grip, yanking her body to his. She felt the evidence of his angry desire hard against her belly.

"Payback's a bitch, sweetheart." He sucked at her neck just short of leaving a mark.

Out-of-control Luke made Jessica all kinds of crazy. Their bed was too far. She wanted him right then, not a second longer to wait.

"Tell me I've been a bad girl, *daddy*."

Luke froze, lips still pressed to her neck. "*What* did you just say?"

"I've been a really naughty girl, big daddy, you need to spank me."

He released his grip on her ass so fast she could barely remember the feel of it.

The elevator doors opened. His long strides took him to the door twice as fast as hers did.

"You've ruined the moment. We may never have sex again."

She felt like a masochist. Her actions left her turned on, yet she couldn't resist. Cold feet over marrying Luke? Not in a million years.

"Luke?" Jessica mumbled.

His sexy, naked fiancée often talked in her sleep.

"Dammit, Jones! Answer your phone."

She wasn't asleep.

"You're on top of me."

She nuzzled her face into his neck. "You love it."

He did. They started their love affair in separate beds then separated by the great wall which came down, leaving an empty gap of complete trust, but one night she fell asleep on his chest. He risked life and limb for a night of her naked body against his. His lips on her head and hands on her perfect ass awoke her the next morning. She didn't flinch. He proposed to her three days later.

"I do love it, but it's 2:00 a.m. and you're demanding I get my phone."

She rolled to the side and he lumbered from the bed to grab his vibrating phone that danced along the dresser.

"Hello?"

"Luke?"

"Who's this?"

"Deborah."

"What is it, Deb?"

Why was his ex-fiancée's mom calling him?

"It's Fran."

He held the phone to his ear with one hand and rubbed the sleep from his eyes with the other.

"Yeah?"

"She died an hour ago." Her voice cracked. Painful sobs bled through his phone.

"I'm sorry, Deb. I really am."

"Y-you loved ... her ... r-ri-right?"

Luke grabbed the back of his neck, looking at the woman sprawled out on his bed—the woman who would be his wife in five days. He never went to see Fran, even when Jessica told him to go. They found a match and she received the heart transplant she needed, but it was never a guarantee and he'd heard from mutual friends that she wasn't doing well.

"Yes. Of course I did."

"The ... the f-funeral is Sat-Saturday. You'll b-be there?"

"I'm sorry, Deb. I can't. I have other plans."

She sobbed harder. "What can be m-more important ... than F-Fran's funeral?"

"I'm getting married. Give Matt my condolences."

Luke pressed *End*. After slipping into his pajama bottoms, he headed to the kitchen. He grabbed a glass of water and stared out the floor-to-ceiling windows at the hazy lights of San Francisco.

Arms swimming in his stolen red hoodie wrapped around his waist. A warm cheek rested on his bare back.

"Fran died?"

"Yes."

"Sometimes life sucks."

Luke loved, with his entire being, the woman who clung to him. He loved that every single one of her imperfections made her absolutely perfect for him.

"Yes." He turned, using his free hand to cup the back of her head, pulling her into his chest. "And sometimes it doesn't. Sometimes we weather the storm, mourn the casualties, and find the sun on the horizon has never been brighter. I'm blinded by mine, and I'm certain for the rest of my life it she—will leave me breathless."

"I hate how much you've lost to get to me."

169

"I feel the same way about you." He kissed her head as she kissed his chest.

"The funeral is on Saturday, isn't it?"

"Yes."

"You're going to think of her that day, there's no way you can't." She looked up at him. "And I'm going to love you even more for it. You hide behind your structured life, a three-piece suit, and the plaques on your office wall, but your heart is so damn big. Everyone who really knows you loves you, it's impossible not to."

"Don't ever leave me," he whispered.

"I have to work tomorrow."

He chuckled. She called his sense of humor dry, but hers was just as dry.

"Oh you meant it more like a stalker, didn't you? Like 'Don't ever leave me ... because I'd find you.'"

"Yes, but not really in that voice."

"Were you good at hide-and-seek? I sucked at it. Jude would talk stupid gibberish while looking for me. Stuff that would make me giggle and give away my hiding spot. He'd say things like, 'I ran out of dental floss so I cut the strings off your tampons. Is that going to be a problem?' or, 'I masturbate in the shower. Don't you think it's odd that you never run out of conditioner?'"

He laughed with her. It was easy to imagine Jessica and Jude as kids because they still sucked at being adults, especially when they were in the same room.

"I dominated hide-and-seek. Especially the seeking part. So yes, I would find you in the most creepy, no-other-man-will-ever-have-you kind of way."

"I should be disturbed by your confession. I should report it to Dr. Jones, but I love to think about you finding me. You've saved me from so much, I can't image a life where you're not there to make it worth living."

He walked to the kitchen, holding her to his chest like a slow dance. After setting down his glass, he lifted her onto the counter. She wrapped her naked legs around his waist, her arms around his neck.

"Hold onto me, Luke. Never let me go."

He slid his hands under the hoodie, feathering his fingers along her abs and up her ribs.

"I've got you. I'll always have you."

She pressed her palm to his chest, over his heart. He closed his eyes because that's exactly where he kept her.

CHAPTER TWENTY-TWO

KNIGHT

Jᴵᴸᴸᴵᴬᴺ'ꜱ ꜱᴛᴏᴍᴀᴄʜ roiled in pain. She didn't have a fat reserve for unexpected kidnappings. Stupid her. After being in the same basement with Claire, that lesson should have been learned. Gandhi went twenty-one days without food and survived. Drifting in and out of sleep and consciousness left Jillian unsure of how many days she'd been in that dungeon, but not twenty-one. Yet.

"You need to eat?"

Knox must have heard her stomach.

"I've been offered maggot-infested dog food. I'm good." She looked down at the IV still in her hand. "She's keeping me hydrated. I've been pissing myself quite regularly, which I'm sure you can smell. I'm so fucking constipated, if I make it out of here alive I'll die trying to shit the redwood-sized cement turd that's backed up in my colon."

Knox chuckled. "Always such a lady."

"Funny, coming from the guy who preached his training facility had to be gender neutral because the enemy killed indiscriminately. I act like a lady in the presence of a true gentleman."

172

"Let me guess. I'm not a true gentleman?"

"You raped me."

"You let me."

She glared at him. All those years she knew he didn't look at it as rape. It's the same reason she didn't—until working with rape victims. Until Luke.

"You had me pinned naked to the ground."

"You could have escaped. I didn't hold you down. Your fear did."

"Two hundred pounds of fear."

He shrugged. "I saved your life that day and you know it."

"Is that how you sleep at night? Is that how you justified yourself worthy of my mother?"

"You killed Edwin Harvey and Matthew Green because I took away your fear that day. You weren't a victim. I gave you power that day."

"I beat the shit out of you. I had power, dumb fuck. Just ask the paramedics that hauled your ass out of the building."

"You had skills, a gun of sorts, but you never would have pulled the trigger. I showed you how to shut off your mind and pull the trigger. You're no longer a victim. Even now, look at you. You're a starving bloody mess. I see the anger in your eyes. I bet Edwin saw it too, but he didn't believe it. You hated him but if it weren't for me, you never would have killed him, not with *forty-four* slashes to his body."

"You don't know me."

"I know you better than anyone. You like the taste of blood and the control that comes with it. That's a part of who you are now. A wedding dress, a fancy apartment in the city, and a big-ass dog won't change that."

"No, but killing you and your Frankenstein bride might

cure what ails me. I'm not one hundred percent sure, but I plan on testing my theory."

He shook his head. "You're going to die in that puddle of piss, sweetheart, and there's nothing you can do about it. If someone removed you from your bindings right now, you wouldn't be able to stand up, let alone kill anyone."

"Get her to let me go and we'll just see what I can do."

"As you can see..." he looked down at himself, completely bound "...I'm not her favorite person either. I don't anticipate her heeding my special requests to let you go."

"Then go ahead and tell me." Jillian closed her eyes, feeling a wave of nausea seize her stomach.

"Tell you what?"

"Make me see what my mother saw in you, because right now I hate you and that makes me hate her for loving you."

Sunny

KNOX MET SUNNY IN KINDERGARTEN. Sunny's bright smile matched her name, just like the ribbons she wrapped around her strawberry pigtails matched the dresses she wore with the same pair of red Mary Janes.

The disheveled ginger-haired boy followed the pig-tailed angel around like a puppy on a leash.

"Knox is a funny name." She giggled.

He did too. "My mama's grand pappy's name was Knox. She says it's a strong name because Grand Pappy was a war hero." He spoke with a lisp from having his two front baby teeth knocked out by his drunken father.

"Sounds like rocks." Sunny giggled more as the other kids chased each other around the schoolyard. Occasionally one would tag Knox or Sunny, not realizing they weren't playing. They had more important things to do, like figuring out a better name than one that rhymed with rocks.

"If you let me give you a new name, I'll let you kiss me."

Knox would have adopted dog poop for a name if it meant he could kiss the most beautiful girl in the world. However, his mama taught him to stand up for himself, even if she didn't standup to his mean daddy.

"I'll let you give me a new name if I get to kiss you every day until I turn six." He beamed at her with a toothless grin.

"When do you turn six?"

"My birfday is tomorrow."

Sunny gave his offer careful consideration then she shrugged. "Okay."

Before he could register her answer, she leaned in and kissed him on the lips and then it was over. He wasn't ready. He was supposed to kiss her, not the other way around.

She giggled. He loved her giggles. His mama took him to church every Sunday, but not once did his Sunday school teacher talk about angels giggling. He couldn't wait to tell her that he'd heard one.

"Mickey."

"Mickey?" He lifted his shoulders.

"Your new name is Mickey. Instead of Micbra. Or Fox instead of Knox."

Knox laughed, holding onto his belly. "You said Micbra."

"That's what our teacher said. Knox Micbra."

"McGraw. My name is Knox Duncan McGraw. Not Micbra."

Sunny twirled her pigtail around her finger, head

cocked to the side. "I'm gonna call you Mickey because I kissed you."

<hr />

From that day forward Sunny and Mickey were inseparable. She loved his red hair that was darker than hers. He loved her red Mary Janes that she wore every day. They both loved the small block that separated their houses—a wonderful discovery that happened on the walk home from school the first day.

That one kiss turned into a daily occurrence. Just one. Always in the schoolyard. Never lasting more than one second. By the fourth grade Mickey made Sunny promise to marry him. She agreed. They were up to two kisses a day and holding hands when adults weren't looking.

At the beginning of seventh grade, Sunny agreed to not question the bruises and occasional fat lip Mickey received from his father, if he promised not to say anything about the "period pads" in her school bag or the bras her mother insisted she wear. Their kisses lasted longer, at least longer than any of their friends who had started kissing. But in all fairness, for seven years Sunny and Mickey had been kissing and sharing food, germs, and colds, even the chicken pox.

"My parents are taking me and my sister to New York over Christmas break. My aunt and uncle live there." Sunny grimaced.

"Sounds like fun. Can I hide in your suitcase and go too?"

Sunny shook her head. Her worried expression deepened along her brow.

Mickey laughed. "I'm kidding." He leaned in to kiss her

as they sat on the couch in her basement, studying, aka their time to make out.

She pulled away before his lips touched hers. "My parents know we ... *kiss*."

"You told them?"

She rolled her eyes. "No. But when my mom asked me, I didn't lie to her. She's not stupid, Mickey. We're always sick at the same time with the same thing. We're attached at the hip. Two plus two equals four."

"So? Are we in trouble?"

Sunny shook her head.

"Oh. Good." He leaned in again and again she denied him by turning her head to the side.

"We're not in trouble. But I've been banned from kissing you until we get back from New York. My mom doesn't want me getting sick."

"I'm not sick."

"My mom's a nurse, Mickey. She said you're usually contagious before you ever have symptoms. It's just a precaution. Don't be mad."

He sighed, flopping back on the couch. "Can we still hold hands?"

"Yes." She giggled and it still sounded like an angel giggling—the most beautiful sound in the world.

He smiled, reaching for her hand. She moved it.

"But we have to wash our hands both before and after."

He grabbed his backpack, slung it over his shoulder, and went home. He lived by his father's stupid rules: take out the trash twice a day, clean both bathrooms even if they're not dirty, make your bed, do the dishes, and never let the old man run out of beer before setting a new one on the side table next to the chair he sat in when he wasn't at work.

With Sunny there had been no rules, until New York. Stupid New York.

THE WORDS "I LOVE YOU" were shared on many occasions over the years, but they took on new meaning by the time they both turned sixteen.

Sunny was a straight-A student and a cheerleader for basketball and football. Mickey played point guard and quarterback. All the anger he carried inside from the constant abuse got released in the game. He showed no mercy. Coaches favored him. His opponents feared him. But Sunny loved him—truly, madly, deeply.

"Promise me we'll get married as soon as we graduate." He rested his head on her lap as they watched TV in her basement.

She feathered her fingers over his buzz-cut hair. "I want to go to college, Mickey."

"Married people go to college."

"What if we don't go to the same college?"

"I'll go wherever you get accepted."

Her legs vibrated from her laughter. "You sound pretty confident that any college that accepts me will also accept you. Need I remind you I'm a straight-A student?"

He grabbed right above her knee and pinched it hard until she jumped with a squeal. "No. I think you remind me of that every day, smarty pants. Need I remind you that I have tons of scouts looking at me for both basketball and football? As long as I keep my grades up, I'll have my choice of schools."

"And you're going to choose whatever school I go to?"

"Yep. I go where my wife goes."

"I hate to break it to you, but I don't think my dad is going to give you his blessing to marry me before I even start college."

"We'll be adults. We won't need anyone's blessing." He turned his head in her lap and inched her shirt up just enough to expose her bellybutton.

"What are you doing?" she asked with a breathy voice.

"Kissing you."

"Kissing my belly?"

He nodded, softly kissing her bellybutton once before dipping his tongue into it.

She swallowed hard as her abs tightened.

"You're so beautiful."

"Mickey ..." she whispered in a weak protest as his hand inched up her shirt.

Touching her felt right, natural, and perfect. He'd loved her forever and he would never stop loving the angel he met over a decade earlier. There had never been anyone else and the only thing he was absolutely certain of in his some-times-miserable life was that there would never be anyone else.

His thumb brushed over the thin material of her bra and his tongue continued to trace along her belly.

"We ... we should ... stop."

His lips pulled into a smile against her soft skin. Her words were less than convincing as she arched her back into his touch.

He dipped his thumb under her bra, circling the pad of his thumb over her hardened nipple. Her full red lips parted as soft puffs of breath escaped. Their eyes locked.

"I want to put my lips where my thumb is." His voice took on a deep, unfamiliar tone.

They'd kissed, hard and long with lots of tongue. He'd

touched her breasts and butt on the outside of her clothes, but that's as far as it had ever gone. He couldn't remember the last time he'd left her house without a raging hard-on. The shower had been his best friend. He jacked off then turned it to straight cold because that one release was never enough for his out-of-control hormones, but it was all he had time for before his father would threaten to knock the door off its hinges if he didn't stop "wasting so much water."

Sunny's breaths chased one another. She swallowed again and nodded.

His mouth worked its way up to her bra. It was torturous. His dick was so hard, pulsing painfully against the confines of his jeans. But he wanted to take it slow with the girl that he loved more than anything or anyone else—the women he would someday marry.

Easing the cup of her bra down to expose her cherry nipple, he covered it with his mouth. She moaned then sucked in a breath as if someone could hear her, but her parents took her sister and a friend to a movie. Mickey knew it was just the two of them for another hour and a half.

"Do you like this?"

She opened her heavy eyelids. "Yes," she whispered, wetting her lips.

He held her gaze, a silent permission, as he pulled down the cup on the other side. Gently rolling her nipple between his thumb and forefinger a few times, he watched her eyes close again. Her hands clenched at her sides. He felt it too. The most painful pleasure. It had been building for several years.

"Mickey ..."

He sucked her nipple.

"Do you want me to stop?"

"Yes ... no ... I don't know."

"Touch me, Sunny. Please," he whispered his desperate plea around her breast.

"W-where?"

He took her hand and guided it between his legs. She didn't move for several seconds and he didn't force her any farther, but he couldn't keep himself from making small thrusts into it. When she finally curled her fingers around the bulged denim, he groaned and nearly came right there.

"Ow!" She tensed.

"Sorry, baby." He lapped his tongue over her nipple after biting it when she squeezed him.

"I'm just so damn turned on and I want you to touch me, but it's almost too much."

"Mickey, I love you, but I just don't know if ..."

"You don't want to have sex. It's okay—"

"No. I'm just ... or we, well, I don't want to get pregnant."

"What if I buy condoms?"

"What do you mean 'what if you buy condoms?'"

He chewed his lower lip for a few moments. "I mean, can we have sex if I use a condom or I'll wear two even ... hell, I'll wear ten if it means we can ..." He kissed the slight swell of her breast.

She grinned. "I think one is sufficient."

He mirrored her grin. "Is that a yes?"

Sunny nodded slowly. He was ready to run out right then and buy condoms, but by the time he'd return their alone time would be about up.

"Take your shirt off."

Her eyes went wide. "I thought we just agreed to wait until—"

He sat up and tugged at her top. "No sex. But there's a lot we can do without actually having sex."

Sunny stared at him, then on a deep sigh she lifted her arms.

Mickey grinned a victorious smile as he pulled her shirt over her head and tossed it aside.

"God, I hope my parents don't come home early."

He wiggled his eyebrows. "The fear of getting caught makes it that much more exciting." He reached around and unfastened her bra.

She held it to her breasts.

"I just saw them. I had them in my *mouth*." He smirked.

Sunny continued to stare at him.

"Fine. Here." He shrugged off his shirt.

Her eyes roved over his torso, not that she hadn't seen it before, but it did feel different with her shirt off too—intimate, sexual.

"I can't believe how much of a man you've turned into."

He chuckled. "You have no idea."

She released her hold on her bra, letting it fall from her chest. "Now what?" Her nerves showed through her shaky words.

"I want to take your pants off."

She shook her head. "I don't think that's a good idea."

"Just your pants, okay. I'll leave your underwear on and I'll leave my jeans on. Deal?"

Biting her lips together, she nodded once.

"Yes?"

She nodded again.

"Lie back."

She scooted her body around and lay back on the couch. He unfastened her jeans, keeping his eyes on hers the whole time. Then he slid them down and off her legs.

"You're beautiful, so very beautiful."

He nearly orgasmed just from the sight of her in

nothing but a pair of white cotton panties, auburn hair fanned around her head. Fear took over her face as he unfastened his belt.

"W-what are you doing?"

"I don't want to scratch you with my belt."

"Why? What are we going to do?"

After dropping his belt to the floor, he pushed her legs open. She resisted him for a second then tried to relax.

He kissed his way up the inside of her leg.

She panted as he brushed his nose over her cotton panties, taking a deep inhale before continuing up her body.

"We're going to practice." He whispered over her lips before kissing her. As his tongue slid against hers, he rocked his pelvis into her. It wouldn't take long, he just hoped he'd hold out until she found her own release.

Sunny moaned into his mouth. He slowly rocked into her, vying for every bit of friction he could get. Within seconds she responded to him, meeting him thrust for thrust, rocking her hips and sometimes circling them, searching for that right spot. He didn't have to search, he was there, waiting on the precipice while praying to God she hurried up.

"There ..." she murmured, breaking their kiss as she arched her back and squeezed her eyes shut. "Oh dear God ... there ..."

He rocked into her three more times, milking her orgasm, then grunting on the final thrust as he came.

They both lay still, breathless. After a few minutes he sat up. Kneeling between her legs. She winced.

"Is that ... *me*?" She stared at the crotch of his jeans.

Looking down, he rubbed his thumb along the dark, wet spot. "Yes, some of it's you ... but I think I'm leaking through as well." He grinned. "How did that feel?"

She covered her breasts with her hands, her whole body flushed nice and rosy. "Like nothing I've ever felt before."

"Good?"

Sunny nodded, looking anywhere but directly at him or his wet jeans.

"I'm going to give you more of that ... for the rest of our lives. I promise."

CHAPTER TWENTY-THREE

JONES

Jackson made no guarantees to Luke, but he said he'd contact Knox and casually fish for information without making it sound like he didn't have a clue as to the whereabouts of his sister. It wasn't much, but Luke took it. He had to jump at any and all possibilities, including looking for clues to places she might be. Ryn suggested they talk to AJ's son, Cage, who was at his dad's place for the weekend to go through everything.

"Follow my lead," Luke said to Lake as they knocked on AJ's front door.

She shook her head. "That's what you said when we stood on Jude's front stoop."

"I did. And then thirty minutes later you were talking about your accident and my wedding day."

"Sorry, but it's hard to keep my leg a secret, and I'm pretty sure Jackson already knew you were going to marry his sister."

"Just ..." He sighed.

"Got it. I'll let you handle it."

The locks clicked and a young man opened the door.

Luke gave Lake a tight-browed glance after she made an indecipherable noise.

"Hi."

"Hi. Cage, right?" Luke asked.

He nodded, looking at Lake.

"I hope we're not disturbing you. We're friends of Jillian's. Could we talk to you about her and your dad for a few minutes?"

Cage shook his head. Luke hadn't anticipated that.

"Oh. Sorry, are you busy? We could come back later."

Cage shook his head again, jaw clenched. "It's too soon. I ... I can't talk about him or them or ... it's just too soon." He cleared his throat.

Luke nodded. Cage's pain was palpable. It was too soon. He would have to let the son be a dead end for a while.

"I understand. Sorry for your loss."

Cage nodded once.

"Mind if I use your restroom before we hit the road again?" Lake smiled.

"Lake you can—"

"That's fine," Cage replied before Luke could finish his protest.

"Thanks." She rested her hand on Luke's arm. "Why don't you go fill the car up with gas and get me a coffee."

The tank was full and he never knew she was a coffee drinker.

"Please."

"O-kay, but I won't be long." He gave her a warning look that, of course, she ignored.

LAKE LEANED her shoulder against the wall to balance as she pulled off her boots. Winter weather made it impossible to hide her prosthetic leg when she had to take her boots off in people's homes. Socks would have been a good idea, but she didn't wear socks with her Uggs.

She glanced up after removing them. Cage stared at her feet.

"I lost my leg." It wasn't like her to state the obvious, but the tall, hunky blond with dimples jumbled her thoughts.

He smiled. It was a melting smile, the kind that could melt a girl's heart, the kind that led her to believe he would make it through the loss of his father.

"I didn't mean to stare."

"I didn't mean to state the obvious." She grinned. Some awkward-girl personality hijacked hers. Lake reminded herself that they were in fact discussing her missing limb. It wasn't flirting. No one flirted over prosthetics. Too bad.

"The bathroom is around the corner."

Lake needed the bathroom reminder since she didn't really need to use it. "Thank you."

After shutting the bathroom door, she rested her hands on the edge of the sink, looking in the mirror at the flushed face of a girl who hadn't given a second glance to a guy since her accident. "He's gorgeous, Lake. Stop thinking stupid shit about a gorgeous guy that lives a million miles away and oh yeah ... he's naturally going to be attracted to gorgeous women with all their limbs intact."

After flushing the toilet and running the water for a few seconds, she gave her reflection an affirmative nod for the needed pep talk and reality check.

Upon opening the door, the large manly form leaning against the opposite wall brought her out of her skin. "Oh God! You scared me." She pressed her hand to her chest.

"Sorry." Cage smiled.

Why was he standing there? Had he heard her talking to herself about the "gorgeous guy?" She stood tall and swallowed her pride, which was easy to do because there wasn't much left if he *had* heard her.

"Better see if your boyfriend is back."

"Boyfriend? Oh, no. No, no, no." She shook her head. "Luke is my brother. Seriously, we look identical, except I have long hair, boobs, and a prosthetic leg." Closing her eyes, she bit her lips together. Someone needed to tape her mouth shut. "I'm sorry. We met like two seconds ago and I can't stop reminding you that I have a fake leg, and to humiliate myself even more I actually mentioned my boobs. I'm just going to go. Even if he's not here, I'll just wait outside."

Cage smirked. Hands crossed over his chest, he seemed to enjoy the *Lake is an Idiot* show. Her plans to ease him into talking about his father and Jillian derailed the second she stepped into the house. There wasn't enough time to back up and steer the conversation in a different direction.

"You live around here?"

Lake shook her head. The less she said the better.

"Are you from New York too?"

Another place she'd never been.

"Yes. Have you been there?" Telepathically she willed him to say no. The last thing she needed was someone wanting to compare favorite places and things to do in New York.

"Yes, but only in transit with the team."

"The team?"

"I play football."

"Oh, that's cool. Which team?"

"Cornhuskers."

Lake nodded. "What position?"

"Quarterback."

She tried not to react to the gorgeous guy confessing he played quarterback for a major college football team, but her eyes widened a bit anyway.

"Are you good?"

Cage shrugged. "I don't know. Some people think so."

"I ran cross country and played volleyball in high school. My mom thinks I should do something with the Paralympic Games." She twisted her lips for a moment. "But I don't know. It's been a crazy year since the accident. Some days I still struggle to climb stairs."

He gave her a slight nod.

"Well, I'd better see if Luke's here and let you get back to ... your stuff."

He looked down, scratching the back of his head. "Yeah, my dad wasn't a collector or any sort of packrat, but my parents were divorced. I'm his only child and my grandparents live in Portland, so I guess it's my responsibility to decide what to do with everything. It's all mine now, including the house. The funny part? I don't want any of it."

"My brother's fiancée died a year ago. Her stuff still hangs in his closet. It's just stuff, but there has to be a finality to get rid of it. I bet you'll feel it when the last thing is removed from here and someone else buys the place. The 'stuff' is the epilogue. The story is over, but part of it lives on like a ghost for just a few more pages. What's left at the end of the epilogue?"

"Nothing."

Lake cocked her head to the side and narrowed her eyes. "Depends on how you look at it."

"And how would you look at it?"

"I'm not sure yet. My boyfriend died in the accident

that took my leg. When I came out of my coma the funeral was over, his parents had cleaned out his apartment, and some other person lived there. I turned the page after the final chapter only to find no epilogue. The author of my life sucker punched me."

"Some would say the author of your life is God."

"And I'd agree. But no amount of faith can truly comfort a grieving heart that can't make sense of such tragedy. I didn't lose my faith, but I did feel like God sucker punched me. No epilogue. But he's God so I'll probably forgive him some day."

Cage chuckled. "I'm sure he'll be grateful."

She tore her eyes away from his smile and those dimples. "I'm sure he's waiting." She pulled on her boots. "Sorry to have disturbed you. We were just looking for Jillian. Her brother doesn't know where she is and thought you might have heard from her. But we'll find her."

Lake opened the door.

"What's your name?"

She turned. "Oh, sorry. I guess after fifteen minutes of talking about my disability, my boobs, and my anger at God, it might be nice to have a name to use when you tell your friends about the crazy chick that stopped to use your bathroom. It's Lake."

"Nice to meet you, Lake. I'm sorry. I have no idea where Jillian is or might be. And for the record, this has been the best fifteen minutes I've had in a long time, so I think when I tell my friends it will be about this hot girl that stopped by and how much I hated to see her walk out the door because really ... the *best* fifteen minutes."

Luke honked the horn. She cursed him behind her smile. Gorgeous quarterback guy just called her 'hot girl.' Her destiny stood before her and she had to leave. Maybe he would never forget their fifteen minutes together and come search for her in *New York*.

Dammit, Jones! Her mind quoted Jessica.

"The feeling is mutual." She began to shut the door then poked her head inside. "Cage?"

He turned. "Yes?"

"You want to know what comes after the epilogue?"

"What?"

"A new book filled with endless possibilities."

He grinned. Yup, the guy would definitely come look for her. In. New. York.

Dammit, Jones!

LUKE DRUMMED the top of the steering wheel with his hands. He was tired of driving around the block.

"You didn't need to honk the horn." Lake slipped in the seat and slammed the door shut.

"So what did you find out?"

"He's gorgeous. He plays quarterback for the Cornhuskers. Oh ... and I think he loves me *and* my prosthetic leg."

Luke pulled out and stopped before shifting into drive, giving her the hairy eyeball.

Lake's smile morphed into a frown. "He said he doesn't know where she is or even could be."

Another dead end. Luke hoped Jackson would find out more helpful information from Knox. The most unsettling feeling in the pit of his stomach kept his mind on Jessica and the belief that she was in some kind of trouble or sending out an SOS that only he could detect.

All they could do at that point was wait, so he headed

back to the hotel. Lake rubbed the top of her leg, staring out the window.

"Your leg bothering you today?"

"No." She stilled her hand. "It's just habit. That's all"

He detected disappointment in her voice. "I have no doubt that you're right."

Lake glanced at him. "What? That it's a habit?"

"No. I have no doubt that you're right about Cage. I'm sure he does love you and your leg. Any guy would be a fool not to."

She smiled and moved her hand to his leg. "We're going to find her, Luke."

He nodded. They would find Jessica. He just wasn't sure what shape she would be in when that time came, or if she'd still be Jessica at all.

CHAPTER TWENTY-FOUR

KNIGHT

JACKSON FINISHED DRYING the last pan while watching Luke and Lake drive out of the development. The Days were no longer dead. Their past had caught up to them. Their past could put everyone involved in danger. It was time to go.

"I have to leave." His eyes stayed focused on the slushy street. "I want you to come with me."

"Sure. Where are we going?" Ryn took the pan from him, hanging it from the S-hook above the stove. "I hope to get a Christmas tree for this place. You could use some holiday cheer around here."

Her comment, although oblivious to the true meaning behind his words, was just one more reason he had to take her with him. The last time Jackson lived in a home with a Christmas tree was his senior year of high school. The beginning of the end of his life as he knew it. He wanted a home, a wife, and a slew of holiday cheer. Jude wanted it too.

They could start over. He would run forever and take on a hundred new identities if they could be together. Jackson's home would be his wife, and as long as they were together ... he would always be home.

"We'll take Gunner and Maddie too."

She laughed, sliding her arms under his and hugging his back. "Gunner won't love tree shopping and it's too cold to leave him in the car. And Maddie? Pfft ... feel free to call her, but I'm certain she will laugh in your face."

He laced his hands with hers. "She can finish school someplace else."

Ryn eased around his body to face him. Confusion lined her brow. "What are you talking about?"

"Marry me."

"I feel like ... we've had this conversation before."

"We did. But most proposals mean 'let's be engaged and eventually get married.' Like putting something on layaway. I don't want to be engaged. I want to marry you—now."

"Now?"

"Well, it's Saturday. We'll have to wait until Monday. Marry me Monday."

Ryn squinted. "Are you pregnant?"

He smiled, just barely. She didn't understand the seriousness of the situation. How could she?

"If I say yes, will you make an honest man of me?"

"Maybe. Are you sure it's mine?"

Threading his fingers through her hair, he bent down and whispered over her lips, "I'm sure *I'm* yours. Just ... say yes."

"Jackson—"

He kissed her. It was unfair. Sexual coercion.

"Say yes." He bit her lip, dragging it through his teeth. If he had to strip her down and use his tongue to make her agree to his request, he'd do it. A yes was a yes. He'd take it and run—run with her and never look back.

Her eyes answered him first. He loved her eyes. They were innocent. In spite of the hell her body endured, her soul had the innocence of a child. Ryn spoke in kindness, loved with a bared heart, and lived with a spirit that not even Preston Iverson could break.

She nodded, pulling her lip from his grip.

She said yes.

"I'll marry you Monday."

Step One: Confess the mercy killing first.

Done.

Step Two: Wait for Ryn to acclimate to Jackson's ability to take another's life.

Done.

Step Three: Make her fall so deep in love with him that not even the assassin confession could drive her away.

Pretty damn close.

Step Four: Be prepared to gently hold her in captivity until she snaps out of her inevitable conniption fit because realistically there is no way Step Three would ever fly.

Jackson felt anything was possible. Ryn surprised him, *amazed* him with her ability to see past the ugly parts. If he were honest, he needed that reflection he saw in her eyes. That man she saw, he liked him. He wanted to spend the rest of his life being him.

"You said yes."

She shrugged. "I have a light schedule Monday."

"Then we leave."

"Honeymoon?"

Jackson shook his head.

"Now I'm confused again. What's going on?"

"By the end of the day on Monday, I need you to have only the things from your house that you can't live without. I'll take care of Maddie."

"What does that mean? You'll take care of Maddie?"

"I assume she's something or someone you can't live without."

She shook her head slowly. "You're scaring me."

"If you're with me, you'll never have any reason to be scared."

Ryn took a step back. "And where exactly is *with* you?"

"I'm not sure yet, just not here."

"This house?"

Jackson shook his head. "Nebraska."

"So the moment I become Mrs. Jackson Knight, we're leaving? And taking Maddie?"

"Yeah ... about that."

"About what?" Ryn's eyes widened. They seemed to dare him to say another word. Her mind had to be at capacity with *everything*.

"You won't be Mrs. Jackson Knight very long."

Ryn took another step back, meeting the window with her back. "I think I rescind my yes then."

"You can't."

"I just did."

"Too bad. We're still getting married Monday. You may not be Mrs. Jackson Knight very long, but you'll always be my wife."

"Oh my God. You're running."

"I like to think of it as relocating."

"This is about AJ."

"It's not."

"Then your past?"

"Yes."

She covered her face with her hands. "I don't know if I'm ready for this."

Jackson agreed. She wasn't, but he no longer had time on his side.

"Don't hate me." Ryn's hands slid down her face, revealing the regret in her eyes. "I want you to be a piano teacher. I want you to be deathly boring, yet wildly sexy. I want to spend the rest of my life in this dream state, the one where I just can't believe you love me. I'm forty and you make me feel twenty, or what I imagine twenty should have felt like."

A tear slid down her cheek. "We don't make sense, but I don't want us to. I can't think of one logical reason to marry you. That's why I said yes. I want to love you with my heart, not my mind. But..." she shook her head "...you're going to make me look back, and I'm afraid ..."

He cupped her face, wiping his thumb along her cheek. "What are you afraid of?"

"I'm afraid if my mind sees your past, my heart won't remember how it felt about our future."

"Ryn," he whispered. "I'm sorry, but I have to tell you *everything*."

THE FLOOR beneath Ryn's feet shook, like every bit of foothold she fought for in her life was about to vanish. She loved him and *that* was enough.

"Don't tell me. I'll go. Just ... I'll go." She nodded like a bobble head.

"You'll go."

"Yes." She stood tall, chin up, resolute.

"You'll marry me Monday and leave here for *forever*, no questions asked?" The disbelief in his voice bathed her in guilt. When he said it like that it made her sound irresponsible—crazy.

"Yes." She cleared her throat. "Now, I'd better get home and start packing." Ryn brushed past him to get her things from the bedroom. Her hands shook. Her teeth chattered. Her heart thundered in her chest.

"I used to be Jude Day." He stood in the doorway to the bedroom.

She fumbled around, shoving her things into a bag. "Jude Day. Jackson Knight. Cute." Too bad she couldn't speak without her voice shaking just as much as the rest of her body. The key was to not look at him.

"I've never lived in New York."

Ryn fished her arm under the bed, searching for her sock. "Just as well. I hear it's quite crowded."

"I was a computer engineer in San Francisco."

"A shame. You're ... you're good at the piano." Sucking in the biggest breath her lungs could take, she squeezed past him toward the front door.

Ten steps. That's all she needed to reach her coat and boots.

"Gunner, come."

Five steps.

Her knees wobbled.

Two steps.

"Jude Day killed twenty-three people."

The floor disappeared, so did the final two feet to her destination. She slammed into an invisible wall, hugging her bag as she collapsed to her knees.

"No!" she cried.

Just. Like. That. He blew up her world.

Step Four: *Be prepared to gently hold her in captivity until she snaps out of her inevitable conniption fit because realistically there is no way Step Three would ever fly.*

Jackson balled his hands, the hands that wanted to hold her. Instead, he watched her sob, folded over on the floor. Gunner lay down next to her, resting his head next to hers.

"I was trained to defend—trained to kill. The people I killed had more blood on their hands than I did. I killed to save lives. I was a soldier in an unofficial army, and I was good at it. That was my life. I hated my mother. She cheated on my father. I hated my father for being so blind. I hated my sister just ... just because I couldn't tell her, and I *needed* to tell someone. Instead, I lived a very lonely life filled with random women, secret missions, and a family that lived a lie."

"Stop ..." Ryn continued to sob.

He hunched down beside her, wrapping his arms around her waist.

"No! Stop!" She fought him.

He fell back against the wall, pinning her arms to her sides and her legs beneath his. Then he waited.

"Our parents were murdered, so we were in danger. There are two headstones with our names on them. We were supposed to be safe ... miles away from our past with no one having any reason to look for us."

At some point the body encased by his gave up its fight. He still held her tight, more for him than her.

"But our past found us. Luke and Lake came to find my sister—*Jessica* Day."

Her body tensed again. Lake shared her brother's fiancée's first name, but not her last.

"Oh my God," she whispered, slowly lifting her head.

He loosened his grip a fraction and released her legs

from beneath his, allowing her to turn in his arms and face him.

"Jillian was going to marry Luke."

"No. Jessica."

"Same—"

Jackson shook his head. "Not the same person. Jessica loved Luke. Jillian loved AJ."

"Who did Jude love?"

He paused before answering. "His sister."

"And now?" Ryn sniffled.

"He doesn't exist."

"He existed the moment you told me his name."

"He died." His jaw clenched a little in spite of his effort to stay calm.

"I'm looking at him."

He released her and stood. Taking a deep breath, he shoved his hands in his pockets. "Believe me when I say Jude Day would not hold you in his arms or give a fuck about your feelings. What happened against your refrigerator would have happened in the bathroom of a bar and then it never would have happened again."

She flinched.

He sighed, releasing enough anger to feel some regret. "I'm sorry. I love you. Jackson loves you."

Ryn grabbed her bag and stood, Gunner heeled. "Well, I love Jude."

"Don't say that." His voice hardened.

"It's true."

Jackson shook his head. "Why would you love someone you've never known?"

"Because he died so I could be with you."

"Dying was the best thing that happened to him. He lived a miserable life."

"I'm sorry."

"The only thing I'm sorry about is what I have to go through to keep him in the grave. I don't want that life back, but Luke and Lake showing up here ... they're trying to resurrect the dead."

Ryn rubbed her temples.

"Headache?"

She nodded.

"Is forever too much to ask?"

Ryn chuckled in spite of the pain etched on her face. "For me? Of course not. But I think what you were trying to tell me earlier is that Maddie would have to come too, right?"

"No. She could stay as long as you don't tell her anything, but ..."

"But?"

On a slow blink he looked down. He didn't want to see the expression on her face when she figured out what he meant.

"When Jillian and I left San Francisco, we knew we would never return, never see anyone from our previous life again."

"Jackson, I can't *never* see my daughter again."

He nodded, still looking at his feet. "I know. That's why there are only two options."

"She can come too or?"

"Or you can stay." He met her eyes again.

"And you?"

"If I stay, my life is in danger and so is everyone I know. I don't have a choice. You do."

"I don't know if Maddie will go."

"It doesn't have to be a choice."

"It does. She's an adult with friends and school and ..."

201

"Her father?"

"Oh my God ..." She closed her eyes again and shook her head. "I didn't even think about *my* parents. I would never see them again either, would I?"

Biting his lips together, he shook his head. "It's only Saturday. You don't have to decide until Monday. Take some time to think about it."

"Time? Are you serious? Basically twenty-four hours. That's what you're giving me to make the biggest decision of my life ... of my daughter's life."

Pulling her into his arms, he hugged her. The love thing hurt so damn bad.

"I'll love you no matter what decision you make."

She looked up at him, eyes brimming with renewed tears. "If Maddie won't go, and I highly doubt she will with no real explanation, then I can't ..." One blink sent them running down her cheeks as her words caught in her throat.

"I know." Jackson gave her a sad smile.

He'd broken all the rules by telling her before marrying her. He would have to break another if he left her behind. She knew too much and in the eyes of G.A.I.L that made her a liability. He'd take his own life a hundred times over before even a spark of a thought about killing her would enter his mind.

He trusted her with his life *and* Jillian's. If she couldn't leave, he would never think of her as a liability, and he would never tell a soul that she knew everything.

CHAPTER TWENTY-FIVE

DAY

Fairy godmothers were real. That's all Jessica could think when she looked at her reflection.

"Don't cry." She smiled at her mom.

Sunny stood behind her, dabbing her watery eyes with a tissue. "This is all I've ever wanted for you."

Jessica slid her hands down the white fitted bodice to the thin satin argyle ribbon tied around her waist. It made her grin.

"Luke is all I've ever wanted."

"Am I going to have grandkids?"

Jessica smirked. "You should investigate Jude's past. It's possible you already have grandkids."

"Don't say that. I don't like to think—"

"About your son being a whore?"

Sunny sighed. "I don't want to talk about Jude right now. I want to just look at you."

Lifting the skirt to her dress, she turned to face her mom sitting in Luke's chair by the window. "Kids were part of a dream that I lost years ago. But Luke is my unicorn. He resurrected my dreams, and he likes to give them back to me one at a time. I'll have as many of his babies as he wants to give me, but don't tell him I said that."

Sunny's smile beamed as much as her daughter's. "Why not?"

"I like to make him work for things." She winked.

"Babe?" Luke called, knocking on the bedroom door. "Why is the door locked?"

She reached for the zipper to her dress as Sunny jumped up to help.

"Uh ... what are you doing back so soon?"

"Look outside. It's raining. Jones is not a water dog. Open the door." He rattled the doorknob.

"Just a sec."

"What are you doing?"

"Hiding my lover under the bed."

"Well then take your time. I'd hate for you to hurry and poke a hole in him."

Sunny slapped a hand over her mouth to contain her laughter as Jessica shoved the wedding gown back into its hanging bag.

"Here." She handed her mom the bag. "Love you. Bye. See you tomorrow at rehearsal dinner."

Sunny draped the bag over her arm and opened the door. "There's my favorite son-in-law to be."

"Sunny."

She blew him a kiss on her way to the front door. "Be good to my baby girl."

"I'll see what I can do," he said, staring at Jessica as she tied the belt to her robe.

"Really? You think the only hot affair I would have is with a blowup doll?"

He smirked, shrugging off his wet T-shirt on the way to

their bathroom. "Trying on your dress again? Thought you did that the other day. You said it fit perfectly."

Jessica followed him to the bathroom and stood in the doorway as he removed the rest of his clothes and stepped into the shower.

"I just … I wanted to try it on again. That's all. You have a problem with that?" She let her robe drop to the floor then removed her panties.

"I'll be quick. Don't come in."

She laughed. "Don't come in?"

He looked like a video in fast forward, soaping up and rinsing off at record speed.

Jessica stepped in the shower.

"I'm done," he said in a quick, jerky voice.

She moved in front of him as he tried to slide past her. He looked at everything but her.

"Does my body offend you?"

He swallowed. "Not at all."

"Then what's up?" Jessica grinned, looking at exactly what was *up*.

"My family will be here in … ten minutes."

"I bet I can get you off in under two."

Luke groaned.

"Go." She let him out with just a hard smack on his ass. "But this is a huge shower, I bet your parents would join us."

"NO! No. No. No," he mumbled from beneath the towel as he dried his hair. "Look. Just like that, my erection is gone."

"You're welcome." Jessica's giggle echoed from the shower.

"Everyone decent?" Tom called as Jones barked.

Luke finished buttoning his navy shirt as he made his way to the door. "Do you really care if we're decent?"

Tom dropped two suitcases by the door as Felicity gave Luke a hug.

"Not really." Tom winked.

"Where's the bride?" Felicity peeked into the kitchen.

"Drying her hair. Where's everyone else?"

"Lake wanted to introduce them to Ben's parents then they'll be here."

"I like his parents. Jessica and I met them two weeks ago when Lake invited us to Ben's birthday dinner."

"We do too. They've stayed with us twice in Tahoe and while I don't want Lake thinking about marriage before she's done with college, I hope he's the one. What would be the chances of all of my kids marrying such wonderful people?"

"Zero."

They turned to Jessica's voice.

"But maybe over time you'll learn to love me anyway."

"Shut up, half pint, and get your skinny ass over here." Tom hugged Jessica, lifting her off the ground.

"Tom Jones. God, I love me some Tom Jones."

"Let her go, Thomas, before you chafe her perfect skin with your scruffy face that you *will* be shaving Saturday morning."

"Yes, dear." He set Jessica back on her feet.

"Louise." Felicity grinned.

"Thelma." Jessica hugged her.

"Not this again." Luke rolled his eyes at their Thelma and Louise thing. He didn't know why they did it, and whenever he asked they both replied, "It's our little secret."

"So what's Gabe got lined up for us tonight? Titty bars or a private 'dancer?'"

"What?" Jessica perched her ass on the counter, shock in her wide eyes, but not the kind that most brides-to-be would have at the thought of their fiancé watching strippers. Her shock was an offended shock, but for an entirely different reason.

"I offered to get you a stripper for you bachelor party, but you said no. What that hell?"

"Jess—"

"You offered to get him a stripper?" Tom asked.

"Yes. Titty Tina. She used to do marathons with us, but then she messed up her ankle. I saw her last month at the store and Oh. My. She has some serious new jugs. Of course, I didn't say anything but she just came out and told me. Now get this ..."

Luke narrowed his eyes at his parents who were completely enthralled in Jessica's story.

"She's twenty-five and decided to go back to law school and she's paying for her new boobies *and* school by stripping at private parties." Jessica shrugged. "I guess she's really good and a lot of rich guys pay a shitload of money to hire her. Anyway, back to my original point. I told her about Luke and I getting married, and she offered to do his bachelor party for half-price."

Everyone's attention shifted to Luke.

"Don't look at me like that. All of you, stop giving me that look. Tina competed with us, a teammate of sorts. I'm not going to watch her strip for me."

"Gabe said he'd be willing to check out her new 'gear' and Kelly is fine with it. She's a nice girl, Luke."

Luke shook his head. Why did not wanting a stripper

for his bachelor party make him into some bad guy in, of all people, his fiancée's eyes? Only Jessica ...

"It doesn't matter now. We're going to a sports bar, having a few beers, and watching a game or two. Even Jude was opposed to the stripper."

"Excuse me?" Jessica's look of shock returned.

"It's true. He said real men don't have to pay to see women naked."

"He misspoke. What he meant was real men don't have to pay for sex. Stripping is different. Women don't strip for him then put their clothes back on and leave. They get *paid* using the barter system. We're no different. If I strip for you, I expect something in return. Does that make you 'not a real man?' No, of course not."

Luke didn't know who to address first: his parents enjoying the back and forth like a good tennis match or Jessica implying that she strips for him to get paid using the barter system. Why did his dad have to mention titty bars and private dancers?

"I will discuss our barter system with you later, in private," Luke said before turning his attention to his dad. "And this is all a moot point because Gabe will be here soon to pick us up. There will be a limo, plenty of alcohol, but no naked women."

Tom saluted Luke. "Yes, sir."

Felicity rested her hand on Jessica's leg as they both laughed. Separately they were manageable, but his parents *and* Jessica in the same room always ended with Luke being embarrassed or on the verge of being committed.

"The bachelorette party tonight has a male stripper, right?" his mom asked.

"Absolutely," Jessica grinned at Luke. "Hope you brought lots of cash, Thelma."

Luke survived his bachelor party. Even with the surprise stripper that arrived in the private room Gabe rented at their final bar destination of the night. Thankfully it wasn't Titty Tina, just a random girl he would hopefully never see again. She gave both he and Tom lap dances, and like the good Jones men they were, they kept their hands to themselves.

"Goodnight, son." Tom pulled him in for an awkward drunk hug before staggering to the guest room.

"Night." Luke weaved his way down the hall.

He eased his bedroom door open. His mom and Lake slept on his bed, with *Jones*.

"Paging Dr. Jones."

Luke whipped around. Jessica stood behind him in argyle porn attire.

"A little birdie tweeted me that the surprise stripper he hired just wasn't doing it for you. I bet she went the Victoria's Secret route, didn't she?"

Without taking his eyes off her, he eased the door shut before his mom or sister woke up. He wasn't aware there was such a thing as argyle nipple pasties, but they coordinated with her pink and white argyle neck tie and matching cotton panties. His beer brain tried to make sense of the women and dog in his bed and the woman before him.

"I've … I've had a lot to drink."

She adjusted her tie. He was drunk, but not too drunk to notice she did a terrible job of tying it.

"Me too, Doc. But I don't have to get anything *up*." She popped the P. "Are you too drunk to … you know?" Her index finger stood erect.

He stared at it for a moment, waiting for it to look like

one instead of a blurred two. "You tell me, Ms. Day." Grabbing her hand, he pressed it to his jeans.

She squeezed his erection that didn't seem to be impaired from the alcohol. A smile formed on her lips, painted in deep red.

"Time to barter." Jessica turned with a bit of a wobble and headed down the hall. She glanced back over her shoulder with a come-hither look just as he read the back of her panties.

Jonesing for Lukey

"Where are you going?"

"Your office."

"Why?" He followed her, not really caring why.

"Because it's the farthest point from our houseguests."

She stopped in front of his desk and turned around. "Shut the door, Dr. Jones."

He wasn't into her daddy kink, and maybe it was the alcohol, but Luke liked the sexy way Dr. Jones rolled off her tongue.

"Now, strip for me."

"What?" He squinted.

"Strip. For. Me."

He fumbled with the buttons of his shirt. Unfastening his jeans was a bit more complicated than usual as well.

Jessica whistled. "That's a seriously impressive erection, Dr. Jones. That's the only head I want you thinking with tonight." She glanced at the wall clock. "Or this morning."

Luke could do that. His other brain wasn't working anyway.

"Now. I think in less than forty-eight hours we're going to spend eternity making love. So tonight I want Dr. Jones to fuck me. Can you do that?"

Luke looked down for confirmation. Yes, he was still in the game. He nodded.

"Good. I have a few rules."

"Rules?"

"Yes. I come first and you can't use your hands."

"You always come first."

She cocked her head to the side.

"Blowjobs don't count."

"Fair enough." She leaned against the desk, drumming her fingers on each side. "I'm waiting, Dr. Jones."

He smirked, taking the few short steps to her.

She *tsked* as he curled his fingers into the waist of her panties. "No hands."

"Then take your panties off." He bent down to kiss her.

She bit his lip, stopping his motion. "You take them off."

"I can't use my hands."

She *tsked* again. "What do you have, like ... ten years of college on your resume? Yet you can't figure out how to remove my panties without using your hands?"

He bit her lip in return, even harder than she bit his as evidenced by her quick intake of breath. The one thing she liked more than being in control was Luke having it, but she didn't like to give it away. She wanted him to take it. That much he knew for sure.

He planted his hands on the desk next to hers and kissed his way down her body. Using only his teeth, he peeled off her panties.

"Spread your legs."

He kneeled before her, keeping his hands on the desk.

A breath away from burying his face between her legs, he looked up. Her hands threaded in his hair, her breaths coming one right after the other.

"No hands."

Her eyes widened a fraction, a silent confirmation that he was taking all the control. She released his hair.

"Now I know why you brought me to my office."

"Why?" she panted.

He loved watching her fall apart from needing his touch.

"Because ..." He smashed his mouth against her, letting his tongue and teeth tease her most sensitive parts.

"Jones!" She shattered his eardrums and left fingernail indentations into the edge of his desk—and within thirty seconds she came first and hard. No hands required.

"Ahem."

Luke shifted beneath Jessica. She didn't want him to move. Sleeping on naked Luke beat any sunrise or hot cup of coffee.

"Ahem." The distant voice got louder. "Sorry to wake you."

"Mom!" Luke began to shift again then stopped.

He must have deemed it better for his mom to see Jessica's naked body than his.

"Sorry, honey. Just wondered if you have any non-dairy creamer?"

"Second shelf in the pantry, toward the back. Now ... go."

Jessica couldn't help but giggle.

"Stop laughing. Stop moving. My back is killing me."

"Sorry, baby. Too old to sleep on the floor?"

"Yes and too old for sex on a hardwood desk."

"I offered to be on the bottom." Jessica rolled off him.

He grunted, turning onto his hands and knees before

lumbering to standing. Jessica slipped into her panties. "I'll see if our guests need anything else."

"Wait."

Jessica turned.

"You're not dressed."

"Oh ... yeah." The topless woman before him grabbed her pasties from the floor and stuck them to her nipples then slipped the argyle tie around her neck, in that same hideous knot. "There, dressed."

"Not so fast." Her grabbed her arm and yanked her away from the door. "I'm not marrying a nudist." He slipped his button-down shirt on her and buttoned every single button. "Better, now go straight to our room and get dressed."

"My wedding gown is more revealing than this."

"Go." He pulled on his briefs and jeans.

The clan arrived and were seated at the table. His other siblings had stayed at the hotel, which was the reception venue, but they all gathered for Felicity's breakfast just like in Tahoe. Lane and Anne passed around their nine-month-old daughter, Gina, while they took turns eating. Lara ate with one hand while resting her other hand on her belly. She was only three months along, but after two miscarriages it seemed like a habit. Her husband, Drake, shared an occasional reassuring smile.

"Where are the youngest Jones kids?" Jessica asked through a yawn.

Everyone turned and smiled as she moseyed into the kitchen before getting dressed.

"Lake is still asleep in your bed with Jones and Liam is still asleep at the hotel," Felicity said while handing Jessica a plate piled high with waffles and fruit.

"Where's Zoe?" Jessica asked as she took a seat next to Tom.

Lara rolled her eyes. "Liam broke up with her ... two days ago."

"Don't worry, I've already found a backup for her spot at the guestbook," Felicity assured.

Jessica wasn't a bridezilla. It didn't matter to her. It seemed silly that anyone had to stand by a guestbook. It was a filler position to make yet another person feel like part of the wedding.

"Are you wearing a tie under Luke's shirt?" Anne asked.

"I am."

Lara laughed. "Why?"

"Because it matches the argyle nipple pasties and matching *Jonesing for Lukey* panties that I'm wearing."

The men choked on their food or tongues as the woman laughed.

"Bedroom. Now!" Luke didn't stop on his way to the bedroom, but his demand silenced the peanut gallery.

Jessica stood, grabbing her plate of food. "My master calls."

Soft chuckling danced in the kitchen behind her as she traipsed down the hall. Lake and Jones met her at the bedroom door.

"We've been evicted," Lake mumbled.

"Sorry, his back hurts from—"

"Jessica!" Luke's voice brought a smile to Lake's sleepy face.

"Yeah, anyway ... go get some breakfast." Jessica smiled back and kissed Jones on the head before closing the bedroom door behind her.

"No food in the bedroom," Luke called from the bathroom.

"You can't even see me. How did you know I brought food in here?" Jessica sat on the bed, leaning against the headboard, legs out, plate of waffles on her lap.

"So did you have fun last night? On a scale of one to ten how hungover are you?"

He appeared in the bathroom doorway, toothbrush in his mouth. "My hangover is a five. What part of last night are you referring to?" Luke mumbled with a mouthful of toothpaste foam.

"Your bachelor party. The stripper."

A few seconds later he returned to the bedroom. She loved him in jeans, no shirt—all Luke, no Dr. Jones.

"The party was fine. The stripper was ... a stripper. Why? Are you jealous?"

"Do you want me to be jealous?"

He lifted her legs and sat on the edge of the bed, resting them on his lap. "Yes. I do. It's such a rare side to you, and I love it when you get possessive of me."

"That's Luke talking. Dr. Jones would never condone jealousy."

He rubbed her feet. "They're not cold."

"I never have cold feet. You know that."

"You're going to marry me."

She grinned over the strawberry she shoved in her mouth. "I am."

"You're going to have as many babies as I want to give you."

Jessica gulped her food down. "You were eavesdropping." She narrowed her eyes.

"I have good hearing, that's all." He smirked.

She rolled her eyes. "You know, I'll cut you off at the knees if you get too cocky."

"I want at least four." He slid his hands up her legs.

She shooed them away. "Three. One just got deducted for your eavesdropping."

One hundred. She knew he saw it in her eyes, even if her words said otherwise. Jessica would have one hundred of Luke's babies. Her dreams were coming true. She loved that man and his whole family.

"Luke?"

"Hmm?"

She set her plate on the nightstand then straddled his lap. "Thank you."

He nodded and it could have been her imagination, but she swore his eyes teared up before he hugged her to him and whispered into her hair, "My God ... I love this woman."

CHAPTER TWENTY-SIX

KNIGHT

Jᴜʟʟɪᴀɴ sᴛᴀʀᴇᴅ ᴀᴛ Kɴᴏx. His story tore her heart apart. It allowed doubt to creep into her conscience, causing mayhem with the memories of her past. Knox didn't deserve that story. He didn't deserve the young innocence of her mother, not when he stole hers so brutally.

"Why?" she whispered.

The trip down memory lane left him equally somber. The hardened man she knew softened before her. Sunny did that. She knew a different Knox McGraw, the ginger-haired boy who loved strawberry pigtails and red Mary Janes.

"Why what?" he whispered.

Jillian recognized something in his voice. Hers had it too. Grief.

"Why am I here?"

"Because Irene wants revenge."

"That's not what I mean."

He inched his gaze up to meet hers, confusion knitted along his brow.

"Why do I exist? Why did Sunny marry Grant?" In the

bigger picture, the one she had yet to understand, they no longer felt like her parents. They were nothing more than a tragic mistake that eventually destroyed everything in its path.

"I didn't realize nothing lasts forever. I took her for granted, and then I lost her."

"She loved my father. I *know* she did. I've felt that love." Jillian swallowed back the pain. "I've had it twice. I know when it's real."

Knox's eyes glazed over as he stared at the floor between them. He nodded slowly. "She did love him. Sunny would never marry someone she didn't love."

"You were mad at her for choosing him. That's why you became such an asshole—a monster."

"And the plot thickens," Irene announced as she threw open the door and pounded her way down the stairs, still wearing combat boots. "My sources tell me your brother is looking for Knox. Seems there's been a breach. Hmm ... let me guess ... I'm guessing that breach would be a certain shrink from San Francisco. He took a flight to Chicago and a car to Omaha. The guy's not exactly James Bond, but I gotta hand it to you ... you've managed to surround yourself with men who would die for you. It's quite romantic—tragic, but nonetheless romantic."

Jillian closed her eyes. She didn't want Luke riding in on his gallant steed. Irene would pierce his heart with an arrow and let his horse run off a cliff. Jillian wanted Luke to forget about her, marry that completely-put-together girl she knew he deserved, and have the four beautiful children he dreamed of having.

She would die. She'd do it to save Luke, she'd do it for Jackson, and she'd do it to take away the pain of losing AJ.

"Don't worry, Knox. Since you're a bit tied up, I'll have

someone reply to Jackson on your behalf." She cackled like an evil witch. "I think we can have him here in say..." she twisted her lips and rolled her eyes to the ceiling "...forty-eight hours."

"He won't come." Jillian coughed, her throat dry and raw.

Irene held up her phone and snapped a picture of Jillian. "Shoot, I think you blinked. Don't worry, I don't actually think I'll have to use it, but it's a nice backup to have. He'll come. I guarantee it." She wrinkled her nose. "I'd love to stay, but it smells like shit down here. Can I get either one of you anything?"

Knox stared at the bowl of dirty water next to him. Jillian had watched him drink from it like a dog then nearly throw his shoulder out of socket to get back up to a sitting position.

The IV kept her alive, but it did nothing for her mouth and throat.

"Very well then. I'll let you two get back to story time. Mickey and Sunny. It's quite touching isn't it?" She glared at Knox before giving Jillian a bitter smile.

He was right. She had eyes and ears everywhere.

As soon as the door shut, Jillian looked at Knox.

"Keep going. Take it full circle. Make me love my mom again and hate you. That's the only happy ending."

Sunny

SUNNY AND MICKEY gave each other their virginities. They promised to be each other's first and last. They loved hard and fought even harder. Mickey felt like Sunny deliberately applied to the colleges with the worst sports teams just to postpone marrying him until after college. The difference between them was she cared about her parents' opinions. He did not.

"I can't wait any longer, Sunny. I've been offered scholarships to six different colleges and I need to decide. *You* need to decide."

She sat up in bed and slipped on his T-shirt as he scooted back against the wall. Sunny's closet was bigger than his bedroom, with a squeaky twin bed and an old metal trunk. He had three shirts he deemed worthy of having on hangers, which hung from his curtain rod because he didn't have an actual closet: his basketball jersey, football jersey, and the only dress shirt he owned.

"I'm not deciding on your future, Mickey. That's not fair of you to even ask."

"My future? Are you kidding? You are my future. Four years. College is four years of my fucking life. It's nothing. Football is nothing. You..." he gathered her long auburn hair in his hand, exposing her neck to his lips "...are *everything*. I love you, Sunny."

She pulled away. "Love won't pay rent. It won't get you a job. It won't buy you a car that you don't have to jump start every morning. It won't get you out of Oakland. You need to play football to pay for college. I need to not piss my parents off so they'll pay for college. They like you Mickey, but they'll hate you if you propose to me the minute we cross the stage. Then they'll disown me for saying yes. We'll be broke, homeless, and what? In love?"

"What did you say?" He grabbed her arm.

Sunny tried to pull away, a scowl stealing her perfect features.

"I said we'll be broke and homeless."

"No, before that." His strength was no match for his. He pulled her into his arms, pouty lip and all.

"What?"

"You said your parents would disown you for saying yes."

"They would."

"But would you?"

She sighed. "Would I what?"

"Say yes?"

With a single finger he lifted her chin, waiting for her to look at him. When she did, he knew the answer.

"Yes, Mickey. Of course I'd say yes. My heart will always be tethered to yours. I choose you today. I choose you always."

He grinned.

She pinched his cheeks together until it hurt. "Don't you dare smile. Just because I'm hopelessly—stupidly—in love with you, doesn't mean I'm not still mad as hell that you're being such a selfish jerk. If four years is 'nothing,' then I don't see the big deal in waiting until we're done with school, *and* if you love me the way I love you, it won't matter if we're at the same college."

She broke free of his hold and searched for her clothes. "Would it kill you to pick up your room? Your dad is going to go apeshit if he sees this mess."

"So let me just be clear on this ... you will say yes no matter when I ask you to marry me?"

"Dammit, Knox! Your dad will be home any minute, and I don't want to be naked when he gets here."

Knox meant business. Sunny rarely called him by his given name, except for when she was ready to explode at him. She'd give him one warning. Saying it twice meant a week or more of jacking off in the shower—no sex, no kisses, rarely even a phone call.

"Here are your clothes." He lifted his pillow. They were wadded under it. "See, I'm much more organized than you give me credit for." His grin just begged to be wiped off his face.

Sunny grabbed her clothes, pulling them on with fire-drill speed. "I'm going home and picking the college with the worst football team ever, you big stubborn ass."

Knox chuckled. "Good idea. They probably need me the most."

She rifled through the clothes and school books covering his floor, searching for her shoes. He could hear her mind cursing at him for being so damn messy and herself for falling in love with a walking disaster. The thought made his smile double because she did—Sunny loved him and it was a miracle.

"I can't live like this, Mickey. I'll divorce you within a month of marrying you if you don't pick up your crap." She tugged on her boots, hopping from one foot to the other. Her nose scrunched as she pulled off her right boot "Mickey! Yuck!"

With frighteningly-accurate precision, she whipped the boot at his head. He ducked and it *thunked* against the wall.

"What?" He grabbed it off the bed. "Oh." His life depended on him not grinning; he nearly lost it. "Sorry, Sun." Biting his lips together, he retrieved the used condom from the inside of her boot. "I just tossed it."

"That's my point. Who just tosses used condoms on their bedroom floor? I don't toss my tampons on the bathroom floor. It's disgusting." Sunny snatched her boot from him and stomped out of the room without putting it on.

"Don't be mad—" The intimidating waste of space that was his father, stopped him in the hallway.

Nicotine and liquor filled his nostrils. The man bathed on a need-to basis, usually when he vomited on himself or had to wash the blood off his hands from beating the shit out of Knox or his mother.

Sunny turned at the top of the stairs. Thankfully, his father let her pass. The evil in his eyes said Knox wouldn't be as lucky.

"Go home, young lady." His father didn't turn to look at her, but he knew she was watching.

"Mickey."

"He's not a fucking cartoon character. His name is Knox. You best remember that."

"Go, Sunny. I'll call you later." Knox packed as much confidence into his words as he could.

He risked a glance over his father's shoulder, but he shouldn't have. The fear in her eyes that day stayed with him forever.

"Mr. McGraw—"

"I said go the fuck home!" He whipped around.

Knox grabbed at him but not before the back of his father's hand connected with Sunny's face.

"No!" Knox yelled, watching arms, legs, and a mess of red hair tumble down the stairs.

"You fucker!" Pain shot in bolts of lightning from his knuckles, clear to his elbow, as he busted his dad's nose.

His father stumbled back, blood running down his face. Knox moved toward the stairs, his heart refusing to beat again until he got to Sunny.

"You're dead, boy."

In the corner of his eye, Knox caught the wrath of the drunken beast coming toward him. He made a fist and rammed his elbow sideways in his father's already broken nose. In less than three seconds the course of Knox's entire future changed forever. His father fell backward, crashing through the railing and plummeting to the first floor, smacking the weathered wood floor six feet from Sunny's limp body.

"Sunny?" Knox skidded down the stairs and dropped to his knees. "Sunny?" He cradled her body in his arms and rocked back and forth. Tears stung his eyes and fear gripped his heart.

Knight

THE STORY KNOX told Jillian felt like another world, a parallel universe. With each word she felt her mother die all over again. She hated and needed each word, each one unbearable yet necessary.

"That scar by her right temple. She said she fell down the stairs and spent three days in the hospital with a concussion and a broken arm."

Knox nodded. "It wasn't a lie."

"It was. She told me she slipped on the top stair."

"Can you blame her?"

Yes. She could blame her mom, and she did. Knox didn't need to know that. Jillian wouldn't give him the satisfaction of seeing her anger, her pain, her vulnerability. Instead, she sat idle, enduring a new kind of hell, the kind that came from having such sacred memories tainted and completely shattered.

Her father had secrets. It was part of his job. Keeping secrets kept people alive. Her mother raised her and Jude.

She folded laundry, scrubbed the floor, made Halloween costumes, and cooked three meals a day. Every Sunday she took them to church. Jessica heard the story of her mother's childhood a million times ... all of it except Knox McGraw.

"She said she was too busy studying, cheerleading, and practicing her violin to keep a boyfriend very long."

Jillian liked the pain in Knox's expression. He deserved it. They shared a mutual disappointment in Sunny for not telling the truth about her past, but for different reasons.

"That day ... when I thought she was dead, I hated myself for ever loving her, for ever putting her at the top of those stairs on that day ... with that man."

"Your dad?" Jillian coughed. She tasted blood, her throat painfully raw. "What happened to him?"

"He was taken out in a body bag."

The words "I'm sorry" sat on her tongue, but she couldn't say them, not to the man she still hated.

"My mother grieved his death for years. I have no idea why. She should have thanked me. Instead, she turned her back on me, blaming his death on my anger management issues even after Sunny backed up my account of the events to both her and the police. Rumors were everywhere and one by one, I lost my scholarship offers. By the time I graduated, I had no means to go to college ... no direction. A few of my buddies decided to get their education via the armed forces, so I did too."

"But my mom didn't end up going to college."

He shook his head, regret heavy in his sober expression. "Her dad, your grandfather, had a heart attack the summer after we graduated. He died on the operating table. Sunny refused to leave her mom and her sister so soon after his death, so she got a job working at the front desk of a hotel."

"She eventually moved to a bartending position in the hotel's restaurant."

Knox looked up. "Yes."

"She told me that's how she met my father."

His expression hardened as he nodded slowly. A few seconds later he closed his eyes, letting his head fall back against the wall. "Yeah, but that's a complicated story."

CHAPTER TWENTY-SEVEN

JONES

"I'M NOT AS EXCITED about Portland. I've been there." Lake stared at the ceiling from the hotel bed, twirling her long dark hair around her finger while Luke typed away on his computer.

"Sorry to disrupt your travel plans. Oh, wait ... you're disrupting mine. Did I mention I'm willing and even eager to send you back to San Francisco? I bet we can still get you a flight out tonight."

"No thanks. You want to know what I think?"

"No thanks."

"I knew you did. I think we should talk to more of AJ's neighbors. Maybe some of them went to the funeral and saw her there. If you don't want to go, I'll do it while you stay here and do ... whatever it is you're doing."

Luke spun around in the desk chair, hands folded behind his head as he arched his back to release the tension from sitting for so long. "How kind of you."

Lake leaned up on her elbows. "I know, right? We could be like Holmes and Watson."

"Mmm ... brilliant, my dear sister. But something tells

me your little investigation has more to do with a certain football player and less to do with interviewing the residents of Peaceful Woods."

She failed to contain her grin. "Seriously, did I mention he's not freaked out by my leg? And he called me hot. *Hot,* Luke. He didn't have to call me that. It's as if he wanted me to know that..." she shrugged "...that ... well, that he thinks I'm hot."

Luke smirked.

"Don't. Don't ruin this for me. Just let me have this dream ... this fantasy. Let me play this out in my head. Can you see it? NFL quarterback shrugs off a throng of groupies after winning the Super Bowl to get to the love of his life and wait for it ... she has a prosthetic leg, but he only sees her as *perfect.* This dream might be it for me. I need more to take back to San Francisco. Thirty minutes, forty tops. Then I'll say goodbye forever. Oh, and of course I'll question the neighbors too."

"I'm so happy that in the midst of my tragedy you can find your own little fantasy."

"So that's a yes?"

"I think Jackson's the only one who will lead us to Jessica."

"Then you should talk to him again."

Luke shook his head. He didn't really trust Jackson to contact Knox. He didn't trust Jackson in general.

"I don't know. If he didn't have Ryn, I'd worry about him skipping town. They're here under new identities for a reason and us being here probably makes him nervous. He's easily paranoid."

"Maybe we should stakeout his place."

Luke nodded. "Exactly. And we could use Cage's bathroom."

Lake rolled her eyes. "Hardy har har. I'm serious."

Luke spun back around in his chair. "I'm not."

"Ugh! You drive me crazy."

The feeling was mutual.

"Okay. I'll make you a deal."

"I'm listening." He typed in his screen password.

"If you let me go 'investigate,' I'll fly back to San Francisco in the morning."

He whipped around in his chair. "Then go. Do you remember how to get there?"

"Yes." She pulled on her boots, her smile stealing her entire face. "I'm going to find the missing clue, Sherlock."

She wasn't going to find any new information, but it didn't matter. His sister would be on a plane back to safety in the morning. That's all that mattered.

<hr />

Lake parked in one of the guest spots several houses down from AJ's.

"Brilliant. Now what?" she mumbled to herself while checking her hair in the rearview mirror.

The bathroom request wasn't going to work twice in the same day. It was a house, not a 7-Eleven. She decided the best plan was to question the neighbors first and maybe he would see her outside in the cold and invite her in for a cup of hot coffee or cuddling with him under a warm blanket.

Three strikes in a row, no one was home. At the fourth house, an elderly gentleman named Marvin Housby told Lake his wife, Greta, might know something, but she was in the bathtub with strict instructions to not disturb her. He grumbled something about "damn new toys."

Lake froze midway down the Housby's driveway. Both

Jackson's and Cage's garage doors opened. A truck with tinted windows pulled into Cage's garage. Jackson opened the door to the most offensive vehicle Lake had ever seen. Just as he started to get in, he zeroed in on Lake. She could feel his laser stare from across the street. However, the hunky guy getting out of his truck stole her attention, and so did the girl getting out of the passenger's side.

Jackson stalked toward her with a menacing scowl. His approach seemed to catch Cage's attention as he stood inside the garage looking at her. She considered fleeing for the Housby's front door again and begging Marvin to let her in to wait for Greta.

"Little Jones girl, what the hell are you doing?" Jackson stood toe-to-toe with her, using his height advantage and deep voice to intimidate her. His freakishly defined muscles and tattoos did that all on their own. He didn't need to invade her space too.

She gulped. "I'm seeing if anyone in the neighborhood went to the funeral."

Jackson looked over his shoulder at Cage still watching from his garage.

"He was there. I thought you and Luke talked to him earlier."

"Well, uh ... we did, but he's not ready to talk about it."

Jackson squinted a bit then nodded once. He seemed to be thinking something that he wasn't willing to share with "Little Jones girl."

"I think snooping around the neighborhood is a bad idea."

"Why?" She lifted her chin.

"Because it's not safe."

She looked around. "You live in a retirement community, in Omaha. I think I'll be fine."

He groaned or growled. It sounded much more like a growl, an angry animal growl. "Stubborn women. I can't handle any more of you in my life." He grabbed her arm. "Let's go."

"What? Wait!" She tried to keep up as he dragged her toward Cage. If there was truly a God, he'd keep her upright and not let her land on her face in front of her dream guy—whom just so happened to have a beautiful girl with two legs standing next to him.

"Young buck, here." He handed Lake off like a piece of property then dug into his jeans pocket. After he retrieved what looked like a couple hundred-dollar bills, he shoved them into Cage's coat pocket, ignoring his look of utter confusion. "I have to run a few errands. Don't let her out of your sight."

The blonde with bangs that kept falling in her face like a sheep dog, gawked at Jackson. If she was a girlfriend, she sure didn't hide her attraction to Mr. Watch After Little Jones Girl.

Cage's gaze shifted to Lake. "Are you on probation?" He grinned.

She could not have been more embarrassed by the situation. If Jackson weren't so menacing, she would have thrown a full-blown conniption fit for being treated like a prisoner. But as she looked at the newly-assigned warden, she couldn't find a good reason to protest.

"Apparently soliciting isn't allowed in this neighborhood. Mr. *Knight* has made a citizen's arrest." She glared at Jackson. "Your sister would *not* approve of your behavior." Looking back at Cage, she smiled. "Jillian likes me. We're sort of best friends."

He nodded, looking at Jackson.

"I'm out of here. Just ... watch her." Jackson shook his head and stalked back to his garage.

"Hi, I'm Lake. Prisoner for the night." She held her hand out to the girl.

"Emily." She shook Lake's hand.

Lake gestured to Cage's coat pocket. "Have you two had dinner? If not, I think my captor just paid for delivery."

Cage smiled, flaunting those damn dimples. Emily was one lucky girl. Lake's quest to add more images of Cage to her fantasy collection took a turn for the weird and a bit creepy in the presence of Emily.

———

CAGE ORDERED pizza while Lake shot off a quick text to Luke informing him of her temporary house arrest. He replied with one word: figures.

With a prolonged stare, Emily noticed Lake's leg the moment she pulled off her boots, but she didn't say anything so Lake decided to not address it either. Cage deserved a break from talking about her leg, boobs, or the death of her boyfriend.

"Pizza will be here in forty minutes." Cage tossed his phone on the sofa and sat next to Lake.

Emily took a seat in the black leather recliner.

"So did the Housby's know where Jillian is?"

"Oh, well ..."

His quick observation as to why she had been roaming their neighborhood caught her off guard.

"Greta was taking a bath and Marvin didn't seem to know anything. I'll check back with her."

"Who's Jillian?" Emily asked, focused on her phone as her thumbs tapped the screen.

"She was my dad's girlfriend. I told you that."

Emily nodded, still not deeming his response worthy of her undivided attention. "I just didn't remember her name. The one who got the mail in her panties and red rain boots?"

Cage grinned, looking at Lake. "Yes."

Lake laughed. She missed Jessica and the thought of her being alive and infiltrating the lives of Cage and his father was both heartwarming and heartbreaking. It was obvious Cage and AJ cared about her, but she belonged in San Francisco with Luke and Jones and the entire Jones family.

"I hope I'm not interrupting your evening."

"No. I just picked Emily up from the airport. Her boyfriend is a buddy of mine and his flight into Omaha got delayed, so I picked her up so she didn't have to wait there."

Best news of the night for Lake. Football player fantasy was officially back on.

"You both live in Omaha?"

Emily looked up. "No. I'm from Minneapolis. Eddie and I attend Texas A&M. His family lives here, so we're spending part of our break with his family then we'll spend the second half with my family. I haven't officially met his parents, so I wanted to wait for Eddie before going to his house."

Lake nodded.

"Eddie was my running back last year and my room-mate. He was injured in the last game of the season. He's done playing football. Emily wanted to transfer to Texas so he followed her."

"Romantic, huh?" Emily winked at Cage.

"No comment."

"He felt bad you know?" Emily gave Cage a sad smile.

233

"He should have. My new roommate has a weird obsession with Minecraft."

"No. I'm talking about your dad. Eddie really wanted to be at the funeral, he just couldn't get the travel arrangements made with the busy holiday weekend."

Lake sank back into the couch. Emily had breached a subject that was not up for discussion, at least it hadn't been earlier that day.

"It's fine. The whole thing was kind of a blur. I couldn't even tell you who was or wasn't there. Except—" Cage hopped up when the doorbell rang. He paid for the pizzas then set them on the counter.

"I think there may be a few cans of beer still in the refrigerator and maybe a can or two of Coke. Help yourself, ladies."

Emily grabbed a beer and slice of pizza before planting herself back in the chair, giving her phone more attention.

"We can eat at the dining room table if it's easier."

Lake shrugged. "Doesn't matter to me."

He grabbed his glass of water and one of the pizza boxes then motioned toward the dining room. Lake followed, not questioning why they didn't just sit at the small table in the kitchen.

"So you are definitely a pleasant surprise tonight."

Lake felt her skin heat from his compliment that took her by equal surprise.

"Thank you. I haven't been anyone's pleasant surprise in a long time. Probably not since my mom found out she was pregnant with me." She gave him a small smirk. "I wasn't exactly planned. I honestly don't think any of my siblings were either. Our parents just can't seem to keep their hands off each other. Even now, after five kids, they embarrass us with their excessive PDAs."

Cage laughed, wiping his mouth with a napkin. "What do they do? Are they retired?"

"No. They own a bed and breakfast in T—" She grimaced. "Times Square."

"In Times Square?"

"Uh ... yeah, that's in New York."

"Yeah, I know."

Lake blushed from her own crazy statement.

"I just didn't realize there's a bed and breakfast *in* Times Square."

There probably wasn't.

"I meant in walking distance." She looked for confirmation on his face that a walking distance bed and breakfast was feasible.

His forehead still held lines of confusion.

"Or driving distance." She nodded. Surely that would pass as a plausible explanation.

"So basically they have a bed and breakfast within the state of New York?"

No. Tahoe.

"Yes." She nodded again. *Dammit. Dammit. Dammit Jones!*

"So you must do more than play football. What are you studying?" She needed a subject change, STAT.

"I'm in elementary education."

"Holy shit, you're kidding?"

"Um ... nope. I'm not."

"You like kids?"

He chuckled. "I do. I think it's a requirement for my major."

Lake shoved a big bite into her mouth, chewing on it as well as thoughts of the perfect—no, beyond perfect—guy before her. Getting a job was no longer an option. She would go home and spend at least forty hours a week dreaming about Cage Monaghan.

"Girlfriend? Oh God..." she covered her mouth and finished chewing "...did I say that out loud?"

Cage had a cool persona. He never fumbled his words or acted nervous or awkward. Yet, he wasn't cocky. He was the guy that was truly "all that" but had no idea.

"No girlfriend right now. Just casual dating."

"Yeah." She nodded. "Me too." Her nod shifted into a head shake. "Actually, that's a lie. I'm not casually dating or dating at all for that matter."

"Really? I'm surprised."

She returned the "come on, be serious" look. Her, look-at-my-leg-or-lack-there-of speech hung on the tip of her tongue. She swallowed it back down. "I'm a bit of a handful."

Cage laughed, the kind of laugh that felt like the warm sun on a bikini-clad body sprawled out on a beach in Southern California—not that she had done that since the accident. But she still remembered the feeling.

"I kind of gathered that from the two hundred dollars cash in my pocket. Babysitting you pays much better than teaching."

The doorbell rang again. Cage's brow furrowed. "It's too early for Eddie to be here." He excused himself from the table. Guys his age didn't do that. Lake quickly added manners to her He's Perfect list.

"I've posted bail, Sis. Time to go."

She narrowed her eyes a fraction at Luke, just enough that only he would detect her displeasure. "How did you get here? I have the rental car."

"They're called cabs, Lake. There's a ton of them in New York too."

She loved her brother, but that remark earned him her best fuck-you smile.

"Thanks for dinner." She stood and tossed her napkin on the table.

"Thank Jackson." Cage grinned.

"Nice to meet you, Emily."

"You too."

"I'll have to look up your parents' B&B in Times Square when I'm there next time."

She ignored the look she knew Luke gave her behind her back. "Yes, the one in driving distance of Times Square."

Cage chuckled. Luke did too, but his was condescending.

"Here." She tossed Luke the keys. "Go warm up the car. I'll be out in a minute."

"One minute."

"Go."

"Oh … have you talked to Dodge and Lilith?" Cage asked.

Luke shook his head. "Who's that?"

"They live in the first unit of the development on the North side. Jillian does some odd jobs for them and watches Lilith several days a week. She has some health issues. She and Jillian are close. Maybe they might know more."

Luke nodded. "Thank you."

After the storm door shut behind Luke, Lake gave Cage her best apologetic look. "So I'd say I'll see ya around or I'll see you later, but I somehow think this is it." She tried to hide her disappointment behind a forced smile.

He stepped out the front door behind her, shoving his hands deep into his jeans pockets. "It's been fun. I needed you today." Cage grinned. "I know that sounds weird, but it's true. I felt pretty shitty when I woke up, but now ..." He lifted his shoulders. "Not so shitty."

"I've had a shitty year, but after today ..." She mirrored his shrug. "Not so shitty. Thank you."

He had a sexy smile, the kind that she could feel. "Bye."

Lake nodded. "Bye." She turned, her heart begging with each pounding beat to say something—do something—anything to ease the disappointment of ending the best day of the entire year.

"Give me your phone number," he called.

She stopped and closed her eyes for a moment, wanting to just savor the feeling. Then she turned. "I can't."

Cage deflated. "You can't or you won't?"

"Both. No, really just ... I can't."

"So you're just going to leave me with nothing."

Her mind screamed "screw it." She walked back and grabbed his face with both of her gloved hands, pulling his cheek toward her lips. At the last second he turned and his lips pressed to hers. She wasn't going to kiss him on the lips. He did it. He turned into her kiss. Neither one of them moved. It wasn't a passionate, open-mouthed kiss, but it wasn't a peck either. Their lips simply locked, idle like a statue, neither one wanting to end the feeling because it was The. Best. Feeling.

However, life was ... life. Time didn't really ever stand still. And just as quick as it happened, it ended with yet again, the honking of a car horn.

Dammit Jones!

CHAPTER TWENTY-EIGHT

KNIGHT

IT TOOK BEGGING and insinuating a possible life or death situation to get Maddie to Ryn's for dinner on a Saturday night. She arrived with an annoyed frown plastered to her beautiful face. Ryn couldn't remember the exact moment her little girl became so bitter. It seemed to happen in a blink. One day they were each other's everything and the next Ryn was the unstable woman who ruined her marriage and her daughter's dreams.

"Who's dying?" Maddie stabbed her fork into her salad.

Ryn was too nervous to eat. She pushed her plate away and rested her crossed arms on the table. "How are things with your professor?"

Maddie shrugged. "Fine, I guess. I have a shit grade in the class, but I'm going to pass. Please tell me that's not what was so urgent. We could have had this conversation over the phone."

"If I moved what would it take for you to come with me?"

"I'm not moving." Maddie laughed as if the idea was absurd.

"Why?"

"Why? Are you serious? I'm in college. I have friends. Dad is here."

"But what if I weren't here?"

Maddie shrugged. "I'll come visit you when I can."

"Is there anything I could say or do or ... give you to make you come with me?"

She flipped her long blond hair over her shoulder. "What, like a bribe?"

"No. Just an incentive."

"Nope. I'm not leaving."

Ryn's heart ached. The crushing reality left her fighting back emotions.

"Maddie ... do you hate me?"

"What? Why would you ask me that?"

"Just answer the question."

With a roll of her eyes, she shook her head. "No, Mom. I don't hate you. God, you're so insecure."

"Shut up," Ryn said. It was nothing more than a whisper, a leaked emotion not meant for Maddie's ears.

"*What* did you just say?" Maddie leaned forward.

Ryn shook her head, years of defeat bearing down on her.

"Did you tell me to shut up?" Defense escalated in her voice.

"I just want to feel your love, but I don't feel it—ever."

"Well, I'm not feeling your love either. Wasting one of the few Saturday nights I have off, to ask me to leave my life, then adding 'shut up' on top of it is not the best way to *feel my love.*"

Ryn clenched her teeth, breathing slowly through her nose. "I gave you life, and then I gave you mine—completely. Do you get that? Do you have even an inkling of what my life has been like? No. You don't. Because I've given *everything* to protect you from the truth, from the ugly, from the nightmare that has been my life."

Maddie stood. "I'm not listening to this. I'm not listening to your sob story. I'm sorry you had some mental breakdown, but it wasn't my fault. Get over it. Stop living in the past. Watching you hate my father is getting old."

She followed Maddie in her pursuit to the front door. "Don't you dare walk out that door. I'm not done."

Maddie laughed. "Well, I am."

"He hit me."

She stopped, hand on the doorknob. "No, Mom. He didn't. He told me you lost control and sometimes he had to restrain you from hurting yourself or anyone else, but he didn't hit you."

"He's lying."

"*You're* lying." She turned back around. "You're a fucking maid with no education, barely a dime to your name, a failed marriage, and some psycho boyfriend who is too young for you. What is wrong with you? The last thing you need to worry about is if I love you. What should bother you the most is I don't respect you. My number one goal in life is to be *nothing* like you."

Something unrecognizable took over inside of Ryn. With three long strides she had Maddie's hair clenched in her fist. She dragged her up the stairs. Her little girl with venomous words stumbled and cried in protest. Ryn heard nothing. Her need to protect her child from the ugly, that seemingly unbreakable bond, snapped and so did Ryn.

"What the fuck?" Maddie looked ten years younger with tears in eyes as Ryn shoved her on the bed. Maddie pressed her hand to her head where Ryn had attempted to pull a chunk of hair from her scalp.

"Reality is a bitch, baby girl, and there are some things in life that cannot be unseen. If a picture is worth a thousand words, then I'm going to give you a million words." She retrieved her fire safe key from the dresser drawer and opened the safe in the closet, pulling out several large legal-sized envelopes.

Maddie shook her head while pulling her phone out of her pocket. "I'm calling Dad or the police, you're losing it." Her voice quivered.

Ryn snatched Maddie's phone, opened the window, and threw it outside. "Well, if I am..." Ryn opened one envelope and dumped the contents onto the bed in front of Maddie, followed by a second, and finally a third "...then I think I have a damn good excuse."

Maddie didn't move, not even a blink. She stared at hundreds of photos spread out on the bed. Tears rolled down Ryn's cheeks. She grieved her baby girl. She grieved her lost innocence. She grieved that exact moment because Maddie would never be the same again.

With a shaky hand, Maddie picked up one of the photos. "Oh my God," she whispered, her other hand covering her mouth. Her body shook and then she released a sob.

"I'm sorry, baby. I didn't have time for college. I was busy raising a daughter. I don't have a dime to my name because I chose to leave—chose to live. And Jackson ... he gave me my self-esteem back. I love him, but he has to leave and if you don't come too, I'll have to choose between the two of you. He loves me. You? I don't think you love me and I *know* you don't respect me. But here's the thing. I choose you, Maddie."

She saw her little girl in pigtails playing with Barbie dolls and kissing Ryn's boo-boos. Maddie rarely saw Ryn without something broken, bruised, or stitched up, but by the time she could understand or ask real questions, Preston limited the number of marks he left on Ryn that Maddie could see.

Ryn blinked, time vanished, and her baby girl was a young woman sitting on her bed, sobbing as she sifted through the pictures of her mother with black eyes, a broken jaw, stitches, bruises, cracked ribs—a human punching bag. At the time, Ryn wasn't even sure why she took them and hid them from Preston. She just knew that someday she would need them. It never occurred to her that she'd need them to make her daughter believe her, trust her.

"I only had to show the judge three of these pictures and a copy of my medical records to get the restraining order."

"Mom ..." Maddie said her name with a tenderness Ryn hadn't heard in years.

She always wondered if somewhere in Maddie's subconscious she remembered kissing her mama's boo-boos. The horror on her daughter's face confirmed that she did not remember those years.

"I hate him," Maddie whispered, tears splattering the pictures.

"Come with me, Maddie. Let's start over some place a world away from your father and—"

"No." Maddie shook her head and held up one of the worst pictures of Ryn—her face barely recognizable.

That was a "biking" accident. Ryn didn't own a bike, but Preston caught her snooping through his stuff after he came home from a business trip with everything in his suitcase smelling like perfume. She wasn't proud that the trips to various ERs included questions she couldn't answer. When the nurses or doctors asked what had happened, she always looked at Preston for the explanation. He always had one, perfectly recited, not so much as a breath of hesitation.

"What do you mean 'no?'"

"You never told me. Twenty-one years and you never told me."

"I did. I told you—"

"Just recently." Maddie's voice grew angry.

"And you didn't believe me."

"You didn't show me these."

Ryn ran her fingers through her hair fisting it. "What if I didn't have these? Jesus, Maddie! I'm your mother. I raised you, cared for you. I love you. I've never given you any reason to not trust me. If you told me someone harmed you, I would believe you. I wouldn't need proof. The day you told me about your professor I didn't once think you were lying. I jumped to your defense." She grabbed a photo of her eye swollen shut and held it in front of Maddie's face. "Nobody should have to see this shit, Maddie!"

"Your father has used you as a weapon against me for years, and the second I stood up for myself he pulled your college funding. He's the reason you're not in medical school, not me. How can you be so smart and yet so stupid to not see that? You question everything I do right down to the shoes I wear and the way I style my hair. But never ... *never* have you questioned a goddamn thing about the man who has been nothing more in your life than a sperm donor —the biggest mistake of my entire life."

Maddie stood, tipping her chin up, teeth clenched. "Well, if he was a mistake then clearly you must think I was too."

Ryn sighed. "That's not what I mean."

"You can't have it both ways. Either we were both a mistake or neither of us were. Which is it?"

"We were both drunk ..."

"So a mistake. Is that your final answer?" Maddie punched holes into Ryn with her contemptuous glare.

"I don't know how to make you understand."

"I hate you both. I'm nothing more than the product of a drunk night between two people who didn't love each other. Neither one of you wanted me." She ran out of the room.

Ryn let her go. Words did not exist to explain her feelings toward Maddie. How could Ryn tell her she regretted that night with Preston, yet loved Maddie more than life? It wasn't black and white. Maddie's conception and her entire childhood was a shade of gray: her daughter the light, her husband the darkness.

CHAPTER TWENTY-NINE

DAY

THE BRIDE-TO-BE STRETCHED in all directions. A smile crept up her face like the gentle rise of the early morning sun. An intense floral scent overwhelmed her senses as she took a deep breath. Jessica opened her eyes.

"Oh. My. God." She sat up.

Her bed. The top of the dresser, Luke's chair, and every inch of the floor was covered in a kaleidoscope of rose petals.

On her nightstand, amongst the petals, was a cup of tea with a sticky note.

Good morning, Miss Day. <—Enjoy it while it lasts.

Her face already hurt from smiling. She took a sip of tea and slid out of bed, curling her toes into the velvety floral confetti. Cinching her robe sash, she spotted a hot pink sticky note stuck to the full-length mirror next to the closet.

See you at the altar. I'll be the guy at the front wearing the shit-eating grin and chanting, "I can't believe she said yes."

Jessica grabbed the note and held it to her chest. "I'm getting married today. I'm getting married today!"

She jumped up and down, squealing like a little girl. Then she bent down, grabbed two fists full of petals and threw them in the air while twirling in a circle. "I'm getting married today!"

"Yada, yada ..."

Jessica stilled. Her unexpected visitor startled her.

"What are you doing here?"

Jude heaved himself onto her bed, sending petals flying. He picked one up and brought it to his nose. "I'm in charge of getting you to the church. That is ... if you're still going to marry the shrink." He shrugged. "It's not too late to skip town. I'll take you anywhere you want to go."

She narrowed her eyes at him.

"Sex with the same guy for the rest of your life. Sounds like a death sentence."

Just the thought of Luke almost brought her to orgasm. It would take a million lifetimes—minimum—to feel a breath of boredom with him.

She flopped down onto the bed beside him, forcing his arm behind her head for a pillow. "I want you to find this, Jude. Finding someone who loves you and accepts you, the real you, it's everything. I'm just a girl with Luke. I know it sounds crazy, but I feel safe with him. Maybe that's it. The thing that's been most exhausting to protect has been my heart, but I gave it to him because I trust him explicitly. And when we're not together I don't feel alive. It's like I'm holding my breath."

"You trust him more than me?"

"Yes."

"Ouch." Jude pressed his free hand to his chest. "Way to not even hesitate."

"Luke and I don't have secrets. Well ... at least by the end of this weekend we won't have any secrets. But you..." she jabbed her finger into his side "...you're not telling me something. I know it. I feel it. It's eating you up inside. Why won't you tell me?"

"I got a tattoo on my penis and it's infected. I fear it's going to fall off. Hopefully not during the wedding."

She giggled. "Shut up."

He smiled.

"What did you get tattooed on your penis?"

"Open wide."

Jessica rolled to her side, burying her face in his neck. "Oh my God ... I can't breathe." Her body shook with laughter.

"Go." He gave her a playful shove. "Go shower. Some Vanessa person is waiting in the living room."

Jessica bolted up. "Vanessa is here? Why didn't you tell me? Shit! She's doing my hair and makeup." She ran into the bathroom. "I can't believe we were talking about your little wiener while Vanessa was waiting on me."

"I can assure you Vanessa doesn't think it's little."

Jessica gasped, peeking around the corner. "You *did not* fuck my stylist. Did you?"

"Shut up and shower."

She threw off her robe and stopped at the shower door. Another pink sticky note.

I've got you. I'll always have you.

Jessica mouthed the words *I'm getting married today* and did a silent, naked dance before hopping in the shower.

"Cold feet?" Jude asked as they pulled into the church parking lot.

"Hot vagina. Let me out. Park the car and keep your dick in your pants the rest of the day."

"Whoa, whoa, whoa ... just until after the ceremony. It's tradition for the single groomsmen to have sex with the single bridesmaids in a dark corner at the reception."

He stopped the car along the sidewalk near the back-door of the church.

Jessica pointed a stiff finger at him. "My bridesmaids are Kelly and Luke's sisters. Dick. In. Pants."

Their mom opened Jessica's door. "There's my baby girl. Your dress is inside and Luke is locked in a room on the opposite side of the church until he has permission to come out. The coast is clear."

"Hey ..." Jude grabbed Jessica's hand before she got out. "I love you ... but more than that ... I'm happy for you."

Tears stung her eyes. "Fuck you." She tried to laugh to keep from crying. "I just had my makeup done."

Jude's smile was soft and heartbreakingly sincere. Jessica got out but ducked her head back into the car before closing the door.

"I love you too."

"Bummer, sweetie, it looks like rain," Sunny said as she ushered Jessica into the back of the church.

"I don't care. I'm marrying Luke today."

"Well, we have thirty minutes to get you dressed and ready to walk down the aisle. I expected you two to be here earlier."

"If you wanted me to the church on time then you shouldn't have put Jude in charge of getting me here."

"Your dad's idea, not mine."

Her mom opened the door to a large room with a few

folding chairs and a full-length mirror that someone must have brought in there for the day.

"Hi!" Jessica squealed as Kelly, Lara, and Felicity saw her.

"Get in here, take off your clothes. You're late." Kelly shook her head as she unzipped Jessica's dress bag.

"Where's Lake?"

"Not here yet." Felicity rolled her eyes. "She wanted to ride with Ben instead of coming with us. Those two are inseparable. I tried calling her cell phone, but she didn't answer. It's probably shoved into her purse, which is probably shoved into the backseat or trunk of Ben's car."

"Oh my gosh!" Lara laughed, staring at the back of Jessica's panties as she stepped into her wedding gown.

Jessica looked over her shoulder and winked. "You like?"

"Luke's going to die."

Her light pink and white argyle panties read: Property of Dr. Jones.

Sunny zipped and buttoned the back of Jessica's dress. "I love that you wore your hair down."

"I always have it in a ponytail. Luke likes it down."

"Step." Kelly set Jessica's heels on the floor and held up the front of her dress so she could step into them.

"How do I look?"

Nobody answered. They just stared with loving smiles as Sunny pinned Jessica's hair-clip veil onto her. The soft tulle flowed down her back.

Jessica nodded slowly while looking in the mirror. "I'm getting married today."

The door behind them opened.

"Felicity ..."

Everyone turned.

Tom stood in the doorway. He didn't make eye contact with anyone but Felicity. The grave look on his face sent haunting chills down Jessica's spine. Tom didn't have to say anything, she just knew that with his next breath he would forever change the memories of that day.

"Lake and Ben were in a car accident. She's been airlifted to the hospital." His voice broke with the final word and tears filled his eyes. The strong man she'd come to love like her own father cracked.

"No ..." Felicity's hand covered her mouth as Lara and Tom hugged her.

"Luke ..." Jessica whispered as she looked at her mom.

Tom looked up as he held Felicity, collapsed and sobbing in his arms. "He doesn't know."

"Go." Sunny's hand pressed to her heart as she fought back her own tears, the tears of one mother grieving for another.

Jessica nodded. "We'll meet you at the hospital." She kicked off her shoes and sprinted to the other side of the church.

"Luke?" She yelled through the hallway, not knowing for sure which room he was in.

"Jess?" Gabe peeked out the door of a room she'd already passed.

"What are you doing? He can't see the bride before—"

"Luke!" She shoved open the door, knocking Gabe out of the way.

"Baby, what are you—"

Her tears spilled over, a lump swelled in her throat the size of a baseball. She wanted to acknowledge how handsome he looked. She wanted to remember the way his eyes took in her dress, seeing it for the first time, but none of that mattered. Those would never be memories of that day.

"It's Lake ... she's been in an accident. We have to go now."

Luke shook his head. "What? What are you talking about?"

"They life-flighted her to the hospital."

Luke patted his pockets with his hands. "My keys ... my keys ... where are my—"

"Here." Gabe handed Luke his keys. "You handed them to me earlier. Lane and Liam are ushering in the guests. I'll get them and make sure they get to the hospital right behind you."

Luke's hands shook as he took the keys. Jessica snatched them from him then grabbed his hand. "Let's go."

Luke followed her to the car, his face blank like a zombie. She opened his door then hurried around to the driver's side.

"Shit!" she grumbled, realizing her veil had been shut in the door. She opened the door and tore the clip from her hair and tossed it onto the ground before shutting the door and squealing the tires out of the parking lot.

"Is she alive?" Luke asked in a voice that sounded defeated—scared.

Jessica honestly didn't know. "Of course she's alive. They don't life-flight dead people." She didn't know that. What if Lake died in transit? They didn't know anything.

"My parents?"

"They're with Lara. I'm sure they're on their way."

He nodded.

Within minutes they were there. Jessica parked the car and they hurried into the emergency room.

"Luke!" Lara called.

They rushed into the waiting room. Luke hugged his sister as she sobbed into his chest.

"Where is she?" he asked.

"They had to rush her into surgery. She was trapped in the car. That's all they've been able to tell us." Tom squeezed Felicity's hand as she pressed a tissue to her nose with her other hand. Both Lane and Liam sat in chairs, hunched over with their heads resting in their hands.

"What about Ben?" Jessica asked, looking around for his parents.

Anne stood next to Lane's chair, bouncing Gina on her hip. She frowned and shook her head slowly. "Ben ..." She pressed her lips together and swallowed. "He didn't make it."

Felicity's body folded over on to Tom's lap. Reality lacerated her heart and everyone in that room could feel it. Best case scenario, she would have to tell her baby girl that her boyfriend died. How could that be the best case scenario? How had the most perfect day turned into a harrowing nightmare?

A doctor in navy scrubs emerged through two large doors. "I'm Doctor Stein. Lake has sustained life threatening injuries to her head and her left leg. It was severely damaged in the accident." He paused for a second. "The prognosis for her leg is not good. She'll never have use of it again and the extensive trauma to it will likely lead to infection."

"What ... what are you saying?" Tom asked.

Jessica squeezed Luke's hand. He cleared his throat. "There is a good chance they'll have to amputate it to save her life."

Dr. Stein looked at Luke and nodded.

"No," Felicity cried, her legs giving out. Liam helped her sit back down.

"We don't have to do it now, but we can."

"What would you do?" Luke asked.

"No." Tom shook his head. "It's not his daughter. Why would you ask him?"

"Dad ..."

"No. You save her leg. You don't know Lake. It would kill her—"

"Dad, she won't ever use it again. We want her alive."

"I need to get back in there." The doctor gestured toward the doors. It was a statement, but also an unspoken question.

Luke looked at his dad. Tom shook his head. "No."

Luke grimaced. "Do everything you can for now."

Dr. Stein nodded.

Luke turned, focusing in on Jessica, her dress, and her bare feet. His eyes filled with tears. "I'm sorry—"

"Don't you dare apologize." She pressed her hands to his clean-shaven face. "I'm going to have Jude bring us other clothes. I don't want anyone thinking about anything or anyone but Lake."

He nodded, folding her into his arms. His mouth brushed her ear. "I hope I never forget how you looked today, but I know I'll never forget the words you just said. Jess ... just ... never enough stars ..."

CHAPTER THIRTY

KNIGHT

Irene added a surgical mask to her GI Jane attire. The stench of infected flesh mixed with fecal matter must not have been her aroma of choice.

"Are you excited to see your twin? I'm going to reel him in and toss him in the cesspool with you two."

"He won't come," Knox said.

"Oh, he'll come."

"Only to take your life. If you see him at the door, I suggest you say your last prayer."

Jillian tried to decipher Knox's motive, if he had one. Irene captured both of them. There was no reason to believe she couldn't get Jackson too.

"Are you suggesting he's smarter than the two of you?"

"Yes." Knox didn't hesitate.

"Do you concur?"

Jillian looked at Irene and then at Knox. She didn't want to join the discussion. "Depends on the day."

Irene grunted, a sly grin curled her lips. "Well, he's not smarter than I am."

"He is."

"Listen, *Mickey,* shut your hole or I'll do it for you."

"Don't you fucking call me that."

There was never a bag of popcorn around when Jillian needed one. The Irene and *Mickey* show captivated her.

"You cheated on me—twice. I'll call you whatever I want to call you."

"I didn't cheat on you."

"You fucked Sunny *and* her daughter." Irene glared at Jillian.

"I did not."

That got Jillian's attention.

"I didn't fuck Sunny while we were married or while she was married, and Jessica ..."

She waited. He called her Jessica. Why?

"It was training. Period."

Knox looked at Irene as if Jillian wasn't in the room. Jillian dared him—needed him—to say that to her while looking her in the eyes.

"I saw the security footage. I *have* the security footage. Did you really think Grant would send his precious little girl to someplace that didn't have eyes? Of course mine are the only true eyes that have seen it. Jackson will come. He will watch it. He will kill you. I will kill him and ..." She cocked her head at Jillian. "I haven't decided what I'm going to do with you and your Dr. Jones. I'm sure it will be mind-blowing."

Jillian stared at Irene and her psychotic-bitch grin that reached her eyes. She couldn't see her mouth, but she knew it was there. Irene's eyes narrowed a fraction. Her brows drew together in a grimace as Jillian sucked in her bottom lip, sinking her teeth into it until blood dripped down her chin.

"You're a sick head case."

Jillian's tongue swiped along her lip. "Don't forget it, bitch."

Irene pivoted in her boots and stomped up the stairs.

"You taste that?"

Jillian looked up at Knox, her face stone, her heart numb, her emotions gone. She nodded once.

"What do you taste, *sweetheart?*"

"Power."

"I sure as fuck hope so … it's the only thing that's going to save you. It's coming … she's going to bring you to your knees with Jackson and Luke as her weapons of choice. Kill or be killed. Do you understand?"

Another nod.

Jones

WITH LAKE safe on a plane back to San Francisco, Luke decided to visit Dodge and Lilith. He also decided to bring coffee and pastries.

The older man at the door gave him a once-over before saying anything. "Is this a special Sunday delivery? Have we been enrolled in the Breakfast of the Month Club?"

"I'm a friend of Jillian Knight."

"Oh, well, why didn't ya just say so." He held open the door. "Come on in."

Breakfast proved to be unnecessary. Jillian Knight was the secret password.

"I'm Dodge and the corpse over there is my wife, Lilith. You'll have to get in her face if you want her to hear ya."

He took the drink holder and bakery bag from Luke.

Lilith smiled and waved Luke over. "I can hear fine out of one ear. Have a seat."

"Thank you." Luke sat on the sofa next to her rocking chair.

"Did I hear you correctly? You know Jillian."

"Yes."

"Am I supposed to share this with you two?" Dodge asked over a mouthful of Danish, a to-go cup in his other hand.

"What's your name, young man?" Lilith ignored her husband.

"Luke."

All remaining color drained from her already pasty-white face. "Downstairs, Dodge. Now."

"'Please.' Have you ever thought of asking instead of ordering me around?"

"Go!"

Dodge grumbled a few expletives that included "old bat" and "bossy cow" as he grabbed the bag and headed toward the stairs.

"Dr. Jones," she said.

He squinted, with an easy nod. "How—"

"She told me everything. Not on purpose at first. Dodge led her to believe that I'm deaf. I let her think it because I wanted to hear the most romantic love story I'd ever heard ... and I could tell she needed to share it, relive it. I think I love you too, but don't tell old grumpy. Or do." She winked.

Luke smiled as something inside of him lit up. Jessica didn't let him go. "Do you know where she is?"

"Oh my goodness. You've tracked her down ... you've come to save her like her knight in shining armor with your trusty steed." She pressed her hand to her chest, tears pooled in her eyes. "That's so ... incredibly romantic. I'm right, aren't I?"

"I don't actually have any official armor and I took a plane and rental car."

Lilith leaned forward and rested her hand on his. With one blink her tears released. Her eyes and smile filled with hope.

He returned a small smile. "Yes. I'm here for her."

She sighed, sitting back in her chair. "You're the one. You know that, right? AJ needed her, but you ... she's always needed you. She must need you now more than ever."

Her words pained him. They confirmed what he already knew—Jessica needed him. But he couldn't find her.

"Do you know where she is or have you heard from her?"

"No. Sorry. Greta Housby, their neighbor across the street, she said Jillian was taking some time for herself. But I assume you've talked to Jackson so you probably already knew that."

"Yes. However, she left her phone at home and Jackson doesn't know where she is so we have no way of contacting her. I'm worried about her. I understand she..." saying it was harder than thinking it "...loved him. So she has to be grieving."

"This must be terribly hard on you? How did you find her? How did you know she's alive?"

"I saw her at a hotel in Houston."

"Oh my. You must have thought you were seeing a ghost."

Luke nodded. "I think I should fly to Portland. I don't want to be insensitive to his family. I'm sure they're still devastated. But maybe she said something to them after the funeral."

Lilith shook her head. "That's not possible."

"Why do you say that?"

"Because she wasn't at the funeral."

"W-what are you talking about? Jackson said she went to the funeral."

"No. She wasn't there. I think his family was a little disappointed, but they understood. AJ left treatment to be with her. She was the last person who saw him alive. We all assumed she was worried about their reaction to her, but they weren't upset. She changed him and everyone saw it. In spite of the tumor, she made him a better man."

"If ... uh ... you'll excuse me. I really have to go." He tried to keep his fear in check. "Thank you for talking with me."

Lilith nodded. "Luke?"

"Yes?" He zipped his jacket.

"I don't know where you'll find her, or what mindset she'll have, but I know one thing with unwavering certainty —that girl loves you like no woman has ever loved a man in the history of the world. She called you her heart. And I believed her."

The words to describe his love for Jessica didn't exist. He smiled in spite of the pain.

Knight

FOREVER DIDN'T COME in a text; it came with a knock at the door. It involved the woman he loved leaping into his arms and kissing him with fervor. Ryn, however, texted Jackson.

Can you come over?

He didn't text her back, but within ten minutes he was at her front door.

Forever didn't have red swollen eyes that refused to make contact with his. He stepped inside. Ryn stared at him, just short of meeting his gaze. She drew in a shaky breath and held it, but she didn't say anything. It seemed as if her words were the only thing holding her together and if she spoke them, she would crumble to pieces at his feet.

"This is goodbye," he said.

She bit her quivering lip and nodded. Pain robbed her beautiful face, and she threw herself into his arms, but not in a forever way. He hugged her back so hard he feared feeling her ribs crack against his. In a matter of days, forever turned into never.

"Maddic h-hates me. I-I can't leave her. She won't … come. I-I love you so much, it feels like … like I'm dying inside. But s-she's my child. If I leave … it will be l-like she died." A broken sob ripped from her chest. "If you leave … it'll be like … you died."

He didn't know what to say. If he stayed he'd put her in danger. Luke's trip to Omaha opened the door for their past to find them. There was no way to stay and guarantee anyone's safety. He'd rather die than leave her, but he'd never be able to live with himself if something happened to her. She needed to come with him, soon, or he needed to get as far away from her as possible—completely dissociate himself from her life for her own safety.

Ryn fisted the back of his shirt, her tear-stained face buried in his neck. "Say something. Please."

"I'll come back."

She shook her head. "Don't say that unless you can

promise me." She cupped his neck and pressed her forehead to his. "Can you promise me you'll come back?"

Her tears dripped between them. He fisted her hair.

"Say it." She sniffled. "Promise me."

"I can't."

Jude would have said that moment—the heart-breaking dream-shattering moment—was the reason to never get emotionally involved.

Not Jackson.

He loved Ryn Middleton with something bigger than his heart. She dug deep and found his soul, and she would forever have a piece of it.

He kissed her, wanting her to be the last thing he ever tasted. He slid his hands up the back of her shirt, wanting her skin to be the last thing his hands ever felt.

"Stop." She turned her head to break their kiss. They stood as one, two bodies clutching each other, begging the world to not tear them apart.

"Let me be with you ... one last time. Let me make love to you," he whispered in her ear.

"I can't." Her body shook in his arms. "I can barely breathe. This hurts so *fucking* bad."

Ryn looked up at him. Her fingers feathered over his lips. He closed his eyes.

"Making love ... knowing it's the last time, would literally Stop. My. Heart."

Step One: Confess the mercy killing first.

Step Two: Wait for Ryn to acclimate to Jackson's ability to take another's life.

Step Three: Make her fall so deep in love with him that not even the assassin confession could drive her away.

Step Four: Be prepared to gently hold her in captivity

until she snaps out of her inevitable conniption fit because realistically there is no way Step Three would ever fly.

Step Five: Let her go.

"Okay." He swallowed every ounce of fucking reality and took a step back.

She hugged herself. He fisted his hands, hating that they would never touch her again. Then he opened the door.

"Jackson?"

He turned.

"Tell me to wait for you."

Forty. The stunning woman before him was forty. She survived years of abuse. Her best friend was a dog. Her daughter hated her. If only one person in the world deserved true happiness, it was Ryn. Waiting for a maybe, a complete shot in the dark, would only lead to more misery. He loved her too much.

A long, slow sigh deflated his lungs like life itself tried to escape his body. Lowering his chin to his chest, he refused to look at her. "Don't wait for me." He said his final words in a thick voice and closed the door.

CHAPTER THIRTY-ONE

Jackson needed to break something or someone. As if the universe heard his need, Luke's rental car was parked in one of the spots between the townhouses. He pulled into the garage and hopped out just as Luke got out and walked into the garage.

"Jess—"

"Inside." Jackson cut him off, leading him in the house. "Jillian has been gone too fucking long. I need to *exercise*. You know how to throw a punch, Jones? Or take one?" He inwardly smirked. That crawling-out-of-his-skin feeling wore on his last nerve. He needed to destroy something. Why not start with the reason for his leaving Ryn?

"I'm not going to fight you."

Jackson shrugged off his shirt and walked into his bedroom. "That's fine. All I really need is a body. I just need to feel the pain of my knuckles cracking against bone. You don't mind, do you? After all, you showed up and ruined my whole fucking life."

"Call Knox."

Jackson grabbed a pair of shorts then pulled at the

button to his jeans. "I did. Haven't heard back. He's a prick that does everything on his time."

"She wasn't at the funeral."

Jackson froze then inched his head up. "What the fuck did you just say?"

"I talked to Lilith. Jessica wasn't at the funeral."

Jackson pulled his phone from his pocket and called Knox again. Again, it went to voicemail. "Where the fuck is she?"

Next he texted him.

I'm coming for you, asshole.

Jackson grabbed a small bag and shoved a few items into it, including his computer and a thick wad of cash from his dresser drawer.

"Where are we going?"

"I'm going to get my sister. You're going home and I don't want to see you again. Are we clear?"

"I'm going with you or you're going to kill me. It's one or the other."

Jackson looked up from his bag. He didn't hate Luke. He hated that life. Luke brought it back.

"I'm tired of living without her."

Jackson nodded. With the fresh image of Ryn emotionally shattered in his arms, he knew how Luke felt, which meant it was best to put him out of his misery. "I can break your neck or I'm good with a knife too. Your choice."

Luke's temporary stay of execution came from a knock at the door. Jackson sighed, aggravation building to an all-time high as he came close to tearing the front door off its hinges. A lethal dose of adrenaline poisoned his bloodstream.

"Open up." Preston Iverson called from the opposite side of the storm door.

Jackson gave him no other response than a slow blink. Preston was nothing more than a tiny dick in a suit sucking air into his lungs that he wasn't worthy of breathing.

"Maddie visited me. She's a little distressed and a lot confused. Seems my dear Ryn has been sharing some things that she should not be sharing. I have this feeling you put her up to it."

Jackson gave him another slow blink.

Preston pressed a photo to the glass storm door. Jackson squinted, leaning forward a fraction. It was a photo of a barely recognizable Ryn with a lacerated lip, one eye swollen shut, and her cheek mottled in hues of blue and purple.

He met Preston's eyes. The little penis in a suit smirked then held open his suit coat to reveal the gun in his inside pocket.

"I'd let me in, jerk-off."

Christmas came early that year for Jackson Knight. He was wrong—the universe's answer to his desperate need was not Luke. It was Preston Iverson.

Jackson opened the storm door and stepped back as Preston came inside, pulling his gun from his inside pocket and pointing it at Jackson.

"You think you can fuck my wife's body and my daughter's mind and get away with it? You think you can just waltz into town with no fucking past and take what's mine?"

"What's going on?"

Preston looked at Luke, moving the gun back and forth between them. "I didn't know you had company. Who's this guy? Your lover?" He laughed. "Buttfuckers."

Jackson raised a single brow. "What are you going to do with our bodies after you shoot us?"

"I'm going to weight your asses down and dump you in the river."

Jackson nodded. "Is that a good spot? Is the river deep? Has it frozen over yet?"

Preston pointed the gun back at Jackson. "Why the fuck do you care?"

It happened in a blink, less than a blink. Jackson grabbed the gun out of Preston's hand like a magician pulling a rabbit out of a hat.

Preston's eyes widened as he held his hands up. "Take it easy. I wasn't really going to shoot you."

"You were." Jackson emptied the clip and tossed it left, then discarded the gun to the right. It skidded to a stop at Luke's feet.

Preston eyed both the gun and the clip as if he stood a chance of retrieving both.

"You're not going to shoot me?" Preston asked.

Jackson shook his head. "Sorry. I'm a bit more hands-on."

"What does that—fuck!"

Jackson started with Preston's nose, his knuckles relishing the feel of crushing bone. "I have a pressing need to attend to..." he landed a fist in his right eye, followed by his left, then a quick upper cut to his jaw that sent him crashing to the floor "...but after seeing that picture of Ryn, I think I can spare an extra sixty seconds to make sure you feel everything you ever did to her." Jackson bent down and grabbed his head, ramming it into his knee, busting out several teeth. Preston gasped and groaned. A click sounded bchind Jackson.

"That's enough." Luke pieced the gun back together

and held it at Jackson's back. "Let's just call the police before you kill him."

"You won't shoot me, Jones." Jackson broke several of Preston's ribs with his foot.

"Argh! Fuck!"

"Stop!" Luke demanded.

Jackson retrieved the photo of Ryn from Preston's pocket and handed it to Luke. "This is Ryn and this is Ryn's ex-husband." He grabbed Preston's arm and twisted it around his back until it snapped. The tortured animal's cries continued.

"He did that to her. If you need to pretend it's Jessica, then go ahead. Just keep looking at it and tell me when to stop and I'll stop."

Bone after bone broke. It really wasn't Jackson's MO to torture someone unless he needed information from them. Preston was an exception. Luke never said another word. Even after Jackson gave the final blow that ended Preston Iverson's life, Luke didn't move. He stared in silence at the photo.

Jackson turned, slightly winded, but also a bit more relaxed. He rested a hand on Luke's shoulder. "Good news, buddy. Thanks to our unexpected visitor, I do believe you're going to live."

He brushed past Luke, pulled on a shirt, and grabbed his bag. "Let it go, Jones. I can hear your thoughts. Look at the picture again. I didn't kill a man, I saved a woman."

On his way to the kitchen, Jackson snatched the picture from Luke's hands. They didn't move—he didn't move.

"Tell me, what would you do to save the woman you love?" He grabbed a Red Bull from the refrigerator and popped the top.

Peeling his gaze from the limp body, Luke focused on Jackson. "Anything."

Jackson nodded then took a swig, content with Luke's commitment to his sister. "I don't know where she is, but I know she would not have missed AJ's funeral. Knox isn't answering me."

"You think he has her?"

"No."

"Do you think he knows where she is?"

"Maybe."

"Then why do you think he's not answering you?"

"I don't think he has his phone. But someone does."

"So where are we going?"

Jackson grinned at Luke's *we* comment. "Are you willing to die for her?"

"Yes."

Jackson finished his Red Bull then tossed the can in the sink. "Last question and don't fucking hesitate. Just answer it."

Luke kept his unwavering gaze on Jackson.

"Are you willing to kill for her?"

"Yes." The darkness in Luke's eyes mirrored Jackson's. It was the need for revenge obliterating all conscience—all reason.

"Then let's go get her."

Luke seemed to snap out of the moment as Jackson grabbed the neck of Preston's shirt and coat then dragged him toward the back door, leaving a blood-smeared trail on the wood floor.

"What are you going to do with the body?"

"I got a tip that the bottom of the river is a good spot." He wasn't used to being the hitman and the cleanup crew, but Knox was MIA. "Don't step in the blood. Just ... don't move at all."

"We're going to San Francisco?" Luke asked after Jackson requested two tickets at the airport ticket counter.

"Yup."

"Is it safe for you to go home?"

"Nope."

"You think she's there?" Luke couldn't imagine making the trip to Nebraska only to discover Jessica was in San Francisco.

Jackson handed Luke back his ID and ticket. "I think the answer is there."

"Why not Portland?" Luke slung his bag over his shoulder and followed Jackson to security.

"Just a hunch."

As they waited to board the plane, Luke stared out the window at the planes taxiing down the runway. He'd heard many first-hand accounts of murder, including Jessica killing Four, but watching Jackson take the life of a human being right in front of him was a life-changing experience. Jackson was right. He didn't kill a man he hated, he saved the woman he loved.

Luke would do the same thing. He would die for Jessica. He would kill for her. He would end ten lives to save one, if that one was hers. It wasn't sane. It was far from rational. But it was love, and true walk-through-the-fucking-flames-of-hell love was unconditional and completely insane.

"Here we go." Jackson focused on the screen of his

phone then he held it in front of Luke. "I've been expecting this."

I have her. Don't be late this time.

"I knew that fucker had her."

Jackson shook his head. "It's not Knox, just his phone." He ran his hand through his hair then squeezed the back of his neck. "Fucking hell," he said on a sigh.

Luke gripped the arms of the chair. "What does that mean? 'Don't be late this time?'"

He stared at the message. "I don't know."

"Well think, goddammit!"

Jackson flinched as everyone around them quieted. Curious eyes put them center stage.

"Calm the fuck down," Jackson whispered. "The last thing we need is a scene."

"What were you late for before? This message is a reference to something. It's telling us exactly where she is."

"I-I don't know." He typed in a response.

"What the hell?"

"Shut it. I know what I'm doing."

I'm busy. Can we set something up for next week?

"This could backfire." Luke grimaced at the screen.

Jackson nodded. "It could."

His phone vibrated with another message.

I'm afraid she won't last that long.

"Jesus ..." Luke closed his eyes as Jackson typed another response.

She's stronger than you think. Next week. See you then.

"And now we wait." Jackson stood, slipping his phone into his pocket as they made the first boarding call.

"Wait? Are you crazy? For what?"

"Her location. If they really want me there, they'll give me more than 'don't be late this time.' But I'm fairly certain I've just pissed them off and they'll need to regroup before sending another message."

"What if she's here? Why are we getting on the plane? We should wait until they message you back."

Jackson shook his head. "This isn't about Jackson Knight. Jude Day was late for something, but he's never been to Omaha, so she isn't here."

CHAPTER THIRTY-TWO

The arctic splash brought Jillian and Knox back to life.

"Rise and shine. Aw, don't look so agitated. Think of it as a bath. You both stink."

Knox glared at Irene as she took a hit from her inhaler. It was his first time experiencing her favorite form of torture. The water wasn't just cold. It felt like a bucket from a snow-fed river high in the Rockies—a heart-stopping jolt. Jillian still preferred it to the heat or even worse, the talk of bringing Luke and Jackson to her immediate depth of Hell.

"Breakfast, darling?" She set a dish of canned dog food next to Knox.

His glare didn't falter.

"Suit yourself." She shrugged then stacked the four empty five-gallon buckets together and carried them up the stairs.

It must have taken her an hour to bring them downstairs, stopping for inhaler breaks. What did it say about Jillian and Knox's physical state that they didn't wake until she heaved them at their face?

"Your shoulder looks infected."

Jillian's gaze shifted to Knox's shoulder. "Yours probably is too, but I wouldn't know. Apparently only *I* need to be naked. I think she's a lesbian."

"I was married to her."

"Let me repeat, I think she's a lesbian."

"Maybe she's just trying to make you feel vulnerable, weak."

"Maybe. The lesbian scenario is more flattering."

Knox chuckled. "You *are* dying. You're in the hallucination phase, falling in love with your captor."

"Stockholm syndrome. It's not hallucinating and I don't have it."

He eased onto his side. Jillian winced then closed her eyes. Knox ate the dog food, just like Claire had done.

"She probably poisoned it."

He continued eating it. After wriggling and grunting back to sitting, brown food stuck to his face, he burped. "She didn't poison it. That's not her style."

"What's her style?"

"She's going to make you choose between saving your brother or Luke. Then she's going to make the one you saved kill himself, threatening to kill you if they don't. For the grand finale she's going to convince you this is all my fault so you kill me and of course ... you will die last."

His words settled like the credits at the end of a tragic movie.

"Maybe that's too predictable. She hates being predictable." Jillian smirked.

"She hates you more than me. She's going to make you kill me then she's going to watch Jackson torture and eventually kill you."

"And Luke?" Knox asked.

"Luke lives."

"Why?"

"Because she knows he's the only innocent one. She's not a monster by nature, Edgar did this to her. You did this to her. The only way she can justify her actions is if she feels like she's somehow ridding this world of sin. Luke walks. It's the only way."

A silent exchange took place. Jillian's meaning was in what she didn't say. Luke was to live ... no matter who had to die to make that happen. Everyone else was expendable.

"Now ... my father. How did he win my mother's heart?"

Knox chuckled. "He didn't."

Sunny

LIFE AND DEATH sent Sunny and Mickey in different directions, but their love never wavered. Knox committed to serving his country in exchange for an education. They had limited time together. She worked full-time at the hotel tending bar and even picked up extra shifts cleaning rooms.

Knox got his degree in four years, serving on the weekends. He took two consecutive tours after graduation. When he came home between tours he promised her "one more year." The broken promises went on for four more years as he worked his way up in rank. Letters, phone calls, and the rare stolen weekend kept them together. He knew she hated him, she said as much in her letters. But the moment he had her back in his arms the hate faded and their love came back as strong as ever.

"How did we get here?" she asked him. Her naked body draped over his. "You were going to marry me right after graduation. Football, long nights studying, and a dinky one-bedroom apartment off campus, remember?"

He kissed her head, relishing the feel of her flawless skin under his fingertips as he feathered them along her back. "I remember. Seems like a lifetime ago. My dad, your dad. I hated life, all of it except you."

"Mickey?"

"Hmm?"

"Why didn't you propose? You never even mentioned marriage again after the ... *accident*."

"What my father did to you was not an accident. I blamed myself. I still do."

She sat up, straddling his waist. Sunny was a beautiful girl. He knew it from the first day he saw her. However, the woman she'd become, as impossible as it seemed, was infinitely more stunning.

"Don't say that. It wasn't your fault."

"I shouldn't have ..."

"What? Invited me to your house? Made love to me that afternoon? What, Mickey?"

Sliding his hands up her legs and letting them settle on the subtle curve of her hips, he drew in a long breath. "I blamed myself for loving you. The smart, beautiful angel I knew would never have been with anyone who didn't love her. I didn't deserve you then and I don't ..."

Sunny shook her head, long auburn hair brushing over her breasts—breasts that only he had touched. His hands owned every inch of her body.

"You deserved me then and you deserve me now. There's no you and me, it's only us. It's always been us. How can you not see that? Six months. Your tour will end and *we* can officially begin. I want to be Mrs. Knox McGraw. I want to feel the flutter of the babies we'll make."

She pressed his hand to her stomach. "I want a life, Mickey, and I want it with you. I'm so tired of waiting to breathe."

"I want it too, baby. I want to give you everything you've ever wanted. If we're just patient, we can have the life we always dreamed of. I've been promoted again, and if I just commit to one more—"

"No!" She crawled off him and slipped on her robe, her hands fisting and cinching the sash as tight as it would go. "Not one more tour. Six months and not one day longer."

"You don't understand."

The life in her eyes vanished under a cloud of anger as she narrowed them. "Don't tell me I don't understand. I didn't go to college, but I'm far from stupid. My ability to 'understand' is perfectly fine. Not everything in life has to make sense, Mickey. *We* don't make sense. We never have, but we're the only thing in this crazy world that *feels* right. How can *you* be so stupid, so ... blind?"

Tears filled her eyes. He sat up, his methodic thoughts warring with his body's desire to grab her, kiss away her tears, and just *be* with her.

"Mickey..." her voice broke and so did the dam of tears "...*you* are everything I've ever wanted. *You* are the life I've always dreamed of. I don't want the money. I want time. I want forever now, not another broken promise."

"I know ... I really do, baby. But what about what I want?"

Sunny pressed her fist to her lips, holding back a sob, then she sniffled. "I'm sorry." She shook her head. "Somewhere over the past two decades I got the impression that you wanted *me*."

That cut deep. Knox tilted his head to the side. "I do want you, but—"

"No. No buts. No more waiting. No more promises. Six

more months, that's what we agreed on after all the broken promises that came before that. I want to be your forever, not your fool." She dressed, the same angry way she did the day his father died and *forever* changed for eternity. "Six months and not One. Day. Longer, Knox."

The door closed to the bedroom. Six months. Tangled in sheets that smelled like her, he had no doubt that he'd end his military career in six months.

One year later ...

THE HIGH THAT came from being promoted, the accolades, the praise, the prestige ... it numbed the pain of missing Sunny. Six months passed, but Knox knew he'd get her back. He'd show her that it was worth the wait ... that *he* was worth the wait. Another year wouldn't matter. What he didn't expect was a bombing that sent shrapnel into his chest, missing his heart by less than six millimeters. Four of his men died that day.

Knox was sent stateside to recover. He didn't want to worry Sunny, so he waited until he was discharged. As fate would have it, one of his former superiors, who left the military to take a job as a DEA agent, wanted to discuss Knox joining the DEA as well. Sunny would be ecstatic to hear of his new job opportunity. They could finally begin their forever—after a lot of groveling and sex. Lots of sex with Sunny.

"Sergeant Day." Knox held out his hand as Sergeant Day stood from the table, giving the waitress a polite nod as she squeezed behind his chair.

"It's Agent Day now, but tonight it's just Grant. How are you, Knox?" He nodded to the chair next to his.

Knox gritted his teeth, trying not to show the pain he was still in as he eased into the chair. "I'm good. Just thankful to be alive."

Grant nodded. "I hope you don't mind, my fiancée will be joining us. A month ago she bought tickets for tonight's symphony..." he looked at his watch "...which starts in ninety minutes. I forgot until she called me about a half-hour ago. She's only mildly pissed off. Anyway, I just wanted to chat with you, kind of get a feel for your plans. I think you'd make an amazing agent. You're smart, fearless—brutal when you need to be—and you have exemplary leadership skills, not to mention years of tactical training. From a hiring standpoint, it doesn't get any better than that."

"Are you officially offering me a job?"

Grant chuckled, taking a sip of his beer. "No. I'm not that guy, but I have some pull. I like to surround myself with men I can trust. We recently lost an agent. He left some pretty big shoes to fill, and when I found out you were heading stateside again, it felt like perfect timing. If you even think you might consider it, I'd love for you to talk with my superior. I've already put in a good word for you."

"Yes, I'm definitely interested. I have a lot of incentive to stay here now."

Grant's brows lifted a bit. "A woman?"

"*The* woman."

Grant grinned. "Even better. And speaking of ..." He stood, looking over Knox's shoulder. "There's the love of my life."

Knox stood and turned. *His* sparkling eyes, *his* long auburn hair, *his* Sunny. When their eyes met, she stopped, crashing into the invisible wall between the present and the past. Her pink cheeks drained to white as Grant hugged her, brushing her hair off her neck and pressing his lips to the soft skin that had belonged to Knox. Not even shrapnel in his chest hurt as much as seeing her for the first time ever in the arms of another man for the first time ever.

"Knox, I want you to meet my Sunny."

She was *not* his Sunny.

"Sunny, this is Knox McGraw. This guy is a goddamn hero. I had the pleasure of having him under my command for my final two years."

"Mr. McGraw." She held out her hand.

He didn't want to shake her hand. He wanted to smash his lips to hers, rip off her clothes, and sink into her until she remembered that there wasn't a 'you or me ... just an us.' Mr. McGraw? Who the fuck was that? Mickey. She called him Mickey.

"Sunny." The weak voice that spoke her name sounded foreign to his own ears. It was something he didn't recognize. It was *him* without *her*.

If there was a God he would have numbed the feeling of her hand in his, but he felt everything. Every touch. Every kiss. Every inch of her body in that one handshake.

"Grant?" She forced a smile.

He might not have noticed, but Knox did. Knox knew everything about that woman. Grant could spend eternity with her and he would not even come close to really knowing Knox's giggling angel.

"I-I need to use the ladies' room, if you'll excuse me for a few minutes."

"Sure." He kissed her cheek.

Knox clenched his teeth as Sunny's gaze stayed fixed to his.

She turned, weaving her way through the tables, her

long white dress flowing behind her.

"I'm going to take off so you two can enjoy your evening."

Grant held out his hand. "So you'll consider coming in for an interview?"

Knox shook his hand, harder than necessary. "Of course."

He traced Sunny's path, stopping at the door of the women's lounge as an older woman came out.

She smiled and nodded at him. He slipped inside. Teary eyes reflected in the mirror. He tore his gaze from hers and checked for anyone else. After he confirmed they were alone, he locked the door.

Sunny turned, mascara bled down her cheeks. "Mickey—"

"Shut up." He took two steps. "Just shut up." Palming the back of her head, he smashed his lips to hers.

She clawed his shirt, pulling him closer, their tongues desperate to reunite. He didn't let her go. He couldn't, not even when her soft moans turned into sobs. Sunny belonged to him. If he had to kiss the life out of her to prove it, to remind her ... he would.

"St-stop!" Sunny fought to push him away. "I can't." She wiped her hands over her black-stained cheeks.

"I'm sorry. I'm so fucking sorry. I messed up. I should have stayed, but I'm here now and I'm not going back."

She shook her head. "It doesn't matter. It's too late."

He cradled her face, bending down a breath away from her lips. "Bullshit! It's not too late. How ... how are you even with him? When did this happen?"

"A few days short of six months ago," she said, her tone bitter, her words daggers to his heart. "I woke up alone. I pulled out the picture of you I kept under my pillow and I said, 'Fuck you, Mickey' as I tore it to pieces, the way you did to my heart. That night, I met Grant at the hotel bar."

He closed his eyes, resting his forehead on hers. "I'm so fucking sorry. I'll do whatever it takes to make this right. I'll spend the rest of my life proving how much I love you. You belong to me. I belong to you. It's *us*. You said it yourself."

"It's too late."

He rolled his forehead against hers. "No. It's never too late."

"It is."

"I love you, Sunny. I'll love you forever. Just—"

She rested her hands on his. Curling her fingers into his, she peeled them from her cheeks, pulling back just enough to meet his eyes.

"Mickey, I'll love your forever too."

A spark of hope ignited in his chest, bringing his heart back from the dead.

"But ... it's too late."

"Sunny, stop saying—"

"I'm pregnant."

Knight

"She wouldn't have married my father had she not been pregnant."

Knox shrugged. "I know that's not what you want to believe, but I had to believe it. It's the only thing that kept me from swallowing the bullet of a .45 caliber."

"So that's it? She was pregnant with me and Jude. She chose my father because you chose your career. You took the job with the DEA and worked side-by-side with the man who took your life. Isn't life a cruel bitch?"

"That it is." He smirked. "The truth? Love is forever, yet waits for no one. He had her hand in marriage and her babies ... but I had her heart. Always."

"Is that why you raped her daughter?"

"Before Jude channeled his natural born killer instinct, he was her ... all her. But you ... you were both. Not just in the way you look, but your personality. It's your dad one day and your mom the next. It's just always been a constant reminder that they shared something that should have been mine. She was supposed to have my babies."

He laughed. "I fucking hated you for showing weakness. It was your mother's compassion showing through." He shook his head. "I didn't want to see it. I didn't want to see her in you because she was my greatest weakness."

Jillian closed her eyes. His words stole her past, leaving a void. Maybe it was better to feel nothing about everything than to harbor the anger.

"Something changed. You treated me like shit during my training, but what you did after the kidnapping ... that was different. That was so much more. Why?" Jillian, *Jessica,* needed to make sense of something. Knox's story crushed her in so many ways.

"She stayed." He closed his eyes.

Jillian hated the door he opened, the one that made her see him as a human. A man in love with a woman. A broken soul. She knew that feeling. That wasn't allowed. There could be no empathy for the man who raped her. Life was a cruel bitch because in that moment a grain-of-sand-on-the-beach part of her heart felt something for the monster, and it wasn't hate. Maybe only another monster who had done some horrifically regrettable things, too, could feel it.

CHAPTER THIRTY-THREE

JACKSON SURVIVED the trip to San Francisco without hearing a word from Luke. It gave him time to contemplate the identity of the man who would step off the plane. As the moist air dampened his lungs upon exiting the airport, he realized the duality no longer existed. The line between his past and present disappeared. Jackson was Jude and Jude was Jackson.

"If you want to go home, I have a few errands to run. I can pick you up later."

Luke squinted. "Don't give me that shit."

"If you end up dead, don't blame me."

"I'll keep that in mind ... when I'm dead."

They took a series of buses weaving them through the city then walked for several blocks.

"What is this?" Luke asked.

"It's where I hide my bones." Jackson tipped over an old bench and dug into the brush and dirt atop a hill in Golden Gate Park.

"Bones?"

"It's a dog reference since I'm digging in the dirt. You have a dog, so I thought you'd get it. Apparently not."

"If you need money—"

"Nope." Jackson kept digging.

"A tracking device for Jess?"

He grinned. "So you think she needs one too? Well, that's something we agree on."

"No. I'm just trying to figure out why the hell you're digging for 'bones' when we need to find out where they've taken her!"

"I know where she's at."

"What?"

Jackson clenched his fingers around a strap and tugged, unearthing a duffle bag.

"Answer me? Where? How do you know?"

He wiped the caked-on mud off the bag. "When we landed, I received a text."

"Well, why the hell didn't you say something? What did the text say?"

"Nothing."

"You received a text that said nothing? That doesn't make sense."

"It was an image."

Jackson refilled the hole and returned the bench to its original spot.

"Well show me the fucking image."

"No." He pulled himself up and sat on the bench, dusting off his pants.

"No? Did you just tell me no?"

Jackson glanced up and sighed. The weight of the image nearly broke him, and he was unbreakable. It would destroy Luke.

"I think you should let me handle this, Preston? The

285

man I killed? I saw the shock on your face. I tasted your disgust. And that was a simple case of taking out the trash. But you felt sorry for him. It was very humane of you."

Luke fisted the collar of Jackson's shirt and pulled him close. "Listen to me," he gritted. "I don't know what you *think* you tasted, but it wasn't disgust. That wife-beating asshole got what he deserved. But I don't want to talk about him. I want you to show. Me. The. Goddamn. Picture!"

"No." Jackson silently applauded Luke's ballsiness, even if it was futile.

"If she dies, it's on you, asshole."

Jackson clenched his teeth. "How do you figure?"

"You killed AJ. You let her leave alone, and then you failed to ask the right questions to the right people. But we don't have time to argue about how I feel about you, so just show me the fucking picture."

Grabbing the bag, he stood, keeping his eyes fixed to Luke's, daring him to blink. He pulled out his phone and clicked on the screen, holding it six inches from Luke's face.

The life drained from his face and his eyes as he swallowed back what had to be the contents of his stomach. It was the *humane* reaction. But he had to give him credit, he didn't blink, not even a flinch.

LUKE COULDN'T BREATHE. Anger was a normal human emotion, but what he felt went beyond anger. He wanted to kill.

It hurt less when she was dead. Seeing her naked, emaciated, bound, bruised, and bleeding ... it was beyond his worst imaginable nightmare. If her sunken eyes hadn't been focused on the camera, he wouldn't have believed she was alive.

"Go home. I'm going to get her. She lives or nobody lives."

"I'm going."

Jackson chuckled, hoisting the bag over his shoulder and walking away from Luke. "You are ... of that I'm certain. Just not with me. When you see her, don't mention my name."

"Wait." His legs came back to life.

"Go straight home, Jones ... and when you get there, don't fight it. They're going to take you and you're going to let them. They're waiting for you ... I'm certain of it."

"What do you mean don't—" By the time he made it to the rotted-out railroad tie steps, Jackson was gone. He vanished, not leaving a footprint or swaying leaf in his wake.

The enigmatic personality of Jessica's brother left little room for trust, but she did. She trusted him with her life. If he couldn't trust Jude, he had to trust Jessica and listen to the whisper of her voice in his head telling him to go straight home.

Home became the proverbial lion's den, but he rushed there just the same. His need to get to Jessica trumped all other emotions, all sense of self-preservation. He typed in his elevator code three times. It didn't make the doors open any quicker, but it did garner a few prolonged stares from the people waiting behind him.

He stepped into the elevator and waited with teetering patience for the other people to select their floors.

"Dr. Jones, haven't seen you in a while." Kim, a former patient who moved into the building shortly after he did, batted her fake lashes at him as she flipped her curly black locks over her shoulder.

"Been busy." He tapped his foot, watching the red numbers climb like a train making a grueling vertical ascent up a mountain.

"You seeing anyone?"

His gaze flicked to hers as his agitation fought to stay hidden. She had no way of knowing he wasn't certain he'd be alive in twenty-four hours, much less able to schedule a date with a former patient. Did she know how unethical it was anyway? Did he?

"I am."

"Oh ... okay." She smiled and waved as the doors opened to her floor.

The next floor was his. He played out every scenario in his head. Someone waited in his apartment. There was no way to prepare to be kidnapped. That's what Jude meant. It had to be. He wanted to kill them. How could he submit to someone he wanted to kill?

He took a deep breath as the doors opened. His neighbor who lived across the hall exited first. The couple next to him stepped back to let him out, or so he thought.

"This isn't your floor, Dr. Jones. The man wearing a baseball cap low to his face shoved the head of a gun into Luke's back, tapping on his kidney.

The woman in a pink hoodie and sunglasses sprayed a white foaming substance on the security camera then stepped behind Luke, opposite of the man. "Sweet dreams, Dr. Jones."

THE UPSIDES to being part of G.A.I.L. were few, but the corrupt side that had infiltrated the humanitarian efforts over the years offered deep pockets filled with drug money. No amount of checks and balances kept any official or unofficial organization free from "justifiable" theft. Some of the vehicles sat in there for over a decade, never being liquidated to feed the homeless or serve any other type of Robin Hood altruism.

On that particular day, Jackson gave thanks for the warehouse in Oakland and the security code to get inside, where he had his choice of vehicles confiscated from deceased drug lords and their circle of thugs.

Jillian would have spent forever deciding which one to take, spewing off useless statistics about zero to sixty acceleration and engine size. Jackson jumped in the first one he came to, hot-wired it, and sped out of the building. She would give him crap about the black Escalade and how only pimps drove black Escalades. At least, he hoped she'd give him crap about it. The other alternative was too unbearable to consider.

The fucking dog food. Had he not seen it in the corner of the picture Jillian's captor sent him, he wouldn't have known her location. Four died and so did Trigger. Someone had a sadistic sense of humor. Whoever had her knew about her past and how torturous it would be to take her back to that tiny basement in San Diego. It all clicked, including the message about not being late. It was someone who knew he waited for his father before going to rescue Jessica and Claire. Those few hours cost Claire her life and Jessica her sanity.

Jude was used to attacking with the element of surprise. Jackson didn't have that. They knew he was on his way. It was possible that he'd been followed, but not a guarantee. He'd mazed his way through San Francisco, including a trip to Wal Mart where he bleached his hair blond and changed his clothes in the bathroom, making sure all his tattoos were covered.

He didn't have the luxury of time, maybe hours or even a day, but nothing beyond that. Waiting was as much of a gamble as ransacking the joint with guns loaded. A few blocks from ground zero he stopped for fuel—several containers of gasoline and a case of Red Bull.

The blackout-tinted windows allowed him privacy in his parking spot under a tree one street over from the old shack, but still allowing him to have eyes on anyone coming and going from the single-car detached garage or front door. After the sun set, he painted all his exposed skin black and emptied the duffel bag arsenal of guns, grenades, and knives on the seat next to him, taking his time to organize them one at a time in his weapons vest and belt.

Then he waited for a sign.

THE END WAS EMINENT. Jillian didn't know what the end would be, but she felt it approaching in Irene's constant checking-up on them and her nervous demeanor that required constant puffs from her inhaler.

"How did you end up marrying her?"

The corners of Knox's mouth turned up a fraction. "It was a marriage of convenience, just short of being an actual arranged marriage. Edgar tired of watching me spiral downhill over the years, pining after a woman I would never have. He knew I had two addictions: Sunny and power. So he fed the latter. His loss led to the creation of G.A.I.L., but my knowledge, connections, and ability to command is what made it what it is today."

"Corrupt."

"Effective."

"How did he know about you and my mom?"

"Love is reckless. We were reckless. The addiction went both ways, like needing just one hit of nicotine. It would have been easier had I not taken the job with Grant. But I did and that kept Sunny in my life, it kept our paths crossing. It was never sex, just years dotted with stolen moments, like that night in the ladies' room—holiday and birthday parties, picnics. It was the most necessary torture. I lived for just one kiss, just one whisper of love. Edgar witnessed one of those reckless, stolen moments. He didn't tell Grant, but from that moment forward he was determined to make sure it never happened again. Irene was a gift of sorts, a promise that someday I would control G.A.I.L. Our skills complimented each other."

He laughed.

"How's that for love? She was smart, but insecure. All I had to do was smile and she willingly said yes to anything. She began to feel restless with the job Edgar gave her. What she didn't understand was that no one left G.A.I.L, at least not voluntarily and not usually alive. He needed her controlled, and who better to do it than the ultimate control freak? I married her. I tamed her."

"And then?"

"And then she found letters I wrote to Sunny, but never sent."

"Why didn't you send them?"

"I wrote them after she married your father. I valued my life too much to send them. Anyway, Edgar assured Irene I wasn't having an affair. Of course she didn't believe him, so she had me followed for months. I didn't get anywhere near Sunny, but those letters ... they wrecked Irene. Edgar insisted she be evaluated for mental stability. You know better than anyone that G.A.I.L can't risk its members suffering from any sort of mental illness. They recommended she take an anti-depressant. She didn't do so well on it. Her paranoia just got worse."

"But it was justified, so it wasn't really paranoia."

He nodded. "But Edgar and I were the only ones who knew it."

"So you had her committed?"

"No. Edgar wouldn't do that. He thought we needed her. She was good at what she did. We managed her the best we could ... for years. But the only thing more unpredictable—more destructive—than Irene was Sunny and Mickey. I waited seventeen years to be with the woman I'd loved my whole life. Seventeen years I watched her raise a family with another man, but never once did my love for her waver. After someone close to her saw us kissing, she decided to tell Grant about us. She told him she was going to leave him after you and Jude started college."

"No."

"It was true. For a breath of time ... it was true. Grant and I had it out, nearly killed each other over one woman. I hated him for taking the family that should have been mine, and he hated me for taking her heart. In the end, neither of us won. You were kidnapped and on the verge of never being the same again. So she stayed for you. She chose him over me. She chose you over me. She completely broke *us*."

Grant and Sunny Day stayed together for their daughter. Of course her mom defended Cathy's affair. She'd had her own affair. It didn't matter that it wasn't sex. In some ways it would be more forgivable had it just been her body, but it wasn't. Her mother gave her heart—her true love—to Knox, not her father. She gave Grant two children, a home, and time. Wasted time.

"You hated her."

"I loved her."

"You raped me after she decided to stay with him ... for me. You *hated* her."

Knox stared at the floor, or the past, or maybe into the void in his heart that used to house his soul. Jillian's words caused him pain. She could see it. He deserved it.

The creak of the door at the top of the stairs brought them out of the past. Irene probably heard everything and was ready to add her take on the unfolding of history.

"Everyone decent?" She called from the top of the stairs, punctuating her question with a cackle. "Of course you're not. Oh well, it's time to welcome our prestigious guest."

Jillian held her breath, not sure if she would ever breathe again.

"Look at me," Knox said through gritted teeth. Gone was the scorned lover. He was all commanding. "Don't you fucking lose it. What she's going to do will hurt worse than anything I ever did to you. Do you understand?"

For the first time they got to see Irene's accomplices as they escorted a new prisoner down the stairs. She didn't recognize them. Maybe because she wasn't looking at them.

CHAPTER THIRTY-FOUR

THEIR EYES LOCKED. His eyelids heavy from being drugged didn't hide the pain. She'd only seen that look once before. It was when she told him about the rape. Even the man whose superpower was masking his reaction had his breaking point, his kryptonite. Luke's was Jessica.

"Set him there." Irene nodded toward Knox. "It will be easier to play truth or dare if they can make eye contact. Besides, she's been pissing herself longer, no need to subject *anyone* to that."

Irene wanted to humiliate her. Jillian didn't need a mirror to know that she had never looked or smelled worse. That certainty, mixed with the probability that Luke hated her for leaving him, was too much to bear. Her gaze drifted to the bow and arrows on the table. Maybe Irene would extend some godly mercy and put Jillian out of her misery.

"Feel free to chat amongst yourselves. I'll be back in the morning."

Creak. Thunk. The door closed, leaving a painful silence. Jillian never noticed it with Knox. They talked. They didn't talk. It made no difference. Had it not been for her mom, there wouldn't have been anything to say. But with Luke ... there was everything to say.

She felt both of their gazes on her. Every second that passed without either one of them saying a word was a gift. Maybe they would both just go to sleep and maybe, just maybe, her body would surrender to death in the middle of the night.

"Jessica, look at me." Luke made the first stab to her heart. Just the sound of his broken voice brought her one breath closer to death.

She didn't look at Luke. Her gaze moved to Knox. Hell had officially risen to meet her. It was the only explanation for her finding courage from her enemy to look at the man who had *unequivocally* loved her.

Knox didn't say anything, no "keep your shit together" or "don't let her break you." Instead, he closed his eyes and rested his head against the wall—a proverbial leaving the room.

"I have to know ..." That voice.

She drew in a shallow breath—all her lungs would allow—then she gave him her eyes. It hurt so bad.

"Were you pregnant?"

"Luke ..." she whispered, her face contorted with pain from that one forgotten detail. "How did you—"

"The receipt to the pregnancy test was in your purse. God ... please just tell me."

The downside to dying without a moment's notice was all the unfinished details: the half-carton of milk in the refrigerator, the unclaimed dry cleaning, and the unshared pregnancy test results.

Day

LAKE LOST HER LEG. A week after the accident, just like the doctor predicted, infection took over, threatening her life. It was awful, but it paled in comparison to the real concern: she'd been in a coma since the accident.

The Jones family rallied; it was all they knew. Tom and Felicity refused to leave the hospital until she came out of her coma, so their other children took turns staying in Tahoe to keep the B&Bs up and running. Luke went back to work half-days and spent the other half at the hospital. On a good day he managed to convince his parents to go back to his place for a shower and a decent meal.

Jessica did what she did best—gave of herself unconditionally. She couldn't cook, but she could order food, deliver it, hold hands, get coffee, share hugs, and listen to their deepest fears while reassuring them that Lake would come back to them.

Both she and Luke devoted their non-working hours to his family. The almost wedding never came up, partly because it didn't matter in the light of a life and death situation and partly because they saw little of each other. Usually one or the other would stay at the hospital to be there for his parents, who seemed to be losing hope a little more each day.

Liam and Lara came for two days and stayed at a hotel a block from the hospital. Jessica suspected Felicity made the suggestion because shortly after they arrived, his parents insisted she and Luke take a couple days for themselves.

They drove home in silence. It had become the norm. There wasn't much to say about the unimaginable.

"I'm going to shower," Luke said as soon as they walked through the doorway to the bedroom. His voice was filled with defeat. He paused in front of the closet where her wedding dress hung from the door. A few moments later his shoulders and head sagged as he continued to the bathroom.

She wanted to follow him.

She wanted to touch him.

She wanted to make the past week disappear, even if just for one night. But the tragic situation left her just as confused and paralyzed as everyone else—just going through the motions of life. The problem was, at the moment, she didn't know what those motions were.

The dress. She had to get rid of the dress. Grabbing it, she took it into the spare bedroom and shoved it in the closet. When she returned, Luke was out of the shower, towel around his waist, bent over the sink brushing his teeth.

Jessica walked into the closet and slid out of her jeans then pulled off her shirt. As she reached behind to unfasten her bra, his hands met hers. She stilled, feeling the heat of his body behind her. Luke pinched the straps, unhooking her bra. His lips brushed her shoulder. Her eyes leadened from his touch. She relaxed her arms, letting her bra fall to the floor.

"Beautiful," he whispered over her skin as his hands slid along her waist, up her ribs, stopping on her breasts.

Her breath quickened, desperate for more of his touch. It was gentle, too gentle. Covering his hands with hers, she squeezed until he followed her lead.

"Yes," she moaned, arching her back into his touch. "Harder." He squeezed and tugged her breasts harder. "Oh. God. Yes." His right hand slid down her stomach, making her ragged breaths come quicker. The numbness of the previous week vanished under his touch. A pulsing pain—need—converged between her legs.

"Tell me you want me."

Her eyes rolled back in her head as his hand slid under her panties. The pad of his finger brushed over her clitoris.

"I want you."

"Tell me you *need* me." He slid his finger a little further, teasing her slick entrance.

"I need you ... so bad."

Biting her shoulder, he slid his finger all the way in as she moaned.

A breath later his hand disappeared, leaving her feeling wobbly and drunk with need. She turned toward him and took his hand, guiding it to his mouth. He sucked her arousal from his finger then she pulled it from his mouth and wrapped her lips around it. His blue eyes faded to black as she sucked his finger.

With a simple tug, she pulled the towel from his waist. Pressing her palms to his bare chest, she walked forward as he retreated a step at a time until the back of his legs hit the bed. The moment she wrapped her hand around his erection, he kissed her. It wasn't soft or patient. It was angry and laced with pain. He pulled her onto the bed and rolled on top of her. His mouth assaulted hers, and she welcomed the raw need.

The only thing she wanted her broken, shell of a man to do was control her because he needed it. She saw it in his eyes. Lake's accident robbed everyone of their sense of control. In the midst of their fucked-up world, she could give him this even if it would be gone in the morning.

Luke pinned her wrists above her head with one hand and shoved her right knee toward her chest as he sank into her. Then he fucked her, fucked the world, fucked the unfairness of life. Amid all the anger, the physical need, and blinding emotions, he made love to her. It's the only way he knew how to be with her—complete, unconditional, earth-shattering love. When it was over, he collapsed onto her, buried his face into her neck ... and he cried.

Control never lasted. Eventually the illusion of time, the pull of gravity, and catastrophic events reminded everyone of their mortality and their utter insignificance in the great big world. Life was nothing more than one long blink. Here today. Gone tomorrow.

"I CAN'T DO THIS."

Jessica opened her eyes, unable to remember when he stopped crying. Her mind shut out the rest of the world and her body became a safe harbor for Luke to let go of everything.

"What can't you do?"

He rolled to his side, taking her with him. At some point his touch became an extension of her own flesh.

"I can't watch her die." His soul bled into his red eyes.

Her hands clenched his hair like his words did to her heart. "Then don't." She released his hair and traced the lines of his face as he closed his eyes. "Watch her live."

He opened his eyes, brows drawn tightly.

"She's strong, so much stronger than anyone can imagine. I know you and your family don't see it, but I do. I recognize that strength. I know you think I'm a fighter, but I'm nothing compared to her. She's healing ... just be patient and let her body heal. When she wakes up you'll be here to help heal her heart."

"It's going to break her."

Jessica shook her head. "Ben's death and her leg ... it will crush her, but it won't completely break her. You won't let that happen." She kissed him. "And if I'm wrong, if it breaks her ... we'll love every single piece of her."

He smiled. "Those were my words to you."

"You have a way with words."

"I have a way with you."

Jessica shoved him onto his back, covering his body with hers. Capturing his bottom lip, she dragged it through her teeth, baring a sly grin. They'd come so far, so far she'd slit her wrists before drawing a drop of blood from his beautiful skin.

"I don't want you to have *a* way with me." She sat up and so did he. Lifting her hips, she inched onto him, both of their breaths catching, waiting, begging time to stop. "I want you to have *your* way with me."

And he did.

They banned all clothing and interaction with the outside world for the rest of the weekend, with the exception of Luke's phone which they agreed he would only answer if it was his family calling, but they never called.

LAKE'S CONDITION didn't change over the next two weeks. Jessica believed with everything inside her that Lake would live. Luke took her optimism and fed it to his parents every day, just enough to keep them going. They needed him, his medical background, his patience, and his reassurance. He became their lifeline. Although Jessica missed the *them* they had for one amazing weekend, she knew his family *needed* him.

Early on a Friday morning, she drummed her fingers on the keys of her computer at work without actually pressing any of them. Between the almost-wedding and Lake's accident, she'd fallen behind with work. Her concentration was nonexistent and the fact that it was Friday made it even more difficult to feel motivated.

Her impatient tapping brought up her calendar. She sighed at all the appointments and dates that lead up to the wedding. The following weekend was blocked out for "honeymoon in?" because Luke wanted to surprise her. She never did ask where he'd planned on taking her. It didn't matter.

She stared at her P day. H days were for hair appointments. C days were for teaching self-defense classes. V days were for taking Jones to the vet. But P day was the start of her period, which according to her calendar was ten days late.

"Shit." Having children with Luke was high on her life's priorities, but the timing was all wrong. She wanted to share that kind of news when he could jump up and down, squealing like a little girl. That would never happen, but the visual brought a smile to her face and that smile felt good.

Bugging out of work early, Jessica stopped by the drug store for a pregnancy test. If it was positive she wasn't going to tell Luke until Lake came out of her coma, if it was negative she wasn't going to tell him at all. That's why she took the test, all three of them, in the bathroom at the drug store. No evidence needed to go home with her.

Pee wait.

Pee wait.

Pee wait.

No more pee. No more tests. She waited.

CHAPTER THIRTY-FIVE

KNIGHT

"THEY WERE ALL NEGATIVE."

Luke blinked, diverting his gaze away from hers. She couldn't read him. Disappointment? Relief?

"I would not have left with your child. I wouldn't have taken something like that away from you."

"But you did."

She flinched. Another stab to her heart.

"I'm sorry. I didn't mean it to sound that way."

"I deserve it."

"You don't."

"I left, but more than that, I left you behind. I didn't have to, I chose to."

"I understand."

"I don't want you to understand." Anger flared in her words, sending tears of regret down her face. "I don't want your compassion, I don't want your forgiveness, I don't want your ..." She bit her lips together.

"My what? My love?"

She nodded, squeezing her eyes shut.

"That's not your choice. It's mine. Don't ever ask me to not love you."

"I'm so tired," she whispered, keeping her eyes closed.

"Jess?" His voice cracked.

More tears found their way out.

"I need you to live."

"I'm already dead. You know that. I saw you ... at my funeral."

Day

THREE NEGATIVE TESTS.

In spite of the timing being all wrong, a pang of disappointment settled in Jessica's heart. It was ridiculous since they weren't trying to get pregnant. She called him anyway, but it went to voicemail. Just the sound of his voice took away some of the sadness.

"Hey, babe. I'm on my way home. Work feels like too much ... work." She laughed. "Just wanted to hear your voice. I guess your stuffy recording will have to suffice. Just a little blue today. Call me if you want me to meet you at the hospital later. Love you."

She stuck her key in the door, but it was unlocked. Easing it open, she breathed a sigh of relief upon spotting Jude.

"I wasn't aware you had a key." She closed the door and kissed Jones on the head. "What's up with the stony expression? Who died?"

"Your parents," Knox said, stepping into view.

"What?" Their joke was cruel and not welcomed after her shitty day.

"Jess." Jude moved toward her, tears pooling in his eyes.

Her life slowed, digging its heels into the ground like she could change the direction of fate before the official impact. Knox's mouth moved. She heard nothing but the thundering echo of her heart, the pounding of doom.

"No. No. NO!" She collapsed into Jude's arms.

It was too much—Claire, Ben, Lake, her parents. No one could endure so much tragedy. It wasn't fair.

"We have to go."

"Go?"

"You know the drill. I'm sorry. You have to make a decision and make it fast."

She pulled away from Jude, glaring at Knox. "A decision?"

"Dad didn't show up to work today. Knox found them at home. Someone shot them."

"No. Stop talking."

"You're next. This life is over," Knox said.

She shook her head.

Jude grabbed her face. "Look at me."

Jessica didn't want to look at him. She didn't want to see him pretend to be strong. He had as many tears running down his face as she did.

"This is what Dad trained us to do."

"He ... they trained us to defend, to ..."

"Stay alive."

"No."

"Yes. It's over. We have to leave. Fin de journée."

Their dad spoke fluent French, thanks to his French mother. He made it seem like a vacation. He joked about moving to Paris if they ever had to flee for their safety. Their temporary life a side effect of his job. After Gail Brighton died, everything and everyone become temporary.

"Luke ..."

"He can come, but he will be dead in his family's eyes." Knox didn't look at her. He seemed to be dealing with his own emotions, a rare side to him that she'd never seen before. Maybe because he was too busy being a monster.

"What? No. I can't. Lake is in a coma. It would kill his parents. They're barely hanging on right now."

"Just you then?"

"No. I can't leave him. He's my ... my ..." A sob ripped from her chest, obliterating her heart. "He's my everything."

Knox looked at his watch. "Every second we wait, puts you one step closer to death."

"Choose, Jess."

"Jude ... I can't. Please don't ..." She fisted his shirt. "Don't ask me to do this. I can't."

"You can. You have to. If you stay, you'll die and he and his family could too. I won't let you stay. I'll fucking drag your ass out of here before I'll let you stay."

"I have to say goodbye. I have to leave him a note. I have to—"

Knox grabbed her purse and tossed it on the counter. "You walk away with the clothes on your back. That's it."

"Let's go." Jude wrapped his arm around her, leading her to the door.

She turned, tearing out of his hold, and hugged Jones. "I love you. Tell Daddy I love him too. Take care of him, Jones." She lowered her voice to a whisper. "Tell him I'm so very sorry."

Jessica took one last look around. "I feel ... numb ... lifeless ... dead."

"You'll be dead by morning." Knox led the way.

Jessica followed, resisting temptation to look back. She could never look back again.

Knight

"Why suicide?"

Jillian looked at Knox, his eyes shut, jaw slack.

"It was the only way. Two unrelated murders would have raised too much suspicion. Suicide confirmed by a paid-off coroner was believable. Tragic, but believable." She coughed.

"Jesus, Jess ..." Luke homed in on the light splattering of blood that landed on her legs.

"My throat is raw. No ... no more talking."

She closed her eyes, swallowing the metallic taste back down. He said no more, at least not in the dungeon.

It didn't take long for her dreams to play. The closer she came to dying, the more vivid her dreams became. In her dreams he spoke to her with love. It was Jones standing guard over the most precious little baby cooing in a white crib. Luke's smile reached his ears. His lips mouthed, "I've never been so happy." The camera in her dream panned out, but the person standing on the other side of the crib wasn't Jessica. It was the completely put-together woman Jessica always knew he'd end up with, the one he deserved. Her hands were snow white, not a drop of blood had they ever taken from another human.

"Oh my ... this is not good."

"Jessica! Goddammit! Stop it!"

Irene. Luke.

Her eyes fought to open. Her teeth chattered. Voices echoed. Jillian was tired or dead. "Is it over? Am I dead?" she whispered. She imagined a light. People talked about a light. Maybe there wasn't a light where she was going.

"There she is." Irene's fucked-up face came to focus first. In her hands was an empty five-gallon bucket. "I fear we're losing you. Five gallons of ice water on your naked body and not so much as a flinch."

"Leave her the fuck alone."

"Luke ..."

"I'm here, baby."

"She's fine."

Knox.

"She's not fine."

"Baby?" Irene cackled. "I'm pretty sure once you decided to fuck your sister's physical therapist, you lost the right to call her baby. What was her name? Charlie?"

"Shut up, Irene."

She glared at Knox. "Tape his mouth shut. It's not his turn to speak."

The guy in the baseball cap placed duct tape over Knox's mouth. Knox gave him the you-will-die look. Jessica had seen it many times before.

"Now where were we? Oh yes, I think we were talking about Charlie."

Jillian met Luke's eyes. She hated the guilt in them.

"It just so happens ... I have some pictures of her." Irene opened one of three large envelopes that sat on the table. She held up a photo of a woman with dark chin-length hair and blue eyes. "She's quite attractive. Wouldn't you agree?"

Jillian stared at the photo, but didn't say anything.

"I asked you a question. Do you need incentive to answer?" Irene nodded at her sidekick.

He pulled out a long knife, but not just any knife. It was identical to the one Four used on Claire. He took a step toward Luke.

"She's stunning," Jillian answered, looking at Luke.

His face tensed with pain.

Irene gave the cutter a nod and he stepped away from Luke. "What about this one?" She held up a photo of Luke and Charlie holding hands while taking Jones for a walk. They were both smiling. "How does he look?"

Jillian watched the guy with the knife. His hand squeezed the handle.

"Happy," Jillian said.

One rule: Luke lives.

"He does, doesn't he? How do you think he looks here?"

She held up a photo of Luke kissing Charlie by the pier, his hands tangled in her hair, hers fisting the back of his shirt.

"Answer me."

"Hungry."

Luke wouldn't look at her. It pissed her off. He had no reason to feel guilty, but the look on his face fed Irene's desire to continue with her mind-fuck games.

"Hungry? I like that. I'd say from how far his tongue is in her mouth that he's starving. Were you starving, Dr. Jones? Did your mouth devour every inch of her body?"

"I didn't fuck her."

Irene nodded to cutter guy, but he didn't move toward Luke, he came at Jillian.

"No. No! Stop!" Luke's eyes widened, his body wriggling against the restraints.

Jillian looked only at Luke. She didn't flinch, not even a blink as the sharp tip of the knife pierced her skin on the swell of her breast. Blood oozed from the one-inch cut.

Luke squeezed his eyes shut, twisting his neck to the side. She needed him to stay focused on her. She needed him to know that she was okay, the pain was hers to take and if it meant saving him, she could take absolutely *anything*.

"Dr. Jones, clearly you're new to this game and not as experienced as Jessica—Jillian—whatever the hell you want to call her. Let's review the rules: Don't speak unless spoken to. Answer only the question asked. And be honest." Irene *tsked*. "If you don't master the rules soon, I fear your *baby* won't last long. Understood?"

He nodded.

"I can't hear you."

The cutter stepped toward Jillian again.

"Yes."

"That's better. Now ... sadly I don't have any more photos of you and Charlie, but I do believe she flew out to Houston to be with you. Am I right?"

"Yes."

"Now you're getting the hang of it. Next question. I know my dear ex-husband spoiled your plans, but if my sources were correct, she was on her way to the hotel where you were staying. True?"

"Yes," he answered through gritted teeth.

"Were you two going to share a room?"

He did it again ... he diverted his eyes. Jillian silently begged him to not look away, to not give Irene anymore control.

"Yes."

"And were you going to fuck her?"

Tears filled his eyes.

Jillian didn't want him to answer, not for her, for him. She'd let them cut her ... forty-four times if necessary to take away Luke's pain.

"Look at her when you say it. It's the only way she'll know you're telling her the truth."

He met Jillian's eyes, a single tear rolled down his cheek. "Yes."

Irene faced Jillian. "How does that make you feel? And don't lie. I'll know if you're lying."

She searched Luke's eyes for something more than pain and regret, but that's all she could see. "Empathetic."

Silence settled over the room as Irene studied Jillian, her eyes narrowed, lips twisted. "I can see that."

She turned and grabbed the other two envelopes, one in each hand as if she couldn't decide which one to open next. "Knox, sweetie pie, you're next."

He grunted as the guy tore the tape from his mouth.

"I know you taught physical torture techniques used to acquire information from less-than-cooperative people, but I've never found them to be near as effective as psychological torture. Physical scars heal. Emotional ones don't. Wouldn't you agree, Dr. Jones?"

Luke glared at her.

"That's fine. Don't answer that now. We'll revisit it later." She opened the envelope. "I had some stills taken from the video footage of the private training session you had with Jessica after her kidnapping."

"Irene ..."

"Knox ..." She leveled him with a stern glare. "First Sunny and then Jessica. You could have just hit me, or cut me, or physically done anything to me and I would have recovered. Those wounds would have healed, but instead you treated me like a whore not worthy of your time, your attention, your love. And then you snuck around with a married woman. Do you know how humiliating that was for me? How *torturous* that was for me? And then this ..." she pulled out several large black and white photos and tossed them on the floor so everyone could see them.

Luke closed his eyes. Knox and Jillian did not. They were there. She wasn't showing them anything new.

"Sunny rejects you so ... what? You fuck her daughter. How did that work out for you? Oh, yeah ... you left on a gurney. And you ..." She shifted her attention to Jessica. "If he raped you, then why didn't you tell anyone? Is it because it wasn't rape? Is it because it was consensual? I watched the tape over and over and I saw what the two of you did to each other. I think you'd have a hard time convincing anyone that it wasn't some BDSM fetish the two of you have."

She bent down and grabbed one of the photos then fisted Luke's hair, jerking his head back until he opened his eyes. "See this? Count yourself lucky that you dodged this bullet. You just about married one sick bitch."

Jillian glared at Knox.

One rule: Luke lives.

She didn't want a single hair on his head injured and it infuriated her to see Knox sit there and allow Irene to touch Luke. She would have lunged at her, intent on further mangling her nose or sinking her teeth into Irene's carotid. Knox just sat there.

"This is upsetting. Wouldn't you agree, Dr. Jones? Could you really blame this man's wife—me—for completely losing it after seeing this video? Look at you. I can see it in your eyes. You want to fucking tear him apart. Does that make *you* a crazy person?"

"You blew up my house."

"SHUT UP! You cheated on me! I read the letters you wrote to Sunny. I saw this video." She shoved the photo in Knox's face. "You brought me to my knees. YOU made me crazy. You and fucking Edgar drugged me, thinking I just needed an antidepressant to 'chill out' about you and your goddamn wandering dick! Then you sent me to a mental institution for five. Long. Years. No visits, just divorce papers." She stepped back, her face taking on a blueish cast as she fumbled though the stuff on the table for her inhaler.

The man with the knife rested a hand on her shoulder. "I'm fine," she whispered after taking a puff. "I need some air." He helped her up the stairs, leaving photos of Knox raping Jessica scattered on the floor.

"If we make it out of here, I will kill you."

Knox chuckled at Luke's threat. "Get in line, buddy."

CHAPTER THIRTY-SIX

Jackson's phone lit up. He was seconds away from raining hell down on that shithole of a house. After seeing Luke bound and escorted inside the night before, he decided to wait until morning for a text and go in if they didn't send one.

A, B, or C?

"Fucking amateurs," he mumbled.
D, E, or FU? He typed back.

A it is then.

That's all he needed to sit back and wait a little longer. He wanted a better sign than letters in the alphabet. Luke would buy him time. Whoever had them was not affiliated with their parents' murder. Drug lords didn't have the time or patience to play games.

Bullet.

Head.

Done.

He assembled his long-range sniper rifle. Next he ordered a pizza, cracked the window, and waited. Forty minutes later his pizza arrived. Jackson paid for the pizza over the phone and left very specific instructions to set the pizza on the porch, ring the doorbell, and leave immediately. To his surprise, the guy did exactly as he requested.

Just as the delivery guy got back in his car, a woman came to the door. She tried to wave the delivery guy down, but he had already pulled away from the curb.

Jackson looked through his scope. He didn't recognized the woman, but with her pink hood pulled over her head and large sunglasses hiding most of her face, it would have been impossible for anyone to recognize her. However, her build was not Jessica's and that's all that mattered. He pulled the trigger and she went down.

"Un-fucking-believable." Through his scope he watched three cars pass by, one slowed in front of the house but then kept going. No wonder Four picked this neighborhood. A woman shot in the head, sprawled across the front porch steps, drew no more attention than a flattened squirrel in the street.

A few moments later, an arm reached out the door and grabbed her leg. Someone, fractionally smarter than the corpse, took cover while dragging the body back inside, confirmation there were at least two involved.

Once again, it was time to wait.

"She blew up your house?"

Knox laughed.

Luke didn't. He said nothing and looked at no one. Jillian wanted to say something to ease his mind, but she knew the worst was yet to come. That third envelope was hers. It had to be. There was little doubt that whatever was in it would destroy Luke forever. AJ would destroy Luke forever.

"Yes. It didn't make the news. Edgar made sure of it. But it was all we needed to put her away ... at least for a while."

"Where were you?"

He chuckled. "In the house. My office was in the basement. Irene didn't realize my office was also the bomb shelter. I fucking crapped my pants, but other than knocking over a gun cabinet and a few things on my desk, I walked away unscathed. You should have seen the look on her face when I showed up at G.A.I.L. The first words out of her mouth were, 'What are you doing here?' Code for 'how the hell are you still alive?' Had we lived in town she would have leveled three blocks. It was pretty amazing she didn't trigger San Andreas."

"Okay, kids. Change of plans." Irene marched down the stairs, her composure back intact. "Brother dearest doesn't want to join the party. So let's just get on with things. I'll deal with him later."

Jackson was close. Jillian knew it.

Irene picked up the remaining envelope while cutter guy cleaned Jillian's blood from the tip of his knife. "What's in the envelope, Dr. Jones?" She waved it in front of Luke. "And bear in mind, I don't like asking more than once."

"Pictures," Luke said.

"Yes, of course, but of whom?"

"Jessica."

Irene *tsked* a few times. "Now, I think someone with your background would realize how dangerous it is for you to think of her as Jessica. I think you will *need* to think of her as Jillian." She brushed away a few strands of hair from Luke's forehead. "You feel guilty about Charlie. Don't you?"

He glanced up, meeting Jillian's eyes.

"Well there really is no need. I can assure you, Dr. Jones. You've been a boy scout compared to your whore of an ex-fiancée." With the toe of her boot she slid one of the photos on the floor closer to Luke.

It made him furious with Knox, but he was about to see something that would make him furious with Jillian. She felt it in her gut.

"Who is this?" she asked Luke.

He stared at the photo of AJ in uniform, hand to his temple saluting someone. Jillian hadn't seen it before, but just the image of him took her breath away. Luke shifted his gaze to her.

"Aric ... I assume."

Jillian nodded like a silent introduction between her ex-lover and her dead lover.

"How messed-up is it that she gravitated toward someone in uniform after her experience with Edwin Harvey? Just ... on a scale of one to ten?"

Irene lost her name. She was straight up Psycho Bitch again.

Luke sighed. "Five."

Jillian narrowed her eyes a fraction. It stung that he thought it was messed-up at all. It hurt that he didn't trust her judgment.

"I would have said ten, but ... whatever." She pulled out

another picture.

Knox smirked, maybe at Irene or maybe at the absurdity of the whole situation.

"Oh ... this is one of my personal favorites."

It was Jillian getting the mail in her red boots, panties, and thread-bare tank top.

"Do you find her sexy?"

"Yes."

"Do you approve of her traipsing around outside looking like a whore?"

"She's not a—"

"Uh-uh ... it's a simple yes or no question."

"No." He didn't blink.

The man staring at her was Dr. Jones. She knew that look and his ability to ignore her over-the-top antics. However, his disapproval still pissed her off.

"God doesn't either," Irene mumbled, tossing the photo onto Luke's lap.

"Here they are on a motorcycle." She held up that photo of AJ driving, Jillian holding on tightly to his back. "Did you ever take Jessica for a motorcycle ride?"

"No."

"That's a shame. You really should have taken more interest in her hobbies. Then maybe she wouldn't have left you. Aw ... here's another good one." She held up a photo of AJ and Jillian next to his Jeep. Her arms and legs wrapped around his body as they kissed.

It was the day they left for Portland and she told AJ to kiss her like he fucked her. She could still taste his lips ... feel his tongue.

"How do they look together?"

Jillian clenched her jaw, but said nothing. It wasn't her turn to speak. Luke showed no reaction. His face still entirely Dr. Jones—neutral, professional, unattached.

"Desperate."

Irene turned, holding the photo closer to Jillian. "Were you desperate in this photo?"

"Yes." It was the truth.

"What about here?" She held up another picture, showing it only to Jillian.

There it was, the end. Jillian looked at the photo and then at Luke. When she blinked the tears came out, an apology to Luke for what he was about to see. Irene was right, psychological torture inflicted wounds far worse than anything physical.

"I love you."

Irene whipped her head around. "Dr. Jones. It's not your turn to speak."

Cutter guy unsheathed his knife.

"Stop! I'm sorry, I won't say it again!"

The tip of the blade punctured Jillian's skin along her temple, blood ran down the side of her face. Dr. Jones vanished. The man before her lost all composure as tears filled his red, angry eyes.

He had no idea how much she needed those three words.

"Say it again," Jillian whispered.

Luke shook his head.

"Say. It. Again."

He continued to shake his head. Irene's eyes flitted between them, enjoyment danced in her smile.

As psycho bitch turned to show the photo to Luke, Jillian let out a strangled sob. "Please..." more tears spilled over "...say it one more time." She needed to hear it because she knew it would be the last time he would ever say those three words to her.

Pain contorted his face as he continued to shake his head. "I love you." He squeezed his eyes shut as the knife carved a new valley in Jessica's skin above her shoulder blade.

She felt nothing but the resonance of Luke's words in her heart.

"Can you still say that?" Irene asked, showing Luke the photo of AJ fucking Jillian.

It was the day she took off on her motorcycle and he followed her to an abandoned dirt road atop a bluff overlooking the city. She was so angry with him for his venomous words. It was a turning point in their relationship. How could she not have known someone followed her ... took pictures of them? AJ stood with the door open, pants and briefs at his ankles. She sat sideways in the passenger's seat, legs spread wide to accommodate his body, her hands clawing his back, her brow tense, eyes closed, jaw slack.

Everything drained from Luke's body—his blood, his dignity, his past, his whole life.

Defeat.

It no longer mattered who lived and who died. Irene won. She ruined Sunny's precious daughter. She found Jillian's weak point and drove a dagger into it.

"Did you enjoy fucking AJ?" Irene asked Jillian, keeping her attention on Luke.

Cutter guy stepped closer to Luke.

"Yes," she said, her voice weak.

So much betrayal lived in Luke's eyes.

"Did you love AJ?"

The knife would hurt him less. Would Luke understand that?

It didn't matter because Jillian didn't want to deny her love for AJ. They shared something life-changing and saying otherwise would tarnish his memory.

"Your brother's antsy trigger finger just put a bullet in the head of my knife-wielding friend's girlfriend. He's ready to kill all of you. I wouldn't push him."

He jerked Luke's head back and pressed the tip to his carotid.

"Yes. I loved AJ."

Luke's eyes shut. A lone tear bled from his right eye.

Knox frowned. It was possible he felt Luke's pain, the kind that came from losing *the one*, the one that was supposed to be *forever*.

"Up." Irene nodded to her disgruntled accomplice.

He dragged Luke to his feet. Jillian used what little energy she had left to fight her restraints. "Where are you taking him?"

"Fishing."

"Luke!" Jillian screamed until more blood came up with a coughing fit. "He's ... he's ..." her voice died.

The door slammed shut.

"Yes. Jackson's going to kill him to save you." The resolution of Knox's words filled the air and buried her alive.

Jillian rolled to her side, the cold concrete pressed to her cheek.

Protocol.

Irene would use Luke as bait to get Jackson to surrender.

He wouldn't.

Never surrender.

Shoot one hostage to make a point and save ten more.

Jackson was selfish. He wanted Jillian alive at all costs. He'd take her broken and desolate as long as she was alive.

"While you were self-absorbed in your own dysfunctional life, one foot in G.A.I.L. one foot out, Jackson killed and he was good at it." Knox nodded. "Better than anyone. Everything has to be black or white. Gray is nothing more than hesitation. He's alive ... and so are you because he never hesitates."

CHAPTER THIRTY-SEVEN

"**J**ONES ... YOU SUICIDAL FUCKER." Jackson watched through his scope as Luke inched into the front yard.

No one else was in sight, yet there had to be another gun pointed at Luke's back.

Protocol.

Shoot the hostage. Always call their bluff and then attack.

"I warned you, Jones."

"Are you willing to die for her?"

"Yes."

The target didn't get any easier. Luke stood completely still, a red dot marked the spot where the bullet would end his life. Jackson took a slow breath. Claire's dead body flashed in his head.

"Let it go," he whispered. A bead of sweat rolled down his face.

Luke closed his eyes, a complete surrender.

"Are you willing to die for her?"

"Yes."

Jackson wiped the sweat from his brow with his arm

then repositioned, the laser finding its target again.

"Take the shot."

Jessica in her wedding dress.

"I'm just a girl with Luke. I know it sounds crazy, but I feel safe with him ... when we're not together I don't feel alive. It's like I'm holding my breath."

AJ.

"I need some time alone to figure out if I can forgive you, because right now what you did feels unforgivable."

Ryn.

"There's nothing about you I couldn't love ... if you just let me."

"Fuck!" Jackson pulled back, the rifle falling to his lap as he tried to catch his breath.

He tossed it aside and got out. With each step he felt his pulse thundering in every single vein. As he crossed the street he unfastened his vest and tossed it in the yard a few feet from Luke, followed by his weapons belt.

"Yea, though I walk through the valley of the shadow of death, I will fear no evil: for thou art with me; thy rod and thy staff they comfort me."

Luke opened his eyes. "Why?"

"I'd rather she love me in Hell than hate me on Earth."

"Move your arms and legs."

Jillian blinked. Cobwebs under the bottom stair came into focus.

"I beat you. I raped you. I sodomized you. I stole your innocence. But. You. Fucking. Survived. Move your arms and legs, goddammit."

She grunted and her arms moved, a lot.

"You don't have much time. Get yourself free. Kill or be killed."

Jillian rolled to her back and wriggled, tugged, and pulled in every direction. Weight loss plus daily drenching had loosened the duct tape. Her legs were still zip-tied but her wrists were not. Irene had to tape them to her sides in order to get the IV in.

"They're coming."

"I can't," she whispered.

"They're going to kill everyone. Do it for Luke. Do it for Jude. Do it for Claire."

Knox had always been ruthless with his motivation. Mentioning Claire was a low blow.

She freed one arm and then the other, ripping out the IV. She was too weak to break the ties around her ankles.

"Take out the guy first."

She glared at him, waiting for him to acknowledge that she was naked, bound at the ankles, battered, bleeding, and strong as a corpse.

"But Irene—" She coughed, not sure if he could hear her voice that was non-existent.

"No. The guy. She won't kill you. She doesn't have it in her, that's why he's here. He'll kill you. The arrows." He nodded to the table. "They're razor tips."

Jillian dragged her body along the concrete floor. Even using the arrow to cut the ties proved to be difficult. She had no strength. Once her legs were free, Knox nodded to the table. "Drink."

Jillian grabbed the half-empty bottle of water and drank it down, burning the whole way.

Just as she moved to help free Knox, footsteps neared the door.

He shook his head. "Leave me."

She hated him and the pictures were still on the floor to remind her why, but for a brief moment she felt the unwelcome emotion of sorrow. "You..." she swallowed, even whispering hurt "...confessed." Her reference was to his admitting that he raped her.

Knox shrugged. "When I see my angel, I want to be able to tell her I tried to right my wrongs. I'm sorry, Jessica."

The door opened. Jillian pulled herself to standing, three razor-tipped arrows fisted in her right hand. She held her head high and took slow, deep breaths to keep from passing out as she hid around the corner. Everything felt weak, including her pulse. She didn't know if she had the strength to kill him. Either way, she'd die trying.

"My eyes."

Jessica nodded.

Four blinks. Her target would be the fourth one to come down the stairs. Knowing where Irene fell in the lineup would have been nice, but she'd improvise. Her heart found some life, pumping blood to her extremities. Four blinks. Four people. Luke was alive.

He rounded the corner first, stopping when his eyes met the empty spot where she had been. Knox shook his head a fraction. Luke didn't speak. Irene shoved him, sending him to the floor before Jillian's absence came into her line of sight.

"Where the hell—"

Jackson saw Jillian first. His eyes made a quick scan of her body. The master at showing no emotion had murder in his dark eyes.

Knight met Day.

The gravity of her time in captivity mixed with AJ, Luke, Knox, and their parents—it was too much.

Life was too much.

Day faded into night ... into complete darkness.

———————

No more games.

No more trying to save everyone.

The photo of her made Jackson's stomach roil, guilt flared in his conscience seeing her standing there a mere skeleton—sunken eyes, bloodied flesh contrasting ghostly skin, her body shaking to the point he could almost hear her bones vibrating.

Life slowed to a crawl. Jessica's breath caught. Her eyes rolled back in her head as her withered body faded to the ground. If that was her last breath ... everyone would die.

Jackson didn't have to think. Jude was back. Instinct took over.

The guy with the guns was disarmed, a bullet in his brain in less than five seconds. The woman Jackson knew as Meredith Baker, his piano student who should have died in Omaha, lunged for her bow and arrows scattered by his sister's limp body.

Bang.

Blood from her head pooled around Jillian's hand. He stepped toward Luke and Knox then stopped, lifting his foot to see what he'd stepped on. His brows drew together, eyes narrowing as the image registered.

Knox McGraw raping Jessica.

The muscle in his jaw ticked like a bomb counting down. He drew his head up. Knox's eyes shifted from the picture to Jackson.

Bang.

Dropping the gun to the floor, he squatted down and retrieved a knife from his boot.

"Hurry," Luke said, keeping his eyes on Jessica.

Jackson cut him free.

Luke lunged for Jessica, feeling for a pulse. "Get an ambulance, now!"

Jackson sprinted past Luke as he pinched Jessica's nose and breathed into her mouth. He left his phone in the Escalade, which felt a million miles away because his sister. Wasn't. Breathing.

CHAPTER THIRTY-EIGHT

Luke sat in the waiting room. When the nurse asked his relationship to Jillian Knight, he didn't have an answer. The truth was, he didn't know Jillian Knight. Only family was allowed to see her. Jackson, he was her only family.

One year.

He was less than an hour away from marrying her and in one year he went from her everything to a nobody sitting in the waiting room—alone. The urge to call someone—Lake, his parents, Gabe—was miserably tempting, but Jackson said it wasn't safe to contact anyone.

The paramedics resuscitated her twice on the way to the hospital. Three hours in the ER and a blood transfusion later, they moved her to a room. When she woke they let Jackson in to see her.

Luke waited.

"She's going to be okay."

Luke stood as Jackson came through the doors. "I need to see her."

"She's ... not ready. Sorry."

"What do you mean she's not ready?"

"Whatever happened down in that basement, it messed her up."

"I'm a psychiatrist, if she needs to talk—"

Jackson rested a hand on his shoulder. "You're not her psychiatrist. I'm not sure you ever really were."

Luke took a step back, collapsing into the chair, resting his head in his hands.

"She was taken while on her way to AJ's funeral. Whether you like it or not, she loved him and now she needs time to grieve. I think she's grieving more than just him, but she won't talk to me either right now."

Dr. Jones understood. Luke hated it.

"For now they're trying to bring her back from severe dehydration and starvation. They might have someone come evaluate her later."

"For?"

Jackson curled his lips and looked at the ceiling a moment. "She doesn't have much desire to ..."

"To what?"

He met Luke's eyes again. "Live."

Luke couldn't speak. He never imagined a world without Jessica, and he certainly never imagined a world with her having no desire to be in it with him.

"I don't want to, but I have to drive back to San Francisco to deal with some stuff. The nurses know how to contact me. You can stay as long as you realize they won't give you any information on her. Or I can take you home."

"I'm staying."

Jackson nodded.

Luke waited and watched for the changing of the guard. By eleven that night he didn't recognize any of the nurses, which meant they wouldn't recognize him.

He first grabbed some coffee from the cafeteria then strolled past the nurses' station like he knew exactly where he was going, even though he didn't know her room number.

"Excuse me, sir. Are you here to see someone?"

He smiled. "Yes. I'm here to see Jillian Knight."

"Are you family?"

"Yes. I'm Jackson, her brother."

The nurse typed Jillian's name into the computer. "Okay, Mr. Knight. She's probably sleeping, but we don't have any visitation restriction for family so you're more than welcome to sit with her."

"Thanks ... oh and one of the nurses from the previous shift mentioned they might move her to a different room. Did they?"

The nurse looked at the screen. "I'm not sure. It says here that she's in room 420."

Luke shrugged. "They must have decided to leave her then. Have a good night."

He stood at her door for few moments to gain something resembling composure. Then he eased it open.

Curled into fetal position on her side, she hugged her pillow instead of lying on it, her arms desperate to hold something, to feel secure. He wanted to be that for her.

After setting the coffee on the windowsill, he pulled the chair as close to her bed as possible. Easing into it, he leaned forward, resting his arms on his legs. His hands ached to touch her, but he didn't.

Instead, he just looked at her. In many ways she was unrecognizable as the woman he knew. Her blond hair, frail body, and a road map of new scars. But the longer he let his eyes settle on her, the more he recognized—the tiny mole below her left earlobe and the way her nose occasionally twitched on its own, the way her eyelashes curled on her cheeks, the rhythm of her breath, and her hands. He knew their strength but never felt anything but love from their touch.

She jumped.

He froze.

But her eyes never opened. She made a soft noise, a heartbreaking noise. Then she silently sobbed into the pillow, but she wasn't awake. He fisted his hand against his mouth, fighting every urge to touch her.

She jumped again, her eyes flew open, her breath held captive in her chest. Luke refused to move, his own breath waiting for her to do or say something. Her eyes filled with tears and she buried her face in the pillow, her tiny body shaking. He'd give his own life to take away her pain, but it wasn't his to take anymore.

His hand moved toward hers. Letting just the tip of his finger touch the end of hers. He inched it up with the softest touch. Then, like a young child, she grabbed his finger and squeezed. Luke felt her touch in the deepest depths of his heart.

Red eyes met his, her chin quivering. She sat up and reached for him with both arms.

"D-don't say any-anything. J-just hold m-me. Please."

Luke lay next to her and held her in absolute reverence. She slid one of her legs between his as if she couldn't get close enough. Words congested his throat. There was so much to say, but he stayed silent. He would do anything to keep her in his arms. His own tears fell to the white sheets. How could she be so close yet an ocean away?

Life. Was. Cruel.

Jillian woke wrapped in Luke's arms. There were no words to describe how it felt. There were also no words to describe the shame, the guilt, the regret, the pain. That pain challenged every breath she took.

In a blink he would be gone again. That was the reality of her life. She had to be Jillian Knight to stay alive, and maybe that's why she questioned her desire to live. Being Jillian Knight was bearable with AJ Monaghan. Without him Jillian Knight felt like a waste of space and time.

"Five minutes." Her voice was still scratchy, but at least she had one.

Luke pulled back a fraction to look at her, his brows drawn tight.

"For five minutes let's talk about anything but us. Let me feel normalcy again for just five minutes."

He continued to just look at her, then he nodded.

"How's Jones?"

"Still big."

She laughed. It felt good, like the smallest spark of life. When the silence enveloped them again, she realized he had nothing to ask her and why would he? He didn't know Jillian Knight.

"How about Lake?"

He chuckled. That felt good to her too. "She's contumacious."

"So, awesome?"

"Pretty much."

"And her leg?"

"She's hell-bent on having one made to be able to wear high heels."

"You should make that happen for her."

"You think?"

She rested her cheek on his chest and fiddled with the collar of his shirt. "Absolutely. She's a young woman. Just because she lost her leg doesn't mean she should lose her right to feel sexy."

He hummed, maybe in agreement or just in thought.

"So ... you sell Lascivio." He nudged the line, a very awkward line.

"I did. I'm not sure what I do now. But, yes, and I was good at it."

"Doesn't surprise me."

"That I sold it or that I was good at it?"

"Both."

"Still have my GTO?"

"I do still have my GTO."

"I miss it."

"Lucky GTO."

She pulled away and forced a smile as she sat up. Pain shot through her shoulder from where the arrow landed, as well as the stitches on her chest and shoulder. Nothing hurt as much as Luke thinking she didn't miss him.

"I didn't mean—"

"It's fine. I think our five minutes are up." She touched her fingers to her throat.

"Can I get you some water?"

She nodded.

"I'll be right back."

Jackson's voice echoed a few seconds before he peeked into her room. "Are you decent?"

"Fuck you."

"So you're feeling better." He smiled, but it wasn't genuine. It said, "I'm playing casual but I have bad news."

"I feel like shit. But let's be honest, I was bound naked in front of everyone. Not that I had much to begin with, but my dignity is gone."

"Luke's getting you water."

"As long as he doesn't throw it on me."

"What do you mean?"

"Nothing." She rested her head back against the pillow and closed her eyes. "Tell me the bad news."

"What makes you think I have bad news?"

"Nine months in the womb together. Just spill it."

"Irene was Knox's ex-wife."

"Yesterday's news."

"She was Meredith Baker too."

Jillian opened one eye. "Seriously?"

Jackson nodded.

"Is this where you give me the lecture about how you should have ignored me and followed your instincts to kill her?"

"That's on the docket, but not today. She spent five years in a mental institution."

"I know."

"Her two accomplices were in there with her. She got out on her own—good behavior and passing the discharge evaluation—but she helped them escape after she got out. In exchange for their freedom, they agreed to help her carry out her revenge."

"What were they in for?"

"He killed his two younger brothers when he was sixteen ... with his bare hands. Blamed it on his ADD meds. She killed her boss after he wouldn't give her a raise."

"Anything else?"

"Yes."

She opened both eyes. He acted weird, even for him.

"It's about Mom and Dad."

"I ... I already know."

"I don't think you do."

"Mom had an affair of sorts with Knox."

"Yeah, I knew."

Her head jutted forward. "You knew?"

He nodded. "I saw them kissing at a fundraiser our senior year of high school."

"And you didn't tell me?"

"I tried. The day you told me about the trip you planned with Claire I was going to tell you, but I decided to wait until you got back home, but then ..."

"But what? She died and I went insane? That doesn't explain *never* telling me."

"You built your dreams on them, their relationship, their marriage. At what point was I supposed to obliterate your dreams?"

"That's what is was ... all those years. You held something inside. I always knew you weren't telling me something. And the women ... I dreamed big, but my God ... you had no dreams at all. It was Mom. That's why you hated women so much."

"I didn't hate women."

"You fucked Irene and then taught her piano lessons without a clue that your dick had ever been in her."

"I didn't."

"You did. In a bar. That's my point." Jillian coughed, pressing her finger to her neck again.

"It's history. That's not what I want to tell you anyway. I no longer give a shit about the affair, their marriage, or any of it. They're dead. Knox is dead."

"You killed him?"

"I saw ..."

"What?"

"Nothing. Let me just say this, okay?"

She nodded once.

"Knox said Mom and Dad were murdered. They suspected Dad's cover had been compromised, but they couldn't prove it for sure."

"Yes ..."

"I had someone at G.A.I.L. pull all of Irene's phone records, emails, texts ... everything since she was released from the mental institution. She started a rumor that went viral through not only G.A.I.L. but the DEA about threats being made against Dad. Several days after it started she texted Amanda and Robbie."

"Who are Amanda and Robbie?"

"They were the couple she sprung from the mental institution. She sent them Mom and Dad's address and step-by-step instructions on breaking the security code. She also wired them fifty grand each from G.A.I.L. and hid it under travel expenses—miscellaneous trips, jet fuel, and pilots that were never actually purchased."

"She went back to working with G.A.I.L. after being locked up for five years?"

"No. But when the brains behind the intel and security leaves, she takes all the secrets with her. She could break into G.A.I.L.'s computer system with her eyes shut."

Jillian shook her head. "I don't understand why you're telling me all this. I don't understand the point."

Jackson sighed. She hated it because it sounded like a sympathy sigh.

"You do understand, you just don't want to hear it."

"No." Denial was the only thing she had left to hold on to.

"I'm sorry. We didn't know."

"We didn't know? Are you kidding me? You and Knox show up and ruin my whole fucking life. I leave *everything,* fake my death, watch the man I love mourn over my grave and you're *sorry*? I was in just as much danger leaving as I would have been staying. The only person coming after us knew who and where we were. Do you see how fucked up this is? How could neither one of you have done your fucking research before destroying my life? You left nothing behind, but I did!" She coughed, a little blood coming up again.

"What's going on?" Luke asked, carrying a tray with water, ice, and something resembling a smoothie.

Jillian glared at Jackson. "Leave."

"I'm sorry."

"I'm not ready for your apology ... for any of it." She didn't say AJ's name, but Jackson's mercy killing had not slipped her mind. It would never slip her mind.

"I died yesterday ... when you weren't breathing. I died. I may make mistakes and act impulsively, but I do it because I love you. When you had the fairytale in your head of Mom and Dad's 'perfect' life, I had nothing but you. When you met Luke, I had nothing but you. But yesterday—in the ambulance—I simply had nothing. So hate me. I'll fucking take it every single day because it means you're alive. I don't need your love. I just ... I just need you."

Jillian clenched her teeth, blinking back her tears. In so many ways the greatest love story of her life was not with Luke or AJ ... it was with Jackson. *He* was the constant in her life. His love defined unconditional. Someday she would tell him ... *someday.*

Jackson left.

CHAPTER THIRTY-NINE

"**W**HEN DID she stop giving you IV fluids?"

Jillian heard Luke's voice, but it was still Jackson's words claiming her every thought.

"It had to have been days ago. They're going to keep you here for several days to replenish lost fluids and electrolytes. They're kind of important to keep your heart beating and kidneys working properly. Your hand and shoulder were infected too. They're treating it with antibiotics."

"K," she whispered.

"Did you hear anything I said?"

She stared at the water and smoothie he set on the tray in front of her.

"I'll take that as a no."

"Sorry." She met his eyes.

"Don't." He sat in the chair next to her bed. "I need you to promise me something."

It felt impossible to promise Luke anything. Their life together was nothing more than broken promises—shattered dreams.

"Don't ever apologize to me."

"Luke …"

"I mean it."

She didn't respond. It was best left hanging in the air. It was an impossible request.

"I need you to do something for me," she said.

"Anything."

"I need you to go home."

The pain of her words reflected on his face, but she wouldn't apologize. He didn't want her to do that.

Luke shook his head. "I can't. You'll disappear. I can't lose you again."

She gave him a sad smile. "You haven't really found me yet."

His eyes searched hers. Only Luke would understand the complexity of her statement.

"I didn't have to leave. Last year? I. Didn't. Have. To. Leave. Irene was responsible for my parents' deaths. It wasn't related to my father's job."

Anger. Luke's features hardened. She understood.

She swiped the tears that fell to her cheeks. "But here's the thing … I did leave. And a lifetime happened in that year. I don't have to be Jillian Knight anymore, but I don't feel like Jessica Day. I just feel lost and angry, and the pain is … *unbearable*. AJ is dead and you're alive, right here, and yet … I'm grieving the loss of both of you."

If she recognized one thing, it was when the man before her fought with the desire to be Luke and the need to be Dr. Jones.

Dr. Jones pulled Luke out of the chair. Luke blinked back his tears. Dr. Jones smiled and brushed the back of his hand against her cheek, catching her tears. Then the doctor and the man she'd love for a million lifetimes walked to the door.

"Jessica?" He didn't turn and for that she was grateful, because she was a breath away from begging him to stay even if it would eventually destroy them.

"Yes?"

"Are we over?"

She clenched her fist next to her heart and swallowed back a sob. "We'll never be over."

THREE DAYS.

They were the longest three days with nothing but her thoughts and grief. Jillian swallowed her stubborn pride and called Jackson to come get her from the hospital when her doctor gave her the OK to go home.

"You wearing that gown home or would you like some clothes." Jackson stood in the doorway holding up a bag.

She walked over to him, her bare ass peeking out of her hospital gown. "I think my skin will reject clothes..." she grabbed the bag "...but I'll give it a go." Lifting on her toes, she planted a kiss on his cheek. "I know you don't need it, but my love ... you have it."

He returned a sad smile.

"Jujube, you were the first boy I ever loved."

His smile grew.

Jillian stepped into the bathroom to dress. "Where do we stand with G.A.I.L.?"

"We don't."

"What does that mean?"

"Our parents died and so did their killers. We don't work for the DEA or any other government agency ... hell, we barely exist. They've 'cleaned up' the situation from the past couple of weeks. I said we wanted out."

"Cleaned up? I didn't want that place cleaned up."

"Don't worry. It's been burned to the ground. I requested a park be put in its spot."

"Did I mention I love you?"

"Yes."

"Though I still don't understand. Nobody leaves G.A.I.L."

"We do. Knox is dead. Someone will fill his shoes, but we're out."

Jillian peeked around the corner. "You're serious?"

"Dead."

"So now what?"

"Now we decide who we want to be. Live within the law and ... I don't know."

"Can you live within the law?"

Jackson smirked. "I can manage."

"No killing."

"I know. I've checked everyone off my wish list anyway."

"You had a 'killing' wish list?"

"I guess 'wish' sounds a bit self-indulgent. It was more like a to-do list."

"And you're done?" She stood in front of him.

"I'm done."

"Let's go then."

THEY HEADED BACK to San Francisco with their freedom. Like all freedom, it was tainted with blood and unimaginable loss.

"Where am I taking you?" Jackson asked.

"The airport."

"Portland?"

"Yes."

"Will you be home for Christmas?"

She shrugged. "Where's home?"

"I think you know."

She did, but home had changed. Like her freedom, it, too, was tainted.

"Where are you going?"

He grinned. "Home."

"She's a good home."

"She's the best home."

Jackson dropped Jillian off at the airport.

"Choose it." He held out two envelopes. One said Day, the other said Knight.

"What's this?"

"It's G.A.I.L's parting gift. How are you going to get on a plane without any identification or money?"

"Good point."

"Pick."

She needed more time, but maybe time wouldn't make the decision any easier. Pulling the envelope from his right hand, she smiled. "New Year's in Omaha?"

"Omaha."

A CAB TOOK her to Willamette National Cemetery. She had no idea where he was, but it felt like part of her journey to find him. Bundled in a coat and gloves under a cloud-covered sky, she took her time searching. Every headstone had a story, some far more tragic than anything in her life.

Then he appeared.

Aric J Monaghan

She touched her gloved hand to her lips as her eyes filled with tears. "Hey, Aric James." She squatted down, tracing the writing engraved into the granite. The days of guarding her emotions were over. The only way to move forward was to water his grave with her tears.

"The napkin ... God ... the napkin. I should hate you so much ... but I don't. I forgive you. I know ... you're probably not sorry, but you should be." Biting her lips, she swallowed hard. Her heart thundered in her chest as if it felt his nearness.

"I never wanted to love you, until I did. Then for a perfectly beautiful moment in time I didn't want to love anybody but you."

She dropped to her knees. "Do you miss me as much as I miss you? Because I do, I miss you every day." Closing her eyes, she let the tears flow and welcomed the pain. It would forever remind her of the love.

"I don't know if I'll ever truly find my path again, but if I do, you'll always be my favorite detour."

"Jillian?"

She turned. Wiping her cheeks, she stood. "Hi."

AJ's parents gave her sympathetic smiles.

"You should have told us you were coming to Portland." Char hugged her.

"I'm leaving tonight. It's just a day trip."

"How are you? We've been so worried about you." Char stepped back, wrapping her arm around Jim.

"About that ... I can't tell you how horrible I feel about missing the funeral."

Char's eyes shifted to the cuts and bruises. "You look ... what happened?"

"I ... I fell into a bit of bad luck on my way to the funeral."

"A car accident or something?" Jim asked.

"Yeah, something like that," she mumbled the last part. "I've been in the hospital."

"Oh my God ... we had no idea." Char reached for Jillian's hand and squeezed it. "You look terribly thin and fragile."

She nodded at Char. "I'm going to be fine. I just ... needed to talk to him."

They looked past her to AJ's grave. "We come every day, but if you need some more time alone we can come back."

"No. I've said..." she batted away a few more tears, drawing in a breath of courage "...all there's left to say."

She turned around one last time. "Goodbye, Aric James Monaghan," she whispered.

CHAPTER FORTY

THE LADY at the gate took her ticket before she boarded the plane home.

"Enjoy your flight, Miss Day."

Jessica nodded. "Thank you."

At every corner, happiness eluded her. Then when it was right there, she still felt undeserving. Luke was at the hospital, he held her, she saw the depths of the love in his eyes, but ... there were still so many buts.

A hotel would have been the smart choice, but at nearly midnight Jessica found herself at Luke's door instead. She wasn't sure why or what she expected.

The door opened, sucking the breath from her lungs.

Luke answered in a pair of lounge pants and a white T-shirt. He squinted against the light, rubbing his sleepy eyes. "Hi," he said in a raspy voice.

"Hi. I ... I just..." she shook her head "...don't know why I'm here."

Luke opened the door wider. "Do you want to come in while you figure it out?"

The instant she stepped inside, Jones trotted down the hall toward her carrying her red hoodie in his mouth.

"Hi, Jonesy." She hugged him, tears stinging her eyes. "I missed you so much." When she released him, he picked up the hoodie and retreated to the guest bedroom, content with her return.

"When did you get out of the hospital?"

Jessica hugged herself, feeling like a stranger in what used to be her home too.

"This morning."

"How do you feel?"

She took a deep breath then released it slowly. "Like I'm going to live."

"I'm glad." His eyes inspected her.

She chuckled, hugging herself. "Me too."

An uncomfortable silence settled between them.

"Where are you staying?"

"Oh ... I ..."

He closed his eyes and sighed. "I don't know how to navigate this. You're welcome to stay here. You know that, right?"

"I don't ... I don't know anything anymore. I didn't even know if you would be alone tonight."

He flinched.

"I'm not being cruel, or at least I'm not trying to be. The day I died, I gave up my right to walk uninvited into your home. I gave up the right to know what you're doing and whom you're with."

"I'm here, with Jones."

"I wanted you to move on. Not for me or any sort of guilt. I just wanted you to be happy. That day in the closet, you promised me you would."

He lifted his shoulders. "I tried, but then I saw a ghost."

Jessica wanted to tell him everything, but she couldn't. Not yet. AJ still lived in her heart and sharing that time with Luke would require her to let AJ go completely. When she opened herself up to Luke, he would flow into every inch of her heart and take everything. That was the only way she could be with him.

Everything.

Forever.

"Can I stay? For tonight?"

"Stay as long as you want." He turned and walked toward the bedroom. "The sheets in the guest room are clean, unless Jones has been on the bed. Sleep wherever you feel comfortable sleeping."

After saying goodbye to AJ, there was nothing she wanted more than a warm body next to hers. She followed him down the hall. He turned into the master bedroom, and she continued to the guest room.

Having nothing but the clothes on her back, she stripped down to her undergarments and slid under the sheets. "Get up here, Jonesy."

He lumbered onto the bed, taking up most of it. She threw an arm and leg over his mammoth body and nuzzled into his neck. "Thank you for taking care of him," she whispered.

MORNING CAME TOO SOON. Luke didn't wake up, he just got out of bed. Jessica being under the same roof again made it impossible to sleep. Jackson called after he dropped her off at the airport, asking Luke to just "be there" for her. She went to Portland to say goodbye to AJ. At some point he

347

planned on allowing his own feelings to surface, but they would wait.

After a shower he decided to make coffee. The moment he walked around the corner to the kitchen, he stopped. The unfamiliar blonde sat at the table wearing nothing but the familiar red hoodie, her legs tucked up into it, the extra six inches of sleeves doubled as hot pads for her coffee. With her back to him, she stared out the large windows, taking the occasional sip of her steamy morning jolt.

He hated the color of her hair. He hated that another man had loved her body and her heart. He hated that she sat ten feet away and yet she felt so out of reach. If he dwelled on all the things he hated, it would make it impossible to love her. And if he only chose to do one thing for the rest of his life ... it would be to love her.

"I missed this view." Of course she knew he was there.

She missed his car, the dog, and the view. Did she miss him?

"It's a breathtaking view today." Luke poured a cup of coffee then leaned against the counter with his legs crossed at his ankles. "Jones has slobbered and chewed on that sweatshirt for nearly a year."

She scooted around to face him. "I just slipped it on. I only have the clothes I had on yesterday. Today might be a shopping day for me."

He hid behind his coffee cup so she didn't see the guilt on his face, the everything-you-owned-is-exactly-where-you-left-it-in-our-closet look.

"It's Friday. I hope you didn't take the day off on my account."

A breathy laugh accompanied Luke's grin. "I've had the whole week off. I flew to Chicago a week ago today."

Jessica narrowed her eyes a bit.

"Then I rented a car and drove to Omaha."

"What was in Omaha?"

He sipped his coffee then rubbed his lips together. "Come to find out ... not much."

"You should have looked me up. I could have given you the ten-cent tour."

"Mmm ... why didn't I think of that?"

Jessica stared at her coffee. "You came for me," she whispered.

"I came for you."

"You could have died." She looked up.

He nodded.

Setting her coffee down, she stood. "I'm going to shower then go buy a few things to wear, maybe some makeup to hide my scars and soften the appearance of my gaunt-looking face until I can gain a little weight. I look hideous."

"You're—"

"So help me, Jones ... if you even think of trying to compliment my looks, I will make sure your face matches mine."

He looked her body up and down, taking note of how much muscle mass she'd lost. "I think for the first time ever I could take you on."

Jessica narrowed her eyes. "Don't test me."

He jerked his head toward the hall. "I'm glad to see you didn't lose your sass. Go shower. I'll take you shopping."

CHAPTER FORTY-ONE

F<small>RIDAY</small>.

Ryn needed a stiff drink and a merit badge for making it though the week. She went from planning a Monday elopement to confessing her past to Maddie in the most graphic way, followed by her daughter hating her, then the cherry on top—Jackson left, forever.

While she cleaned her two houses for the day, Omaha received another eight inches of snow, making the drive home a crawl through the busy late day traffic.

A needed grin crept up her face as she pulled into her driveway that was shoveled and covered in a good inch of ice melt. "Funny, Drew." She rolled her eyes at his attempt to make fun of Jackson's over-the-top ice melt incident. Payback would be fun.

After knocking the ice melt off her boots she opened the door. "Hey, baby," she said to Gunner. Then she flipped on the light.

"Oh. My. God." Her words were barely a whisper. Anything louder would have required her to have air in her lungs.

Breathless.

The walls were painted, the furniture was new, book-shelves, lamps, throw rugs. However, the shocking part was she'd seen everything before because every detail was a photo from her Pinterest boards.

She continued to the kitchen, but she knew how it was going to look before she rounded the corner—new appli-ances, light fixtures, even the wine rack—all from her Pinterest boards.

On the small, white, built-in desk by her back door was a new computer. The screen saver flashed photos of Ryn, Maddie, and even a few of Gunner. She clicked on the mouse, revealing a message on her home screen.

I changed my mind … wait for me.

Ryn swallowed her heart and turned around. There he stood wearing the sharpest black suit and tie she had ever seen.

"Did you wait?"

A million words jumbled into so many questions. Why? How? Are you for real? She shook her head.

"You didn't wait for me?" Jackson's eyes widened.

Ryn shook her head again. "I couldn't. Once you left there was a line of guys waiting at my door."

"Young, no doubt?" His eyes narrowed a bit.

"Mere babes in the cradle." She smirked.

"Jude died. For good this time."

"I'm sorry."

"I'm not. He stood in the way of me being with you."

Ryn blinked back tears, swallowed hope, and waited for the unknown. At some point in her life she forgot how to dream … how to imagine having any sort of lasting happiness.

But … there he stood.

"Are you?"

With just a few slow steps, his larger-than-life presence swallowed the space between them. The pad of his thumb caught her first tear.

"Are you with me?" she whispered, desperate for him to pull her out of the shadow of doubt that loomed over her.

"Forever."

"Jackson ..." Her arms flew around his neck. She held him with all her strength, daring life to try and take him away again.

His hands cupped her face and he kissed her. She didn't care how many people died for him to be with her. His touch made her selfish. She didn't care why he was there. His past didn't matter. He was her future.

Fuck the past.

"You hacked into my Pinterest account and hired an army of help," she murmured.

His lips devoured every inch of her neck as one of his hands laid claim to her ass and the other to her breast.

"I did." He unfastened his pants.

"Are you going to invade my privacy for the rest of our lives?"

He bit her shoulder, a grin playing along his lips. "Yes. There's not a single part of you or your life that I'm not going to invade, dominate ... claim as *mine*." He stood.

"What if—"

He kissed her, swallowing her words of protest.

Taking her into his arms, he backed her against her new stainless-steel refrigerator. Then leaving her breathless, he stepped back.

"Take off your clothes."

The familiar flush surfaced along her skin. She used to hate it, but no longer. It meant the beautiful man before her wanted to see her body. It was crazy, improbable, and utterly flattering.

"You first."

Jackson grinned. He reached for his tie.

"Leave on the tie ... and your glasses."

He raised a brow, his cocky smile taking over his face.

Ryn melted to a puddle on her new floor as he undressed for her. He widened his stance and crossed his naked arms over his naked chest, with the exception of his black tie.

"Your turn."

It took a few seconds for her mind to stop chanting, *mine, mine, mine* ... The tattooed specimen before her was *hers*. That ... she would never completely understand, but for women over forty everywhere—and the greater good— she would spend the rest of her life trying to figure it out— figure him out.

Fuzzy socks, skinny jeans, a pink V-neck T-shirt—she stripped for him. He made her feel sexy, something no other man had ever done. Letting her bra drop to the floor, she slid off her panties, leaving them next to her bra at her feet.

"Pick your panties up."

She stood still, only her eyes shifting with a bit of confusion.

"Do it."

Keeping her eyes on him, waiting for further explanation, she bent down and picked them up.

He stepped closer, so close she could smell his minty breath and intoxicating body wash. Ryn was certain she smelled like lemon furniture polish, but she didn't care in that moment.

"Wad them up in your fist."

"Uh—"

"Just do it." He ducked down and sucked her earlobe, biting it as if to accentuate his demand.

It had to be a fetish he hadn't revealed to her, she just knew it. Jackson would make her stuff her panties in her mouth to muffle her screams while he fucked her. She took a hard swallow and wadded them up, accepting her new life, a sacrifice for his body inside of hers.

The expectant look on his face said he was done talking. She knew what to do and he waited for her to do it.

Slowly ... she brought her panties to her face and parted her lips.

He narrowed his eyes. "What are you doing?"

"Um ... what you want me to do?"

He grabbed the handle to the refrigerator and jerked it open a few inches, forcing her body flesh to his. "I want you to toss them in the refrigerator, *hot pants*."

Ryn's eyes widened in realization while her skin crimsoned with embarrassment. She tossed them inside the refrigerator, attempting to act like she didn't just taste her own panties.

Jackson knew otherwise. He palmed her ass and hiked her up his body. She wrapped her legs around his waist as he kissed her.

"You were going to..." he mumbled over her mouth between kisses "...stuff your panties in your mouth for me." She couldn't respond. She would never acknowledge any such thing.

"That's so fucking hot."

Ryn found her sexy and owned it. Jackson Knight was the lucky recipient of it, and nothing compared to a woman hell-bent on making up for missing out on two decades of not feeling loved, not feeling desired, not feeling *alive*.

He "effed" her in nothing but a black necktie and black glasses. Then he carried her to her new bed and made love to her.

"Tell me you're staying."

He chuckled into the pillow, his arms stretched over his head. Ryn's body cloaked his back, her cheek resting on his shoulder as she traced his inked skin. Naked Ryn touching him—he never wanted to leave her bed.

"I think we've been over this."

"I know, but I asked you on the verge of an orgasm and you answered with half my breast in your mouth. Maybe we should go over it again now that we're sexually sober."

"You're naked, on my back, and tracing my ass with your fingernails. I'm not sure this qualifies as 'sexually sober.'"

"Did you just wake up one day and think, 'Hmm ... I'm going to get a dragon tattooed on my ass today.'?"

"No. It was more of a premonition. I knew someday it would tempt Ryn Middleton into touching my ass."

She buried her face in his neck and giggled. "Is that so?"

"Yes."

Her lips brushed the back of his neck. "Tell me you're staying," she whispered.

"Forever." He rolled over, dragging her on top of him. "Tell me you like your Pinterest house."

Her hair tickled his face as she kissed the corner of his mouth. "It's too much. It took my breath away." Ryn's soft blue eyes gazed into his. "*You* take my breath away. You make all my dreams come true ... and it has nothing to do with any of this. It's just ... you."

Jackson threaded his fingers into her hair, holding her to his face, nose-to-nose. "I hope our baby has your freckles."

Her eyes filled with tears. "What if I can't—"

"Shh ..." He kissed her, his hands gliding down the perfect curves of her beautiful body. "Don't worry about it. I can do this. I used to find all the eggs on Easter before Jessica."

Ryn laughed through her tears. "Just don't drown in my pond before you find the eggs."

CHAPTER FORTY-TWO

BROTHER DEAREST CALLED to share the news of his reunion with Ryn. He had been away from her for less than a week. Did he really think she was going to have moved on already? In his words it was the season of miracles. However, Jessica had yet to witness one. After ten days of living like roommates with Luke, she felt something inside of her begin to die: hope.

His kindness and patience made it worse. He cooked her meals, took her to dinner, joined her for walks with Jones, and talked about everything and yet *nothing*. But he didn't touch her. They hadn't made any sort of physical contact since the night he held her in the hospital.

Every night he told her goodnight and walked to his bedroom—their bedroom—and shut the door. He told her to "stay as long as you want;" he didn't say "stay forever." At first it felt like he was giving her space to grieve, space she needed, but that space seemed to grow with each passing day.

"My family is dying to see you. No pun intended."

Luke smiled as they pulled out of the building, heading to Tahoe for Christmas.

Jessica hadn't seen any of his family except Lake. Luke told them about her year as Jillian Knight, but he asked them to wait until Christmas to see her. Once again, to give her time to grieve and acclimate back into her life.

The trip to Tahoe was bittersweet because he asked if she'd like to come for Christmas with his family. Jessica remembered a time when they considered her part of that family.

"Well, I'm *living* to see them," she replied to his dying comment.

"I'm surprised you didn't decide to go to Omaha for Christmas. Don't get me wrong ... I'm glad you're here."

"Thought I'd give them some privacy on their first Christmas together. Apparently he's working round the clock to knock her up. His words not mine. But I'm glad that you're glad I'm here. It would be even more awkward if you weren't."

"More awkward?"

Staring out her window, she felt his sideways glance, but chose to ignore it. "I didn't mean 'more.'" She lied. Then she acquiesced to his attempt to engage her in more small talk for the rest of the way to Tahoe.

"I'll let Jones do his thing and then bring our bags."

"K." Jessica found her best smile when his family tackled her at the door.

Hugs, kisses, smiles, and even a few tears. For a moment she felt like family.

"I have you guys in the same two rooms as your first visit."

Two rooms.

"Thanks, Mom." Luke gave Felicity a kiss on the cheek.

"I'll take our bags upstairs."

"I've got mine. I might need to reapply some makeup to my skeleton face." She gave his family a toothy grin as she took her bag from Luke.

"You look lovely. Don't even think twice about us," Felicity said.

Luke told them everything—almost—and truthfully she didn't feel an ounce of judgment.

"That's why I love you." She winked. "I won't be long."

Fleeing for her room, she shut the door and leaned back against it. Before she could let her emotions settle, a knock came at her back.

"Yeah?"

"It's me."

Jessica opened the door. "Hey, Lake."

She stepped inside and took a seat on the bed. "Luke told me to check on you."

"I've been up here like ... five seconds."

Lake shrugged. "I know ... and hello..." she pointed to her leg "...girl with the fake leg doesn't love going up the stairs. He's been so weird lately."

Jessica shut the door. "How so?"

"Since your kidnapping he's just been on edge and paranoid."

"Really?" Jessica had yet to see that side of Luke, which meant he'd put on an act with her.

"Yes. I'm not trying to compare it to what you went through, which was just ... horrifically unimaginable. But I think the whole ordeal messed with his head. Do you have any idea how hard it is to mess with the head of a shrink?"

She did, at one time. Since their year apart she wasn't sure if she *knew* anything for certain about Luke.

"Has he said anything to you?"

"Probably nothing he hasn't said to you."

Luke hadn't said anything to Jessica.

"Like?"

Lake twisted her lips. "Like how hard it is to be with you when you're not 'together.'"

"He said that?"

"Yeah, I'm sure it's the same for you too."

Jessica nodded.

"Come downstairs." Lake stood. "You don't need any makeup. You should have seen me after three months in a coma. Besides you already look better than when I saw you last week. Food looks good on your bones."

"DIBS ON LICKING THE BEATERS," Lake said when she and Jessica walked into the kitchen.

Felicity rolled her eyes as Lake snatched it from the bowl of whipped cream. "Some things never change."

Lake moaned. Her eyes rolled back in her head as she licked the whipped cream. "So good. Where's Luke?"

"He took Caleb upstairs to rock him to sleep." Lara smiled. "He thinks he's the baby whisperer." She shook her head.

"He's going to be an amazing dad," Anne added. Her heartfelt smile faded to a nervous one when she looked at Jessica. "I didn't necessarily mean your kids." The smile was a full on grimace. "God ... I didn't mean that either ... I just meant *if* he has kids with ..."

"How's your foot taste?" Lake laughed.

Jessica welcomed Lake's attempt to lighten yet another awkward situation.

"It's fine, Anne." Jessica smiled. "I agree. Luke will be a

great father someday." Her nightmare replayed in her mind of Luke, Jones, the baby, and the woman who was not her.

"Gather the troops. Everything is ready," Felicity announced, carrying the Martha Stewart-worthy turkey to the table.

They took their seats. The baby whisperer slid into his chair next to Jessica as Tom said the blessing. After murmurings of Amen, Lane stood, holding his glass in the air.

"To Jessica. I think we can all agree you are the greatest gift this Christmas."

Jessica looked around the room, fighting back all the emotions. "Thank you. I feel the same way about every one of you."

Luke's hand rested on hers for a moment. She blinked and it was gone, but the way his touch lingered paralyzed her.

They passed around the food. Chattering about kids, the weather, and football ensued. Jessica focused on her mashed potatoes as if she'd never seen them before.

"So, Jess, are you planning on staying in San Francisco or going back to Omaha?" Tom asked.

And just like that ... all her illusions vanished and reality hit her as cold as the still familiar five-gallon buckets of ice water. Luke let her stay. He wasn't taking her back. They weren't "together" and everyone knew it except her.

The potatoes demanded her attention again. She pushed them around on her plate, knowing she'd never be able to take a bite of them with her heart lodged in her throat.

"Um ... I guess I haven't ... I mean ..."

"It's fine. I was just asking. I'm sure it's too soon to know what you want."

She risked a glance. "I guess."

Not even bound and beaten had Jessica ever felt so weak. The thought of a future without Luke sucked every bit of life from her existence.

She gutted down the food on her plate, which was a shame since Felicity's skills rivaled her own mother's cooking.

"Keep eating," Luke whispered for the millionth time.

"If you say that to me one more time I'm going to jab this fork in your eye." She gritted between her teeth with a fake smile to everyone else still sitting at the table. Half of the family had excused themselves to fall into a holiday coma in the living room.

"Dessert?" Felicity asked.

Jessica ignored Luke's yes-you-want-dessert look. "Can I wait a little while?"

"Certainly. I think the kids are antsy to open their presents anyway ... and by kids I mean Liam and Lake. I think they're more excited than Gina, and Caleb is too young to understand."

Jessica pushed back in her chair. Luke stared at her.

"Don't give me that look. I'll eat the whole damn pie later, just ..." She sighed.

He grabbed her wrist before she could get away. "You're upset with me."

No. She wasn't upset. Fucking livid and emotionally broken beyond the destruction of an atomic bomb was a more accurate description.

"I just want to see you get healthier."

"I am. I'm not upset. I'm just full. Okay?"

"I'm sorry."

"Don't." She didn't intend to have an edge to her tone,

but she did. "If I'm not allowed to apologize, then neither are you."

"Fine."

"Fine."

THEY'D PLANNED on staying three days. Luke questioned if it was too long. Jessica seemed distant and angry, but only with him. He couldn't figure out what he'd done to upset her.

"Would you look at this?" Tom said, staring out the back window.

Luke yawned, pouring a cup of coffee, desperate for a jolt. It was only six in the morning, but he couldn't sleep with Jessica on his mind. He hadn't slept much since she showed up at his door.

"I told her I planned on chopping some wood this week-end. She's about finished a day's worth of work in ... hell, I'm not sure. What time do you think she got up?"

Jessica brought the large ax behind her then swinging it over her head, she killed the log in front of her.

"Think she's cold?"

A pair of faded jeans hung too lose from her thin frame. A black T-shirt clung to her sweaty torso. She wore work gloves and a red beanie too. The still unfamiliar blond hair hung in a low pony tail over her right shoulder.

"I doubt it, but she shouldn't be doing that. Her shoulder isn't ready."

Tom chuckled. "There's a six-foot stack of chopped wood out there that says otherwise."

"You should tell her to come inside."

"Me?"

Luke sipped his coffee. "Yes. She won't take it well coming from me."

"Bad?"

"Not good. I don't know how to talk to her or what to say. I'm so damn afraid she's going to leave."

"She should talk to my son. I hear he's a brilliant psychiatrist."

"Some days I think I'm the one who needs a psychiatrist."

"Why don't you?"

"I'm not ready to think about me yet. I need to know that she's going to be okay."

Tom put his hand on Luke's shoulder. "Maybe she needs you to be okay first."

Luke didn't respond. He knew there was truth to his dad's words. His fear held him back from being okay.

"I'll drag her skinny ass inside."

"Thanks, Dad."

"I'M NOT GOING to have an excuse to duck out on laundry this weekend if you chop all that wood."

Jessica dropped the ax and wiped her brow, smearing dirt along her forehead. "Sorry. I feel out of shape and Dr. Eat and Don't Exercise won't let me do anything because of a few little injuries that are just fine."

"Felicity coddled him too much." Tom leaned against the shed and blew at the steam spiraling from his coffee mug.

"How did he react?"

He studied her. "When you died?"

Jessica nodded.

"He was devastated. We all were. We'd been drowning in the fear of losing Lake and the news of you was like this goddamn freight train that came out of nowhere, barreling through what was already a shitload of wreckage. Luke was numb for months. He just existed—barely. Then Lake came out of her coma and we had to relive everything again with her: the wedding, her accident, Ben's death, her leg, your parents, and you. I know people say that God won't give you more than you can handle, but I think He did. I'm still not sure my boy is okay. He's scared right now. I see it in his eyes, like any day he could break."

"Scared of what?"

"You."

CHAPTER FORTY-THREE

Luke suggested leaving a day early. Jessica didn't argue. The harder she tried to hold it together in front of his family, the more she felt herself falling apart. The events of the previous month taught her one thing: death came in the unsuspecting arms of silence. Luke didn't speak on the drive home. Even small talk seemed to be too much.

"I'll take Jones for a walk." Luke set their bags on the floor.

"Want company?"

His three-second delay said everything. It was the truth before the lie.

"Sure. If you want to."

Jessica picked up her bag. "Maybe I'll just unpack."

"Okay."

She took her bag to the guest room. The slam of the front door was another stab to her heart. Luke didn't slam doors. He controlled everything.

After sitting on the edge of her bed, staring at her bag on the floor for almost thirty minutes, she decided not to unpack. Maybe she'd outstayed her welcome.

On her way to the kitchen to get a drink—a real drink—she noticed Luke's bag on the floor. Leaving things on the floor was also something he didn't do. What had happened to her Luke?

She grabbed his bag and took it to his room. Tossing it at the end of the bed, she stood there taking in everything that felt so familiar. Why did that familiarity, that comfort, hurt so much? Moving toward the closet like sneaking up on the enemy, she opened the cracked door and the light came on.

"Oh my God," she whispered.

All of her clothes were exactly where they'd been when she left—when she died.

Jessica died.

Jillian lived.

She loved another.

And Luke never let go.

"I lied."

Jessica closed her eyes at the defeat in his voice behind her.

"When I told you I'd move on and love again if you died ... I lied."

"Luke," she whispered.

"I don't expect anything."

She turned. Every word he said intensified the pain and flared her anger. "Jesus, Luke ... I put on a wedding dress, I went to the church, I didn't have cold feet, I didn't even have to think. Being with you was as easy and *necessary* as breathing."

"I don't know what you want me to say or do or—"

"I want you to expect *everything* and say anything."

Tension pulled at his brow as he shook his head. "I can't."

"We need to talk about AJ."

"I can't." He swallowed, jaw firm, gaze set on the floor between them.

"That picture—"

"Don't." He continued to shake his head as his expression hardened. "I can't."

With a blink, her tears broke free. Irene wanted to destroy everything dear to Sunny and Knox. She wanted to destroy Jessica. She did. The moment she showed that picture to Luke, she took everything.

They stood a chance if all he had was the idea, the verbal confession that she had loved AJ. But that image would be in his mind forever, eating at him—at them—like a slow death.

"Tell me how you feel."

"I can't." His voice cracked. "It would end us."

"There is no *us*! You haven't touched me since I asked you to in the hospital. You're miserable and so am I. It can't get any worse. If we can't save us, then at least save yourself. If you don't say what you're feeling, it will kill you. I can take it. I'm so much stronger than you think I am."

He said nothing.

"Five minutes."

Luke looked up.

"I'll give you five minutes to say *everything*. Don't think ... just say it. For once don't protect me. Give me the part of you that hurts the most. And then we'll never mention any of it again. But what's happened between us feels worse than any death, and we both need closure."

She lost him, but even more than that ... he lost himself in her. Luke wouldn't acknowledge her at all. That hurt the most.

"Fine," she whispered. "Don't tell me, but please tell someone. Then get rid of my stuff and choose to *live* because you're not ... not like this." She walked past him to the bedroom door. Love wasn't enough ... not for Mickey and Sunny, and not for Jessica and Luke.

"I haven't had my five minutes yet."

Jessica stopped breathing. She didn't recognize the icy voice behind her. It held no love, only a year of anger that would cut her to the bone.

Turning, she held her head up in spite of her tears. She would die from his words before she'd let him live with the pain of harboring them. Fisting her hands, she imagined them taped and ready for Jude's unforgiving jabs. The difference was she wouldn't fight back. Luke was about to knock her out without even touching her.

"You destroyed *us* when you died without giving me a choice. Knox said I could have come with you. I know you did it for my family, but that's just it. *You* made the choice. I know how fucking selfish it sounds, but I would have chosen *us*. I would have left, even with Lake in a coma."

Jessica blinked.

Words cut.

Emotions bled as tears.

He knocked her down. She got back up.

"That picture is branded into my memory, and I want to physically cut it out of my brain. Another man touched you. Another man loved you. Another man made you *feel* and *love* and it wasn't me. You let him have you, and it should have been me. I never knew him, yet I hate everything about him including the part of your heart that he took to his grave. I can never have that. And I'm selfish because I want *everything*."

Jessica bit her quivering lip until she tasted blood.

"I hate the color of your hair. I hate the name Jillian Knight. I fucking hate the whole goddamn state of Nebraska." His voice escalated. Each word cut deeper as he let go of the rawest, deepest, most painful emotions. He stepped toward her.

"Is that what you want to hear? That loving you has turned me into a selfish bastard." He blinked and just like that ... his own emotions bled down his face.

"I *hate* myself for feeling this way. I *hate* myself for wanting to rip off your clothes and fuck you until I can no longer see that photo, until you can no longer remember his touch, until I've reclaimed every part of you right down to your soul." He stepped closer, as close as he could get without touching her. "In my head I know what you did was selfless and amazing and ... the most beautiful gift to him. And the rational part of me is so damn proud of you for finding the part of you that I've seen all along."

She swallowed hard, refusing to shy away, no matter how hard he punched.

"But with you, my feelings don't come from my head, they come from my heart. My love for you is selfish because I don't think you need it anymore. I've been walking around here on pins and needles, so afraid that you're still grieving him, missing him, needing him. I'm so afraid my touch will scare you away. But I'm So. Fucking. Selfish. Because it doesn't matter whether you need my love anymore ..."

He released a sob and so did she.

"Because I *need* to love you." Drawing in a ragged breath, he shrugged. "It's all I know," he whispered.

Knocked out.

Luke reached into her chest, pulled out her heart, and said, "If I can't have it, no one can have it."

She wanted to tell him that her love for AJ was real. She wanted to tell him that she regretted nothing. She wanted to tell him that fate took her away from him because AJ needed her more, if only for a mere breath in time. But she didn't because it didn't matter. AJ died ... and so did Jillian Knight.

"Time's up," she whispered.

Five minutes. He killed her in five minutes.

Defeat pulled his gaze to the floor. "I don't know what you want me to do."

Jessica took his hand and placed it over her heart. "Touch me."

His eyes locked to hers. "Jess—"

She kissed him. Time was up.

It was the longest five minutes of her life. It was the most painful five minutes of her life. Like all the other odds in her life, she survived and they would never talk about it again. Jessica died to be with AJ ... but she *lived* to be with Luke.

"Dammit, Jones!" She grabbed his hair because he stood there, hands limp at his sides. "He borrowed me, but you *own* me. You. Fucking. Own. Me. Take back what's yours and don't *ever* let me go."

He kissed her—really kissed her. Eager hands tore off clothes. Within seconds of hitting the bed, he filled her on a painfully emotional groan.

"Luke ..." She surrendered everything.

He captured her lips and reclaimed the woman that had always been his. In that moment Jessica couldn't remember AJ's touch. She let the memory of it die. She let Luke erase it.

In a life filled with monsters, their love was a survivor.

EPILOGUE

One Year Later

"I'M CURED?"

Dr. Harper looked over her red-framed reading glasses. Bangs of gunmetal gray streaked with white fell across her forehead as Jessica spun in the desk chair, dark hair flowing behind her.

"You're functional." Dr. Harper closed her laptop and slid it onto the desk.

"And Luke?"

"You know I can't discuss my other patients with you."

"Why didn't you ever suggest counseling us together?"

"Neither one of you did anything wrong. This hasn't been about apologies and reconciliation. It's about acceptance, but not of each other. It's accepting the past ... the things you can't change."

God grant me the serenity to accept the things I cannot change;

courage to change the things I can;

and wisdom to know the difference.

Jessica nodded. "The Serenity Prayer. I think it's become my mantra."

Dr. Harper set her glasses on her computer. A grin played with the corner of her mouth. "You're not the most troubled person I've worked with in my career, but you are unequivocally the strongest. There are some things that can't be taught. Either you have it or you don't." She nodded slowly. "You have it."

Jessica planted her feet on the ground and crossed her arms on the desk. "Have what?"

"A will to live that goes beyond circumstance and possibly even reason. You find something from nothing and feed off it. You're that flower that sprouts through a crack in the barren granite face of a mountain. You feel what everyone else has to see to believe. You sense the sun before you see its light, and you do it subconsciously. That's a gift. That's why you're still here—alive—with me today."

A smile grew on Jessica's face. "You shrinks have a way with words. Luke has said the most profound things to me over the years and I don't even think he expects his words to affect me the way they do. What you just said? It's haunting yet flattering and ..."

Dr. Harper stood. "The truth."

Jessica grabbed her purse and walked around the desk. "The men in my life have been that *something* I've found from nothing."

Dr. Harper pulled Jessica in for a final goodbye hug. "Hold on to them and the memories. Happiness moves you forward, but pain keeps you balanced." She held her at arms' length. "Okay?"

"AJ will keep me balanced?"

Dr. Harper shook her head. "His memory is a promise. A promise that should anything ever happen to your beloved Luke, you will survive. Life will go on." Narrowing one eye, she held up her index finger. "Mickey and Sunny ... those memories will keep you balanced."

Jessica frowned. "Mickey and Sunny ..." She sighed. What could she say? So many lives had been affected because one day, many years ago, little Knox McGraw met a giggling angel in red Mary Janes on the playground.

"My mother once said, 'Love is reckless because true emotions are immune to logic. The most beautiful love stories are often the most tragic.'"

"Mmm ..." Dr. Harper smiled. "Your mother told you the story of her life in just two sentences."

A HANDSOME—ALBEIT cocky bastard—stood at the entrance to Samovar Tea with the most beautiful baby girl nestled to his chest in a red Ergo carrier.

"Give her to me." Jessica held out her hands and wiggled her greedy fingers.

"No way." He opened the door.

Jessica shot him a glare as she walked inside the restaurant.

"Two?" the waiter asked.

"Yes." Jessica pointed to a booth in the corner. "Over there please."

After she shrugged off her coat, she held her hands out again. "I mean it. Give her to me."

The cocky bastard's chuckle accompanied his smile as he shook his head. "No. Sorry. If you wake her we're both screwed."

She plunked down into the booth. "You've always sucked at sharing."

Tatted arms hugged the little bundle tightly as he eased to sitting. "Ryn ran a few errands. She took her breasts with her so I've got nothing if Livy wakes up."

"She should have left a bottle."

"We're not using a bottle for another three weeks. Nipple confusion."

Jessica laughed. "Never thought I'd live to see the day where my brother was an expert on nipple confusion."

Jackson pressed his lips to Livy's tiny head. She had his dark hair and lots of it. "You'll understand soon enough." His eyes, the ones that matched hers, looked up. A smile pulled at his lips still pressed to Livy's head.

"We'll see. Dr. Overprotective insists on no babies until my doctor gives me the okay. Apparently the whole starvation then dying thing, followed by six months of no menstrual cycles makes me a poor candidate for getting pregnant or having a healthy pregnancy."

They gave the waiter their order. Jessica's gaze stayed glued to Livy. She adored her.

"San Francisco." She smiled, shaking her head. "I still can't believe you sold Ryn's place after everything you did to it, but I'm glad you did. I love having you living here again."

Jackson bounced Livy gently as she stirred then settled back into him, resting her other cheek to his chest, her tiny fist at her mouth.

"Her parents were willing to move wherever we moved, but it was still a hard sell until Maddie took that job in Baltimore."

"I never want to ask, but how are they?"

Jackson lifted his shoulders. "Maddie is ... Maddie. Stubborn. Young. Immature. Defiant. And unforgiving. But she's smart so she'll do well with her job, marry some guy who can tolerate her attitude, and if she has a child of her own someday, I suspect she'll come crawling back to Ryn."

"And she'll welcome her with open arms because a mother's love is unconditional."

Jackson stared at Livy, his face stone. "I still can't forgive her."

Jessica felt that familiar pang in her chest that came every time they talked about their mother. She thought of Dr. Harper's words. *Your mother told you the story of her life in just two sentences.*

"Mom's dead. I don't think she's spending her afterlife worrying about you forgiving her, because I don't think she regretted any of it—not with Knox, not with Dad, and not with us. The same way I don't regret mine."

"The unconditional love?" He looked at her. "It's gutting."

Jessica smiled. Livy would break him some day ... one boyfriend at a time. "Yes, yes it is." She glanced out the window. "Oh she's coming ... gimme, gimme, gimme."

Jackson followed her gaze to Ryn walking toward the building. He smiled. Jessica loved the way he looked at Ryn, like each time he fell in love with her all over again.

Before he could protest, Jessica had the Ergo latch unfastened and Livy in her arms.

"God ... I love how she smells." Jessica held her close, inhaling the essence of her niece. Livy's blue eyes blinked open as she sucked at her fist.

"There's my beautiful wife." Jackson stood, freed the carrier from his body, and hugged Ryn, palming her ass and kissing her like they were the only two in the room. But they weren't and there were plenty of wide eyes staring at them.

"Daddy's ready to give you a little brother already ... right here in Samovar," Jessica baby-talked to Livy. "Maybe they should go work on that in private and we'll go visit Jonesy."

Ryn giggled with Jackson's greedy lips still pressed to hers. "Hi, Jessica." She freed herself.

Jackson adjusted himself before sliding back into the booth next to Ryn.

Jessica shook her head and rolled her eyes.

"What?" Jackson took a sip of his tea, hiding his cocky-bastard smirk.

"So how was your last day with Dr. Harper?" Ryn asked, stealing Jackson's sandwich and taking a huge bite.

He gave her the hairy eyeball.

"Sorry, baby. I'm starving," she mumbled. "Think of it as feeding your daughter."

Jessica widened her eyes at Jackson. For all the years he gave Luke crap about submitting to Jessica, there he sat—no testicles—lovesick for his wife and utterly smitten over the bundle in Jessica's arms.

"I'm cured. My words, not hers."

"Is Luke still seeing her?" Ryn wiped her mouth as Jackson reclaimed the rest of his sandwich.

"Yes." Jessica laughed. "The guy had me iron his socks to take to Goodwill. You can't fix that kind of crazy overnight."

The twins shared knowing looks. Luke not only had AJ to deal with, he had the memory of watching Jackson deliver a violent death to Preston Iverson. After two months and still no Preston, Ryn asked Jackson if he killed Preston. In true Jackson style, he replied, "Do you really want to know?"

Ryn shook her head and they never discussed it again.

"Speaking of crazy ..." Jessica glanced at her phone next to her plate. A photo of Luke pinned beneath Jones on the floor lit up her screen with the caption "Play time. Where are you, Mom?"

"Looks like it's time for Livy and me to head home." She stood.

Jackson cleared his throat, but it sounded more like a growl.

"Fine." She handed Livy to Ryn.

"Get your own." Jackson smirked.

Ryn elbowed him. "Don't be mean."

Jessica typed a message into her phone. "No, he's right. I plan on remedying this situation as soon as I get home."

Jessica: *I'm on my way. Get your dick out. I want a Livy too.*
Jones: *Still waiting for your doctor to give us the go ahead.*
Jessica: *Dammit, Jones! Meet me in the GTO in 20. Dick. Out.*
NO CONDOM!

"There. I just sent Luke a love letter. Wish me luck. I'm going to get Livy a cousin."

Jackson and Ryn laughed.

"Bye." Jessica winked and blew them a kiss before floating on her dreamy cloud all the way home.

"So REMIND ME ... why aren't they married?"

Jackson chuckled, stealing Livy from Ryn. "You know I don't speak woman."

"Yeah, yeah ... and I don't speak Jackson, but I got you something anyway." She pulled a box from her purse.

"You're too late. Christmas was last week." He sucked on Livy's fingers.

"I felt bad that your glasses were lost in the move." Ryn smirked.

"And by lost you mean tossed."

"I didn't throw away your glasses. *Anyway* ..." She grinned.

Jackson loved that grin, those freckles, and her eyes that lit up just for him and the miracle he held in his arms. But without a doubt ... he knew she threw away his glasses.

Ryn opened the box and pulled out a shiny pair of black Clark Kent glasses.

"You can't buy someone glasses as a gift. You don't even know my prescription."

"Pfft ... drop the act. They were vanity glasses and we both know it. I looked through them ... they weren't prescription."

"It was minor."

Ryn slipped his new glasses onto his face. Then she cocked her head to the side, lips twisted. "They just don't look the same without the tape."

"If and I mean *if* in the most hypothetical sense ... *if* my glasses were vanity glasses, then why would you buy me new ones?"

Ryn shrugged then leaned in to kiss Livy's chubby cheek.

"Unless ... the glasses are for you."

She scoffed. "Why would the glasses be for me?"

"Because you like me to..." he pressed his fingers over Livy's ears and whispered "...fuck you wearing nothing but those glasses."

Even after nearly a year of marriage and the birth of their first child, he could still make her blush from nose to toes.

"And we're one week from *the* day."

Ryn cleared her throat. "The day?"

"I've noticed the past few days you've wandered into the bathroom, opening and closing drawers for nothing in particular, at the exact time that I'm showering. I've watched you ogle me."

"Livy's extra diaper supplies are in our bathroom and the ogling to which you are referring is me glaring at you because you *get* a shower. Since you went back to work two weeks ago I've had three showers."

"Sorry, my new job is demanding."

"You're a computer geek and you work from home."

Jackson shook his head. "You don't even know what it is I do, and I would offer to help more but I don't have boobs."

"She doesn't eat twenty-four hours a day."

"Yes, but she fusses easily."

"So?"

"So ... I don't like it when she's upset with me."

Ryn laughed. "She's not upset with you. She's a baby. Babies cry."

"Because they want boobies."

"Oh my God ... let's go."

As if on cue, Livy started crying. The second Ryn took her and held her to her chest she stopped crying.

Jackson held the door open with one hand, diaper bag and carrier in his other hand. Ryn narrowed her eyes as she walked past him. "Boobies," he mouthed.

"Shut it," she whispered.

He let the door close behind him and just stood there for a few extra seconds, watching Ryn toss a blanket over Livy on the way to the car. With a long sigh, he looked up at the bright clearing in the late afternoon sky. Beyond all certainty he knew there was a God, one who didn't keep score. One who, in spite of all the lives Jackson had taken, still found him deserving of *everything*.

He loved her. No ... he adored her. That was the only explanation for Luke leaning against the door of the GTO when Jessica arrived home.

"We're not having sex in my GTO."

She smirked. "And yet ... here you are."

"I just came down here to tell you that." He stood with his back straight, arms crossed over his chest.

"Today was my last day with Dr. Harper."

"I know."

"Did you also know that last week my pussy doctor gave me the green light to get pregnant?"

"I know that Dr. Brannon is an OB-GYN, not a 'pussy doctor.'"

"Says the shrink." She curled her fingers into his front jeans pockets.

"How can we have a baby if you think marrying me is bad karma since Lake's accident?"

Jessica knew it bothered Luke that they weren't married yet. She wore the ring but they never set a date. Too many plans in her life had taken a turn for the worst. No plans with Luke. Just one day at a time.

"You went to medical school, yet you don't know how to make a baby?"

"You know what I mean."

"I do. I also know that my parents married before my mom had me and Jackson and their life together—although filled with moments of happiness—was tragic. Then there is the story of Tom and Felicity Jones. Now, I do believe you were at that wedding and how are they doing this many years later?"

"We are *us*. Do you get that?"

Jessica nodded and held up her hand to show him her ring. "One day at a time. We'll get there. But right now I want a Livy. Jackson is terrible about sharing."

She could see him, *feel* him thinking. Luke's mind was incessant and logical, but with her his thoughts were visceral.

"Don't overthink this, Jones. Get your ass in the back of the car."

Luke looked around.

"Overthinking ..."

He grumbled something and she was certain it was "contumacious."

"Don't worry, Dr. Jones..." she smacked his ass as he crawled in the backseat "...we'll keep it discreet in case someone drives by. I know you have a pressed argyle sock reputation to uphold in the building."

"We have a perfectly good bed upstairs. This makes no sense."

She slipped off her shoes and undressed from the waist down then straddled his lap. "I have my reasons." Smashing her hungry lips to his, she unfastened his jeans, bringing him to life the second her hand stroked him. He closed his eyes and moaned into her mouth.

Once the windows fogged over and she felt him possess her whole existence, she whispered in his ear, "Tell me you love me."

Luke nuzzled her neck, brushing his fingertips along her bare legs. "I adore you."

"Show me."

He showed her, twice for good measure. Luke's head fell back, eyes closed, sweat beaded on his brow.

She giggled, nipping at his ear lobe. "This is fate you know."

"You think?"

"I do. We may have just conceived a child in the same backseat as you were conceived."

Luke's eyes popped open.

Sorry, Thelma ... I had to tell him.

The End

ACKNOWLEDGMENTS

"God gave you a gift of 86,400 seconds today. Have you used one of them to say thank you?"
~ William Arthur Ward

This has been a crazy, incredible journey. I have a huge cast of real-life characters to thank.

My husband and three boys: If you didn't bring out the crazy in me every day, I would have been too sane to write the Jack & Jill series. You are my heart—never enough stars —I *adore* you. <3

Mom: I write for myself, and the world now, but I write *because* of you. You have always been my biggest fan in life, and for that, I am yours too.

Dan (Dad) and Roger: Thank you for being you! Your laughable antics and old-man ways brought Peaceful Woods to life.

Kambra: Thank you for taking on any task I threw at you—proofreading, beta-reading, Social Media PA ... and the list goes on. I can't wait for my readers to know you better.

Jyl: As aways, thank you for being my BFF, beta-reader, sounding board, fellow squirrel chaser, and travel companion!

Sherri: Thanks for reading my words at their worst and still seeing the diamond beneath the turd.

Shauna: Our personal messages and random confessions are a highlight of my day, every day! You are a true name queen, a true fan, but more than that ... you've become a true friend. I know we'll be talking much ado about nothing for many years!

Monique: You are my #1 bitch. <—Can you believe I really wrote that? I know someone will steal you because you're just that awesome. However, I will continue to work tirelessly to get you back. I can honestly say NO ONE has even come close to working so hard to get my books into the hands of readers. It's such an honor to call you my friend.

Max: Words are my thing, but it's hard to articulate how incredible it feels to write something that reminds you of why you do what you do. Your words, not mine. You are a true teacher and I love being your student. I should mention that you are my editor at The Polished Pen, but I don't want aspiring writers to hire you and compete for my spot on your busy schedule.

Kiezha: Librum Artis Editorial Services is my top find of 2015! I am the luckiest author out there to have such a brilliant editing team. Thank you for proofreading Middle of Knight and Dawn of Forever.

Ella James: Oh. My. Goodness! Thank you for befriending me when I needed it the very most in my writing career. Your guidance has been invaluable.

Thank you, Lisa with TRSoR Promotions and Neda with Ardent Prose, for organizing the publicity and promotions.

Thank you to every single blogger who took a chance on this series and loved it! My jaw is still stuck to the ground. You magnify my words to the world!

Finally, thank you to every reader who opened their mind and their heart and invited my characters into their own imagination. It is the ultimate privilege to write for you.

ALSO BY JEWEL E ANN

Standalone Novels

Idle Bloom

Undeniably You

Naked Love

Only Trick

Perfectly Adequate

Look The Part

When Life Happened

A Place Without You

Jersey Six

Scarlet Stone

Not What I Expected

Jack & Jill Series

End of Day

Middle of Knight

Dawn of Forever

One (*standalone*)

Out of Love (*standalone*)

Holding You Series

Holding You

Releasing Me

Transcend Series

Transcend

Epoch

Fortuity (*standalone*)

The Life Series

The Life That Mattered

The Life You Stole

Receive a FREE book and stay informed of new releases, sales, and exclusive stories:

Mailing List

https://www.jeweleann.com/free-booksubscribe

ABOUT THE AUTHOR

Jewel is a free-spirited romance junkie with a quirky sense of humor.

With 10 years of flossing lectures under her belt, she took early retirement from her dental hygiene career to stay home with her three awesome boys and manage the family business.

After her best friend of nearly 30 years suggested a few books from the Contemporary Romance genre, Jewel was hooked. Devouring two and three books a week but still craving more, she decided to practice sustainable reading, AKA writing.

When she's not donning her cape and saving the planet one tree at a time, she enjoys yoga with friends, good food with family, rock climbing with her kids, watching How I Met Your Mother reruns, and of course...heart-wrenching, tear-jerking, panty-scorching novels.

www.jeweleann.com